BETTER THAN CHOCOLATE

SUSAN WAGGONER

BETTER THAN

𝓌𝓂

WILLIAM MORROW

An Imprint of HarperCollins*Publishers*

BETTER THAN CHOCOLATE. Copyright © 2005 by Susan Waggoner. All rights reserved. Printed in the United States of America. No part of this book may be used or reproduced in any manner whatsoever without written permission except in the case of brief quotations embodied in critical articles and reviews. For information address HarperCollins Publishers Inc., 10 East 53rd Street, New York, NY 10022.

HarperCollins books may be purchased for educational, business, or sales promotional use. For information please write: Special Markets Department, HarperCollins Publishers Inc., 10 East 53rd Street, New York, NY 10022.

FIRST EDITION

Designed by Jennifer Ann Daddio

Printed on acid-free paper

Library of Congress Cataloging-in-Publication Data

Waggoner, Susan.
    Better than chocolate / by Susan Waggoner.—1st ed.
        p. cm.
    ISBN 0-06-053977-1 (alk. paper)
        1. Women—Fiction. 2. Success—Fiction. 3. Chocolate—Fiction.
    I. Title.

PS3623.A3535B47 2005
813'.54—dc22   2004055964

05   06   07   08   09   WBC/BVG   10   9   8   7   6   5   4   3   2   1

For

ELSA LINDQUIST WAGGONER,

*who believed every four-year-old
should have a library card*

Chocolate is no longer for me

what it was, fashion has led me

astray, as it always does.

BETTER THAN CHOCOLATE

Chapter 1

TOUJOURS WALLEYE

Anyone who still has the October 2002, issue of *Martha Stewart Living* can see, on pages 27 through 31, the story that has made the "Pumpkins!" issue something of a collector's item. Twenty dollars on eBay, although for this you will also get articles on Bedlington terriers, maple syrup, player pianos, acorn crafts, and macaroni and chevre, the *new* comfort food.

The magazine didn't usually do personalities, and this made the spread all the more eye-catching. *Here's* someone I should know about, readers must have thought, gazing at the woman wearing a garnet chenille sweater over black silk trousers. The best of the pictures shows the woman at a pickled-oak worktable, one foot twined pensively around a chair leg. The table is fifteen feet long and bare except for a computer, a bowl of green and golden pears, and a ream of blank paper that is supposed to be mistaken for a finished manuscript. Beyond the table is a row of windows, beyond the windows a sweep of green lawn, beyond the lawn a dock dipping down to a blue expanse of lake. The woman at the table gazes across this vista thoughtfully, as if inspiration will rise from the thin mist hugging the water.

The lake is Minnetonka.

The woman in the garnet chenille is me. And the entire spread— "Annie Wilkins at Home"—glows with what can only be described as, well, star power.

It wasn't planned that way. Initially, Martha was going to fly out to interview me herself. I'd been thrilled by the news, heady at the prospect of rubbing elbows with the woman whose tips for embedding violets in ice cubes and basil leaves between sheets of ravioli represented an altogether different world from the peanut-butter-and-jelly-encrusted planet I lived on. But when that day in midsummer actually came, Martha was ensnared in her own problems. Like a saucepan full of homemade caramel, the ImClone stock scandal had reached a surprisingly swift boil, and Martha had stayed home to preserve an appearance of unruffled normality. She might as well have made the trip, because being grilled on *The Early Show* as she tried to shred cabbage did her no good at all. In fact, so reversed were our respective poles that week that someone actually thanked me for "saving" the October issue.

I don't think it was quite that extreme—the Bedlingtons article and a recipe for homemade marshmallows could easily have carried the day—but I did add a certain pizzazz to the issue. Perhaps it was the slant of light. Or the Vivaldi the photo-shoot boys had brought on their boom boxes. Or the espresso we were swilling out of huge French coffee cups. For whatever reason, I looked as close to ravishing that morning as I ever would. My hair had the high-quality gloss of a good ganache. My sweater hung casually from my collarbone. My breasts were apples of garnet chenille.

I say all this without fear of boasting because, of course, it was all illusory, as handcrafted as the acorn Pueblo people on page 68. On the day I go back to now, the day on which this story begins, the *MSL* spread was months in the future. Ditto my collarbone. Martha Stewart had no idea who I was and wouldn't dream of sending Neil, her personal person, to Minnesota to do my hair and makeup, as he did that morning. Strangers were still inhabiting the house on the blue lake, scattering toast crumbs over countertops no longer to be theirs, desecrating my future pantry— their mudroom—with salt-and-snow-caked boots, curling ribbon and attaching bows in the gift-wrap room we would convert to an emergency office equipped with microwave and minibar, networked laptops, and a distressed leather chaise said to have belonged to Milton Hershey—a fact mentioned, if you read them, in almost every one of the stories written about us that year.

On the day this story begins, my highest achievement in the world of glossy culinary/lifestyle magazines was an article in *Gourmet* entitled "Baby Goes Bistro: Provence with Your Toddler." It had been published at the height of the Peter Mayle frenzy, and despite numerous follow-up pitches, I'd failed to sell them anything since. I had, however, gotten other assignments because of it, mostly from regional magazines who considered a *Gourmet* writer living among them something of a catch. Which is why, on this day in question, I was sitting in half a bedroom in suburban Minneapolis—half a bedroom made into an office by virtue of a rented wall—contemplating a rather scattered array of notes. My article "The Walleye: A Fish for All Seasons" had yet to acquire the *je ne sais quoi* so highly prized by my editors at *Minnesota Menus*. It had yet, in fact, to acquire any words at all.

Beyond the rented wall, in the half of the room that remained her bedroom, my four-year-old daughter, Sophie, was amusing herself with a box of crayons and a roll of butcher paper. Like Picasso before her, Sophie was working through a blue period, her pockets filled with the periwinkle, cornflower, blizzard blue, and cerulean she had worn to nubs. The air was thick with creativity and the smell of Crayolas. Our Labrador retriever, Scout, hovered nearby, indifferent to art but always on watch for the stray graham cracker. I heard the crinkle and rasp of paper and Sophie's running narration. "I like this one best," Sophie informed Scout. "See? This one is no good. Now I'm going to make a new one. It's going to be the *best* one. See how I'm making this lady's hair? It goes up into the sky."

I heard a click of dog nails and a thump as Scout, art critic at large, slid to the floor in a stupefied drowse. Sophie could go on like this for hours. She was a self-driven little engine, and this would be my first word of advice to anyone seeking to be a writer—if you must have children during this period of your life, try to get hold of a self-sufficient model like Sophie. She even enjoyed our office arrangement, though half her toys were now stored under her bed and playing dolls with more than one friend at a time meant that somebody had to set up camp on the floor of the closet. (Insisting this was the glamour spot, Sophie made everyone draw lots to see who got it.) We even had an office routine, and from time to time, Sophie's head would pop around the door frame and announce, "Juice break."

I was the one who had reservations about our cramped little slice of suburbia. Especially after a dream I'd recently had that, like a goldfish in a teacup, Sophie had simply stopped growing.

"What happened then?" my husband asked when I woke him up with my panic.

"What do you mean what happened then? Sophie was a . . . a *midget*." I was too upset to fish for the politically acceptable word of the moment.

"No," Tom said calmly, rolling over to face me. "Dreams are like movies. They have settings, actions, *events*. So aside from Sophie's being short, what happened?"

"I don't remember," I said, but a picture was assembling itself in my head. "Okay, in one scene she was *short*. Then, later, you and I were on a cruise to Tahiti. Sophie and Jeff weren't with us. But then when we got off the boat, Sophie *was* there. She was"—I gasped as the horrific memory flooded back to me—"she was Hervé Villechaize."

"Was she happy?"

"She waved at us from the beach. I think she was organizing a scavenger hunt."

"There you go then. She's happy, we're off the hook."

"It was my dream, I *let* myself off the hook."

"Annie, how tall is Sophie?"

"Thirty-nine inches."

"How tall was she last year?"

"Don't you remember? They had that yard-tall party for her at preschool? She brought home a paper beanstalk?"

"Normal growth pattern, then?"

I made a that-isn't-the-point click against my teeth. Somehow, I'd never convinced my scientist husband that empiricism isn't always the way to go, especially when your daughter will soon be sleeping with her feet in the hall. Although I did, I admit, feel better, and told him so.

"What did it look like?" he asked drowsily, relaxing into my calm.

"What did what look like?"

"Tahiti."

"A lot like the Mall of America. Without Camp Snoopy."

Two and a half years earlier, when my husband and I decided to leave academia, our rationale and game plan had seemed foolproof. Tom, a research chemist, had found himself doing less research and more administrative work. There were budget cuts and support-staff cuts and endless harangues over grade inflation, an irritant common to us all.

"Look," I told him, "I have the same pressure. A dozen times a semester I give out As that would have been Cs ten years ago."

"But you're in the history department," Tom said. "What if I give a bogus A to some kid who decides to make nuclear energy his life's work? Twenty years from now, boom, Chernobyl two. You give an A to a kid who doesn't know if Dien Bien Phu was a person or a place and so what? What's the downside for society?"

"Doris Kearns Goodwin?" I volunteered.

But my hubby continued to frown. The grades issue truly bothered him, and you had to love a man who felt that way. That spring the state legislature cut funding again, scotching any hopes of imminent pay raises. Staring down the loaded barrel of taxes, braces, school tuition, and our own base desires not to acquire second, third, and possibly even fourth jobs, we threw in the towel. Tom got a research job with International Milling in Minneapolis, the world's third-largest producer of processed foods. I would try my hand at writing full-time.

Unlike Tom, the gem of the hard sciences, I had never quite taken to university life, nor had my colleagues taken to me. Ten years ago, I'd committed the scarlet sin of writing a dissertation that was a commercial success. For a few years, it had reigned as a cult classic and then, like almost all the books ever written, slipped completely out of sight. But memories are long and bitter in the academic world, and long after my book was out of print, I myself was regarded with suspicion, as if I was still trundling in royalties by the cartload and greedily monopolizing a job that by rights belonged to a needier, worthier scholar. I watched my colleague Arnold Ammerton make the leap from turgid, incomprehensible journal articles to turgid, incomprehensible historical fiction, an effort for which he was not only congratulated but promoted. *Of course,* he admitted with a self-deprecating dip of the head, he *could* have written a racy, Crichtonesque best-seller if he'd wanted to, he'd had that time-travel idea *years* before, but in his own words, Arnold felt "the world deserved better." To all of which I said, unfortunately aloud, unfortunately at a faculty pizza night, unfortunately correctly—B.S. Sun-dried tomatoes froze to the roofs of mouths. Beer turned warm in its pitcher. Such silence had not been heard around a table since the Green Knight crashed King Arthur's New Year's bash a thousand years ago. And I knew that I had, academically speaking, broad-axed my own career.

Needless to say, the idea of leaving academia took on fresh appeal. Out of the campus cauldron, I could stop wondering if my fringe status would eventually hurt Tom's career. I could stop worrying that this particular pterodactyl would come home to roost in the rooftop of our happy marriage.

Once word got around that we had unhooked ourselves from the ICU that is academe, our colleagues let it be known that, in their eyes, we were checking out against medical advice. Nils Holmquist, the ruddy, Santa Claus–size chair of my husband's department, pulled me aside at our farewell barbecue. "Annie, Annie," he said sorrowfully, taking my hand in his enormous, oven-mitted paws. "If only you could persuade Tom to stay. Such a mind, such a shame." His white beard trembled with disappointment. "Is there a chance we still might save him?"

Poor Nils. He was clearly unaware of the role I'd played in fomenting our defection. I didn't have the heart to set him straight.

Nils, at least, seemed genuinely sorry to see us go. Others, and I am sad to say they were mostly in my department, sent us off with the kind of glances generally reserved for those swimming away from the raft of the *Medusa* with the only available life vests. What a cranky, narrow-minded tribe we dwelt among. I could almost hear the boos and hisses as we loaded the kids and the dog in the car and slunk out of Dodge—or, in this case, St. Cloud, bound for the northwest suburbs of Minneapolis. Surprise number one: we weren't going to miss our headily cerebral friends half as much as we'd thought we would.

Surprise number two was harder to absorb. Although Tom's salary at International Milling was nearly double his teaching salary, we somehow had less to show for it. Not only was everything more expensive, we needed more expensive things. Bicycling home with your groceries wasn't a chic, Greenpeace kind of thing to do in Oak Creek Park, it was dangerous. You couldn't fob off cheap wine and NPR's "Classics at Night" on your new friends or they'd wonder what kind of boho idiot you were. Nor could you rely on some eager grad student to baby-sit for free in exchange for access to your LexisNexis account—you had to shell out ten bucks an hour plus pizza. And who knew that a Silicone Prairie boom had sent the cost of housing in the Twin Cities area soaring, forcing us into a split-level rambler whose biggest selling point was a basement that could, one day, be turned into a bedroom?

A few months in, our decision looked dubious at best. We were living in the suburban equivalent of a mud hut. The savings account we'd smugly named "College $" had failed to thrive and, in fact, had an IOU sitting in it for roof repair. Then came 9/11, bringing with it the comforting knowledge that we'd moved our children from a safe, out-of-the-way haven to a metroplex that, Twin Cities newscasters cawed proudly, ranked near the top of the terrorists' wish list. The same newscasters suggested we keep a full tank of gas, three months' worth of food and water, and an extra four or five thousand in cash around the house in case of a biological, chemical, or nuclear "incident."

Just like moving from one country to another, migrating from academia to the United States of Corporate required a currency conversion, and we were the ones holding Canadian dollars.

All the more reason to get going on that walleye article.

———

By mid-afternoon I'd written five hundred words about the history of Chippewa spear fishing. For me, this was the important part of the article, but I'd done enough pieces for *Minnesota Menus* to know that, to them, it would seem mere breading. No matter how interesting it was, they'd ask me to shorten it to free up extra room for walleye-on-a-stick, a hit new-comer at last year's state fair. "Maybe you could add a sidebar on *dipping* sauces," I could already hear Jean Raymonds, my editor, suggesting. Right-o. Sweet-and-sour walleye it would be.

But even as I began to type, I felt my energy flag. I was no M.F.K. Fisher, wandering effortlessly from prose to recipe and back again. The truth was, I had no particular interest in the recipe part of this at all, and like a balky pony, I stopped flat and tossed my mane. How had I ended up at this particular jump anyway? Unlike half the women I met, I had never fantasized about being a food writer. I did not wonder why a cruel twist of fate had kept me from being the wife of, say, Ming Tsai or Tony Bourdain. I wasn't yearning for a Dacor range or a Kyocera chef's knife, and I'd never given a single thought to learning to make artisanal cheese in the Rhône Alps. It was just that food writing was the dime romance of our time, the stuff they were snapping up like Pringles (which I guiltily pre-ferred to IM's TatoBakes); if I could hang a bit of history on it, well, pass me the white-truffle oil.

I was wondering how to get from the shores of Gitche Gumee to wall-eye ceviche when I remembered that George Redquill, the tribal elder I'd interviewed, had given me a perfect segue. His ancestors, the Sokaogan Chippewa, had come west because their prophets promised them a home "where food grows upon the water." In other words, Rice Lake, Min-nesota, where—and this was the lucky part—Schultzie's Supper Club was still serving up plates of pan-fried walleye and wild rice on a nightly basis, just as it had a century ago, when Earl Schultz's grandfather opened the place.

It was a little more trouble to work in my other big interview, Buck Birnbaum, born in Brooklyn, now of Lake Osakis. As a boy, Buck had learned to make lox and smoked whitefish from Grandpa Shmuel on Atlantic Avenue. "So I come here after the war," Buck told me, "'cause I fell in love with a nurse from Osakis, and when I get here, I see the lakes are jammed with fish but there wasn't a whitefish salad in sight. Herring, that's all you had. No kasha *varnishkas* either." Buck married the nurse, who turned out be a natural with kasha, and they opened a combination bait, tackle, and deli on the strip of road that led from town to the lake. To accommodate local tastes, he offered bagels with a choice of butter, cream cheese, or peanut butter and jelly. And his smoked walleye with onions and horseradish sauce was out of this world.

I portrayed Buck as yet another follower of the walleye, not unlike the Sokaogan prophets or the grandfather of Earl Schultz, who'd set out from Bremerhaven. By the time the article was finished, the walleye—not the forests or the farms or even the running highway of the Mississippi—would emerge as Minnesota's true drawing card. I hummed with satisfaction.

And that was where Buck, Schultzie, the Chippewa, and I parted company. I didn't finish "The Walleye: A Fish for All Seasons" that afternoon or even, due to the momentous turn of events, the afternoon of the next day. By the time I finished the article three days later, the poles of our lives were in mid-shift, jerking us from the torpid equator up to the headier latitudes. On the last perfectly normal day of my life, I kept working until I heard my son come home from hockey practice and realized that October dusk was beginning to clump in the corners of the windows. I shut down the computer, gathered my office mate, and headed downstairs, followed by Scout, who at some point in the afternoon had gamely consented to have one of his ears shaded with sky blue, giving him a van Gogh-ish look.

Halfway down the stairs, I saw that Jeff wasn't alone. Hulking behind him was a tough-looking kid with a shock of brown hair who looked like the sixth grade's answer to Marlon Brando in *The Wild One*. I nevertheless put on a nonjudgmental smile and greeted the new friend brightly. He returned my "Hello, Luke" with "Everyone calls me Blade."

As adaptable as Sophie was to any situation, my son, Jeff, was the opposite. At St. Cloud State University, where Tom and I had been on the faculty, Jeff hadn't quite fit in with the sons and daughters of the cloistered few. He preferred football to soccer, real camp to science camp. He hadn't joined the Tree Musketeers in their campaign to end logging in North

America. As far as we knew, he was the only one in his class who wasn't hoping his sixth-grade graduation present would be a surprise trip to Tuscany. It was a school counselor who'd tipped us off to the magnitude of our error—Tom and I had tried to give Jeff the carefree, clueless childhoods we ourselves had had. Not that you didn't mean well, the counselor explained bluntly, but that paradigm no longer exists.

We'd hoped leaving academia would help Jeff find his footing, but as I stood in the entryway watching him with Luke-a.k.a.-Blade, I saw we'd missed the mark again. The two boys could have been a photo essay called "American Youth: Then and Now." Jeff, with his father's fair coloring, was a blush of bright face between stocking cap and blue muffler. Blade had the collar of his leather jacket turned up and stood with a slight hunch to his shoulders, as if ready to light a cigarette in the wind.

While Jeff was taking off his boots—Blade didn't wear any, of course, just wildly strobing Nikes—Sophie darted forward waving a blue-crayoned drawing in Jeff's face.

"Who's the kid?" Blade asked.

"My sister. Wow, that's really good, Sophie. Can I have it?"

Blade looked puzzled. "Your whole sister? Like, your mom and dad are her mom and dad?"

"Yeah."

"Cool. Hey, what about—"

Jeff looked at me anxiously. "Mom, can I show him The Room?"

"Jeff, we've—"

I didn't have the heart to do it. We'd told Jeff time and time again that The Room was part of Dad's work, not a tourist attraction. We'd explained that anyone who wanted to be friends with him would be friends with or without The Room, because he was a good person and fun to be with. Which was a lie. Because, while Jeff was everything we told him he was, the other boys were more like Blade, with friendship meters finely attuned to PlayStations, Air Jordans, and personal paging devices. The Room was Jeff's ace in the hole. Besides, like the rest of us, he was paying a price for it. If The Room hadn't taken up all of what was supposed to be the master bedroom and bath, Tom and I would have been able to sleep there, Sophie would have had a bedroom to herself, and Jeff would have had the larger room Sophie and I shared as office and bedroom.

"Oh, all right," I said, wondering if there was something in The Room I could plunder for dinner. "But you know the rules. If—"

"I know, I know," Jeff interrupted. "If we want a snack, you have to call Blade's mom to make sure it's okay."

"She won't be home," Blade offered.

"No? Does she work, then?"

Blade shrugged, and I realized it probably wouldn't matter whether we got hold of his mother or not. I began to feel ever so slightly sorry for him, which was probably why Jeff had brought him home in the first place. Jeff, like his father, could go through life without ever knowing who the stray dog was.

"Let me get the keys," I said.

_____

Chapter 2

IT

I swung open the door of The Room and pocketed the keys. As usual, the moment rivaled the opening of Tutankhamen's tomb, with Jeff in the role of Howard Carter. He flipped on the light switch. Blade stood transfixed, jaw agape. Which, I'd noticed, was the common reaction.

The Room was filled with rows of eight-foot-tall gray metal shelves, the kind you'd expect to see in a stockroom. Industrial strength, they'd been supplied by International Milling. IM had also supplied the hundreds of packages and boxes filling them.

"C'mon," Jeff said, pulling Blade into The Room. "What do you want? Mom, where are those chocolate-covered potato-chip things?"

I opened the three-ring binder chained to the shelf unit nearest the door and looked up the code for MudSpuds. "A-567," I said.

Blade was so excited I could hear him breathing through his mouth. While the boys toured the shelves, I looked around for something to whip up for dinner. Handy, having a minimart in your master bedroom.

At St. Cloud State University, Tom had been heavily involved in the chemical composition of synthetic substances, with special research in the area of artificial oligosaccharides. I wasn't sure what that meant, exactly— I only memorized it so I could answer with crisp enthusiasm when someone asked, "What's Tom into these days?"—but it had something to do with man-made carbohydrate molecules and their various behaviors. Far more scientifically savvy than I was, International Milling took one look at Tom's CV and snatched him up for their research-and-development department.

Tom's new job was easier for me to describe. It was to invent nothing. Good tasting, satisfying nothing, but nothing nevertheless. International Milling held the patent on a number of synthetic substances—fats, sugars, salt, gluten, you name it, all cleared by the FDA and just waiting to find their way into delicious, 100 percent nutritive-free comestibles. Synfoods, as IM called them, would be *the* wave of the twenty-first century, banishing obesity, diabetes, and high blood pressure while leaving mankind free to cavort at the trough of nonstop grazing. IM saw itself racking up millions in sales. Leaving number two competitor, General Mills, to dither in the dust. Leaving number one competitor, Canfield Brands, so outgunned in the synfood wars they'd raise the white flag.

For the lucky researcher whose product made it to market, there were perks, bonuses, and royalties to beat the band. I saw proof of that early on, at a meet-and-greet cocktail party held in our honor.

"That's Barney Oldenfield," Tom whispered in my ear as we did our turn through the room. I'd already heard much of the legendary, nearly mythic Barney. He was the Oppenheimer of shelf-stable foods, the Bill Gates of reconstituted carbs. Or rather, reformulated and much-tinkered-with potatoes. MudSpuds were nothing compared to his most recent creation, the Dip-*IN*-Chip, a little purse of potato chip that, when bitten into, rewarded the snacker with a creamy burst of dip. Available in French onion, barbecue, roasted garlic, and bacon horseradish. How the dip stayed creamy (not to mention safely edible through the year 2008), and how the chip stayed crisp, were Barney's secrets, and the reason why, on our way in, we'd passed a Ferrari convertible with license plates that said "SPUD-DR" in large blue letters. He was a pulsating beacon of inspiration to every researcher in the room—an imperfect simile, perhaps, because Barney was easily a head shorter than trophy-wife number three on his arm. Now *she* was a beacon.

Of course, there had been a few synfood failures as well, disappointments whose unfortunate creators were no longer in the employ of IM. Pizza in a tube hadn't set the world on fire. Macarooni, meringue-filled chocolate pasta, was similarly a dud. And the first try at nutritive-free bread had to be abandoned because vermin continually mistook it for nesting material. But Tom, I knew, would steer clear of such disasters. He'd already had modest success with an unsinkable cornflake and now was working on an item so exciting, so potentially lucrative, we couldn't even bring ourselves to call it by name. For months now, we had simply been referring to it as *It*. And when *It* was invented, we too would be on the way to Barney Oldenfield-like heights. Fingers crossed, we might even be able to trade up to a house large enough to breathe in.

In the meantime, The Room considerably eased our dining and entertainment budget. Besides their fledgling synfood division, IM still made plenty of traditional packaged foods. As trusted—or at least willing— members of the IM family, we were supplied with box upon box of foods in various stages of testing and refinement. Packaged in clear cellophane or plain white, each stamped with a coded number, we were encouraged to share these items with our friends. In return for this largesse, we had to fill out and return the "Observation and Comment" sheets dispensed with the items. IM was a stickler about this, and failure to complete the sheets in a timely way left you guiltily scrambling to invent guests and their reactions. I'm sure there are people in market research who are still thrilled to contemplate the fact that such a solid citizen as Mr. S. Wilkins—distant relative of ours, native of Labrador, now holding down a full-time job as a security guard—was so taken with the Beef Teezers that he consumed eight of them in a single sitting. After that, we took care to keep Scout out of The Room.

I grabbed a box of chicken-and-portobello pilaf and a Peaches 'n Dream Dessert Mix. I congratulated myself on having a bunch of real, honest-to-goodness broccoli in the refrigerator, and fleetingly wondered if my family would recognize anything as exotic as fresh produce, much less eat it.

"Are you boys ready?" I asked. At the door, I did the usual check-out routine. "Okay, show me what you've got. Pockets inside out, please. I'm sorry about this, Blade, but this is very, *very*, top-secret stuff, you know? You'll have to eat that candy bar before you leave today, and I have to make sure you haven't taken anything with you."

All this wasn't strictly necessary, but Jeff had hinted—broadly—that his friends thought the maximum-security treatment was cool. In Blade's case, it might also be routine. He looked ready to go up against our country-goose wallpaper and spread 'em. I snapped the Observation and Comment sheet into his hand as if giving him his parole papers.

"Your mom *rocks*," I heard him whisper to Jeff as I went off down the stairs.

If you grew up, as I did, with unrestricted access to TV and a too steady diet of *Little House* and *The Waltons*, you may have formed the idea that the harmonious family at the table, not the splitting of the atom, was the defining achievement of the American twentieth century. I certainly did. I believed that people who loved one another produced happy families, and happy families invariably partook of happy meals, the kind in which members eagerly asked after one another's days and, in concert, agreed that tonight would be a good night to pop popcorn or, better yet, sweep the floor and beat the rugs so Ma could take a nice bath in the old tin tub Pa had brought all the way from Ohio. One month into my marriage, when the NFC championship game coincided with our dinner hour, I realized on what a thin foundation my faith rested. The subsequent arrival of each child only multiplied the odds that on any given night someone would be cranky, teething, vomitous, sullen, premenstrual, or otherwise unable to hold up his or her end of things.

Tonight it was Tom's turn. From the minute he walked in the door, he exhibited a strange and anxious quiver, an antsy-ness so intense I wondered if someone in R and D had said, *Hey, Mondays are a drag, let's all do amphetamines.* When I saw his briefcase sitting on the bench in the entryway, I knew something was seriously amiss. This may seem like small potatoes, but my husband has a scientist's mind and mien. He's as far from the stereotype of the absentminded professor as Katie Couric is from an original thought. His ordinary routine was to carry his briefcase up to our bedroom, deposit it by the bed, and change out of his work clothes. So the sight of a briefcase left on a bench, let alone a briefcase with one latch undone, gave me pause. I tried to catch his eye all through dinner. Without success. Instead we heard a thrilling recital by Sophie about the virtues of indigo blue over navy blue, along with a request that we write the Crayola company to ask them to stop making navy blue because, in a word, it was "stinky." Jeff told Tom about Blade and Blade's suggestion for a new flavor of Korn Klippers—tequila shot.

"It would be way cool," Jeff said, "because, like, you could party hearty and never even need to buy booze. You could just get bags and bags and *bags* of Korn Klippers."

I roused myself from my distraction over my husband's state. *Party hearty? Booze?* Where did this come from? At St. Cloud State, everyone sipped white wine. In Oak Creek Park, Tom and I had the occasional cocktail. No one in the family, except for a second cousin of Tom's who'd once been arrested on an episode of *Cops*, drank "booze." And we relaxed. We entertained. We had people over. We did not "party hearty." I looked to Tom for help, hoping he might hold forth on how alcohol breaks down during cooking, but he was moving his pilaf around on his plate the way Richard Dreyfuss had pushed his mashed potatoes around in *Close Encounters of the Third Kind*.

"And so these tequila-shot Korn Klippers would be alcoholic?" I asked Jeff. "Would you need an ID to buy them?"

"Well, I . . ."

"Could kids buy them?"

"Well, *duh*, Mom. Not if they have alcohol in them."

"So you couldn't sell them in grocery stores?"

"Of *course* not."

"Where would you sell them, then?"

Jeff thought. "Liquor stores, I guess."

"So," I said thoughtfully, "let me get this straight. We're going to sell tequila-shot Korn Klippers so people won't have to bother to buy liquor.

But they'll have to go to a liquor store to buy them, so why won't they just buy the liquor while they're there?"

Jeff shrugged. Now *he* was beginning to make mini-Pyrénées out of his pilaf.

"I'd say Blade has a lot to learn about market economy," I concluded, starting to gather up the dishes. Tom's absenteeism was really beginning to bother me.

I finally established contact with Tom while Jeff was reading Sophie her bedtime story. Unlike houses ripped by the blood-curdling screams of sibling rivalry, ours was a placid little patch, and Sophie adored her big brother. He had been the only one who could rock her to sleep when she'd had colic, and if she woke up scared in the middle of the night, she went to his room first, not ours. Jeff didn't mind his role as designated reader. He had such a warm, caring nature that I sometimes felt I'd given birth to a human version of Lassie who, with Tom's fair, thatchlike hair and my brown eyes, Jeff actually resembled a bit.

Losing the bedtime-story gig had been a bitter pill to swallow at first. What had we done? Why couldn't we be the ones sitting in the ring of soft lamplight watching Sophie's dark ringlets shake with delight? It was the biggest perk of the preschool years, one of the few jobs that did not require endless patience, a flair for discipline, or an indifference to ripe and smelly odors. All it required was a sense of fun and a persistent fondness for the smell of books and freshly washed offspring. But Tom and I had been fired. To salve our feelings, we had taken to sitting out story time over wine or coffee and having what we racily referred to as AC—adult conversation. "You going to tell me?" I asked the minute the coffee was poured.

Tom's eyebrows lifted, his blue eyes widened. At thirty-six, the age when most of us are beginning to look a little shopworn, Tom still had his brightness, that fresh, you-don't-say look he'd had a decade earlier. Not a handsome face, but something much better—an honest and, most days, cheerful face. If you don't think that beats handsome, you've never been married.

"Oh, come on, Tom. We both know you can't keep a secret. What's the deal?"

"*It.*"

"*It?*"

"A new version. I think I've got it this time."

I felt deflated. What had I been hoping for? A bonus? A raise? An HGTV moment when he told me he was driving by a fantastic five-bedroom, 2,500 square footer that had just gone on the market for such a fantastically affordable price that he'd put in a bid? Or, on the other hand, that he'd been fired, that IM was closing down the synfoods division, wary of carcinogen-inspired lawsuits twenty years down the road? Or that he'd been longing to dress in women's clothes for years and had finally decided to share his very special secret with me?

Yes, I guess I was expecting all of those things. I was expecting something big. And though *It* was a big idea, yet another trial version of it, of which there had been many, hardly rocked my world.

Tom saw my disappointment. "No, Annie. This batch is . . . well, you'll see."

"You brought some home?"

"Smuggled it past security."

Technically speaking, products at this stage of raw development weren't supposed to leave IM's premises. But on this project, I was Tom's muse. Not only his muse but his arbiter of taste. For *It* was a substance I knew a great deal about, a substance I had spent years sampling and choosing and eventually studying.

Left to his own devices, Tom might have focused on creating artificial shredded wheat or beets made from a seaweed derivative. He often wandered down the corridors of what was scientifically interesting rather than what was commercially viable. But I—I brought him back to reality.

"If you're going to invent fake food," I'd told him, "invent something people already love, something they're dying to gorge themselves on." Something that will make us some money and get us a bigger house, I'd added silently.

"What would that be?" Tom had asked.

I couldn't believe he didn't guess. The answer was right in front of us. But men can be curiously obtuse about food, never realizing there are some items worthy of genuflected worship.

"Chocolate," I told him.

"Chocolate?" He'd blinked slightly, as if hearing the word for the first time.

"A good, semi-bittersweet chocolate," I'd said, warming to my subject and, I admit, beginning to drool just a little. "A chocolate that tastes good on its own but is also hospitable to the addition of nuts and caramel. A chocolate versatile enough to be chunked into cookies or wrapped around a nougat center."

"Annie," he'd said, inspiration lighting his features. "Annie, that's *it!* And I've been working on a polymer-coated molecule that bonds at room temperatures but dissolves over moderate heat . . ."

When we made love later that night, it was with the kind of passionate, dirty-minded zeal that I adore. Besides many silly, double-entendre references to *It,* there'd been a scenario about a good little girl who would be a very bad little girl in exchange for a candy bar. And this is one of the things I loved most about my husband—that even though he thought of himself as too plain and too tame to be exciting to women, he knew he was exciting to me, and that was the self he always brought to our bedroom.

Remembering all this, I was freshly enthused about the new version of *It.*

Tom made me wait another hour, though—"Until both children are in bed, Annie"—and then brought a wrapped object the size of a Filofax out of his briefcase. I peeled back the wrappings and inhaled.

"No scent."

"I can fix that."

"You'll have to. The smell is half the pleasure. And the color should be a shade darker too."

But the first cut was a *wow*. Like real chocolate, this particular version had just the right amount of resistance, with little splinters that fell away from the edges as I sliced. I picked one up and tasted it.

"Mmm. Creamy." I rolled my tongue around in my mouth. "Really good, intense flavor. No chalkiness, either." Chalkiness had been a problem from the outset, giving Tom's inventions an unappealing, crumbly quality, like talcum powder mixed with cocoa and held together with soap. He'd made progress, but had yet to completely overcome a tendency to crumb.

"Well?" Tom asked eagerly. "On a scale of one to ten?"

I put more of the slivers in my mouth. Then I cut a sizable chunk. Each piece seemed better than the one before. I felt that I'm-falling-in-love feeling certain foods engender. "God, this is wonderful. Cut me some more."

But Tom snatched it away and folded the chunk back into its wrappings. "No more," he said. "Remember the time you got that rash?"

"Just one little sliver," I begged. My face was flushed and I felt like throwing a tantrum. God, this stuff really *was* like chocolate.

"You can have more tomorrow," Tom said, hiding *It* at the back of a cupboard. "But only if you're a very *good* little girl."

"Or a very naughty one," I said, picking up the crumbs with my fingertips. "Tom, look," I said suddenly. It was astonishing, really. *"Look!"* I waved my smeary fingertips at him.

"Want a paper towel?" he asked.

"No, that's not it. Look at my fingers. Look at the way it *melts*—in your mouth *and* in your hand, just like chocolate."

"Oh, yeah," Tom said, "I gave it the same melting point as cocoa butter. I could make it higher. Or lower. Whatever you want."

"No," I said, "this is *perfect*."

I woke up at three A.M. with a strange but familiar longing. I felt calm and languorous but also *desirous*. Sex? No, we'd had that several hours ago. It was something very close to sex, though. Something that was making my whole body sigh. Slowly, the source of my yearning floated from my subconscious into my conscious mind. It was like trying, with both patience and excitement, to keep yourself from guessing a very pleasant surprise, until at last the prolonged moment ripened and fell into your hand. *Yes, that's it!*

I slipped out of bed, hurried downstairs, and rummaged in the cupboard until I found what I was after. *It*. Just like real chocolate, *It* had seduced my palate and bewitched my entire body. *It* had left its calling card the way a lover leaves behind a cuff link. *It* had left me wanting more in the way that good chocolate—real chocolate—invariably does. I peeled back the foil and cut a rich, satisfying bite, unfurling with pleasure as Tom's creation slid down my throat.

Chapter 3

THE FEW, THE PROUD

I admit it. I was so excited about Tom's discovery I completely forgot about "The Walleye: A Fish for All Seasons" until the night before it was due. From midnight on, I was scrounging the Internet and back issues of the Sunday magazine for recipe inspirations. At least one concoction, lifted from the *Onamia Lutheran Church Cookbook,* seemed downright bilious to me—walleye Stroganoff?—but I was short on the goods and grasping at straws. I even sank so low as to scale the type size up a point, an incredibly childish trick and one I knew would come back to haunt me. *You need more recipes? You're kidding. Wow, I thought they were taking over, so I weeded several out. No, it's not a problem, I'll just work them back in. I can turn it around and have it in your e-mail tomorrow morning. Don't worry about it, no, no thanks necessary.* Lie, lie, lie. What can I say? I was obsessed with *It.*

By the time my walleye swam through cyberspace as a fifty-KB e-mail attachment, I was working my way through my second block of Tom's synchocolate. Not that I'd eaten it all. No, though I'd eaten plenty. Mostly, I'd become fascinated with playing with the stuff. The first day I melted it and watched it cool to room temperature, perfectly regaining its solidity. The next day I poured a melted cupful on a cookie sheet, spread it out with a spatula, waited for it to cool, and used our pizza wheel to cut it into firm but deliciously silken little wafers. Another day I had fun dipping various nuts and fruits into it. A hit every time. The stuff was simply amazing. There was almost nothing you could do to ruin it.

The second batch Tom brought home was even better than the first, having acquired the proper scent (deep yet subtle) and shade (just this side of coffee). He was, he told me, working on a richer, lighter-hued milk-chocolate version as well, but was having trouble with IM's synmilk derivative, which kept separating during the mixing process and rising to the surface in an unattractive scum.

By the time the third block came home, the children were clamoring to try it. Since I'd been snacking for ten days with no problems, I gave them sparing portions. Young systems, as we'd learned when we served a prototype ice cream at Jeff's last birthday party, can be significantly more sensitive than adults.' Fortunately, there hadn't been any hospitalizations, although there was a great deal of absenteeism in class the next day. Most parents wrote it off as childish gluttony, and I'm ashamed to say we let the kids take the rap. One set of parents was initially irrate but brightened up when we delivered our apologies in person with a case of Quacker Snacks, the cracker that whistles. So despite both Jeff and Sophie's clamoring, *It* was meted out sparingly.

When a week went by and even the children suffered no ill effects, Tom took the news to his bosses.

"And?" I said when he came home that night.

"And they liked it."

A slow grin broke across my husband's face, lighting his eyes and making crow's-feet-crinkles in the corners. For someone with Tom's low-key nature, this was the equivalent of throwing his hat in the air, or roaring up the driveway with a new car whose vanity plates said "$$-R-US."

"Really?"

"Oh yeah. Really. They said—" Tom made an effort to retrieve the exact words. "They said they're 'extremely hopeful' about its 'market potential.' "

I felt the tiniest, meanest pang of disappointment. I wanted Tom to get fanfare and a hero's parade. I wanted the corporate chiefs of IM to appreciate the brain they had hold of and carry him around the office on their shoulders. I wanted to hear that production of *It* would start tomorrow, that my husband would get a bonus, a promotion, a promise of things to come. Enough money for a down payment on a house we could all fit in. Was that so terrible? I caught myself just in time to unstitch the frown lines forming between my brows. I wasn't going to rain on Tom's parade. I hugged him. "Just wait till those CEOs take samples home to their wives. You'll be the hottest thing since sliced bread."

"Well, *It*'s just a little fake chocolate, Annie." He brushed his hair back, forgetting, as he has for several years now, that he no longer sports the hairstyle of a young Han Solo and that this gesture is no longer required. I found it endearing anyway. "Maybe we shouldn't get our hopes up too high."

Too late for that. My hopes had already skimmed past the space shuttle.

Predictably, *Minnesota Menus* wanted the historical aspects of "The Walleye: A Fish for All Seasons" pared down and the recipes plumped up. Ordinarily, this would have depressed me beyond measure and become a bone of contention, but I was now so distracted by what IM was or wasn't going to do with *It* that I responded to my editor's requests with the robotic good cheer of a Stepford wife. My article now compressed time, galloping past the evolution of the walleye and the Sokaogan Chippewa and creating the impression that history had begun with the arrival of the white man and, shortly after it, the implementation of fishing season. In addition to adding recipes for walleye almandine and walleye à l'orange, I came up with a sidebar they flipped over, an explicit but not overly gory step-by-step guide to cleaning and filleting your own catch. Tom was my source on this, and I decided not to include a reverie about how very, very much my children enjoyed playing with the air sacs in a pan of water. If nothing else, *It* was smoothing my sometimes truculent relations with *Minnesota Menus*. My editor must have wondered what kind of happy pills I was on.

An hour after I e-mailed off the final revisions, Tom called.

"Annie," he said, and then fell silent.

"What's up?"

"They want us to come to a meeting." I didn't have to ask who. "*Both* of us."

I felt a curl of excitement that began with my toes, which suddenly began to perspire. I was right. I was right! *It* was going to be big. "When? What time? Why do they want to see *me*?"

Tom ticked off answers like points on a lab sheet. "As soon as possible. Time flexible. And why you, I'm not sure, except I think"—and here he lowered his voice—"except I think it's something good. They want to know if you're free early next week."

Aside from carpooling for Sophie's preschool two mornings a week, I was pretty much free until Jeff's high school graduation seven years from now. I told Tom I didn't think finding a sitter for Sophie would be a problem and I'd call him back in a few minutes. It was while I was securing the sitter that my gaze fell on my reflection in the mirror. I'd always considered myself mildly pretty in a good-to-see-you, nonthreatening sort of way. But, let's face it, writers aren't held to the highest glam standards in the world. I was always looking at the endless stream of heels, suits, blouses, trousers, and "office" jewelry my friend Astrid bought and thinking, I am lucky, so lucky, not to be in the corporate whirl. Well, here I was, about to enter—for an hour at least—that very whirl.

Let's start at the top. Good hair, a nice, thick brown, but, at the moment, caught in an unfortunate time warp. What had I been thinking all these years? my newly discerning self inquired. Okay, remain calm. My eyes, deep brown, with a nice little upward slant, always made up well, and I was sure, if I really searched for them, I still owned both an eyelash curler and tweezers. Lipstick was always a problem, since anything too colorful made me look like I should be telling fortunes and selling lucky charms, but perhaps a nice pale winter rose shade . . . I hurried on. True, my outfit-of-the-day—jeans, Eddie Bauer T-shirt—screamed stay-at-home mother—but the body beneath it, I'm proud to say, was still respectable. Looser and wider than it once had been but, at thirty-five, possessed its own kind of ripe, post-childbirth niceness. So a stylish hair-cut, a few painful sessions with the tweezers, a new outfit, and I'd be ready to go. Oh no, really, I heard myself saying, I'm only *one year* younger than Tom. Thank you, though. Just lucky genes, I guess.

As I wheeled into the IM parking lot the day of the meeting, I had the confident glow of those women you see in Dove or Oil of Olay commercials—women meant to astound you with how good they look for their ages. It had not been easy. In a misguided attempt to strike out toward something different, I'd bypassed my usual hairdresser and gone to a salon I thought of as hip and youngish. I was halfway on my way to Liza Minnelli-dom—Spikes! For the *Older* Woman!—when I called a halt to the madness and, through shrewd bargaining and a hefty tip, emerged with something I actually liked, a chin-length, slightly tousled cut, with a sexy little fringe tickling my cheekbones.

The clothes story was its own nightmare. The last time I shopped for clothes, constructed clothes did not exist. There were no blouses with darts, not to mention belts with anything, and if you really needed a size large, you had to beat all the size-two girls to the racks before they got them all. Swing tops, one-size-fits-all pants, sweaters that measured sixty inches at the bottom edge—need I say more? But that era, I discovered in the harsh glare of dressing-room lights, was long gone. Not only did the blouses have darts at the bust, they had them at the waist. The sleeves were either waferlike little winglets or altogether missing. And instead of a ten or a twelve, my sizes through the swing-top era, I discovered I wore a fourteen. The pants experience I won't even go into. Finally, a gaminelike salesgirl showing off her ultratoned arms in a gauzy little number suggested I might try the Eileen Fisher section two floors up, which I did, and left with trousers, shirt, and lightly quilted jacket in ravishingly coordinated shades of stone, pebble, and carrara. And so what if I'd settled on the large? I asked myself. I was five-six, and *lots* of women my height wore a fourteen. *Lots* of them.

If only it were summer! I could have impressed everyone on my way into IM—a worthwhile task since the company's headquarters were in a majestic Frank Lloyd Wright building tucked into a nest of forest overlooking a private lake. (Okay, so Minnesota has ten thousand of them—it's still impressive to get one all to yourself.) But it was the second of November, so I settled for ditching my coat and boots in Tom's office, stepping into the low heels I'd brought, and enjoying a purr of approval from my husband. I wanted to ask him if he'd gotten a better idea of what this meeting was about, but before I could, we were called for and ushered two floors up to a conference room.

A conference room? To call it a conference room was akin to calling Versailles a house. Certainly this was *the* conference room, the one reserved for oh-so-special meetings. Three of the walls were flagstone, but the fourth was glass, cantilevered so that you felt you were actually hovering over the lake. The furniture had that spare but comfortable arts and crafts look, all earth tones and brushed copper. I congratulated myself on the Eileen Fisher outfit—my stone-pebble-carrara trio fit right in.

Then my glance fell on the oak conference table and I realized that this was indeed to be one of those life-changing meetings. Arranged at the dozen places, I saw a dozen copies of my dissertation, the book version, but where did they find it? It had been out of print for over a decade. *The Coming of Chocolate* by Anne Manning Wilkins. For a moment, I felt the momentary flutter of unbearable happiness I'd felt the very first time I'd seen it. Tom and I had been married a little over a year. We both had our Ph.D.s and I'd just found out, the month before, that I was pregnant with Jeff. I remember opening the advance reading copy from the publisher and first sniffing, then laying my cheek against, the cool pages. I was filled with a sense of having found my starting point in the world, a better starting point than I had ever imagined.

Beside each book was a matte-black folder printed with swirling gold letters that said "Better Than Chocolate." And beside that, a small bar, wrapped to resemble gold bullion and embossed with the IM logo and the words "One Ounce Fine Goods."

I wanted to squeeze Tom's hand, but he was already being seated across from me, on the other side of the table. For the first time, I noticed how many people were in the room and that they had all risen as we entered.

"I'm Ed Lundquist, senior corporate VP," said a very tall man who once, Tom had informed me reverently, been a lay-up ace on the U. of M. basketball team. "Let me introduce you to everyone else."

I had a hard time keeping the myriad vice presidents and officers straight—marketing, innovation and technology, sales, human resources, corporate communications, advertising and brands management—and was relieved when we got to the only other woman in the room. Her name was Kate Hawkins and there was something crisp and deeply reassuring in the nod she gave me.

"Are we all here?" Ed asked.

"We're still waiting for Lucie," said Bob Kovacek, head of advertising and brands management.

"Now *there's* breaking news," Kate said. I thought I detected a slight heavenward eye roll.

"Shall we start without her?" Ed asked tentatively, glancing at Kate.

"Let's. She'll be along soon." Kate smiled a mockingly sweet smile. "I'm absolutely sure she'll be able to find a few minutes for us in her busy schedule."

As we found our seats, I took a closer look at Kate and tried to recall what department she was in. Advertising? Merchandising? Market research? Sales? Ten or fifteen years older than me, she was definitely a woman after my own heart. Not only was Ed the lay-up ace deferring to her, but her amiable sarcasm broke the waves of formality that had begun forming around all of us. It was like watching Eve Arden wisecrack her way through *Mildred Pierce*.

"Now," Ed began, "Tom here has come up with an exceptionally exciting product. Tom, you really knocked our socks off with this one. We've known for some time that Canfield Brands has been working on their own line of synfoods." He glanced at me and explained, "Synthetic foods made from proprietary, FDA-approved synthetic ingredients. Canfield's basic materials are essentially similar to ours, but, to date, we've been a little ahead of the curve. Not that they haven't scored some successes."

"*Satin!*" said the innovation and technology VP, and everyone groaned. I recalled that Canfield's synthetic milk, available in "rainbow flavors," was a huge success.

"It's the snack-size packaging," Kate said. "Stroke of genius, those pink plastic udders. Not surprisingly, prime consumers are males ages thirteen to twenty-five."

I suppressed a smile. Kate had clearly passed the age where being a nice girl mattered to her. I found myself wanting her to like me.

"Huge success," said Ed without a trace of irony.

"Yes, it is," Kate agreed. "Huge."

"But," said Ed, bringing us all back to the point, "not in the same league with this chocolate stuff." He held his little gold bar aloft and surveyed us solemnly. "This, we feel, could be *bigger than pizza*." He let his words settle in the quiet room. Outside, I saw, it had begun to snow, happy little whirls of flakes that had shown up just to look in on us. "Bob and his team have convinced me that this product, this very *special* product, should have an equally unique market strategy. Tom, Annie, are you with me?"

We both nodded. I had that feeling you get when you are at the very top of the roller coaster, right before you go hurtling down with your stomach flung against your ribs.

"Good. It's all outlined in the presentation folder, but let me lay out the basics before handing it off to Bob. We feel, IM feels—"

Suddenly, the double doors swung open and a young black woman stepped into the room. "Sorry I'm late," she said breezily.

Bob Kovacek stood up. "Tom, Annie, this is Lucie Kinneman, the other half of my best-brands management team. She and Kate have come up with a remarkable strategy."

Lucie was tall and slim and as graceful as a gazelle. She sprang forward and put her hand in mine. "Lucie," she said. "As in Port Saint L-u-c-i-e."

I found it hard to believe she and Kate were part of a team, let alone had dreamed up a strategy together. They were each other's diametrical opposite. If Kate Hawkins was a gal in shoulder pads, Lucie Kinneman was someone you just *knew* had a ring in her belly button. Lucie's salmon pullover was dazzling with her eggplant miniskirt. Five belts, each a different color, sat at rakish angles on the nodes of her hips, giving her the look of an unusually tall and colorful ring-toss game. When she sat, her legs folded gracefully in their saffron tights and high clogs. Lucie's hoop earrings danced, her head was a bouquet of corkscrew curls. She was stupendously adorable, intimidatingly hip.

"Lucie, it's so good of you to make time for us," Kate said. "I hope we aren't wreaking too much havoc with your crowded schedule?"

In the Minnesota I grew up in, our idea of ethnic diversity was someone whose grandparents were Polish rather than Swedish or Norwegian. Catholics were strange people who lived mostly in St. Paul, and exotic cuisine meant meatballs and spaghetti that didn't come out of a can. This left us wildly ill-equipped for the great influx of the 1980s. We didn't know how to deal with anyone who didn't grow up knowing that the smelt ran in late April and the Vikings couldn't score inside the red zone. Confronted with people whose features screamed I-am-a-stranger-here-among-you, the response of most Minnesotans was to smile politely and wait to see who made it through the winter. No sense in going overboard for softies who'd turn tail the minute the thermometer dipped beneath minus twenty. But those who lasted met an even chillier politeness in the spring, as anyone who wintered in Minnesota by choice was surely more than a little off the beam and therefore to be given the widest berth possible.

I looked around the table to see how Kate's comments to Lucie were flying. People seemed simultaneously uncomfortable and gleeful, as if they were weighing the disaster of a hostile-workplace lawsuit against the satisfaction of seeing Lucie called on her obviously habitual tardiness. Lucie herself remained oblivious to all the nuances.

"Sorry. I have been *so swamped*. Did I miss anything?"

"Lucie is often late," Kate said, glancing at me with a slightly raised eyebrow, "but her sheer brilliance makes up for it."

"Why, *thank* you," Lucie said, flashing a radiant smile.

"As I was saying," Ed Lundquist continued, gathering our attention back to him, "IM feels that Better Than Chocolate—that's what we're tentatively calling it—is *better than* advertising. We want to give the product a more meaningful rollout. Do you want to take it from here, Bob?"

"Thanks, Ed. Okay, does anyone remember that coffee campaign, ten or so years ago? Where that couple met and romanced through a series of commercials? We want to take that concept one step further."

"We want to leave out the commercial," Kate said. "We want to make Better Than Chocolate more than just a product."

"We want to make it a *lifestyle*," Lucie finished breathlessly.

"That's where you would come in, Tom, Annie," Bob said. "You are a very typical, very attractive young American couple. Striving. Achieving. Two kids, big dreams. Tom, as the product's father, is a natural spokesman. And your background, Annie, is, well, it couldn't be more perfect. Everyone, I'd like you all to read the book in front of you over this weekend. *The Coming of Chocolate* was Annie's dissertation." He glanced at me and smiled warmly. "Annie parlayed her history background into a career as a food writer."

I wondered briefly what my other former colleagues in the history department would say to the idea that my Ph.D. had been a mere springboard to *Minnesota Menus*. Sellout, for starters. But I still wished they were here to see the ripple of interest that ran through the room as necks craned toward me.

"We've developed what we feel is a unique strategy," Bob continued, "a *lifestyle-oriented* approach that positions our product as the key that opens the door. We've already done some preliminary market research and are now in the process of refining and developing a multilayered approach for—"

"Oh for goodness sakes, Bob," Kate interrupted, "just cut to the chase. Traditional ad campaign, out. Tom and Annie, in. We want to go right to the heart of our market—upscale, health-conscious adults in the twenty-five to forty-five demographic. Through a series of interviews and personal appearances—primarily television and food and lifestyle print media—we will create a *story* and, in the process, enormous product interest for Better Than Chocolate."

I was liking Kate better by the minute. My initial evaluation had fallen short of the mark. She was way, way smarter than Eve Arden.

"Have I got it right, Bob?" she asked.

"Yes," Bob conceded. "In a nutshell, that's it."

"So I hope we can persuade you to sign on," Ed Lundquist added, looking from Tom to me and back to Tom. "Of course, we'll have to work out the details, but I can pretty much assure you that the terms will be very, very favorable. And Kate will explain about the house later."

The house? The *house???* I wanted to walk around the table, pull up a chair, and grab Ed Lundquist by the tie until he answered my questions. What house? But I saw Tom—who still remembered my critique of Arnold Ammerton at that faculty pizza party—frantically trying to catch my eye, so I gave him a don't-worry-darling smile and stayed in my seat. Barely.

"Now if you'll excuse me," Ed Lundquist said, "I have another meeting to do, so I'll leave you all to get on with things. Tom, Annie, we'll be in touch."

It occurred to me as he left the room that he'd sat through the whole meeting just to say those words. Not to see us, not to sign off on the project—those things had already been done. No, he'd come just to assure us that there would be enough money, oodles of it, to forestall any silly impulses on our part to say no.

It was beautifully orchestrated, the way that, the minute Ed left, a girl sailed in with a cart laden with beverages, fresh fruit, muffins, and croissants. Apparently, we were taking a little break. Or maybe the muffins were just to loosen up the atmosphere.

"So," Kate said, her gray-eyed gaze suddenly on me, "tell us what you know about chocolate, Annie."

"What I know about chocolate?" I echoed. "HOUSE" was still flashing in gaudy neon in my brain, and it took a moment to reel myself in. I reached for a croissant. Did I see Lucie frown slightly over her fresh cantaloupe cubes? "Well," I began. My voice sounded dry and reedy, like a student preparing to deliver an oral presentation she was not at all certain of.

"Will someone get Annie some coffee, please?" Kate asked, and coffee miraculously appeared beside my croissant. "Yes, Annie. How did you become interested in chocolate? Why did you choose it as your dissertation topic?"

Everyone, including Tom, was looking at me. Clearly, this was not the time to tell the whole truth and nothing but. Because the truth was,

I'd begun to write about chocolate, and food in general, by default. History is one of those commodities that is made very slowly but consumed at a breakneck pace, and by the time I came along to do my dissertation, I discovered that all the good ideas, and a lot of the not-so-good ideas, had been taken. I'd had three topics turned down—the first on widows' rights in seventeenth-century England, the second on trade in late-medieval Genoa, and the third on the footwear of the Renaissance—all on the grounds that the topic had already been covered. I was in a particular funk when I learned that someone had even beaten me to the shoe story, and I whiled the day away in the campus library in an orgy of reading whatever the hell I felt like. I was deep into the Marquise de Sévigné's fascinating letters to her daughter when I was struck by a thread running through several years' worth of correspondence. The formidable marquise had an intense love-hate relationship with chocolate, one month recommending it as the curer of all ills, the next decrying it as a purveyor of fever, lighting the way to death itself. The marquise was addicted! And so, I discovered with a little further research, was all of Europe. Suddenly, I saw chocolate washing from South America to Spain, from Spain north across Europe, in a huge tsunami. I had my topic.

For Kate and the IM team, I made my rebellious library browse sound like a voyage of purposeful intellectual curiosity. "Food has always had a transforming power in society," I explained. "The opening of the spice route is a good example. It not only changed the cuisine, it changed the culture. The more research I did, the more I saw that chocolate, during the seventeenth and eighteenth centuries, had similar power. It could shape men's actions. It spawned subsidiary industries and crafts. Like a king, it could enrich or impoverish."

I glanced around the room. Several people were scribbling like mad.

"And so," Kate said thoughtfully, "do you see Tom's—our—product as a betrayal? As an unsatisfying substitute for the real thing?"

Did she think I was nuts? That I would say yes, quite right, Tom's chocolate is a sham, thanks for the croissant, I'll be going now. No, I realized. She was gauging my reaction to the unrehearsed moment.

"Not at all," I said, thinking quickly. "In fact, just the opposite. You see, innovation is very much a part of the chocolate tradition."

"Go on," Bob Kovacek said, glancing at his secretary, who had entered the room behind the refreshment cart. "You're getting this, Betty?"

I went on. "Well, you see, in its natural state, the cocoa bean is pretty unappetizing. Not only do you have to crush the bean and extract the paste, you have to add a whole host of things—sugar, fat, flavorings—to make it palatable. Did you know that the chocolate Europe went mad for was what we call cocoa? That chocolate bars didn't even exist until just before the 1800s? That milk chocolate didn't come on-line until 1875? All because someone did something *innovative* with the basic bean." I looked around the room. I had my audience. "So what Tom has done, you see, is really no different than the work of a Rudolphe Lindt or a Jules Sechaud."

"That's *very* interesting," someone said.

"Way cool," Lucie Kinneman added.

"Tom," Bob broke in, "do you—or you, Annie—have any questions?"

"Well," Tom said, "I guess I'm kind of wondering how this will all work out. I mean, I won't have to give up my lab work, will I?"

I felt a rush of wife-love for my earnest husband. Also a mad desire to kick his shins.

"Oh no," said Jim Curtis, Tom's boss. "I've made that clear already— I don't want to lose you down in R and D."

"We see you and Annie making appearances and doing interviews in *harmony* with your current schedules," Lucie said, although I was fairly certain she hadn't a clue as to how difficult this might be to arrange.

"Do *you* have any questions, Annie?" Kate asked.

"Yes, one, at least, that I can think of. What, exactly, would the personal appearances entail?"

"We're looking into national television," Bob said. "Betty, have we heard back from the *Letterman* people yet?" He saw the look of surprise on my face. "Don't worry. When this product rolls out, *Letterman* will be calling *us*."

"And with your background in food," Lucie added brightly, "we think cooking demonstrations—making items from the product itself—would be absolutely *perfect!*"

Exactly what I'd feared. The deal breaker. Having a dim memory of the Watergate era, I decided to come clean right way. "I should explain then," I said, "that I'm not a gourmet cook. I write about food, I know something about it, and I love to eat it, but I am not known for my culinary skills."

Now it was Tom's turn to look surprised. "But, honey, you're a *great* cook." He looked at the rest of the room. "She is, really."

Well, yes, in a Midwest-casserole sort of way, he was right. My dinner rotation included such delights as Tater Tots hotdish, turkey lasagna, and stack-a-roll Stroganoff. "I don't think they mean *that* kind of cooking, Tom."

Kate made a dismissive gesture with her hand. "It doesn't matter," she said. "We've got a dozen chefs on staff. They'll develop the recipes and teach you whatever you need to know. Well"—she stood up—"I think we're ready to go on to the next stage now, unless anyone has anything else?"

I stood up too, hoping Kate would spirit Tom and me—or at least me—off for a little postgame wrap-up. But to my dismay, she, Bob, and Jim Curtis ushered Tom out of the room, and I found myself alone with Lucie, her assistant, Matthew, and assorted levels of secretaries, advisers, gofers, and *people*. "Let's go to my office," Lucie suggested. "Much more private."

Something in the way she said this triggered a slight sense of misgiving. As did her next sentence. "I don't know if Bob or Kate mentioned it to you, Annie, but one of the roles I play around here is image consulting."

We went down a curving flight of stairs and a long corridor. Lucie dismissed Matthew and asked him to hold her calls, then ushered me—alone—into her office. After a few pleasantries, she asked me to stand and turn slowly, a full revolution. Her legal pad was already full of notes, but she continued to write as I turned. Self-conscious, I stood straighter, threw back my shoulders, drew in my stomach. Clenched my buttocks.

"It's all right, Annie. This is just, you know, to get a kind of basic line on some things. Could you walk over to that chair and sit down?" When I did, she held a lens to her eye and looked at me for some time. "Face left. Good. Now right." She lowered the lens and made some more notes. "We'll have to fix the hair. I can give you the name of my stylist. And, um, do you think you could lose some weight?" she asked.

Do you think you could be more rude? I answered, but only in my head because the answer would be yes, of course, she could be much, much more rude.

"How much weight?"

She looked at me thoughtfully, as if measuring yardage for a tent. "Twenty pounds. Twenty-five."

I was aghast. *"Twenty?"* The most weight I had ever lost in my life was twelve pounds, and I still remembered that particular era with a sort of *Mein Kampf* bitterness.

"It's for *tele*vision," she said in a reverential whisper that was meant to explain everything. "Look, Annie, it's not that you're *fat*. If this were . . . seed corn or something, I'd be the first to say hey, no problemo. But this is chocolate, Better Than Chocolate. To get across the . . . *health* aspects, everyone on the team has to look trim. Lean, mean, Better Than Chocolate eating machines." She leaned toward me in what I recognized as Full-sharing Mode. "Look, it isn't that hard. Before I came out here, I worked in Hollywood. Big agency. *Lots* of hot bodies. I took seven pounds off Joan Rivers. That might not sound like a lot to you, Annie, but on a tiny woman like Joan, well, just that smidgen of weight . . ." She talked on, soothing me, buoying me, listing any number of clients she'd reduced. "Benjamin Bratt before *Piñero*. Tom Hanks during *Philadelphia*. Renée Zellweger after *Bridget Jones*. Russell Crowe . . . well, you can't always . . ." She frowned, then brightened. "But we took thirty pounds off Jennifer Aniston."

"Jennifer Aniston can afford not to eat," I sulked. "She makes millions."

"We'll make millions."

I looked at her, astonished. "Millions?"

"Yes—but only a thin we."

"How long would I have?"

"Well"—Lucie consulted her notes—"they want to launch you ASAP. We can't make the Christmas season but definitely want to hit before Valentine's Day. That means print ads done by . . ." She counted backward on her fingers and scrutinized me. "I suppose we *could* put them off for a few weeks, or start you on *Oprah*—she's in a fat orbit just now, so you might look fine—of course, it could backfire . . ."

I felt like the *QE II*. Only larger.

"We could give you a month, I think." She saw my doubtful look. "We'll get you whatever you need. Personal trainer. Pills. Hypnotherapy. Stomach stapling."

"Stomach stapling? For twenty pounds?"

"I'm just saying."

"Isn't that a lot in one month? Twenty pounds? Is that healthy?"

"Oh, all *right.*" She gave an exasperated sigh and picked up the phone. Her first call was to someone named Koli, in traffic, who apparently was the last word in deadlines. Then she speed-dialed again. "Luba, *golubushka*. How are things in legal? Have we poisoned anyone? Well *that's* a relief! Listen, I'm here with Annie Wilkins. Um, yes, yes, that one." She lowered her voice. "Well, no, not drab, exactly. But we're going to have to do a fat clause here. How much are we authorized for? Wonderful." Lucie put the phone down and looked at me. "You're going to be pleased. I got you eight weeks and"—her eyes lit up—"half a mil. Five hundred thousand if you're camera ready by January first."

Visions of fully paid college tuitions danced in my head, where the word "house" was still strobing. "Deal," I said so swiftly I swallowed the word and started coughing.

While Lucie was out of the room getting me a glass of water, I glanced at the notes she'd made. "Mousefrau" it said in slanting backhand and, beside it, in heavily circled rings, "$1M OK."

Chapter 4

LUNCH WITH LUCIE

Lucie had a present for me. For *me!* And high time too, I thought as I dropped Sophie at preschool and reminded her that she was going home with Natasha and her mommy because I had a business meeting.

"Binness, binness," Sophie singsonged, scrutinizing me gravely. "It's always binness with you, isn't it?"

I wondered where she got that particular phrase, and if there was some subtly subversive anti-working-mother sitcom out there I should be monitoring. But she tucked her new purple portfolio under her arm, advised me to eat vegetables for lunch, and waved me off cheerfully. I sighed at the thought that I had gotten away with it one more time. I had kept myself from saying that "binness, binness" actually meant rich, rich, *rich*.

Tom and I had decided not to broadcast, in the sixty-point type we felt, the news of our impending upturn in fortune, especially to Jeff and Sophie. What would they think if they saw us in the nonstop cavort we felt? What would happen to our careful teachings about money not being everything, about toys and possessions not being what life was all about? Instead, we explained that there would be some changes soon, and that we would probably be moving to a bigger house. Jeff was disgruntled about the prospect of changing schools in midyear.

"I like Willow Lane," he protested. "I don't want to go to a different school. I have cool friends here. Where else am I going to meet someone like Blade?"

Where indeed? I wondered and returned to the real estate section with renewed zeal.

We didn't tell our friends either. Not just because IM had sworn us to secrecy, but because it was, well, crass, to call people up and shout, "We've hit the jackpot! We're loaded!"—even though that was the line going off like fireworks in my brain twenty-four hours a day, alongside the Roman candle of "we get a new house" and the perky sparklers of "couch without dog stain," "dishwasher that does not flood kitchen," and "car with work-ing heater." It was acceptable to crow a bit over these things once we could spread the largesse around, but to throw our future in the faces of all and sundry while still parading around in old T-shirts and eating at Dog 'n Suds with everyone else would have been, as my mother would say, put-ting on airs.

In fact, that was exactly what my mother *did* say, on a long-distance line from Spain. Friends were one thing, but Tom and I decided we had a duty to give our families a heads-up wealth alert.

It was a little anticlimactic. Tom's mother, a farmer's widow who never trusted luck further than the next day's weather, let fly with an enthusias-tic, "Well now, that'll be different." Then, without missing a beat, she wondered if Tom could drive down to Worthington and look at her cold frames, because she thought there was something wrong with the heating cable and she wanted to "get a jump on it" before spring.

It was no use pointing out that we were just now eating the last rem-nants of Halloween candy, and spring, even if you were an optimist, was a good six months away. It would have been wasted breath. Just recently, Carol had finally given up keeping chickens for the egg money. She hated to part with such a going concern—"Those weekend folks pay twice as much for brown eggs, God knows what they think they're getting"—but, at age sixty-three, she'd finally gotten tired of caring for animals whose young were too dumb to drink unless you dipped their beaks in water. She still worked part-time at the city library, though, and made extra money cooking noon meals for the farmer who rented out the five-hundred-acre spread surrounding her house. She also raised truck produce, flowers, and bedding plants she sold to a local nursery. In the dozen plus years of my marriage, I'd only seen Carol sitting down twice, though she had seen me sitting down plenty, and her mere presence usually made me feel like a pampered trophy wife who was addicted to the action at the local nail salon. To be fair, I don't think Carol actually felt that way about me, but I still hid the Hamburger Helper whenever she came to visit, and told Jeff and Sophie to say that we never, ever, called Pizza Hut for dinner.

Given this, and the fact that she herself was sitting on 1.5 million dollars' worth of farmland, I guess I shouldn't have expected too much in the way of enthusiasm. My own parents, though, were a different story, and I felt subtly betrayed by them.

I blamed it on Spain.

Since I'd been brought up with strictly middle-class aspirations, in a suburb not far from the one I was currently living in, I assumed that when my parents told us they'd like to spend the first years of their retirement "somewhere warm," they meant the edge of a golf course in Arizona. Instead, they threw away the script and bought a villa near Calpe, Spain, and for the last two years had been living the high life on the Costa Blanca, where the sunshine, friendly locals, and excellent food were ruining them forever.

Soon after they relocated, my father had begun going down to watch the fishing boats come in every day. Over the satellite bounces of our phone calls there was a lot of enthusing over the "simple life" and "good, honest, outdoor work." Before I knew it, Dad had shed thirty pounds, acquired a permanent tan, and begun to discover his inner Hemingway. I still felt bad about that mix-up at the airport last spring, but how was I supposed to recognize him in that white beard and those hemp sandals? And my mother in that four-tiered skirt and nubbly chenille cape—a cape, she informed me, she'd woven herself on her brand-new, grand-piano-size floor loom, which wasn't, she swiftly added, one-tenth as expensive as the boat my father had his eye on.

"It's so great," I hollered into the telephone, trying to drum up enthusiasm after I'd explained Tom's coup to them. "We're finally going to have a house with a guest room."

"But it sounds like so much *work*, dear. Are you sure you want to commit to something like that? When Jeff and Sophie are still so young?"

"Your mother's right," my father's voice echoed somewhere near the phone. The concept of having an extension was, apparently, well beyond the ideals of the simple life. "You want to stop and smell the flowers."

"But you'll come visit?" I persisted. "When we get settled in the new house?"

"I don't know, dear. There's Don Diego to consider. He can't possibly be left alone."

"But—"

"Parrots aren't parakeets." My mother sniffed, as if personally offended. "They *pine*." This from the woman who had made a latchkey child of me. "Why don't *you* come visit us? It's so lovely here, and Jeff and Sophie would absolutely *adore* . . ."

That left my older sister, Barb. But telling her seemed like a violation. Five years apart in age, we'd always been partners at the bottom of the economic heap, me because of my foray into academia, Barb because she'd had the guts to marry a musician. Jay taught music during the day and lived for the nights when the Kings of Swing, the big band he played in, performed for just enough money to keep them all in sheet music. Barb was a medical transcriptionist for the Osceola Medical Center, a job she relished for the Zenlike monotony of it. There were days, she claimed, when she positively couldn't wait to begin tapping her way through the play-by-play of some retiree's bowel obstruction. Barb and Jay had three boys, the youngest two years older than Jeff, the middle in junior high school, the oldest about to finish a fast-track B.S. from the U. of M. Barb told me there were nights when two dinners over the course of an evening were sometimes not enough for them. The grocery bills were staggering, as was the need for sports equipment, electronics, and, of course, books and a dissectable pig carcass for Rob, who was determined to become a veterinarian.

The afternoon I called Barb, she had just finished stuffing a dozen pork chops with four boxes of Stove Top and chopping three heads of broccoli for dinner. Both bread machines were hard at it as well.

"What's that noise?" I asked. "Sounds like someone crying."

"Well, it could be me," she said. "But it isn't. Rob's home this weekend. He found some abandoned kittens on 494 and we were just bottle-feeding them and they're fussing a little." My older sister not only loved animals, she had the softest heart in the world. This was a lethal combination in a small town, where you were quickly pegged as someone who would take in almost anything. Over the years, she had nurtured birds, squirrels, raccoons, pond turtles, ducks, wolverine cubs, carnival ponies, and the occasional monkey in need of deep rehab before being passed along to an animal sanctuary. Fortunately, their house was large, if somewhat fur matted. "You don't know anyone who wants a cat, do you? These will be ready to adopt in a few weeks."

I held two fingers up in the shape of cross. "God, no. Everyone I know who *wants* a pet *has* a pet." We had this conversation on a near monthly basis. My sister enforced a tough no-kill policy and so was always looking for friendly homes.

"Okay, okay. What's up? How're you guys doing? Did I tell you Rob got really good feedback on his interview at Ames?"

Her voice was equal parts pride and worry. Iowa State University had the best D.V.M. program in the region. It also, if you lived out of state, had a whopper of a price tag. I wished I could tell her no problem, don't worry, we'd be glad to bankroll Rob's degree. But I couldn't, so I backed off even the wimpy half announcement I'd planned to make and told her that Tom was in line for a kind of promotion, and if we got enough money for a down payment on a bigger house and bought new furniture, would they be interested in any of our current stuff? I also said we'd think about taking one of the kittens.

That conversation with my sister ushered in what I came to think of as the starving-in-good-faith era. I was starving to take off the twenty pounds, pass go, and collect my $500,000 cash prize. I was showing good faith by proceeding to do this without benefit of a signed contract.

The week after our first meeting with IM, there was a second meeting to discuss the specifics of the contract. Tom and I would each get a whopping salary for the duration, a lump sum for the down payment on a new house, an allowance for furnishings and a decorator, and a lot of other entrancing perks. All we had to do in return was select a domicile "congruent with IM's needs and marketing goals" and turn over most of our lives to them. We agreed to everything without blinking an eye, and I naively thought this would guarantee the contract's arrival in a few days, two weeks tops. But, although Tom and I had signed two intent-to-sign-the-contract contracts we had not, as yet, signed *the* contract, and the promised treasure trove of goodies had yet to spill into our laps. (We *did* receive a double shipment of Bangers 'n Smash, the first shelf-stable breakfast sausage with a Saturday-morning TV tie-in, but did that count?)

I had, of course, forgotten the lawyers. There were in-house lawyers and out-of-house lawyers, our lawyers and their lawyers. The lawyers had lawyers and the lawyers' lawyers had accountants, financial advisers, and tax planners. While they hashed it all out and took each other to expensive lunches, the rest of us proceeded on the assumption that there would one day be a finished contract that, even after the legal fees, would generate enough money to make us all happy.

My chief activity for the last month had been not eating, which takes a lot more time and energy than anyone would suspect. In the moments of idleness sandwiched between frenzied moments of not eating, I'd written several articles for IM, which, as Lucie phrased it, could be "rolled out" and "dropped" at just the right moment. On the personal front, I'd had a less-than-perfect tooth filed down and built up with laminate, had my eyebrows laser plucked into clean, perfect curves, and a mole near the corner of my mouth removed. I'd always thought the mole gave me a slightly Cindy Crawford-ish air. Half of the focus groups they tested footage of me on agreed—and commented that I was an annoying Cindy wanna-be. The other half, men and women over fifty-five, labeled the mole distracting. A few worried that it might turn cancerous and said it made them feel anxious. I'd also had my hair highlighted and then, after some test footage, *un*highlighted. From time to time, I heard the uplifting word "wardrobe" spoken and my ears would perk up like a setter's; but the word was inevitably followed by a discreet whisper from one edgy handler to the next—"Let's hold off until she drops the weight"—and I would poutingly return to the task of caloric abstinence. So when Lucie said she was taking me to lunch, and casually mentioned that she had a small gift for me as well, I felt I'd earned a reward. It was only my due, and long overdue at that.

I was percolating with frothy excitement by the time I pulled into my new, nifty, personal parking space at IM—although, in my state of extreme, Atkins-induced ketosis, it might only be light-headedness; I could never tell these days. I nosed up to the little sign that said "Reserved for Annie Wilkins," wishing once again they had gone for something headier, like "Mme. du Chocolat"—a no-go since, in an unnerving show of what I hoped was only paranoia, IM confided their worry that Canfield Brand's satellite, high overhead, zooming in and clicking away, would home in on the sign and allow our competitors to put two and two together. I locked the car and made the short walk to the building without gaping upward like a bit player in a *Twilight Zone* episode.

Lucie had told me to clear my afternoon, as she had a big surprise for me in addition to the gift, so as I passed my security card to the guard and waited for the matching image to materialize on his screen, I wondered what, exactly, my day held in store. Lunch at a swank downtown restaurant? The long-awaited wardrobe revamp? Or maybe a green-mud wallow at a day spa followed by a revivifying massage at the hands of a strapping, blond Hessian named Gunnar? And would Lucie drive or would we go in a company limo loaded with champagne?

"Ready?" Lucie greeted me when her person delivered me to her office. With the delicacy of a grasshopper freeing itself from a spiderweb, she disengaged herself from two cell phones, a headset, speakerphone, Palm Pilot, mainframe, laptop, and a nimbus of other electronics whose function I could only guess at. *"Ciao,"* she called out, waving to the eyeball cam on top of her monitor. "Catch you later."

"Does Ilya Kuryakin know about this?" I asked.

"Who?"

"Never mind." Clearly, she'd never been stuck at home with two young children and the Nickelodeon channel.

Lucie picked up the fringed leather bag that matched her buff-suede cowgirl outfit. For no justifiable reason, the ensemble looked extremely fashion forward on her. She grabbed my elbow and steered me down the corridor. "I was going make reservations at Eloise, but I had a better idea."

What? Was there someplace swankier than Eloise that I didn't know about? Someplace where the *bisque de homard* was smoother? Where the *côtes de veau papillote* were more *belle?*

"I remembered," she said, pressing the elevator button, "about your diet. So we're eating here. No temptations. Besides, we have *so* much to talk about. I can't *wait* to tell you."

At least, I consoled myself as we got off the elevator, we were eating in the corporate dining room, not the employee cafeteria. Maybe I'd run into my husband there. Or Kate Hawkins. According to Tom, they ate there often, whiling away many a happy noon hour over flaky spanakopita and marketing plans. Tom had now spun off both milk- and white-chocolate versions of his creation and was well on the way to perfecting Better Than Chocolate's Better Than Hot Fudge ice-cream topping. IM's dilemma was whether to flood the market with lots of products at once or go for a more orderly, stepped introduction. Neither Kate nor Tom was in the dining room, and, except for a table of executives I didn't recognize ("the animal-feed division," Lucie whispered), we were more or less on our own.

I'd like to report that Lucie was one of those girls—sure to have beaten you at push-ups in the seventh grade—who was willow-wand thin but ate like Diamond Jim Brady on a bender. Oysters by the dozen. Hamburger rare with a pat of butter on top. Chocolate mousse for dessert or crème brûlée? Oh, let's try them *both*. That, alas, was not the case. The case was far worse, and infinitely more annoying.

Our Lucie, it turned out, was one of those girls who chows down on a bowl of radicchio leaves (sprayed with a fine mist of fat-free vinaigrette if she's feeling *very* naughty), sends back the bread basket before you even get your napkin unfolded, and halfway through this repast, leans back, pats her nonexistent stomach, and tells you how *absolutely stuffed* she is.

In the face of this admirable mortification of the flesh, I could hardly order the *carbonara* Tom had told me was so excellent, or even the spanakopita. I settled for the steamed trout and, at Lucie's suggestion, tardily substituted steamed asparagus for the wild rice *aux jambon*. My sacrifice earned a smile from Lucie.

"I can see you're really trying with this diet thing. What have you lost now? Five pounds? Six?"

"Fourteen."

"Really? I guess the weight around the face is the last to go, huh?"

I toyed with the notion of reaching across the table to give one of those adorable corkscrew curls a good, sharp yank. How far would it stretch? And how much would it hurt? Should I yank upward or downward for maximum pain?

Unaware of her near peril, Lucie speared a forkful of greens. "I don't know what's wrong with me today. I'm *so* famished I'm going to have dessert. The yogurt here is really good. Do you want one?"

What I wanted was to tell her that, in a few years, when she was married and had kids, yogurt would morph into something forever reminiscent of baby spit up. "No, thanks."

"Oh, well, if you're not having one . . ."

"No, really, go ahead. Enjoy it."

And enjoy that rodeo roundup outfit as well, Luce, because in a dozen years, you'll look like Ma Kettle in it. Except, I conceded with a sigh, Lucie was probably the type who would *never* look like Ma Kettle.

"Are you sure?"

She looked so abject, I felt guilty and nodded vigorously. "And I meant to thank you, Lucie, for that ab-cruncher board you sent over. It's really been useful." In a roundabout sort of way, at least. The last time I'd seen the ab board, Sophie was coasting down the snow-slicked slope of our backyard on it.

"Fab," said Lucie. "Oh, I almost forgot. Your present."

Since I hadn't seen any gayly wrapped boxes, I'd half-convinced myself that the gift was indeed unwrappable, the size not of a bread box but of a house. Now Lucy opened her Natty Bumpo bag and extracted a small gift bag with a bow stapled to the top.

I seized the gift and tore through layers of multicolored tissue paper until I came to what looked like a folded-over diaphragm made out of peanut-butter-colored felt. A fuselike string protruded from its folded smile, making me wonder if it was some bizarre new style of tampon. Or perhaps the prototype of some new food product.

"What is it?"

"Pull the string."

I did and the thing snapped open. Nestled inside was the tiniest note-pad I'd ever seen, with munchkin-size printing on every page. I picked it up and squinted at it. Not only was the type crammed onto an area the size of a postage stamp, it was written in an italic so ornate it was almost impossible to decipher.

Butterflies never eat. They are nourished by their own beauty.

I looked at the next page.

D-I-E-T is not a four-letter word.

Then, with mounting horror, the next page and the next.

Firm your tummy, then your thighs, and the mind will follow.

I love myself enough to say no to me.

And finally, the most dispiriting of all,

Today is the first day of the rest of your diet.

"Don't you love it?" Lucie beamed. "It's an affirmation fortune cookie! A friend of mine makes them. Her business is called Smart Cookies Squared, meaning smart cookies for smart cookies. I told her I want to rep her if she goes national. She gave me one for each of us. Only, you know, because I don't really diet, well, I mean, I'm always dieting so . . . anyway, she gave me the one called the Smart Cookie for Smart Cookies Who Work Too Much."

"What's mine called? The Smart Cookie for Smart Cookies Who Eat Too Much?"

"Well, um, yes, actually."

I tucked my cookie away in its bag. "Thank you, Lucie. Has your friend thought that maybe for dieters a big felt fortune cookie might be a little off point?"

"I see what you mean." She whipped out a personal recorder the size of a Bic lighter. "Camilla, cookie shape could be food trigger. Can felt shape be something else? Miniskirt? Martini glass?"

"How about a magic uterus?" I suggested, going back to my first impression. "A sort of message from the inner inner woman."

A few other pictures came to mind. Baked potato. Empanada. Hostess fruit pie. Thickly buttered dollar bun scrunched in half.

"Oohh, a magic uterus would be terrific," Lucie cooed into her recorder. "Get purple felt. *Perfect* for women with fertility issues." She reached across the table and touched my hand lightly. "I *knew* we'd be a great team, Annie. When I walked into that first meeting, it just hit me that we were on the same wavelength. If there's anything I can do, I mean, any favor or anything . . ."

Suddenly, I felt an intense need for adult company. "I'd like to say hi to Tom while I'm here. Kate too, if she's around."

"Oh, no can do. Tom has a full load today. He and Kate went to Oceanaire for lunch. Then they were going to Brooks Brothers, then to pick out new office furniture, and then I forget where, but somewhere." Lucie must have seen my lower lip begin to droop, because she added, "Don't worry. I told you—I've got a surprise for you. And it's a whole lot better than Brooks Brothers."

My surprise was waiting on the third floor, the floor the employees' cafeteria was on. The cafeteria was the size of a school lunchroom, with a glass wall fronting the corridor. I admit I felt a ruffle of *Yess!* when we passed and a few hundred heads swiveled in our direction. I was already a celebrity! At least on the IM premises. I glanced at Lucie to see if she'd noticed, but she was about a quarter mile ahead of me down the long corridor. I hurried to catch up, and after a series of mazelike turns, we crossed a glass-topped walkway and entered a wing of the building I knew was off-limits to everyone except executives, VIPs, and Girl Scout tour groups. The IM test kitchens.

According to IM's official publicity, there were seven test kitchens. In reality, there were at least three dozen, though I may have missed a few as we walked along. The maze was so vast and confusing there were actually street signs at corridor intersections, pointing the way to various kitchens. The Hacienda, Northwoods Cabin, and Twelve Oaks were on Laura Ingalls Lane. Winnebego Wonderland, Cape Cod Cottage, and Welcome to L.A. were on Mary Richards Place. The space was staggering, a cuisine convention, a Forbidden City of countertops and ranges. There was every conceivable combination of equipment there, from the wood-burning stove I glimpsed in Appalachian Springs (off Mondale Drive) to the triple-decker configuration of conventional, convection, and microwave ovens at Mira Lago (Woebegone Boulevard). There were, I noticed, no tributes to Tammy Faye Bakker, Minnesota Fats, or Prince.

We ended up at a door without a nameplate. I felt like a summer camper searching for her cabin.

"Which one is this?" I asked.

"This," said Lucie, pushing the door open, "is yours." She mistook my stare of horror for speechless gratitude. "Remember when we talked about the cooking demos? And giving you some help in that department? Well, we keep our promises!"

Oh yes, *just* what I'd been hoping for. Another kitchen to slave away in.

But, I had to admit as we stepped inside, it *was* lovely, with its gleaming-white tiles and red and blue accents, a permanent Fourth of July. "Patriotism is *in*," Lucie commented. "And red, white, and blue read well with chocolate."

"We'll be doing shoots here, then?"

"Oh, absolutely." She squeezed my arm enthusiastically. "You'll be spending *lots* of time here, Annie. Isn't it just the *best?*"

By the time I picked Sophie up, got home, and started dinner, I was feeling extremely sorry for myself. There's a scullery maid deep in every woman's soul and IM seemed to have located mine. I pictured a future in which Tom was eternally lunching at Oceanaire while I, starved and unappreciated and locked away in my kitchen, melted mountains of synthetic chocolate. Two and a half glasses of wine into this train of thought, I was on the verge of tears, and Jeff took over the dinner duties.

"Go lie down, Mom. It'll be all right."

Just as I was wallowing my way to the bedroom, Tom walked through the door.

"Hi, honey."

I set my wineglass down behind a stack of books and stared at him. Something was different.

"Tom, you look . . . amazing."

He smiled and hung the three Brooks Brothers suit bags he was carrying in the hall closet. "I had a terrific lunch," he said. "With Kate."

Tom had lost his harried academic look. The crinkles at the corners of his eyes looked interesting rather than tired. But there was more than that. There was a sort of vitality. My husband positively *glowed.*

"Did you get a haircut?" I asked.

"Well, uh, not exactly. Kate took me to this place, this kind of consultant . . ."

Beneath his tan, I caught the faint edge of a blush. What tan? It was November. We were all as pale as bean sprouts. We had been this morning anyway. Now only three of us were.

I got closer. I think I even sort of sniffed him.

"Hon, are you wearing makeup?"

"Just a little bronzer. It was kind of an afterthought."

"An afterthought to what?"

"The hair thing. You know, the highlighting."

"They highlighted your hair?"

"Yeah. Remember when they shot the test footage? Right after you had your hair done? They decided I should stand out more, so they unhigh-lighted you. They told you that, right? They unhighlighted you so you would fit in the background better?"

"No, they didn't tell me."

"Oh. Sorry. Where're you going?"

"To get some more wine." Another few jugs should about do it.

Tom followed me into the kitchen. "How was your lunch with Lucie? She told me she had something to give you, some kind of gizmo. What did you get?"

"What did I get?" I took a deep sip of my wine. "Three ounces of steamed trout, some steamed asparagus, no rice, no sauce, no bread, no butter, no dessert, a felt fortune cookie that looks like a diaphragm but might become a uterus, and a kitchen in which I am to live out the best years of my life. That's what I got."

"Geez, that doesn't seem fair. Sorry, hon."

I felt my voice wobble and I actually might have squeezed out a pathetic tear or two if the phone hadn't rung.

"Lucie," Tom said, handing it to me. "For you."

"Ann. Annie. Sorry, but I forgot to mention something. We were hav-ing such a good time, it just slipped my mind. Can you get away tomor-row? Or Thursday? I know you need to find a sitter and I should have told you earlier, and it will mean an extra workday on short notice, but . . . well, IM thinks we should start looking at houses." She paused, her voice heavy with anxiety. "Actually, I need to have a preliminary properties report to them on Friday morning, so . . . ."

A giddy grin spread across my face, and Tom grabbed my wineglass before it could pass the tipping point. Lucie, Lucie. Poor little upside-down Lucie. Poor little Lucie who'd sat all day on the one bit of news that would have made me complete putty in her hands.

"It *is* short notice," I agreed, letting her sweat it out for a few more minutes. "And I don't know if my regular sitter's free, but, well, I *think* I can line someone up for tomorrow."

Chapter 5

THE HAPHAZARD OF
NEW FORTUNES

Sitting next to Lucie in her racy little car the color of marigold, I was something akin to deliriously happy. Despite the heavy morning traffic and the fact that we were surrounded by a phalanx of SUVs and big rigs, we were not ants about to be crushed but gazelles leaping cleverly past all obstacles. Somewhat to my surprise, Lucie was an expert driver—a truly expert driver, as she was not only driving but was, as usual, wired into a web of electronic devices.

Watching the stream of SUVs was like watching a flickering hologram of my hitherto life. Children fought in backseats. Dogs devoured untended bag lunches. In the car immediately to our right, a glassy-eyed boy Jeff's age had his headphones turned up so loud I could hear reverberations of "I tote guns, I make number runs" through the rolled-up windows. His mother, wisely, was sporting the thickest, furriest pair of earmuffs I'd ever seen. In another car, a mother I felt a leaping pang of sympathy for had clearly pulled her coat on over her robe and kept stuffing the pink terry-cloth cuffs back into her sleeves.

I leaned back and enjoyed the thrill of not driving. What a treat not to have a momload full of preschoolers or budding jocks roiling in the backseat. What a positive luxury not to worry that any sudden braking action would mean being whacked in the back of the head with flying Egg

McMuffin wrappers or drink boxes full of juice. How wonderful to know that no one would throw up during our brief ride, or need the Kleenex I was certain not to have.

"I think we'll look at Forsythe Knolls first. Even though it's tract, I hear they're very distinctive." I wasn't sure if Lucie was talking to me or whoever was on the other end of her headset, but it didn't seem to matter. "There're some Kenwood properties I'd like to see, and Claire faxed me the specs on a house in Prior Lake. There isn't a problem with lakefront, is there?"

Lakefront. Kenwood. Forsythe Knolls. The words plunked into my mind like golden coins. At breakfast Tom had told me that whatever I wanted would be fine with him, as if I were off to buy a new lamp or a rug for the kitchen. Now I imagined returning triumphant, tossing out the fact that our prospective house would have a three-car garage and boat access. Visions danced against my sun-warmed eyelids. I imagined a canopy bed for Sophie and a study alcove with a new computer for Jeff. I imagined Christmas in a great room with cathedral ceilings and a twelve-foot Christmas tree. To be completely truthful, I also imagined myself as Elizabeth Taylor in *Giant,* handing a complementary Christmas stocking to James Dean, who was still in love with me in spite of having had a spectacular fistfight with my cattleman husband. I must have looked the way Scout did when he drowsed in the sun, paws paddling and tail twitching. Until this morning, my highest aspirations had been to four bedrooms and two baths in Maple Grove. But Maple Grove had earned a dismissive snort from Lucie, who muttered something that sounded like "high prol," shifted gears, changed lanes, and shot us toward Edina.

At Forsythe Knolls, we were met by a woman I picked out as a real estate agent before she was even halfway out of her Lexus. She had that fortyish and tastefully frosted look, along with a Pashmina shawl large enough to wrap Nefertiti and all her descendants in. Beneath the shawl was a dress coat in Hillary Clinton blue, and beneath that a velvet-trimmed suit I was fairly certain I'd once seen on Barbara Bush. It was as if, on leaving office, first ladies opened a secret wardrobe workshop for licensed female Realtors. But Claire Holmes, I was informed as we all shook hands, wasn't just a Realtor. She was a "relocation coach."

"With a background in semiotics," Claire added. She led us down a wide sweep of street-under-development. The finished boulevard, I estimated, would be only slightly narrower than I-94. "This is the first Forsythe Knolls house I've shown, and I don't know if it will work for us or not. I want to make sure we get the message right."

I smiled enthusiastically. Yes, I was all for The Message. I was a big supporter of The Message. Every meeting I'd been to at IM over the past weeks had, in some way, been about The Message. And though it had never been articulated in so many words, I now realized I'd incorporated it like a DNA code. *We're happy. We're active. We live in the house of our dreams where we entertain, enjoy quality family time, eat healthfully nutrition-nil chocolate, and avail ourselves of the many benefits of a low-density community with spacious parks, no crime, and excellent schools. Please join us in this wonderful lifestyle! (Hint: Start with the chocolate!)*

"And, of course, I'll help you transition," Claire tossed back over her Pashminaed shoulder.

"Tom's worked at IM for a while, so I don't think . . . I mean, we're not really relocating."

I caught the upward motion of a carefully brushed eyebrow. "Oh? Where are you living now?"

"Oak Creek Park."

"*Big* transition."

Suddenly, I felt like Granny about to be shown her first ce-ment pond.

"Claire's helped *lots of* our top executives transition," Lucie put in quickly.

We headed toward a house set on a slight rise on its own cul-de-sac. In fact, all of the houses in Forsythe Knolls seemed to be set on their own cul-de-sacs. We'd passed Robin Hill, Soames Court, and Old Jolyon Drive and had entered Stanhope Gate. The house had an imposing front—two and a half stories with a soaring columned arch above the front door that reminded me of Taco Bell gone millionaire. There was a picture window on each story, one aligned atop the other, leading me to speculate about the sumptuous prospect of an extra living room on the second floor. Once we were inside, I saw that both picture windows opened onto the ground-floor living room, an enormous, lovely living room with twenty-foot ceilings and cream drapes that pooled like melting ice cream on the thick cream carpet. All I could think about was how did you climb up there to wash the window, change the lightbulbs, and dust the padded cornice boards?

A wide, curving staircase led to a second-floor gallery that, when I got up there, offered a breathtaking view of the living room. I slipped off one shoe and treated my right foot to a discreet romp in the thick carpeting.

"Three bedrooms on this level," said Lucie, consulting the prospectus, "home office and guest bedroom on the ground floor. Of course, you could switch them around."

There was also a formal dining room on the ground level, which flowed into a kitchen finished in cherry wood.

"There's no family room," I said in a kind of panic. "We can't buy a house that doesn't have a family room."

"Of course there's a family room," said Lucie, handing me the prospectus.

"Oh, right. Finished basement."

Claire touched my shoulder lightly. "Houses like these don't have basements. They have lower levels or, in this case, a semisubmerged level."

And indeed, the semisubmerged level boasted a cavernous family room, a second fireplace, a weight and exercise room, and a laundry area far nicer than many places I'd lived in. I was giddy with desire.

"What does this house *say* to you?" Claire asked, tapping a manicured fingertip thoughtfully against her chin. "What is the essential message here?"

Actually, I thought the message was *Buy me,* but I gathered from Claire's frown that I was supposed to pick out some obvious fault.

"Well, uh, I suppose it lacks, hmm . . ." I couldn't think of a single thing this house lacked.

"It's a McMansion," said Lucie.

"Exactly." Claire beamed approval at the star. "It's a McMansion. It says, '*Anyone can live in me.*'"

"But it's a *lovely* house," I sputtered.

"Of course it is. Lovely. Nothing wrong with it at all. However . . ."

She paused to make sure she had my attention. "However, the way Lucie has explained this acquisition to me, and the role your house will play, this house just won't do."

"No?"

"No. This is a house that, with hard work and conservative investing, far too many people can afford. We need something your target customer aspires to but will never achieve."

Lucie nodded vigorously, her corkscrew curls bouncing. "They see the house, they want the house, they know they will never afford it, so they complete the association by buying Better Than Chocolate instead."

"It's the rechanneling of sublimated envy," Claire amplified. "The primal transaction of all market economies."

I was about to say this was ridiculous when I identified myself as a frequent rechanneler of sublimated envy, usually to the benefit of Restoration Hardware, the Pottery Barn, and Martha by Mail. So I climbed back into Lucie's sports car and we followed Claire Holmes out to Prior Lake Road, where an A-frame chalet awaited us.

To say the house was "on" Prior Lake Road was like saying the Twin Cities were "on" the Canadian border—true only if you were looking at the globe from, say, Saturn. Twenty minutes after turning off the road, we were still traveling on a rutted drive through an intensely gloomy expanse of forest primeval. In fact, the road had narrowed so much that pine boughs were now brushing the windows. I would have worried about getting lost in the deep and seemingly permanent twilight except that Lucie and Claire had had the foresight to don headsets and establish communication with each other before we set out, so Lucie's periodic murmurings of, "Slow down, wait, okay, I see your taillights," gave me hope that we would not end up as the subjects of a statewide helicopter search.

The A-frame, Claire told me when we finally arrived, was owned by an avant-garde sculptor who was moving to Santorini to be near his spiritual center, Atlantis. Also, the tax situation was more favorable there. The unkempt, pasturelike yard was littered with hulking pieces of jagged metal, welded haphazardly and swaying precariously every time the wind lifted. I imagined my children impaled beneath them.

"Will the owner be clearing out these scraps before he goes?"

"I expect so," Claire said. "These pieces are worth *millions*."

Inside, the house had all the charm of an operating room. Glass brick made up an entire wall and a surprising amount of the furniture. The staircase, devoid of anything as prosaic as a balustrade, was also glass brick. Tucked high up in the ceiling were tiny constellations of halogen lights. If you stood directly beneath one, the illumination was blinding. Step two feet to the left or right and you had to grope your way along.

"Amazing chiaroscuro," Claire observed, narrowly missing a sheet-metal coffee table that would have required stitches, blood transfusions, and probably a tetanus booster. "The owner's been exceptionally playful with light and shadow, don't you think?"

"Who is the owner again?"

"Ah, well, I can't say exactly. He's well known and prefers to remain anonymous."

Who could blame him?

The kitchen, when I finally stumbled into it, was genuinely beautiful. The gently curving countertops consisted of layers of glass in varying shades of blue, giving the impression of a deep, free-flowing stream. Perhaps this was the point of the whole house, to make the living space so dangerous and unappealing that arriving at the kitchen would trigger the kind of relief and near euphoria I was now feeling. Perhaps it was the sculptor's metaphor for life. As I was wondering what the bedrooms might look like, I inadvertently leaned my elbow against the countertop and the microwave whirred to life.

"Careful," Claire said. "That's a membrane panel. You can turn anything in the house on from that section of the counter."

What wonderful news for anyone with a four-year-old. I imagined Sophie running our electric bill into the millions.

"I think the message of this house is a little too austere, don't you?" I asked carefully, picking my way through the Esperanto of semiotics. "It doesn't say *warm*. I'm not reading *family*."

To my relief, both Claire and Lucie agreed.

"Blue and food don't mix anyway," said Lucie with a sigh. I couldn't tell if it was the homeowner's ignorance that bothered her or the need to vacate a kitchen so perfectly calibrated to suppress the appetite.

The next listing was the A-frame's opposite, a restored farmhouse whose mahogany woodwork and leaded glass were beautifully intact. Claire wrinkled her nose and didn't even bother with the second story. "Too much country," she said.

I ran my hand along a sideboard built into the length of the dining-room wall. "We're closer to town than that A-frame was," I said, loving the way the smooth mahogany felt beneath my hand.

"But that house was modern in the country. This is Victorian in the country. We're not looking for Old Stourbridge Village here, you know, and when you add the location to the house, the sum total screams, 'Over the river and through the woods.' We're trying to create the elusive juxta-position, what I call time-traveling architecture. No one *really* wants to live in the country, they just think they do. They want a sort of idealized country fantasy. So we appeal to them by speaking the modern dialectic with a country accent."

"Or vice versa?" Lucie asked.

"Or vice versa. Take your pick."

"In other words," Lucie simplified, turning toward me, "we want country in the city, or city in the country, but never country in the country or tech in the city. Very smart, if you think about it."

It was. Very smart. And I had to hand it to Lucie. She'd caught on a lot quicker than I had.

I was the first to nix the next house. The minute we got inside the front door, I decided it was too small and not nearly special enough. Claire nod-ded approval at my discernment. I'd come a long way in five hours. At nine A.M. this house would have filled me with desire. Now I was turning my nose up at almost a million dollars' worth of real estate.

Claire paced back and forth on the hardwood floor. "I think I'm seeing the problem here. In the price range you gave me, we're right on the cusp between ordinary and extraordinary homes. If we were able to go up, say, just a quarter of a mil, the added value would be enormous."

The way she flung out "just a quarter of a mil" gave me the bends, but not Lucie. "Let's try it," she said. "Let's have a look at a few. If I could go back to IM with the right property, I think we could get approval."

Claire nodded, whipped out the smallest laptop I'd ever seen, and within minutes was scrolling dozens of homes a minute. I admired her ability to do it without inducing some sort of brain seizure.

Lucie put on her headset, got out her cell phone and Palm Pilot, and called in for her messages. "Well, *show* me the layout, then," she said, squinting at the minuscule screen of her cell phone. "Ohmygod. Yes, *yes*, it has to go back. I told them they *could not* keep that peach background. No, it's peach, I don't care what they call it. Annie oranges out in it. Pill tan. God, she looks like George Hamilton."

Lucie drifted out of the room, which was just as well because, really, I didn't want to hear more about how very much I resembled George Hamilton. Claire had pulled something the size of a steno book out of her briefcase, plugged it in, and was printing out directions to several properties, so I was free to wander around the house on my own.

Secure in the knowledge that we weren't going to buy it, I could enjoy its high points. The view from the kitchen was definitely at the top of the list. The backyard was old fashioned, and I mentally congratulated the owners who hadn't felt the need to erect a redwood deck the size of the *Forrestal*. Wisely, they'd left the old-fashioned flagstone patio in place. I imagined them as Mr. and Mrs. Anderson, our neighbors when I was five, grandparenty people who would let hollyhocks bloom in summer disarray and who made sun tea on the back porch. The lot gave way to a stand of brush and hardwoods, the kind of place Jeff would forage in and spend hours exploring. Maybe build a secret retreat, a tree house or a fort. I could be very happy with a backyard just like this. *Could have been,* I corrected myself, feeling a surprising pang of melancholy. Or maybe it was hunger.

A subtle movement near the trees caught my eye. At first I thought it was the wind brushing through bare branches, but then the movement turned and offered a bright spot of color. It was Lucie. She had her coat on, but it was a thin, stylish thing, something that should never have been sold north of the Iowa border without a warning label. Shoulders hunched, she was trembling against the cold, and I wondered if under-dressing was part of her grim, endless plan to burn the maximum number of calories possible. I let myself out the French doors and crossed the brown, winter-dead lawn.

"Lucie? Shouldn't we stop for lunch or something? It's past one."

She folded both arms around herself. She stopped pacing, rummaged in her shoulder bag, and offered me a power bar. "Here, you can have my lunch."

"Share?"

She shook her head. "Not hungry."

For the first time, I noticed that her headset was down around her neck. Her eyes were glassy with tears.

"Lucie? Is something wrong?"

A tremor ran through her shoulders as she turned toward me. "I got a phone message. It's my brother."

A brother? Had she ever mentioned a brother? I remembered her say-ing she'd worked in L.A. before landing at IM. Visions of South Central blossomed in my mind. Things fell into place—studied hipness, the focused control, the erasure of anything even vaguely ethnic. God. Lucie, game little striver. Her brother was probably a gang banger. "Is it a, um, legal thing?"

She shook her head. "Sickle cell."

I was still thinking "cell," as in L.A. County and it took a while to sink in. "Your brother has sickle-cell anemia?"

"My big brother. He had to go into the hospital again."

"Are you going back to L.A.?"

"L.A.?"

"Home."

"Oh. No. I'm from Madison. My brother's a professor at UW. Like my dad. They even teach in the same department."

So much for gang bangers. I felt ashamed of myself. "But you'll want to go home to be with your family, won't you? Won't IM give you time off?"

She looked at me in a way that made me feel absolutely clueless. "Of course IM would give me time off. Besides, I've got three years' worth of vacation coming. But my brother was diagnosed when I was five years old, and if I went home every time he was sick, I wouldn't have a career. Step off the track, you might never get back on. Of course, IM would be very, *very* understanding, but I'm not dumb, Annie. Kate would have some protegée of hers sitting at my desk by the time I got back, and all IM would do is shrug."

I felt so sorry for her I let the jab at Kate go. "But you're . . . you don't have it, right? Sickle cell?"

"Nope." I was about to congratulate her when she went on. "I'm what they call an 'unaffected carrier.' I have the gene but not the disease. Which kind of puts a crimp in my dating life."

"I'm sorry, Lucie."

She blotted each eye with her index finger, careful not to smudge her makeup. "No, I'm sorry. This isn't your problem. Unprofessional of me." She was staring at me thoughtfully, as if there was something more she wanted to say.

"What is it, Lucie?"

"Nothing, just—"

"What?"

"You've really, *really* lost weight, Annie. From this angle, in this light, it almost doesn't look like you have a double chin at all." She fished up a pale smile for me. "Did Claire find some houses for us?"

"Probably, but after all this, maybe you'd rather not—"

"No, I'm fine. Really. Let's go."

I noticed she left her headset down and her cell phone off for the rest of the afternoon.

I was determined not to like the next house, not only because a show of house lust seemed crass in the face of sickle-cell anemia but because I was childishly affronted by the double-chin remark. (*Did* I have a double chin? I'd never thought so.) I was wondering how I would manage to suppress my delight over a property that Claire told us had a full-lake view when I noticed yards of heavy plastic tarp spread over the roof. In this case, "full-lake view" was literally true, as the house lacked not only a finished roof but a rear wall. Apparently, the owners had embarked on a messy divorce mid-renovation, and the house was now the pawn in their custody battle.

Despite the fiasco, the house lifted all our spirits. *If only it had a wall and a roof, it would be perfect.* What a difference that extra quarter mil made.

"We're getting closer," Claire said brightly. "Let's try one more."

Fifteen minutes later, I was standing in a turn-of-the-century beauty with the kind of wraparound porch I'd been dreaming of since I was seven years old.

"This is perfect." I tried to sound casual, although I was fairly panting with house lust.

"It might be," Claire agreed. It was her most enthusiastic comment so far, and I began to hope.

"The lot's kind of small," Lucie said, "and we want to create a feeling of spaciousness. But I think we could get around that with camera work."

"Not too Victorian?" I asked Claire cautiously.

"No. The built-ins give it more of a prairie-school feel, which we can carry forward with furniture. Lose the Aubussons, no camelback sofas. I'm reading overstuffed leather in a sort of tobacco color."

I began to feel the tug of ownership. This house *was* perfect. The walls were a pale, lit-from-within shade of butternut. Six floor-to-ceiling windows fronted the wraparound porch. Two dramatically wide, polished walnut steps led up to a dining room whose skylight shed a Tuscany-like light over the room, as if you were standing in a courtyard. For the first time in my life, I began to understand the real meaning of the phrase "showcase home."

When we got to the kitchen, I remembered another phrase, "crushing disappointment." Clearly, the owners never cooked at home. Small, dark, and cramped, the kitchen made me want to cry. All the more so when Lucie pointed out the obvious.

"It would take an extension and a complete remodel," she said. "Total demolition. We'd never finish in time."

And that was that. Good-bye to my wraparound porch and courtyard dining room. Farewell backyard lily pond and side-yard lilac hedge.

"I think I should do some prescreening on these listings," Claire said. "Now I have a much better sense of what we need."

When we got back to IM, Lucie wanted me to see the layouts in which I did or didn't orange out, and since I was curious to see how my chin was photographing, I agreed. Was it my imagination or were people giving us a wide berth as we walked past security and through the lobby? Was it accidental that everyone chose the elevator that arrived next to ours?

When we got to the third floor, the receptionist had just enough time to whisper, "*Where* have you *been?* Kate's been trying to get you for *almost an hour!*" before we were surrounded. Kate, Tom, Ed Lundquist, Bob Kovacek, and several other people I recognized as part of the happy wallpaper of our very first meeting. Only no one was happy now. There was so much communal angst in the air you could almost smell it, like nitrogen after an electrical storm.

"What is it? What's wrong?" Lucie looked terrified. I wondered if she was thinking about her brother or the fearsome consequences of being out of the loop for the last ninety minutes.

"Kate's uncovered some disturbing news," Ed Lundquist said. He'd lost the tanned glow of our first encounter and now wore the worried this-is-what-they-pay-me-for demeanor of a *Fortune* 500 exec.

"*Very* disturbing," said a woman I later learned was the head of legal liabilities and personal damages.

"We may have to pull the plug, and pronto."

"On looking at houses?" I quivered with dread.

Tom caught my elbow and propelled me toward a conference room. "On the whole damn thing," he whispered. "Sorry, Annie. Chocolate looks like a no-go."

Chapter 6

SLOUCHING TOWARD
SHANGRI-LA

"Isn't Mom getting up today either?"

I heard the voices outside my bedroom door. Tom fending off Jeff, Sophie wanting to call her preschool and tell them she couldn't come because she had to stay home to take care of me.

"I'm getting up," I said. "I'm getting *up!*" But my voice was weak and I felt like someone calling out from the Thermopylae battlefield. I lurched out of bed and yanked open the door. Relief broke across all three faces. "I'm up. I'm fine. *Really.*"

I wasn't fine, but I maintained the appearance until everyone was out the door. Then I sat down and read Kate's handout one more time. Kate, who had sources everywhere, had gotten an advance copy of a research paper due to be published in the January issue of *Nerve & Tissue*. And Tom was right, once the world got wind of it, Better Than Chocolate would be a no-go.

Through Tom, I had long been aware of an active cabal of foodies, neo-hippies, greenies, and scientists perennially gunning for food additives. Tom called them the "Twinkie defensers"—the kind of people who blamed every illness and misdeed on the modern food supply. The sugar lobby, the American Beef Tallow Association, trial lawyers, and, more recently, politicians had jumped on the bandwagon, so enthusiastically that, in the last year, a countermovement had gained a foothold. Opposing the Twinkie defenders were libertarians, radio talk-show hosts, corporations like IM, working mothers horrified at the idea of paying a 15 percent sin tax on convenience foods, and a group of postmodern utopians called the TCRM, or Total Caloric Replacement Movement. According to TCRM, synthetic foods were our only hope, the only chance we had of halting America's alarming obesity epidemic. TCRM's goal was to have tasty, viable, 100 percent nutritive-free foods on 40 percent of America's grocery shelves by the year 2020. Not only would this slim down a nation at risk, it would allow millions of calories, no longer needed in America, to flow to Africa, North Korea, India, and other famine hot spots.

The *Nerve & Tissue* paper was about to put a bee in everyone's bonnet. It summarized a series of recently completed studies that demonstrated, fairly convincingly to my novice eye, that aspartic acid had hitherto unquantified, potentially lethal side effects. Aspartic acid, the key ingredient in every decent-tasting artificial sweetener on the market, was considered an "excitotoxin" by the Twinkie defenders, a substance so stimulating it caused cells to vibrate themselves to death in a kind of overreactive ecstasy. Allegedly, these mass cell deaths could cause a wide range of disorders, from eyelashes that fell out to psoriasis, kidney failure, coma, and death. FDA tests consistently failed to find such a link. Even rats given unlimited access to artificially sweetened water, which they much preferred to Evian and drank to the exclusion of everything else, did not produce the morbidity rates the Twinkie defenders had hoped for. In some tests, the tested rats outlived control-group peers, who found plain water so uninteresting they didn't take enough of it in and suffered from high blood pressure, obesity, diabetes, rheumatoid arthritis, and elevated cholesterol.

Now, however, *Nerve & Tissue* was set to report an alarming new discovery. According to a three-year multisite study conducted by the Allied Universities of Medicine Research Foundation, authentic foods containing a single synthetic ingredient were one thing. But when additives were ganged together to create nutritive-free foods, the results were disastrous. "Without the buffering effects of legitimately nutritive ingredients," the paper asserted, "the potential side effects of individual synthetic ingredients aren't merely increased, they're exponentially increased at a rate surpassing the ten-fold increase of the Richter scale. In our sample groups, the ingredient most likely to make its effects felt was aspartic acid, which comprises up to 50 percent of the ingredient load in popular artificial sweeteners." The paper went on to state specifically that physically healthy subjects participating in the study had experienced bouts of persistent, diffuse anxiety alternating with mild to severe mania, which, in a handful of cases, had led to psychotic breaks and at least three attempted suicides.

The Allied Universities of Medicine Research Foundation. I pictured a gathering of white coats, letterheads from Johns Hopkins, Harvard, Duke, U. of Penn., and Columbia. A good-guys version of Don Corleone's meeting with the five families, only this time it was us they were coming after. The paper concluded with a strongly worded recommendation for the immediate ban on aspartic acid and a handful of other additives, pending further study by the FDA.

Aspartic acid, of course, was the key ingredient in IM's patented sweetener, Asparmé, and Asparmé was used in particularly large amounts in Better Than Chocolate to buffer the cocoa's bitterness. No wonder crepe had been hanging from the windows and desks. *Nerve & Tissue* would publish in January. Then science writers would translate the findings into everyday English and add a hefty sprinkling of words like "smoking gun" and "national health crisis." By February, coverage would be wall to wall. TV newsrooms all over the country would see it as a Valentine's Day tie-in and run sweeps-week promos with scary voice-overs saying, "Sweets for your sweetie? Or boxes of pretty poison? When Valentine's treats become a deadly trick. Tune in at ten."

As Kate's prefacing memo said, we were dead. Our key ingredient made you want to kill yourself. We were about to be banned by the FDA. And even I knew that, in sci-speak, "further study" meant not months or years but decades.

I'd spent all yesterday in a wallow of self-pity. The only time I'd even left the house was to pick Sophie up from preschool and stop at Rainbow Foods for a satisfyingly large McGlynn's cake, whose decorative carrot made of cream cheese frosting I scraped off and ate in the sticky ecstasy of one-who-is-no-longer-dieting.

Now I had a bit of a sugar hangover and, looking around my cramped house, I simply couldn't believe that we had to go on living here. My future stretched before me not as *my* future but as something from one of those who-will-survive television shows. Could Annie Wilkins endure the rabbit hutch she and her family had been thrust into? Would she be able to convince the *Minnesota Menus* editors that she hadn't *really* been ignoring their calls for the last month? Would she assure them that, in fact, she'd be *thrilled* to write about anything they chose, including the upcoming holiday sensation, applewood-smoked plum pudding, grilled and smothered with a sharp Wisconsin cheddar sauce?

I knew I should call *Minnesota Menus*. I *had* to. But when I picked up the phone, I dialed Tom's old number at the university instead. I wasn't going down without a fight.

Considering how against our leaving Nils Holmquist had been, Tom's department head was remarkably sympathetic to our plight. He told me to fax him the paper and he'd try to read it before the weekend.

He called me back an hour later.

"You read it already?"

"I didn't really have to." I felt a stab of disappointment. "But I read it anyway. That name—the Allied Universities of Medicine Research Foundation—got me going. Ever heard of them?"

"No."

"Me either. I've got a former student doing a fellowship at *Nerve & Tissue,* so I gave him a call and asked him to get me some more information. It turns out, as I suspected, the Allied Universities of Medicine Research Foundation is a commercial research group. You know, the kind companies hire when they're hoping for certain results. Four out of five dentists recommend—that kind of thing."

"Does that make the study invalid?"

"Not necessarily. Some commercial research shops are very good. But this particular outfit is headed by Glen Milton." Nils gave a soft chuckle, and I pictured his large, comforting belly quaking gently. "Glen Milton. I haven't heard of him for years."

I felt a butterfly wing of hope unfurl. "He's unreliable?"

"Oh no, he's reliable to the hilt. Tell him what findings you want and he'll be sure to get them for you, invariably delivered in such a slick package even people who should know better won't notice that the research is bogus."

"And you think that's what happened here?"

"I think if you follow the funding trail on this, you'll find someone who wants aspartic acid off the shelves. Probably a competitor. Someone who makes a less popular sweetener that isn't based on aspartic acid, or has a product that uses the alternative sweetener. Why fight your competition if you can get the FDA to do it for you?"

I wondered who the intended victim was. Diet Coke? NutraSweet? Us? "Any ideas who?"

"Nope. I would have once, but all the action's in transfatty acids these days. Did you see my clip on Court TV? I did a day as an expert witness for Nabisco. Some nitwit was suing Oreo cookies."

I was still marshaling my case against Milton. IM would want a lot of answers, especially if I couldn't tell them who'd funded the study or who the target was. "But this is a multisite study. How did he pull that off?"

"It isn't that hard, especially when you're dealing with conditions like anxiety, and depression, which are not only hard to quantify but already present in any random sample of the human population. Did you notice that the trials were multisite, but didn't run concurrently? The New York/New Jersey trial, the last to be completed, is referred to in the paper as a 2001 trial. But when you read the fine print, the trial only lasted six weeks, from September fifteenth through November first of this year."

"Right after the World Trade Center attack."

"Right. Milton was purposely drawing from a tainted pool. Everyone between New York and Washington was under stress and should have been rejected. And the New Jersey study was conducted at the Baywater

Health Center. I looked it up. There's a Bayswater, New Jersey, but no Baywater. The Baywater Health Center is a walk-in clinic in Middletown."

I remembered the name because, at the time, it had seemed so heart-breakingly prosaic. Middletown was a bedroom community that had lost a staggering number of husbands and fathers on 9/11. Again, a population so skewed by external events they should have been exempted from the study.

"I suspect," Nils continued, "if you delved into each of the populations studied, you could find some local stressor that skewed the results. A factory town with high unemployment, a town recovering from some sort of natural disaster. The effects from factors like that can affect wide sections of the population for years. Or Milton could have deliberately weighted the samples. For example, he could argue—correctly—that since single women are the prime consumers of no-fat, no-calorie foods, samples should consist primarily of single women. However, single women also report more symptoms of anxiety and depression in general, not necessarily because they *are* more anxious or depressed, just more cognizant of their emotions, not to mention more sensitive to cuing. You know how the old saw goes—'women end up in therapy, men end up in jail.'"

No, I didn't know that particular old saw, but I wrote it down. I'd been writing down everything Nils said for the last ten minutes.

"But what about the foundation itself? Isn't there a truth-in-labeling law or something? Can they call themselves the Allied Universities of Medicine Research Foundation if there are no universities involved?"

"Oh, there probably are universities at some level. Just not accredited ones. And probably not in the U.S."

"So you really think this paper is invalid?"

"Yep. I told Tom Branch so, and he's probably already sitting down with his senior editor. My guess is that *Nerve & Tissue* will hold publication while they revisit the issue, ask Milton to supply data he won't be able to come up with, and eventually the whole thing will go away. This paper will never see the light of day."

Which wouldn't do Tom and me much good. As long as IM thought there was a chance Milton's paper would get printed, Better Than Chocolate was going nowhere. One other thing was bothering me as well.

"If Milton's such a hack, how does he get away with this?" Nils had recognized his name; why hadn't anyone at *Nerve & Tissue?*

"His usual MO is to lie low until the dust settles. He rises up, causes a stink, then sinks out of sight until everyone has forgotten, when he reinvents himself and reemerges as if nothing were wrong. The last time, though, he really dropped out of sight. I'd thought he was gone for good."

"What happened?"

"Do you remember a lawsuit against Novalix Pharmaceutical in the 1980s? Novalix produced one of the first synthetic insulins for diabetics. Milton was the lead author on a five-year tracking study suggesting that Novalix's insulin caused serious and irreversible side effects—retinopathy leading to blindness, sudden blood-sugar plunges, that sort of thing. There was a huge class-action lawsuit, and Novalix's stock tanked. But Milton's timing was off. His client, the company who'd underwritten his so-called research, got impatient. They had a new insulin in the pipeline, and their aim had been to take Novalix off the map first. But their FDA approval came sooner than expected and they couldn't wait. Betram Drug Company ended up marketing their product before the lawsuit had been settled. Betram's good fortune seemed a little too coincidental to the Novalix lawyers, who went snooping around and came up with the goods on Milton and Betram. As sci-med scandals go, it was huge. Milton's been MIA ever since."

"If I wanted to document Milton's role in the Novalix escapade, do you think I could find a trail on-line?"

"Too long ago," Nils said. "There wasn't an on-line world back then. At least, not like today. But a student of mine cited the case extensively in her dissertation, "The Prince's Dilemma: Negotiation and Rationale in Funded Research." Sandra Ellenberger, but she hasn't done her defense yet."

"So I can't get a copy on-line?"

"I'm on Sandy's committee. I'll have her e-mail the relevant chapters to you. The bibliography should sway a few minds."

But I knew corporate America was as skeptical of academic America as academia was of them. I was only going to get one chance to make my case to IM, provided I got any chance at all, and I wanted all the ammunition I could get. "Nils, suppose I had to make a case without Sandy's data, with just what I could dig up from the Net. Would I have a shot?"

"Mmm, that could be tough. You know, I used to think that papers and libraries would put their archives on-line. Logically, it makes sense. Would free up acres of space. But they didn't, so . . . wait, I know what we can do."

The "we" cheered me instantly. People didn't get behind a bad idea with a we. As I'd gathered, Novalix had been only one of many corporate victims Milton had gone after with his research. Nils named others, ranging from the manufacturer of infant seats made of allegedly flammable materials to a toiletries company whose hair-in-a-can for men was supposedly linked to low sperm counts. The pattern was always the same. Milton threw the bomb, then ran in the other direction as batteries of greedy consumers, personal-injury lawyers, government-regulatory agencies, and self-appointed protectors of the commonweal took the bait.

"The amazing thing," Nils said, "is that none of Milton's findings have ever been upheld in a court of law. Not a single product has been banned. Not a dollar has been paid in court-awarded damages. But the targeted companies have lost millions in product holdups, legal fees, and bad publicity. I'd like to see this guy nailed, Annie. So here's what we're going to do."

And while I wrote, he gave me his password to casebase.com and a list of names to search. While research journals and newspapers might not put their archives on-line, legal databases cited cases that went back to the inception of the American legal system. I was off and running.

First, I called Tom and told him to schedule an all-hands-on-deck meeting as soon as possible. I just hoped that Sandy Ellenberger's dissertation would arrive in time, and that casebase.com proved as richly rewarding as Nils had promised me it would be.

The following Monday I made my presentation in the private conference room that was part of Ed Lundquist's office suite. Malon James, the company CEO, wasn't there, but his second in command was. So was the head of legal and what looked like about half of the legal department. Jim Curtis, IM's chief chemist and Tom's ultimate boss, sat directly across from me. The table was strewn with an intimidating snare of recorders and microphones and, I noticed, the videotape was also rolling.

The funny thing was, I wasn't intimidated. I wasn't even nervous. Between the information Nils Holmquist had given me, Sandy Ellenberger's dissertation, and the citations I'd found at casebase.com, I was full of confidence. Tom had helped me pull out the most relevant sections and frame them in plain English. His grasp of the complex material was, naturally, far better than mine, and we toyed briefly with the idea that he should make the pitch. In the end, we went back to plan A. If we went down in flames, it would be better that I'd challenged IM's decision-making process, not Tom. And, as Tom cheerfully admitted, between the two of us, I'd always been better in front of a class. So last night while I'd printed, collated, and rehearsed, Tom had taken the kids to the mall for dinner and then to Office Depot to pick up folders for my handout. Tom wanted to get clear polyfilm, Jeff chose a shade he described as "electric snot green," and Sophie, still in her blue phase, seized the aquamarine package and shrieked, "Power color! Power color!" until they gave in. Along with the binders, they brought me two hot Cinnabons and a latté guaranteed for hours of high-wire brain activity.

Though the latté had long since worn off, as I began to talk, I realized that I hadn't been this jazzed since I'd left St. Cloud State. It was like teaching D day, when I began by asking my students to imagine the worst hangover of their lives (the closest I could get to seasickness), then telling them we were going to drop into the Mississippi at full-flood stage, wearing backpacks, and see who made it to shore without drowning. Those who did would move on to round two and get to climb the riverbank while the rest of the school fired on us from various campus buildings. Inevitably, someone would say it was a bad plan and we'd get slaughtered, and I would say that didn't matter, it only mattered that five or six of us got through to give cover to the next group, so six or seven of them could get through and give cover to the group behind *them*. By the end of the day, with luck, more people would be getting through than dying. What luck? someone else would grumble, and I would tell them about Rommel being home on leave, about Hitler dithering for hours before launching a counterattack, about the British gunners turning back the German panzers at Périers-sur-le-Dan. When the hour was over, my students exited in silence, and I felt a small thrill of triumph.

I felt the same thrill now. Ten minutes into the meeting, I knew I had them. Ed Lundquist was nodding at me briskly. Jim Curtis had thrown his pen down the minute I uttered Glen Milton's name. The legal department looked smug, and advertising and PR were newly afroth, gleaming with the kind of excitement only a superproduct can deliver. And was it my imagination or was Kate Hawkins looking at me with the alert, focused attention of a bird dog at work? Her keen gray eyes seemed to be *bravoing* me across the table, or at least concluding that I was more than just a convenient writer of Better Than Chocolate puff pieces. I felt flattered, the way I'd felt as a student when teachers singled me out for special projects, special praise, special attention.

I stopped speaking after fifteen minutes because there was no point in going on. I'd crossed the Delaware to surprise the British on Christmas night. I'd torpedoed the Russians at Port Arthur. I'd shocked the pants off Custer at Little Big Horn. Okay, okay, I'd only delivered a modest proposal to save our future, but it had worked.

"Any questions?"

"Just one. Even if the research is bogus, it will still be out there. Creating doubts, stirring up lawsuits, throwing red meat to the whole-foods crowd, getting the FDA in a tizzy. That's still a highly negative climate to bring a product out in."

The question was Kate's, which didn't surprise me. It was the smart question to ask. And, of course, I'd saved an answer for it.

"Well, the fact is, this paper *won't* be out there. *Nerve & Tissue* has pulled it pending a thorough review. As you see from the data, it's highly unlikely that Glen Milton and the Allied Universities of Medicine

Research Foundation will even remotely satisfy a rigorous investigation. The paper will never be published, not by a reputable journal, at any rate."

"I'll need to go over this material in some detail," Ed Lundquist said, "and float it by a few others, but I think we can safely assume that BTC is back on track." He was smiling. Everyone was smiling. Lucie flipped me a perky thumbs-up. It was the first time I'd seen her since the afternoon in the garden, and I felt that a curtain, briefly lifted, had come down again. Whether her brother had improved or she'd simply bulldozed her way back to the land of even keel I didn't know.

There was a light but assured touch on my arm. "Well done, Annie," Kate said, steering me deftly to the side. "Lucie has been keeping you all to herself and I'm a little jealous. Why don't we get together for lunch? Are you free Wednesday?"

"I can't," I said, and explained that I'd run through my share of good-will baby-sitting by other mothers. Besides, I missed Sophie, and I'd promised her a girl's day out.

"Why don't we make it a threesome?" Kate suggested. She dipped her head so that only I could see the impertinent little gleam in her eye. "I have a company gold card and absolutely no qualms about using it. Rain Forest Café for lunch? Pedicures for three at L.A. Nail?"

Sophie would love it. And so would I. No doubt about it, I'd definitely won Kate's gold star for the day. Glancing across the room, I saw Lucie. For a millisecond, I saw a flash of disappointment on her face as she looked from me to Kate. Then the flash was gone, the klieg-light smile was back in place, and the flirty little skirt, a parody of a Black Watch kilt, sailed off on the high-hipped body to join the cluster around Tom.

"This is so *great,*" I heard her say.

Above the scrum, I saw the fluff of Tom's newly lightened hair.

Chapter 7

THE BRINGER
OF CHOCOLATE

I dipped my wide, glossy, and brand-new paintbrush into the tray of Crème de Patrician and painted a smooth swatch across the wall. A few buttery flecks scattered across my new (size ten!) jeans and the crisp white shirt that was tied just above my waist, below my newly rediscovered rib cage. Tom was a few feet away on his own ladder, painting the crown molding with Versailles Vellum, Crème de Patrician's complementary trim tone. For a moment, neither of us moved, and I was aware of being held confidently aloft in the glowing shell of our bedroom, within the snug sphere of our new house, in the snowy, evergreen beauty of our new neighborhood. My eye caught Tom's and we smiled. It wasn't hard to spin out a strand of visible, beaming satisfaction.

"Oh, that's great. Hold. One more. Annie, can you turn a little on the ladder? Tom, keep looking at her, into her eyes. Right. Perfect. Okay, that's it. Strike it."

Cindi, the makeup girl, rushed forward to blot drops of paint off my cheek with a small, pyramid-shaped sponge. Someone grabbed the paintbrush out of my hand and someone else took the paint tray and began pouring the Crème de Patrician back into its can. I ducked into the bathroom (*my* bathroom—Tom had his own on the other side of the room), changed clothes, and handed the shirt and jeans to a wardrobe person who studied the paint drops and began creating similar spatters on a duplicate outfit, the just-in-case backup.

Kate and Lucie were going over a storyboard propped on an easel. Thumbnail sketches filled a catacomb of squares, most of which now had check marks to show that they'd been completed. I knew the text copy penciled below each square by heart, having spent much of the past week writing it.

—*Tom and I enjoy working on our new home together.*

—*It's a great way to save money and, with our busy schedules, an ideal way to relax and reconnect.*

—*Growing up on a farm, Tom learned to do a little of everything for himself, including carpentry.*

And:

—*Christmas means friends and family to us. I love a big crowd and find it as easy to make two turkeys as one!*

This year, Christmas, two weeks ago last Wednesday, had meant packing crates, Chinese takeout, and a "Christmas Eve" photo shoot on January 3 with catered food heating in the ovens and rented furniture standing in for the custom dining set that would not arrive in time. Even our close friends and family were borrowed, and to this day I don't know who the interesting and photogenic people in that spread were. Actors, I presume. At least that's the conclusion I drew when Sophie began lobbying for her own eight-by-ten glossies a few days later.

By the time I finished changing my clothes and joined the crowd at the storyboard, the strip of crown molding was down, two men were carting the wall away, and another man was folding up the dropcloth onto which nothing had been dropped. Because, of course, it was a fake wall, and the paint was just for looks. Even I knew, the first time I saw it, that this was not the kind of house you painted yourself.

It's a good thing I'm not a novelist or I'd be tempted to resort to a cheesy cliché here. Something like, "The days rushed by in a head-spinning blur." Or, if this was a movie, I might go for the old trick of calendar pages flying away in a gale-force wind. But that's a cheat to real life, isn't it? In the press of momentous events, people remember more details than they ordinarily would—so many details that their perception of time stretches to accommodate them. I did a paper on that once, "The Erroneous Hourglass: History, Time Perception, and Eyewitness Fallibility." I interviewed people who'd lived through historic events, asking them to estimate time spans between key moments of the incident. The shorter the length of actual time, the greater the elongating distortion. Most people clearly recalled a gap of "several hours" between the bulletin of JFK's shooting and the news of his death. The actual time between the bulletins was less than an hour, give or take a few minutes depending on which station you were tuned to. For rememberers, the hour was stuffed with a kind of hyper-recollection. Several people recalled being at lunch when, in fact, they had already returned from lunch. But the meat-loaf sandwich they ate and the bit of office gossip they heard had been retrieved and reshuffled to occur within the frame of the event. It's the days when nothing happens that pass in a blur. Add a momentous event and you're stuck with a Pandora's box of detail.

Which is why I remembered, in fly-eyed detail, everything about the moment when I first heard this house mentioned.

It was the day Kate, Sophie, and I went to Mall of America. Still replete from lunch (Caribbean Coconut Shrimp for Kate, a Rumble-in-the-Jungle Turkey Wrap for Sophs, and the Leaping Lizards Lettuce Wrap for me), we'd just come out of L.A. Nails and were sitting on a bench watching Sophie, barefoot, with cotton balls between her toes, walk on her heels and wave her socks dramatically at her grape mist toenails. I was sure she'd understood my explanation that "shiny" didn't necessarily mean "still wet," but she was going for the drama. I figured in another five minutes we'd pack up her inner Sarah Bernhardt and be on our way. A woman in a red car coat was crossing in front of us, holding a perfectly well-behaved four-year-old by the hand. I remember feeling vaguely sorry for her.

Then Kate turned to me and said, "Do you have to get home right away? Because, if you don't, there's a house I thought we might look at."

An involuntary frown, a remnant of the headache I'd ended up with the day I went house hunting with Lucie, must have traced its way across my brow because Kate shot me a lightly mocking smile. "I thought you might want to see at least one house without deconstructing its own very special message."

"Claire Holmes won't be meeting us?"

"No, she won't. If we're to believe that's her name."

"It isn't?"

Kate tipped her head to one side and furrowed her brow earnestly. "Hmm, let's see. A woman who is not just a real estate agent but an expert in semiotics. Claire Holmes. Claire. Holmes. Oh, right, it *has* to be a coincidence." She flipped open her cell phone. "Should I call the agent?"

"And the agent's name . . . ?"

"Ivy Hornbostel. Thick glasses. Drives a Ford."

"Perfect." I corraled Sophie and got her socks back on. "Let's go."

I felt a little thrill of excitement as we skirted Lake Minnetonka, then a plummet of disappointment when we turned down a driveway. Even from the outside, I could tell that this house was way beyond anything we'd looked at, even after Lucie had gone up another quarter million. I wondered why Kate wanted me to see something we so obviously could not afford.

On a few occasions, Lucie had told me, with a gravely lowered voice and a look of wizened disillusionment, that Kate had—gasp—An Agenda. I dismissed this as part office rivalry, part Youth Contemplating the Bust of Reality. Of course Kate had an agenda. Who didn't? An agenda was the only reason otherwise sane people got up in the dark to swill coffee, leap into panty hose, and scrape frost off their windshields. Truth be told, I was still proud to have gotten *on* Kate's agenda. The bouquet that arrived the day after I outed Glen Milton and his bogus aspartic-acid study had been from IM but the handwriting on the card—"Thrilled we're back on track!"—was definitely Kate's. Clearly, I'd crawled onto her radar screen. I felt that, for the first time, Kate saw me as more than an acceptable-looking wife with a convenient dissertation and a knack for writing about walleye on a stick, deep-fried dill pickles, and the culinary chaos that ensues when a Hmong girl marries a third-generation Finn. She now saw me as clever, resourceful, and definitely a person worth knowing.

So where did this house fit in? Ivy Hornbostel sped out to meet us as if waiting for Kate's call, so it probably wasn't a spur-of-the-moment idea. Maybe Lucie was right, I thought with a chill flicker. Maybe Kate didn't see me as a Person Worth Knowing at all. Maybe she saw me as competition. Maybe she thought I was taking my IM parking space way too seriously. Maybe she thought I wanted to be co-president. Maybe she was dangling this house in front of me just so she could put me back in my place when she yanked it away. From Hades Lane thou came, to Hades Lane thou canst return. But as long as we were here and Ivy had the door so invitingly open, there was no harm in looking, was there?

The impressive thing about the house was that no one had tried to make it impressive. There was no marble foyer with balustrade and rotunda, no twin set of spiral staircases swirling down from the east and west wings, no artificial stream running playfully beneath a glassed-over section of the kitchen floor.

"It's really quite a simple house," said Ivy, who lived up to Kate's description of her. Ivy Hornbostel had mouse-colored hair and spoke with the unhurried hush of a librarian. There wasn't a Pashmina in sight. In fact, she was wearing mittens, which she pulled off and stuffed in her pocket. "Do you want to see both floors?" she asked, as if unwilling to impose. "And the boathouse?"

I sure did, even if I could never own them. It would be like flirting with Colin Firth at a party all night long (not the comfy *Bridget Jones* Firth but the ruthlessly sexy Firth of *Valmont*) and knowing you'd go home with your husband anyway—but in the meantime, so what? You'd still get three or four hours to fill your eyes. So I ambled along behind Ivy, admiring the skill that had gone into making such a spectacular house seem unpretentious and even casual. I agreed that yes, it *was* convenient to have a wood room with both interior and exterior access, and the idea of connecting the two children's rooms with a walk-in closet designed like a playhouse— inspired! Determined to maintain an air of sangfroid, I ignored the soaring feeling the exposed-beam ceilings gave me as diligently as I would have ignored the Firthian forelock and chin cleft. To no avail. By the time we reached the back of the house, which faced the shoreline, I was besotted.

The great room, which would eventually make its appearance in

Martha Stewart Living, bowed outward, lapping after the blue of the lake. A curving row of windows ran its length and wrapped around one corner. The other end of the room flowed gracefully past an island into a kitchen of cream-colored brick and pickled oak.

I made one last stab at indifference. "Isn't the kitchen a little small? For what IM wants?"

Kate gave an amused little snort. "Oh, this is just the family kitchen."

Multiple kitchens, apparently, were the latest thing in luxury living, and this house had two of them, three if you counted the one in the boathouse, and three and a half if you counted the kitchenette off the sunroom on the second floor.

"This kitchen is more for everyday informal cooking," Ivy explained apologetically. "It has everything, of course, but on a smaller scale. The wine refrigerator, for example, is only a half cabinet."

So that's what that thing was. I thought it was a dishwasher with a see-through front.

"Look at this," Kate said.

Beyond double doors that I'd assumed led to a pantry was what Ivy described as the working kitchen, a vista of brushed metal and pale celadon ceramic tile that had given up its amateur status and gone professional. The refrigerator alone looked like it could sleep six. Three skylights splashed light around the room, a luxury in Minnesota in November. Along one wall, a recessed alcove held an enormous old library card file, its wood polished to dark honey by age and use.

"Too heavy to move, so it comes with the house," Ivy explained. "I love this part." She pulled open a drawer and the scent of mace filled the room. The forty-eight-drawer file was the kitchen's spice cabinet. I peeked in. In the mace drawer alone there were four different kinds of mace, whole and ground, domestic and imported.

I suppose I should have found the sheer excess of three and a half kitchens morally dubious, but I didn't. I loved the idea of having a perpetually clean kitchen to dazzle my friends with while the real kitchen, full of soaking pots and scattered flour, abattoir of gourmet dreams, remained out of sight. I pictured myself with a champagne flute in one hand, sliding trays of perfect canapés from the spotless oven. My life would be one big GE commercial, except that the appliances would be Thermidor, Viking, and Sub-Zero.

"The wine refrigerator in this kitchen," Ivy was saying, "is much larger than the one in the family kitchen."

Oh yes. Our cellar collection of Ernest and Julio should fit quite nicely. With about ninety-six slots to spare.

Sophie bashed through the swinging doors. "Mommy, ducks! Ducks!" She pulled me back into the great room and pressed desperately against the windows. "*Can't* I go see the ducks? *Please?*"

Just beyond the dock, thirty or forty loons had settled on the open water of the unfrozen lake. Loons are shy, solitary birds, each pair taking up a small lake or a corner of a larger one, and I'd never seen more than two together at a time. Here was a whole flock, their elongated beaks and glossy black heads bobbing like sideways teardrops against the navy blue water. I wished Jeff were here to see this. Awesome, Mom, he would say. Triple-mega awesome.

"Can't I go out and see the ducks?"

Sophie was still grasping my hand.

"No, honey. They'd fly away."

"Why?"

"Because they're busy. They're on their way someplace warm for the winter."

"Migrating."

"Do you know that word?"

"I've known it for*ever*," Sophie said. "Can we see them when they come back?"

Someone else would be living here then, and I felt ridiculously sad about it. I caught Kate's eye. I had to get out of here.

"You don't like the house?"

"I *love* the house. It's perfect."

"Then—"

Even with the bonus I would get for losing the weight, Tom and I wouldn't have enough to make an offer. Our current house, with its small down payment and two years' worth of equity, would barely cover the move.

"Come on, Kate. It's way, *way* off the charts. There's no way IM would go for this."

Kate's silence filled the room. Ivy wandered off, tactfully out of earshot. "I'm not sure they'd say no, Annie," Kate said at last, her voice meditative and deliberate. "It wouldn't be easy, but there are ways."

"How?"

She took a deep breath. "Do you really, really love the house, Annie? I mean, would you be willing to be house poor for a few years?"

I nodded, and Kate, satisfied, shifted into high gear. "All right, then. One. I've done some research. The owners just retired to Florida. They're paying two mortgages, the luxury-home market has been hurting since the dotcom crash, and we could probably get them to shave a few hundred thousand off the top for starters. Two. I can use the dual-kitchen thing as a selling point. It makes the house much more usable to IM. And the setting is perfect—the Minnesota lifestyle, family fun on the lake. There ought to be lots of opportunities for cross-promotion. Three. Would you be willing to commit more personal time to IM? To give them more access to your family life?"

"We've already pretty much agreed that they can have us lock, stock, and barrel," I admitted. "We don't have a whole lot left to bargain with."

Kate shot me a wicked grin. "Never say that, dear. It's all in the presentation. We just have to do some repositioning."

"Sure, but I know the ballpark numbers we've been talking about. They're not going to double what's on the table."

"No," Kate said patiently, "but there are lots of ways to structure a contract."

"Are there?" I was so, *so* afraid to want this house.

"Well, Tom gets a royalty for Better Than Chocolate products, right? And you get pay-pers for personal appearances? We could negotiate both those things down. Take a smaller royalty percentage on the products, agree to do appearances on an as-needed basis in return for a larger up-front sum. Lots of tweaking we can do, Annie, and I haven't even gotten to foreign sales yet."

"Less royalty on product? I don't know if we could . . ."

My voice trailed off as I watched Sophie focus again on her ducks. In all the talks we'd had with IM, it was clear that the bulk of our income would derive from royalties. They were our chance to salt away money for college, for retirement, for savings, and for emergencies. I pictured Jeff at eighteen in the same fix my nephew Rob was in, uncertain whether he could afford eight years of college or not. It was one thing growing up knowing the score, as Rob had, but how would Jeff feel if we told him there was no money because Mom had to have the house of her dreams? Well, I knew the answer to that one. *It's okay, Mom. I didn't want to go to med school that much. Driving a cab isn't so bad. Really. Do you and Dad, like, need some money? Until you start getting Social Security?*

"Kate, I just don't think we can give up all that much—"

"Not give up," Kate said briskly, "*defer*. Have you ever heard of a stepped royalty? Let me explain."

So Kate told me how you could structure a royalty so that on the first x-number of goods sold, you got so much. Then at certain stages—after, say, a million BTC bars—the royalty escalated. It kept on escalating, sometimes to unheard-of percentages, but by that time, there was so much money flowing in nobody cared.

Maybe, I thought. *Maybe.*

"Do you think they'd go for it?"

Kate tossed me her cell phone. "Call Tom. Tell him to come see his new house."

I sat on a folding chair and studied my revised biography while Tom changed out of his painting clothes. The new-and-improved Annie Wilkins was quite a girl, and I needed to have her down pat before we went to New York to launch Better Than Chocolate the week before Valentine's Day.

For starters, I was now a gourmet cook. There was nothing I found more relaxing than holiday entertaining. I looked upon a three-day recipe for Beijing duck as a "road map to adventure." Lucie had written that line, and my attempts to take it out had been completely unsuccessful. I also now had an artistic flair and, hence, could be said to embrace home decorating (magazines), painting (finger, with Sophie), and flower arranging (I owned a vase). My church was important to me (since two weeks ago, when we hastily joined). I enjoyed sports (well, yes, because without the Vikings the malls would be jammed on Sundays) and going on fishing trips with Tom and the kids (true, although I didn't think laughing hysterically while Sophie bounced her minnow on the water and shouted, "They call him Flipper, Flipper," quite put me into *Old Man and the Sea* country). Yes, I *did* miss teaching and was hoping to give back to the community (property taxes weren't enough?) by doing some volunteer tutoring in the near future (*surely* they were kidding). In my spare time, I was a voracious novel reader (the classics before I married Tom, the *New York Times* bestsellers after, chick lit when I was pregnant, and since we had the kids—?).

When Tom emerged from the bathroom, I tossed the list into my purse, knowing it would join the menacing, ever growing school of unheeded lists circling through a Sargasso Sea debris at the bottom. I needed to round them all up, sort them out, and make a master list. But I needed a list to remind me to do it.

"I can't keep up with her," I said.

"Who?"

"Her. Me. Annie Wilkins. According to IM, she's a whirlwind. You don't think they'll really want me to volunteer-tutor, do you?"

Tom lifted the hair off the nape of my neck the way I loved. "I don't know, babes, but if they want you to—better brush up on those high points of American history. We can't turn back now, you know."

True. As soon as Kate stepped in, having apparently committed Donald Trump's *The Art of the Deal* to memory, things had moved fast. We signed our contracts with IM the day before Thanksgiving and closed on the house less than a month later. We wouldn't have a whole lot of liquid

cash, at least not until Tom's royalties paid back the enormous down payment IM had made for us, but we did have the most perfect house in the
world, and how could you put a liquid cash value on that?

The last time we'd moved, we'd spent weeks begging boxes from grocery stores, asking friends to save their Sunday papers, and doing our own
packing. This time, IM deployed a fleet of packers and movers who
swarmed through our house like locusts. They packed the homework Jeff
left on the kitchen counter for five minutes. Not that he cared much. He got
a lot of mileage out of saying, "The movers ate my homework. Ha! Ha,"
and was changing schools anyway.

We didn't even have to show and sell our own house—IM would take
care of that. In the interest of speeding things along, they said, but I think
the real reason was that six months from now they didn't want anyone
identifying us as that rumpled, harried couple from the house on Hades
Lane. Our new bios didn't even mention Oak Creek Park but hinted that
we'd lived in some hipper, trendier suburb. Or maybe it was our furniture
they wanted to dissociate us from—the couch with its removable, wash-
able Ultrasuede slipcover, the coffee table Scout had eaten a corner of in
his adolescence, the bounced-on beds and nicked dressers familiar to anyone with children and a five-figure income. Most of it was going to my sister, Barb, anyway. I was shipped off with IM's decorator (excuse me, home
interiors consultant) to shop for new pieces. A dream come true, surely. So
why did the fifty-dollar rocking chair that we'd bought at a garage sale the
weekend I found out I was pregnant seem suddenly so dear that I snuck it
out of the scrap heap, wrapped it in a mover's blanket, and labeled it
"Louis XIV chair?" And how did the bookcase Sophie had crayoned her
name on become "antique end table"?

I twisted around and looked at Tom. "Listen."

"I don't hear anything."

"That's because they've all left. They've *gone*. This is the first time
we've ever been here alone." I had an idea. "Do you have to go back to
work right away?"

"I should."

"Let's christen our house first." I jumped up and grabbed his hand. "Come on. Let's plant the flag. Let's take possession!" I led him down the stairs, then down the softly gleaming bead-board hallway that reminded me of an old farmhouse. "This is going to be great," I whispered.

I could still muster it, the sense of over-the-top wonder I'd felt that first day, when Ivy Hornbostel pushed open the door directly across from the wood room. I was expecting a linen closet, a bath, or maybe a guest room. Instead my eyes filled with light, late-afternoon light pouring in a torrent through the sloping of glass roof that curved over to become a glass wall. Late-afternoon light glinting off the water of an indoor pool. Not an over-size hot tub, not a swim-in-place pool shooting jets of water for you to work against but a lovely, fifty-foot pool with blue ceramic tile and wedding-cake steps at the shallow end. I was so dazzled I didn't even think about the safety aspects until Ivy showed me how to activate the child-proof security keypad by the door and pointed out the windows at either end of the room, one that looked in from Tom's study, the other from the great room. You could also, Ivy added, see into the pool room roof from several of the second-story rooms.

I tugged at Tom's belt. "Let's go skinny-dipping. In our new pool."

"You're a naughty girl."

"And you're easy."

"That's why I love you."

"Same here. Come on, big boy, off with 'em."

He pulled me close. "You do it."

Instead, I stripped off my own clothes and waded in. "Let's swim first."

And we did. In my newer, thinner body, I felt like a sylph, a water sprite, the goldfish flirting her tail in the original *Fantasia*. And Tom—maybe it was the blur of chlorine haze, but he looked truly buff. I swam up and grabbed a bicep. It was firm. And large.

"Wowie zowie. What's this?" It occurred to me that I hadn't seen my husband naked in a while. We were so tired these days, we fell asleep with the lights on. Besides, there were so many packing crates stacked around our house that you couldn't stand back far enough to see anyone naked.

Tom pumped his muscle. "I've, uh, I've been working out in the employee's gym on my lunch hour. Weight training."

"Every day?"

"Three times a week." He looked sheepish. "Tuesdays and Thursdays there's a step aerobics class."

"Step aerobics?" This was the guy who I'd never gotten on a dance floor. Even in college. And only once at our wedding. Now he was bouncing up and down off a plastic stool twice a week while Ricky Martin and J.Lo rocked on with it. "How did this start?"

"Um, Lucie thought it would be a good idea. She and some other girls do it, so I thought, why not?"

I laughed. "Are you the only boy in the class?"

"No. Sort of."

"Well, I like the muscles. Pretty hot." I stopped treading water and wrapped my legs around him. I felt him go hard against me. "No shrinkage problem?"

"Apparently not."

"Then let's misbehave."

We tried making love in the water, which never works, so we fumbled our way onto dry land and tried again on the poofy, striped cushions of the double-wide chaise. *That* worked. More than worked.

"I love you, O bringer of miracle chocolate."

Tom rolled onto his back and stared up at the sky through the glass roof. " 'She is the heart of my heart and the light of my home.' " He was quoting from our wedding vows. "She is the mother of my children and the source of my laughter. And she can melt my chocolate anytime she wants."

How was it that he could still make me laugh and cry at the same time? I reached toward him but got only a handful of air.

"Oh hell. Damn it." Tom had scrambled to his feet.

"What's wrong?"

"We don't have towels, do we? I'm soaking wet and I've got to get going. Did they leave a dropcloth or anything?"

I stretched lazily. To be honest, I didn't stretch, I undulated.

"Don't do that, Annie. Really. I've got to go."

"Okay, okay." I was still aglow with love. "Dry off with my clothes. I'll throw them in the dryer after you go and it'll work out fine."

But when he left, I drifted off in the warm patch of sunlight and my clothes never did make it to the dryer. I dreamed that my sister, Barb, was holding a Tupperware container full of fruit salad and I could see all my favorite bits, strawberries and pineapple, cantaloupe and honeydew. We were having a picnic, and she was saying that I didn't eat enough healthy food, and I was saying it was hard to hear her over the doorbell. Except there were no doorbells on picnics, which is how I realized I was waking up, and the doorbell was ringing madly.

At first, I ignored it. We hadn't officially moved in yet. I wasn't obligated to answer. And who rang doorbells in neighborhoods like this anyway?

The doorbell pealed again and again. Then I realized it had to be Tom. I still had the only set of keys. Maybe something was wrong or urgent or he was having car trouble. I jumped up, grabbing my wet clothes. My chlorine-stiffened hair dripped cold water down my back.

"I'm coming," I yelled. And louder, "Coming!" I gave up struggling with my jeans and settled for just the shirt and panties. "Hang on!" My feet were freezing. My hair was a wadded mass that felt like an abandoned papier-mâché project. And people wonder why the romance goes out of marriage. "What *is* it?" I yanked the door open so forcefully it smashed against my kneecap.

"Oh, I'm sorry. I didn't know you were having private time. I'm Estelle Mackenzie. Mudjekeewis Lane, just around the corner. I saw your car and wanted to welcome you to the neighborhood. My husband and I run the Mackenzie clinics. Addiction, cognitive therapy, and behavior modification. Am I getting you at a bad time?"

Of course she came in, although I don't actually remember asking her to. Estelle was a take-charge type. No wonder so many celebrities sobered up at Mackenzie. She slapped it right out of them.

"I'm sorry I can't offer you anything," I said, trying a graceful reentry after I'd left and gotten my clothes on. "We haven't really moved in yet. I don't even have a coffeepot. Or coffee."

No problem. Estelle had packets of Sanka in her briefcase. Also a collapsible cup. All she really needed was my In-Sink-Erator instant hot-water tap, which I didn't know we had until she pointed it out to me. Estelle seemed cozily at home in my kitchen.

"Did you know the people who lived here before?"

"The Esterlys? Absolutely! Everyone knows everyone here." She leaned toward me, *over* me, actually. She was at least six feet tall. "We're a very close community here. A little village, really." She looked at me brightly. "There's a bit of a buzz about you already, you know."

"There is?" I hoped it didn't have anything to do with Tom's and my performance on the chaise. I'd assumed the wall of evergreens screened the poolroom, but maybe I was wrong. Maybe Estelle had a cupola and a pair of binoculars, close neighbor that she was.

"We hear you're a food writer. And your husband works for General Mills."

"International Milling."

"Even better. Do you know, your Gator Tators have the most calming effect on hyperactive children? Counterintuitive, but it's come up so many times I'm thinking of doing a paper on it. Maybe a book." She snapped her fingers. "We could do it together! *Eating to Live: Rules and Recipes for the ADHD Child.* Do you have children?"

"Two."

"Hyperactive?"

"No."

"Are you sure? So many children these days don't *have* symptoms. We call them the silent sufferers. It's only when a teacher or counselor alerts parents to the problem . . . Have you had them evaluated?"

"My children are not hyperactive."

"Oh. Well." Estelle looked momentarily disappointed. "It would have lent a nice personal note. But I'll give you my case notes—you can create some composite studies, flesh them out, develop thirty or forty recipes, and we'll split the money! Brilliant!"

Shoot me. Somebody. Please. Shoot me.

Estelle finished her Sanka, smashed the coffee cup flat, and put it back in its little tin case. "I'd love a second cup, but I can't. I just don't have time for these kinds of indulgences. How do you manage it? You'll have to tell me what it's like sometime. You know, when you commit your life to giving to others, the one person you never have time to give to is yourself." She glanced at her watch. "God, my manicurist will kill me. Anyway, I really stopped by to make sure we get you onboard. You and——?"

"Tom. Onboard for what?"

"Our gourmet club. It's informal, really, just neighborhood families getting together to de-stress. We all bring something gourmet. No problem for you, I know. You'll probably think we're at the tuna-noodle-casserole level of cooking anyway, but we'd love to have you."

"But——" I was about to explain my lack of tony cooking skills, but remembered my bio and the fact that the new Annie Wilkins adored these little chances to show off in the kitchen. Estelle extracted a Blackberry from a postal-size leather bag and began punching and scrolling furiously, making a racket I didn't know was possible with a handful of plastic. For the first time, I appreciated Lucie's dexterity with all things wireless.

"I'll slot you into the Esterlys' place." She pulled on her coat and tapped the Blackberry one more time. "There. I've e-mailed the whole gang. They'll be thrilled. Let's see, what were the Esterlys down for? Oh, easy. Just dessert. It'll be a snap for you. Ten adults, a dozen or so children. No strawberries. Kathy Haines's daughter says she's allergic to them. See you Saturday at seven, then."

"*This* Saturday? But——"

"Don't worry. We'll love you. We're a very unsnobby crowd around here. We don't judge. Mudjekeewis Lane, 2688." Estelle shot out the door and was halfway down the walk before she turned back. "Bring something chocolate! The year *Fargo* came out, Joanne Blessner made the most fantastic Paul Bunyan out of bittersweet mousse."

And she was gone.

Chapter 8

THESE LITTLE
TOWN SHOES

"For the first year we lived here, I used to sneak back to Cub to buy groceries because I thought Byerly's was too expensive. Which drawer do you want this in?"

Lyn Vickers was the whirlwind of efficiency I was not. Since nine A.M., she had been bobbing around my kitchen putting towels in drawers, mixing bowls on shelves, and plates in cupboards. My informal kitchen, that is. The working kitchen had been professionally equipped by IM. So far, I'd counted fourteen wire whisks and twice as many spatulas in there, along with an array of baking sheets, rings, molds, crimpers, and cutters so bewildering I'd left immediately and hadn't ventured back since.

"You can't let the money overwhelm you. Should I have it, is this right, this isn't right, if I feel guilty, will it be all right?" Lyn moved so quickly her voice seemed to trail a few seconds behind her fluff of short, white-blond hair. "Just enjoy your house, because if you didn't have it, someone else would, so why not you?"

Lyn was giving me a short course in moving up the socioeconomic ladder. Like Tom and I, she and her husband, Dan, had leapfrogged the system, going from being scrabbling software developers to the creators of Doggit!, the software program that retrieved all those files you knew were somewhere on your computer but had no idea where, making it unlikely you would ever see them again. The genius of Doggit! was that it got to know you. The longer it was in your computer and the more often you used it, the more it learned about your haphazard, idiosyncratic approach to storing files. So you saved the image of a couch you wanted to your income-tax folder, because you'd been working on your taxes the day you browsed furniture on-line. Five months later, when you were ready to buy the sofa, you had no idea what you'd called the file and whether it was a .jpg, a .bmp., or a .gif. You didn't remember the name of the site you'd gotten it from, and it was anyone's guess which of the thousands of folders and subfolders you might have chucked it into, except that you had eliminated the one tidily named "House Ideas" because it certainly wasn't there. All you had to do was type a loose chain of free associations into the Doggit! search box (sofa, green stripe, image) and it would find the file in ten seconds or less, two to five seconds if Doggit! had been installed and running at the time of the original save. Microsoft had bought the rights to bundle Doggit! with Windows, and Lyn and Dan had bought the house at the end of our block.

Now Dan was working on an even more innovative program, one that would revolutionize how computers were used. Tentatively called Bark! (presumably to keep the doggy theme going), the program would be distributed free, on a disk, to everyone who wanted one. With the disk, you created a floor plan of your primary locales—home, office, car, yard, whatever you wanted. Then you attached specially encoded peel-and-stick minidots to the items you were most likely to mislay, such as car keys, cell phone, wallet, checkbook, briefcase, purse. If you wanted, you could put peel-and-stick dots on every single thing you owned, and all for free. When you mislaid an item, you booted up Bark!, typed in the item name, and the program went into action. The peel-and-stick minidots emitted a signal that the computer detected, identified, and located. It threw up a floor plan with a cute barking dog on it to show you exactly where the missing item was. It was at this point that the program ceased being free. Every time you used Bark! to locate a mislaid item, it was logged into your computer and, the next time you went on-line, relayed to a mainframe server that would bill your credit card $1.50 per search. And really, what harried mother, late for work and desperate to find the keys her toddler may well have fisted deep into the Diaper Genie, would hesitate to fork over a few bucks? Oh yeah, the Vickers were going to retire on this one.

Lyn wanted no part of developing Bark! and could hardly wait until Dan joined her in semiretirement. "Do you know how many hours of my life I spent entering code? Scary. I just want to stay at home while Emily's still a kid. I want to buy tubes of cookie dough with holiday designs in them. I want to watch Christopher Lowell and *Trading Spaces* on TV."

Who could blame her? For the last two days, when the confluence of moving vans and delivery trucks had made our new house resemble a jumping-off town along the Oregon Trail, I had been incredibly happy. Not just the happiness of feathering a new nest but the happiness of not having to deal with IM. I'd passed the test, gotten through a rehearsal interview with my new Annie Wilkins demeanor intact, and had been put on parole while they worked with Tom, who still suffered from deer-in-the-headlights syndrome whenever the bright lights came on. A blue-eyed deer in the headlights, in this case. Tom's eyes had been deemed insufficiently dramatic and he was now adjusting to azure contact lenses that made his eyes ache. Twice I'd had to retrieve a lost lens that slid onto his sclera. I admit that a mean little part of me, the part that was still eating lettuce with a spritz of fat-free vinaigrette for lunch, took grim satisfaction in the fact that he, like me, had to suffer for this gig.

Lyn and Dan, like most of the other couples we'd met at the Mackenzie's, were surprisingly normal. Like us, they seemed to have shown up because it was easier to stuff some artichokes and put in an appearance than it was to resist Estelle. And, having shown up, they remembered that the whole thing was actually sort of fun. Most of the children got along, and at least it didn't mean forking over $10 an hour to some teenager who would be yakking to her boyfriend in Brazil on your cell phone while your children experimented with microwaved peanut butter and jelly on potato chips, creating a mess that might well necessitate replacing the entire unit. Aside from the Mackenzies themselves, who were from New York, the only other non-Minnesotans in the group were the Culpeppers, who were old-money Charleston and referred to their six-thousand-square-foot natural-stone Tonka Bay home as a "little house on the ice-strewn prairie." Lyn told me that early in their residency, at a gourmet night conducted amid the wail of summer tornado sirens, the Culpeppers had become terrified and screamingly drunk and hadn't been quite the same since. Now at the first sign of fast-moving clouds, Tiny Culpepper would grab her children and begin a frantic search for shelter.

Lyn and I had bonded over a look of shared horror when Estelle announced that her twelve-year-old son, Bengt—an intellectually gifted child, we were informed, challenged not only with genius and with hypercreativity but with double doses of ADHD and bipolar depression with tendencies toward pyromania—was making our shrimp flambé entrée.

"We believe in providing constructive opportunities for him to interact with fire," Estelle explained just before Bengt appeared table side in a miniature white tunic and toque. "When you have an IQ as high as his, finding the right outlet is a challenge."

Bengt was a round, miserable-looking child who added more and more bourbon every time the flames began to die down. Finally, his father, a Bengt on a larger scale, told him to cut it out, and Bengt bowed slightly, bid us, *"Bon appétit, mesdames et messieurs,"* glanced forlornly at his mother—who by this time was lost in a conversation about the stresses of caregiving—and left the room. The funny thing was that the shrimp was delicious.

Lyn and I bonded again when we both took minuscule portions of my flourless chocolate cake.

"It looks delicious," Lyn explained, "but I'm dieting from my last pregnancy."

I felt an unaccountable pang of nostalgia. "When did you have your baby?"

"Emily. Almost five years ago."

I laughed. My kind of woman. Then we realized our daughters were the same age and that sealed the deal.

When we got home, I asked Tom what the men were like.

"Fine. We talked about ice fishing, the T-wolves, and building an indoor grill, which I think we might want to consider at some point. Rob Mackenzie's a little odd, though. Do you know, he thought we'd moved here from out of state. Then he took my hand and asked which of us had come for treatment."

The only social soft spot of the night had been Jeff who, predictably, had taken Bengt the flame thrower under his wing.

"He doesn't have any friends, Mom. It's sad."

I wondered if it was time to tell Jeff that some people didn't have friends for perfectly good reasons, reasons you should pay attention to. That way, you would never have to face a TV news crew wanting to know why your seemingly mild-mannered friend had just been arrested with twenty gallons of gasoline and a diagram of the state capitol.

I unpacked another box of glasses.

"What about Emily?" I asked Lyn. "Do you worry that she'll grow up too materialistic?"

I already worried that we'd gotten off on the wrong foot, bargaining with Jeff and Sophie in an effort to make up for Christmas. Sophie cashed in her chips first, and now two kittens named Bonnie and Clyde, dropped off by Barb a few days ago, were on the lam in the great room with Sophie and Lyn's daughter, Emily, in hot pursuit. Jeff proved a tougher negotiator. He started off asking for a computer, and when we agreed too quickly, he upped the ante. He wanted us to get Tivo as well, and a new DVD player, and when I pointed out that our family present was going to be our trip to New York for IM, he told me, in a voice that I didn't like at all, that New York didn't count because it was work.

"I mean, don't you worry that she'll get a skewed image of the world? It's not exactly multicultural central here."

"Oh please," Lyn scoffed. "It doesn't take a village. You're the one in charge of your kids, not the Greater Minnetonka Homeowners Association." She tucked a strand of pale, springy hair behind her ear and looked at me long enough to read my mind. "Your kids are *not* going to turn into Bengt Mackenzie. Besides, there's nothing really wrong with Bengt. He's just an ordinary kid."

"In a toque. Who wants a blowtorch for Christmas."

"To get his mother's attention. Don't you see? Estelle will not tolerate ordinary. Bengt has to be 'gifted.' And 'troubled.' He's doing his best to make her dreams come true."

She paused to smooth my new shelf paper down. "A little too successfully, maybe. Bengt really *was* a nice, ordinary kid until the separation."

"What separation?"

"The Mackenzies. Rob moved out last summer. You don't know this because I don't know this and no one knows this but of course we all do. Rob Mackenzie moved out and is living with his psychoanalyst—well, former psychoanalyst; she dropped him as a client."

"Are they going to get a divorce?"

"Uh-uh. They don't want to divide the business, or risk the bad publicity. The worst part, and how warped is this, is that they're paying Bengt—paying him an actual salary—to do his part in maintaining the happy family front."

"You're kidding."

"Nope. Apparently, Estelle explained to him that we all have jobs in life, and if we do our jobs well, we're paid accordingly, and right now this is Bengt's job. Along with managing his bipolar ADHD, which he doesn't have, and getting straight As."

"Does Bengt get straight As?"

"Nowhere near."

Poor old Bengt. "How do you know all this?"

"He comes over to my house a lot after school. He's not allowed to be in his alone, and sometimes the nanny of the week—they don't last long with Estelle—doesn't show up."

"Why can't he be in the house alone?" My mind leaped. "Fire risk?"

Lyn shook her head. "Eater. Apparently, he'll cook everything in the house and eat as much of it as he can before he's stopped. Probably because Estelle practices strict portion control and thinks a growing twelve-year-old boy should eat exactly the same amount of food his forty-two-year-old mother does."

I wanted to ask her more, like whether or not Bengt might sneak into the walk-in refrigerator in my working kitchen and die there, but the phone rang.

"I've got the most incredible news!" Lucie bubbled. "Are you sitting down? We got the Super Bowl!"

"Great," I said. Then I wondered. "What does it mean? We got the Super Bowl?"

"We got you a cutaway spot at halftime. You and Tom. They're giving us thirty seconds from your living room. Live! How great will that be? I mean, do you know what the halftime audience is? Millions!" I wasn't sure if she was talking viewers or airtime cost, but I wasn't sure I needed to know. "That's fantastic, Lucie."

"Just one thing, Annie. We have to move the New York trip up. *Click!* will only take us if they get a worldwide first. Since the Super Bowl is international, we need to do *Click!* ahead of it."

"But we can't! Tom's not ready. I haven't packed. I haven't even *un*packed. We're too clacked to *Click!*"

I thought this was passably amusing, but all it got from Lucie was a sharp intake of breath. "Do you have any idea how many women watch *Click!*, Annie? Women who are dieting? Women with PMS? Women who would kill for calorie-free chocolate? *Any* idea how big that audience is?" Lucie's voice threatened to crescendo up a couple of octaves. "And do you know how many favors I had to call in for this? Not just getting *Click!* to switch your dates but everyone else. The Food Network, *Live at Five*, Letterman, Matt and Katie."

"You got Letterman to switch?"

"Yes. Not easy. So we're going to New York. Thursday morning six A.M. Right?"

"Right," I answered weakly and fumbled the phone back into its receiver. I wondered how Tom was taking this, but I didn't dare call him until I could keep the panic out of my voice. "Oh God. We're screwed."

"Sit down a minute," Lyn said, quickly moving a pile of dish towels. "Put your head between your knees. You look awful. What's wrong?"

When I told her, she grabbed our jackets and got Sophie and Emily into theirs. "I know exactly what you need," she said. "This is an emergency. You're light-headed from chronic caloric depletion and lack of animal fat in your diet. Give me your car keys."

"Where're we going, Mommy?" Emily asked as Lyn gunned the engine.

"Krispy Kreme."

Half an hour later, I was sitting in a state of satiated, cream-filled serenity.

"I'll probably gain fifty pounds," I said, lazily noting the complete lack of concern in my voice. Deprived for so many weeks, I'd gone a little wild, insisting we try at least one of every single flavor. "Do you think I overdid it?"

"Nah," said Lyn. "You were following the overload theory of weight control, so you should be okay."

"Overload theory?"

"It's like, if you have a package of cookies, you should eat them all in one day and be done with it, because your body can absorb only so many calories at once, and the rest just slide on through. Eat those cookies one day at a time and they'll be part of you forever."

"Makes sense to me."

It didn't, but I didn't much care. The surge of panic I'd felt at Lucie's call was buried beneath a *pousse-café* of custard, jelly, chocolate, and baker's glaze. New York? No problem. We'd handle it. We'd be brilliant.

Because I'd never been on a corporate jet before, I got up at four to fill a carry-on with juice boxes, sliced apples, and little bags of granola. Which my children completely ignored because, although they'd never been on a corporate jet before either, or even on an airplane, they somehow knew there was a galley aft and discovered the chilled orange juice, fresh fruit cups, and basket of muffins before we even taxied for takeoff. They spent the first minutes aloft pretending their oversize leather seats were starship command centers, then settled in with their complimentary packets of activity books, Day-Glo gel pens, and handheld games. When that paled, there were personal DVD players. So *The Color Kittens* book I'd bought for Sophie and the *Kids' New York* I'd packed for Jeff remained in my carry-on with the mushy, rapidly browning apple slices.

"Muffin?" Cindi, our makeup and hair person, rattled the basket at me. "Better eat now. It'll be hectic when we land, and once I get your makeup on, you won't be able to."

In addition to Cindi, we had a wardrobe person named Ralph (pronounced *Rafe*, like the actor) and three food stylists in charge of five cartons of the first bars of Better Than Chocolate, two milk, one bittersweet, and two with crispies. In addition to the bars we'd display, gift bars would be sent, along with a press release, to every newsroom in town. There was also a camera crew, a still photographer, and half a dozen copywriters and account executives who would run focus groups (rating Tom and me, not the candy bar) and measure East Coast responses against simultaneous groups conducted in the West, South, and Midwest. The copywriters and AEs—youngish and clearly overworked—had fastened their seat belts, kicked off their shoes, clamped their mp3 earphones over their heads, and fallen asleep before we reached full altitude.

Lucie, still nervous about how Tom would perform on camera, was sitting with him in the forward part of the plane, trying to tell him that the average television viewer would not follow a lengthy explanation of the mesmerizing dance oligosaccharides did to become Better Than Chocolate.

"But you said you wanted me to talk more," Tom responded in a baffled tone.

"We do, just not about oligosaccharides. Or any other chemicals, for that matter. Remember the message. This isn't fake food. This is *better* than food, Tom. *Better*. Got it?"

"Oh, okay. Let's try again."

It was too painful to watch. I'd done my part to boost Tom's confidence. So far on the making love scorecard, we were four for six in our new house, with special emphasis on me as the slave girl and Tom as the sexy sheik, me as the captive novitiate unable to resist the marauding Viking, me as the uptown girl hitching a ride with the leader of the pack, and, finally, me as the pretty woman to Tom's Richard Gere (a little tame but always Tom's favorite). If this didn't put his ego over the top, nothing would. Least of all Lucie's high-strung inquisition. She was like Torquemada on uppers.

I got up and made my way to the back of the plane. Kate had her shoes off and her feet up, a stack of magazines and newspapers beside her and little red Chinese slippers on her feet. Much more like it.

"I think Tom may push Lucie out the emergency door."

"There's nothing wrong with Lucie a few martinis won't fix."

"I don't think she drinks."

"But I do, and that's where the martinis come in. I always try to get hold of something on the rocks before we take off." Kate folded her *Investor's Business Daily*. "Have a seat. Magazine?"

I glanced at the stack: *Forbes. Wall Street Journal. Business Week.* "What are you doing, getting ready for a corporate takeover?"

"No, just feeding the fantasy that one day I can blow this popsicle stand and live on my investments."

I gave a short, cynical snort. Now that Tom and I could finally contribute to all those jazzy 401ks and Roths and growth funds, now that we should be learning to distinguish between a muni and a T-bill, they were all dropping through the floor. "Who's your broker?"

"Toulouse-Lautrec. Was. Now I am. When I trade my way back to even, I'm throwing a party and not inviting him. Unless of course someone wants to play pin the tail on the donkey."

"Or hangman." We both laughed. I picked up the *WSJ*. Apple Computer reported a decline in Q4 profit, but holiday sales came in above forecast. Was this good or bad? I hadn't the foggiest. "Everyone says Tom and I should start investing, even in this market. Maybe you can give me some pointers."

"Avoid the brokerage house of Mistaken, Misjudged, and Misbegotten, for one." Kate took off her reading glasses and looked at me. "Are you really interested?"

I nodded. I could think of about a million things I still wanted—*needed*—for the house.

"After the market crashed, a bunch of us formed an investing club. We meet at my place about once a month. Toasted cheese, quarterly reports, and gossip. We've had some successes. I'll let you know when the next meeting is."

I spent the rest of the flight wondering what Kate's place was like. Did she own a house? Rent an apartment? I pictured her in an updated version of Katharine Hepburn's apartment in *Desk Set*, with Spencer Tracy popping in for a game of canasta.

I felt the plane begin to drop away beneath me. "There's Manhattan!" I said.

"Long Island, actually. Manhattan's that little blob over there."

Besides never having been on a corporate jet before, I'd also never been to New York, and wondered if I was going to spend the whole weekend wearing a Rube City T-shirt while Tom, the kids, and everyone else cast distressed looks my way. Would I entangle myself in the subway turnstiles? Become convinced I could beat the three-card monte dealer? Burst out singing "New York, New York" in the middle of Times Square?

Well, guilty on the last count. By the time I got back to the kids and told them we were almost in New York, I was thrumming with excitement. The majestic wheel around the Statue of Liberty, our slow pull up the island with its concrete canyons and tallest windows sparkling gold in the morning light—it all *did* make me start singing "New York, New York."

Only to be critiqued by Jeff.

"That's so lame, Mom. It's '*blues*,' not '*shoes*.' Everybody knows that. Melting away! Ha ha!"

Chapter 9

SEX IN THE CITY

According to Lucie, *Click!* was the single most-watched show in the world by women ages eighteen to forty-five. It was the first international talk show, attracting a staggering 1.5 million viewers a day. "New Talk for the New Millennium!" proclaimed the pink, orange, and yellow posters plastered on countless buses and billboards across the country. The show had been so successful in its first six months that it had already been on the cover of *Time* and *Newsweek*. Entertainment writers wrote headlines like "New Girls on the Globe" and "A Fresher, Friskier View" and did in-depth profiles of the three co-hosts—Sally Marshall, the American entrepreneur whose Marshall Plan cosmetics line had just been bought for millions; gorgeous Devi Singh, of Bollywood fame; and Marika Whetu, the Maori jazz-fusion vocalist.

"They're fabulous," Lucie said confidently. "You'll love them. You won't even remember that a million people are watching. So don't be nervous, okay?"

And I wasn't. At least not until that moment on the Triborough Bridge when I looked across the river and saw Manhattan so unarguably *there*. Then I developed a whopping case of nerves that lasted all the way to the studio. The greenroom experience didn't help, either. While *Click!* was beamed around the world in English, most countries ran it with closed-caption-style translations into various native languages. So as we sat, supposedly relaxing, my eyes were riveted to a bank of monitors that spanned one wall of the room. There was Sally in Chinese! Devi on Japan's NHK! Marika translated into what seemed to be Hungarian!

"How many people did you say watch this?" I asked Lucie.

"One and a half million. But that's only live. In a twenty-four-hour cycle, with repeats and tape delays, it's probably double that." Her smile was bright. "Isn't that great? By this time tomorrow, the clamor for BTC will be worldwide!"

I felt my nerves expand into a state of full-blown anxiety. No! I absolutely *had* to calm down. Because if I got stage fright, who'd bail Tom out when he turned to stone in front of the cameras?

Lucie flipped us a thumbs-up and suddenly, in the breathing space of a commercial break, we were standing in the middle of a set that looked like a country kitchen, a three-sided country kitchen lit to the brightness of a solar flare and chilled to just slightly above freezing.

"The way I like it," Sally Marshall said in her broad Texas contralto while someone blotted her forehead. She was majestically tall and had down-to-her-waist hair that gleamed like a well-cared-for Heywood-Wakefield. As she glanced at the display of Better Than Chocolate bars fanned artfully on the butcher-block table, I saw in the slight dilation of her pupils how right the IM packaging team had been. They'd gone the original Hershey's packaging one better, wrapping the bars in gold foil and using bright, glossy red for the paper wrapper. "Better Than Chocolate" was stamped on in flowing, gold script.

"Hi. You're the chocolate people, right?"

"Right," I answered. My throat was so dry the word sounded three syllables too long.

Sally gave my arm a quick squeeze. "Don't be nervous. It's just us."

Right. Just us, and a few million gal pals.

Then they counted us down, we came out of commercial, and Sally asked Tom to explain what synfoods were. I prayed that he wouldn't use the words "artificial," "glycosylated," or "sialic acid" in his answer.

He used them all, and threw in "not necessarily carcinogenic" for good measure. I edged closer, hoping to cut him off.

Sally had the same idea. "Well, I don't know a saccharide from my backside, but—"

"But you *should* know," Tom said. "Saccharides are among the most important macromolecular substances in the universe."

It was as if Tom had committed Lucie's what-not-to-do script to memory and was now perversely following it. This was going all wrong, and if it kept up, we would easily place ahead of the charge of the Light Brigade and the Crusades on the All-Time Disasters list. I searched frantically for Lucie in the shadowy murk beyond the set. Unbelievably, she was nodding contentedly. When I caught her eye a second time, she pointed to the bank of monitors. I looked up. There was Tom. A glowing, eye-pulling, move-over-Harrison-Ford version of Tom. His nose, a little too pointy to start with and crooked ever since he'd broken it in a faculty softball game, looked rugged and interesting, the kind of nose you would trace with a fingertip after making love. The slight crease between his eyes suggested that he was worrying about the world, freeing you from the need to do so. Even the way he dipped his head to keep the bright lights from bouncing off his contacts seemed winning rather than awkward, and when he did look up, the effect was—well, to be honest, *sexy*. And that, believe me, is not a word most wives use to describe their husbands' public demeanor after a dozen years of marriage. No wonder Lucie was smiling. It didn't *matter* what Tom said, only that he looked fantastic.

Sally picked up one of the bars. "It says 'no fat, no calories, no sugar, no carbohydrates.' *This* I've got to try." She ripped open a milk chocolate with crispies, broke off a large piece, and popped it in her mouth. For a minute, I thought she was having a stroke. Then an orgasm. Then she opened her eyes and shouted, "Girls, you want to get over here and get a piece of this." And she reached out and pinched Tom's butt.

That started the stampede, and within two minutes, the set was overflowing. Devi demolished an entire bar with rapid, ladylike nibbles. Marika wanted to know when it would go on sale and if she could take Tom home with her until then. One of the guests, a starlet just coming out of a nasty breakup, said she needed several cases as soon as possible. An investment guru publicizing his book predicted a four-point bounce for IM.

Then a women in the front row shouted for Tom to throw her one of the bars.

"No, throw it to *me*," someone a row behind her yelled.

A large woman in a pastel jogging suit leaped to her feet. "Me! Over here!"

"No, here!"

"Back row! Up here!"

"I'll give you five dollars."

"Ten!"

"I'll give you—"

They were on their feet, their individual voices merging in a tangled roar. "Choc-late! Choc-late!" It was a female rant, a Greek chorus of pent-up desire. The men in the crowd looked terrified as the women spilled into the aisles and surged toward the set, stopped only by security guards.

Suddenly, I saw Tom wince. A lipstick tube bounced off his shoulder and landed on the table. He reached to throw it back but grabbed one of the Better Than Chocolate bars by mistake and lobbed it in an arching curve. It landed in the seventh row and there was a skirmish for possession.

Other items sailed toward us. More lipsticks. A package of wintergreen Life Savers. Earrings. Pens with business cards and phone numbers clipped to them. Several purse-size calorie counters. Dozens of low-fat power bars and rice cakes. Shoes. A cell phone ringing out the *William Tell* Overture. A Three Musketeers bar.

I saw the show's producer signaling that no, we would *not* go to commercial. I saw IM's camera crew swing into action. I saw Lucie pull out three cell phones and, fanning them like a winning poker hand, dial them simultaneously. Later, she told me who she'd called—Page Six, E! TV, and FoxNews on the first round; David Letterman, New York 1, and Liz Smith on the second; Eyewitness News, Newsradio 88, and AP on the third. While she was talking, the first pair of panties sailed toward Tom. Then another and another. Then a garter belt and a Miracle bra. A Japanese grandmother threw her obi. More panties were tossed, lace-trimmed bikinis and modest pastel silks and naughty black thongs. Bloomies and Hanes for Her and Victoria's Secret. A pair of pink cotton briefs that I thought for a dazed second might be Sophie's, until I saw her and Jeff safe on the side-lines between Kate and one of the security guards.

I will always wonder who the Spiderman boxers belonged to.

"Do you know what just happened out there?" Lucie asked when the melee finally died down and we got off the set.

"Not a clue," I said.

"Sex," she said. "And it was *huge*."

There were so many messages waiting for us at the hotel that Kate called a temp agency for help. The sitting room of our suite at the Essex House—the one I'd imagined Tom, Jeff, Sophie, and I launching sightseeing sorties from—was turned into battlefield headquarters, with Kate and Lucie as Eisenhower and Montgomery.

In fact, if Kate had been in charge of reconnoitering D day, things would have gone a lot more smoothly. Not only could she size up exactly what the troops would need, she had a way of getting the supply lines to move. Within an hour, she had us equipped with a six-line phone bank, two printers, a fax, a copier, three more television sets, cable connections, VCRs, and all the blank tapes we needed. Not to mention coffee, sand-wiches, and a fruit basket compliments of the hotel.

Lucie, meanwhile, was doing battle on the phone, her favorite arena. "I don't care if you have to buy them first-class tickets, or charter a plane, for that matter. I'm telling you, we need two dozen cases of Better Than Chocolate bars here by tomorrow afternoon. Right. No, I'll send someone to pick them up. *Letterman*."

Tom, still a bit shell-shocked, was flipping channels. "Annie, look—there we are."

It was hard to see us. After the show, three or four dozen women had waited in front of the studio, refusing to disperse. The minute we opened the door, they'd surged toward us—or, more accurately, toward Tom. Lost in the general swarm, I'd fought to stay near my husband and failed. I couldn't even see myself on the news tape. And all I saw of Tom was a quick ducking motion as he tried to avoid the hands that grabbed for him.

"—and if you weren't watching *Click!* this morning," the announcer was saying, "you can catch the most wanted man in New York tomorrow morning on *Fox & Friends* starting at six eastern."

News to me, but I didn't doubt it. Kate and Lucie had drawn an hour-by-hour schedule on a legal pad. Every time one of them hung up the phone, a new slot was filled in. Instead of taking the kids to see Rockefeller Center and eating dinner at the Hard Rock Café, we were doing an interview for next Sunday's *New York Times Magazine* and stopping by *Live at Five*. Kudlow and Cramer wanted us to discuss the business aspects on CNBC, and *Prime Time Thursday* was already running heady promos—"Tonight, in studio, the couple whose miracle cure for chocoholics sparked a near riot on the streets of New York . . ." And when the American news cycle spun down, there was the BBC, Sky News, and the ABC (not ours, Australia's). We'd be free to do what we wanted about two A.M., which should leave us a good three hours before *Fox & Friends*, Katie and Matt, and Regis and Kelly. Did I mention *Good Day Live?* I think the only talk show we weren't appearing on was *Crossing Over* with Jonathan Edwards. Although that might change if one of us dropped dead before tomorrow.

We were already scheduled to do *Letterman* tomorrow night, and now I watched as the hours in front of it were eaten up. I watched as our trip to the Statue of Liberty gave way to a meeting with a cookbook editor who might want to do a book on cooking with synfoods. I saw our walking tour of Wall Street, Little Italy, and Chinatown replaced by *People* magazine and a taping for *Larry King Weekend*.

Jeff saw the same thing. "Mom?"

I looked helplessly at Lucie and Kate. "What about the kids? We'd planned to—"

Lucie tapped the makeshift schedule with the tip of her pen. "These are the plans now. We're on a roll here, Annie, understand? You can't buy publicity like this, and we've got to make the most of it. I'm pretty sure the hotel has day care or sitter services. If not, we'll find someone."

I'd been avoiding the word "day care" for weeks, the way a dentaphobe with a toothache avoids the word "dentist," but it was taking an increasing amount of energy to preserve the illusion that I could avoid it indefinitely. Now here it was, in the middle of the city I'd always planned on showing, my children myself.

"A *baby*sitter?" Jeff spat out the word. "No way."

Kate saw my distress. "What if I took them tomorrow? Lucie has everything in hand, and we could go to . . ." She glanced at Jeff. "What are you up for? Ellis Island? Chinatown? The Bronx Zoo? IM has a corporate box at Madison Square Garden. Who's in town tomorrow night, the Knicks or the Rangers?"

"Rangers!"

"Well, we can go if you want."

For a woman without children, Kate had a knack. Then Lucie added her own dash of maternal insight.

"We'll get Jeff and Sophie a cell phone, so you can be in touch. It'll be like being there."

It wouldn't, but I didn't say so.

Like most Midwesterners, I never really understood the whole media-feeding-frenzy concept. It isn't something Minnesotans ever did, except for the time Bud Grant came out of retirement to coach the Vikings for a final year. Then two dozen reporters, awaiting his return, staked out the Northwest Airlines terminal.

I think it's a matter of geography. In the Midwest, news spreads out and melts away. But New York is so concentrated, there's no place for the news to go. It bounces around and heats up and expands until, like the Blob, it ensnares everyone within a ten-mile radius, which puts you well into New Jersey.

Lucie understood the media thing, though. Wherever we went, she took just enough BTC bars to spark a frenzy. Our camera crew filmed the outbreaks and sent the tapes off by messenger. The Better Than Chocolate furor became a mini–soap opera, and by the time we got to the Ed Sullivan theater, where Letterman taped, there was a huge crowd waiting for standby tickets.

"This is perfect," Lucie told us, collapsing her headset with one hand and tucking it in her purse. "I just talked to Letterman's crowd-control person. The headline guest is Johnny Depp, so half of the crowd is teenage girls. Plus, we've got five busloads of women from New Jersey. Halvah? Hadassah? Something like that. Tons of women, anyway. So here's the plan. Tom, you hand out the chocolate. We'll drop you off at the end of the line, so work your way forward. Toss out a bar every four or five people and end up in front of the theater doors. And don't worry, you'll be fine. See those two bikers over there? Bodyguards. They've been shadowing us all day. Kate's idea. Brilliant, no? If the crowd goes postal, they'll jump in."

Tom hesitated. "But what about Annie? And you?"

"We'll go in the back and meet you in the greenroom." She looked exasperated. "This isn't about Annie, Tom. It's about you—you and BTC and whatever it is those women are missing in their own lives. So get out there."

The limo slowed to a rolling stop and Lucie practically pushed Tom out, along with two twenty-four-bar packs of BTC. The last thing I saw as we rounded the corner of Broadway and Fifty-third was the two bikers shouldering their way toward my husband as the crowd engulfed him.

Later, after the taping, Lucie denied having anything to do with Jennifer Aniston calling in during the show and asking for an emergency shipment of BTC. Sitting in the back of the limo, Lucie looked completely exhausted.

"I'm canceling dinner."

We were slated for Tavern on the Green, where we would just happen to get the most visible table in the house. For two people about to lose such a table, Tom and I both looked insanely relieved.

"Really?"

"Really. I mean, we've gotten more publicity in the last two days than anyone expected. *Letterman* was brilliant. Did you see those two women slamming each other with handbags? I think there was even some hair pulling. But there's a thin line between in demand and overexposed. You know? Like someone who can't leave a party and suddenly discovers everyone else has gone? So I'm making the call here—mission accomplished. We've got some print interviews in the morning, then that meeting with Kate's book-editor friend, then we can go. We're out of product anyhow. I called Kate while you were finishing *Letterman* and she signed off on it. And—" She fished in her bag. "Damn, which one has the text message? Oh, here. Jeff says the second period just started, the corporate box is awesome, and you should come."

Sophie had fallen asleep on the couch at the back of the box by the time we got there. Jeff looked a little woozy but was clearly not going to miss a minute of life at the top. He had his feet propped on the window ledge, a slice of pizza in one hand and a remote control in the other.

"Look, you can watch the game down there and on TV at the same time. How neat is that?"

"Pretty neat," Tom said, sitting down beside him. "Did you have a good time with Kate?"

"Yeah. We went to the dinosaur museum and to the *Intrepid* and to NBC and saw them rehearsing *Saturday Night Live*. We rode this sort of cable-car thing that goes over a river. You could see into people's apartments. And we had"—he looked questioningly at Kate—"what was the stuff we had for lunch?"

"Kung Pao shrimp."

"Yeah, and Kate taught us how to use chopsticks."

"Mommy, I saw Eloise."

Sophie, flushed from sleep, climbed onto my lap. "Did you, sweetie?"

"The picture in the Plaza," Kate explained.

"And we sent a postcard to Emily and her mommy for taking care of Bonnie and Clyde and Scout. And we went to a big toy store and I got a new Barbie."

I felt a little jealous. "Is there anything you and Kate didn't do?"

"Lots," said Kate. "We didn't make it to the Statue of Liberty or Chinatown or Little Italy or the Empire State Building." She waited until Jeff was distracted by the game and Sophie started nodding back to sleep. "I did change some reservations for you, though. You ended up not getting to spend any time with your kids. We're flying back tomorrow afternoon, but you don't have to. The suite's yours through the weekend; there's a Northwest flight that'll put you in Minneapolis around seven Sunday night, so why not stay over?"

It must have been exhaustion that made my eyes go suddenly teary. I felt irrationally grateful. "Kate, you're a genius."

"Some days. By the way, did you see tomorrow's *New York Post?*"

She tossed the tabloid to me. The cover showed Tom in front of the *Letterman* studio and the two biker bodyguards holding back a tide of women. In three-inch type it said "THE EMPEROR OF CHOCO-LATE." And in smaller print at the bottom, "What this man knows about science, saccharides, and what women want."

I was a little worried that we might be spotted on the streets. But with two kids and dressed as ourselves—without the benefit of special lighting, tinted contact lenses, Cindi's makeup work, or the continual fizz Lucie had kept frothing around us—we went unnoticed. The only person who stopped us during the rest of our time in New York was a hotel security guard who concluded that we were too grubby for the place and asked to see our room card. Of course, we lost the limo too, but that was fine with me. We got on buses and subways and hailed cabs and wheeled through Central Park in a carriage. We stood in line for tickets and bought ridiculous souvenirs, including huge, goofy sunglasses with Empire State buildings jutting up off the frames and green foam Statue of Liberty tiaras. Sophie was disappointed that I clung to her waistband throughout the show at Radio City, thwarting her attempts to join the Rockettes onstage, but other than that, it was nonstop fun. Women weren't mobbing my husband, no one was scheduling twenty interviews a day for us or fussing over how we looked or handing us a cell phone so we could shout a fleeting hello to our children. No one knew or cared who the hell we were and it was perfect.

"It was great to be us again," I told Tom Sunday evening as I fished for my front-door keys. Sophie, sound asleep, was flopped over his shoulder, and Jeff had gone over to Lyn's to pick up Scout and the kittens.

"Aren't we always us?"

"You know what I mean."

"Yeah."

I breathed deeply. Minnesota was in the midst of a rare January thaw and the air smelled moist and almost balmy. If you used your imagination, the promise of spring was there. I felt a little skip of excitement. In a few months, Sadie's loons would be coming back.

I pushed the door open. Oh terrific. "There must be a leak somewhere."

A dark water stain, by-product of the thaw, spread across the entryway ceiling.

"At least it isn't dripping. I'll have to call a roofer tomorrow. And get the painters back."

"I'll call the roofer. And the painters are coming anyway. To do the upstairs hallway."

"Do what to the upstairs hallway?"

"Paint. I told you, remember?" I wasn't sure I had but, even if I hadn't, how could he not have noticed? "It's the wrong color. It's supposed to be kind of a pale saffron. It's a—I don't know, almost a nutmeg."

"But it was just painted."

"The wrong color."

"It looks okay to me. I mean, it isn't hideous."

I took Sophie from him and started unbundling her. "Not hideous. But this is our *house*, Tom, and with just a little extra effort, it'll be perfect. How could you not want that?"

Chapter 10

MY BLUE HEAVEN

I watched as Sophie and Minka, our new au pair, played fox and geese in the backyard. The January thaw had lasted just long enough to slick the surface of the snow, then freeze it to a sugary crust, and, over the last few days, it had acquired a dusting of new powder. Sophie shrieked with excitement as she chased Minka around the pie-shaped wedges they'd outlined.

I turned away from the window and luxuriated, yet again, in the relief of having found someone trustworthy, affordable, and free of both tattoos and a prison record. Through no valorous effort of my own, I admit. But at least it was one item I could cross off my to-do list. Which left only 67 urgents, 98 pressings, 326 importants, and 5,831 must-get-around-tos.

We came back from New York to a barrage of messages from Lucie. No need for me to come in to IM for a while, she said, as they were waiting until the post–Super Bowl focus-group data came in before they decided how to fine-tune the campaign. In the meantime, she'd be e-mailing me a daily task list.

Lucie's memos had file attachments in a format I didn't even recognize. Neither did my computer, because I tried opening them with every program I could think of without success. Instead of confessing my computer illiteracy to the hardwired Lucie, I called Lyn Vickers and asked her what the heck an .mdb extension meant. She hauled Emily over on a sled, took a quick look at the computer, and told me the program I needed was a basic Microsoft feature that had never been installed.

"Disks, please," she said. And before Sophie and Emily even had their Barbies set up, the installation was up and running. She showed me how to open Lucie's file, which I took one look at and promptly managed to lose completely.

"Look," Lyn said tactfully, "I think you'll feel more comfortable if someone comes out and shows you how to use this program." She did a few quick right-click moves as well. I didn't even know you *could* click on the right. "Whoa—have you ever defragged this system? Guess not. Or even done a disk cleanup?"

Windows were snapping open and shut like umbrellas. Then the screen went black and we were in outer space without oxygen. I started to hyperventilate. "Did we lose everything?"

"What? No. *No.* I'm just checking your system. It looks like you've never done any maintenance."

I felt the same way I feel whenever the dentist tells me I'm not flossing enough—guilty, marginal, and possibly diseased. "I, uh, I mean, we just walked into a store and bought the thing one day. I only use it for word processing and some on-line research. I'm not sure I even know how—"

"Well, time to learn." Lyn grabbed a pen and wrote down a name and number: "Janusz Datka." "Janusz," she said, giving it the thrilling, Zsa-Zsa Gabor-like pronunciation, *zha-noosh*, "is the best computer guy I know. Dan and I have used him for years. Have him come and take a look. You should have a firewall, for starters, and your virus definitions are about two years out of date. Do you know that absolutely anyone can sneak into your system when you're on-line? Do you know the risk you're taking?"

Not only was I not flossing, I was apparently practicing unsafe sex as well.

"Janusz is a sweetie. He can teach you how to use Access and anything else you need to know. Call him."

Janusz arrived two days later, by which time more to-do files from Lucie had piled up. I dreaded opening them so much I almost canceled the appointment. Lyn was right, though, Janusz was a sweetie and made Microsoft's Access, with its alien fields and warp-speed scrolling, seem like something I could master. He was also, as far as I could guess, about twenty years old.

"Lyn said you've worked on her computers for years?"

"Right. Nine years."

"But you must have been . . ."

"Fifteen. The Vickers lived across the street from us then, and Dan let me start running the maintenance programs on his computers and doing stuff he didn't have time to do. The Vickers are very cool people. Could I please have a glass of water? And some fruit if you have any?"

Two liters of Deer Park, three pounds of apples, and four toasted-cheese sandwiches later, Janusz had my computer running so smoothly I thought he'd installed new hardware. He'd also convinced me that he could build a better computer for Jeff than the Gateway we'd been think-ing about ordering. He assured me that we'd want to install broadband throughout the house and, like Lyn, exhibited shock and dismay over our fly-by-night ignorance of virus updates, firewalls, cookie crunchers, and regular maintenance. I liked him and signed on. For what seemed like a very modest retainer, I also purchased his 24-7, 365 premium service—access to a special hot line with a guaranteed response time of four hours or less.

"Here," he said, handing me my receipt, along with a laminated card.

58-23-6244449

DATA BY DATKA

JANUSZ DATKA, PRESIDENT AND CEO

"This is the phone number?"

"My cousin Ludwik in Gdansk. He takes the calls and pages me. His English is very good. He'll understand you, no problem."

"*Gdansk?*"

"Don't worry, it's a free call. You won't be charged."

"Your cousin makes a living handling your phone calls?"

"Of course not. He also takes calls for my cousin Adrian in New York, Blue Rain Computer; tell your East Coast friends. Also my uncle Janek, a plastic surgeon in Los Angeles, Uncle Dymitr, an electrician in St. Paul, and his wife, Stella, who is board certified if you need an excellent cosmetologist."

"Anyone else?"

"My fiancée, Minka, who is a nanny and is sadly out of work just now because the family moved to Florida last week."

And that's how I met Minka. At first I'd had misgivings about hiring both Janusz and Minka, especially as Minka would have to stay overnight if Tom and I had to be away. Not long ago, WCCO had run a series chronicling the many sins of the contemporary nanny. Called "While Mom's Away," hidden cameras showed the high-paid help doing everything from whacking toddlers to drinking on the job to having a relatively innocuous but nonetheless creepy romp-and-sniff through both spouses' underwear drawers. Would Janusz and Minka be skinny-dipping while Jeff, unsupervised, turned into the kind of hacker the FBI goes looking for? Would Minka be surfing the Net for wedding gowns while Sophie cracked the code to the poolroom keypad? Would she fail to hear the house-wide, ear-splitting shriek the device made if you failed to punch in a second code within thirty seconds of opening the door? I'd voiced a toned-down version of these fears to Janusz, who'd looked wounded.

"Mrs. Wilkins. I am a professional. Minka also. We would never . . ."

He was too overcome to go on, and I was too in need of an au pair to pass up a promising lead, so I'd called Minka. And was still pinching myself over how well things had worked out. During our initial two-week trial period, I'd watched intently but, I hoped, discreetly. Minka never plopped Sophie in front of the TV set but actually did things with her. She was inventive and patient and had a way of monitoring Jeff's after-school whereabouts that made him feel important rather than tracked down.

There was another big plus Minka had going for her, and that was her ability to drive our new SUV. We'd enrolled Sophie in the same preschool Emily Vickers went to (Lyn said it was the least obnoxious in the area), and after riding shotgun with Minka on several school runs, I concluded that she was a better driver than I was, especially when it came to that Minnesota specialty known as "wintery mix"—the simultaneous explosion of ice, wind, snow, and sleet that always leaves me clinging, white knuckled, to the steering wheel. Minka was unperturbed and had the benefit of younger, faster reflexes. After several school runs, I turned the job over to Minka without qualms. Lyn as well, who paid Minka to ferry Emily to school along with Sophie.

To tell the truth, both Minka and Janusz were more mature than Tom and I had been at their age, and the only disagreement I'd had with Minka to date had been, of all things, over her frugality. I'd come in one day to find Sophie happily smacking down a peanut-butter-and-jelly sandwich for lunch. What happened to the far healthier, protein-loaded sliced turkey breast I'd bought at Byerly's the day before? And the fresh pears? When I hauled the turkey out of the refrigerator, Minka sniffed and pointed to the deli label stuck to the plastic. "Seven dollars and ninety-nine cents a pound," she said, "is not lunch, is Sunday dinner." As for the pears, ignored in their bowl on the counter, they were so expensive she assumed I planned to use them for a centerpiece of some sort.

Other than this tic of personality, Minka fit right in. Jeff and Sophie loved her, and, after the first month, asked that if anything happened to us, could they live with Janusz and Minka instead of Aunt Barb and Uncle Jay? I'd found the perfect nanny. And I hadn't even had to call Cousin Ludwik in Gdansk.

I immediately regretted learning how to open the to-do lists Lucie sent me. Delivered spread-sheet style, various columns denoted the task title, action needed, deadline dates, venues, people and contact numbers, goals, tips for getting the job done, and whatever other thoughts were spiraling through Lucie's head that day. I suspected more than one case of, literally, crossed wires when I read, in Lucie's "Notes & Comments" column, reminders to pick up dry cleaning, return the call of someone named Reba, and remember to last-minute bid on the 1966 Mary Quant gym-slip dress (tags still on!), item 2336144473 on eBay. Tasks were color coded—

magenta for urgent, orange for pressing, lime green for important, and a nice, soothing blue for the must-get-around tos. At the end of the week, I got a combined version of the week's lists, minus whatever tasks I'd managed to complete, with all the urgents ranked at the top and some urgents going to red-alert status as the deadline neared.

One of those red-alert deadlines was blinking on the computer screen behind me now, a Sunday-supplement advertorial, due in days. I was supposed to be writing about the new and exciting age of miracles in which we lived, with special emphasis on the potential of Better Than Chocolate to improve all our lives.

I was having some trouble.

It wasn't that I didn't believe in Tom's idea of using BTC as a "loading ingredient" for doses of vitamins, vaccines, and antibiotics. The technique would revolutionize not only pediatrics but medicine throughout the entire third world. I also looked forward to Better Than Thin, a product that, if talks went well, would be paired with Hastings-Delano Labs' Pamera, making it the most pleasant-tasting weight-loss drug of all time. I hoped they hurried with that one. I'd gained about five pounds in New York and was having a hard time not eating. Despite slaking my sweet tooth on bar after bar of BTC, I was perpetually hungry these days, and a nice thick bar of BTC bittersweet loaded with an appetite suppressant was my idea of heaven.

So what was my problem?

Tom had come home late almost every night this week. Twice there were corporate dinners (Oceanaire, I suspected), and once he'd done local TV. When he got home, I pointed out that he'd missed the Welcome New Parents night at Jeff's new school.

"Come on, Annie, I'm really tired."

"Poor baby."

I'd meant to be sympathetic, but the words came out with a sarcastic edge and we had one of those frosty little moments you have when you're both trying not to fight. Our life of activity! fun! togetherness!—the one that looked so swell on the Super-Bowl remote—was proving a little elusive. But even that wasn't the real reason I was irritated with Tom that night, or why I was having a hard time with the advertorial. The real reason was that, ever since New York, I'd felt a subtle shifting of the landscape. Why hadn't those corporate dinners involved both of us, the Wilkins, that hip young couple? Why hadn't both of us been called on for the *Twin Cities Tonight* TV spot? Why was I sitting here like an ungrateful Boswell?

For the umpteenth time, IM's Cheezaritas screen saver came on, a cascade of rumba-crazed crackers shaking green-olive maracas at me. I pushed the mouse and got my work screen back.

CHOCOLATE THAT'S GOOD FOR THE WORLD

What does the future hold? If you're Mary Poppins, or her twenty-first-century equivalent, chances are you'll no longer need a spoonful of sugar to help the medicine go down . . .

"Mrs. Wilkins?"

Despite my requests to be called Annie, Janusz insisted on a formality he apparently thought befit my age. "Yes?"

"I'm ready to put this computer on the network now. I'll have to shut it down."

"Right now?"

Janusz glanced at his watch. "Well, Jeff will be home from school in an hour for his lesson, so if I don't do it now . . ."

Computer lessons from Janusz were about the tenth thing Jeff had whittled out of us with the rationale, "We never had Christmas. This'll be my Christmas present, okay?" And really, what was the point of giving him a jazzy computer if he didn't know how to use it?

"Why is it again that I want my whole house networked?" I asked Janusz as he set to work.

"It's the world of tomorrow today." He was beaming. "You can access any computer in the house from any other computer. No need to copy files on a disk and take them to the other computer. If Jeff is on-line upstairs, you can flash him instantly, no need to e-mail or message."

"I could also just go upstairs and knock on his door," I pointed out.

Janusz was disappointed by my failure to see the possibilities. "You can all use the Internet at once with just this one cable connection—think how much money you are saving—and you can see what sites your kids are looking at while they're on-line."

Which, I admit, seemed like a pretty darned good idea. "Okay," I said, "go for it."

"And in a few more years, appliances will be wired into the network as well. You'll be able to turn your oven on from up here, or reset the time on your outdoor lights. If you want, I can also connect this network to the one at—what is the name of your company again?"

"IM, but no thanks." The idea of Lucie being able to check my progress, or lack thereof, made me blanch. As did the vision of Sophie e-mailing a big "I love you, Daddy" to everyone at IM, along with pictures of Scout and the cats.

I went downstairs, found today's edition of the *Wall Street Journal*, and settled down to a serious read, notebook in hand. Ever since attending my first meeting of Kate's investment club, I'd been determined to become a "smart investor," a term whose meaning, I guessed, designated someone who made money rather than losing it by the bucketful.

Kate certainly struck me as a smart investor. Her town house on Lake Josephine only seemed modest. When you looked closely, you noticed that the place was loaded with pricey collectibles. Not eBay kitsch, but the kind of antiques only the dogless, catless, childless, and mortgageless among us can indulge in. As well paid as she no doubt was by IM, I doubted her salary had funded the little trinkets stashed and scattered about—the collection of small seventeenth- and eighteenth-century carved crystal and porcelain boxes that nestled in the early American curved glass cabinet, for instance, one shelf above a half dozen very Fabergé-looking enamel cigarette cases and pill boxes. Or the clearly original art on the walls. Or the imported, hand-painted tiles marching with devil-may-care abandon around the kitchen backsplashes.

Kate caught me ogling the goods and seemed to appreciate my notice.

"Yes," she said lightly, "smart investing *does* have its little rewards. And, I find, it's kept me from becoming bitter."

"Bitter?"

"You know, the whole men-make-more, glass-ceiling rage. Buying Pepsi at thirty-five and selling it at fifty takes the sting away. Almost."

It wasn't that I envied Kate. I never truly envied anyone because that would mean wishing away Tom, Jeff, and Sophie. But there was something in her calm and complete self-assurance that I'd certainly like to borrow. I doubted Kate had spent the 1980s in a frantic search for Mr. Right. Looking around her town house, at its forthright and uncompromising Kateness, you got the idea that Mr. Right—*any* Mr. Right—would just never have fit in. He would have been in Kate's way.

At Kate's, I listened as, over a splendid sandwich loaf, a dozen or so women mixed gossip, makeup advice, and hot stock tips. In all of which I was way, way behind. A secretary who introduced herself as Sheila from personnel patiently explained investment basics and gave me a list of suggested reading. A project manager named Suki held forth on why she felt Toll Brothers home builders, in the low teens, would continue to benefit from low interest rates and break thirty by summer. Another woman, from accounts payable, felt GM's pension and benefits obligations would significantly detract from the stock's worth and dividend payouts in the coming years, and urged us to look for selling opportunities for all or part of our holdings.

Unlike other investment clubs I'd read about, which pooled funds and bought stocks, Kate's group was more entrepreneurial. This way, Kate explained, those with less to invest wouldn't feel pressured, and those with more were free to buy a wider variety of stocks and take more speculative positions. The women simply researched companies that held personal appeal or interest for them and swapped information. Apparently, the approach worked. Despite the fact that the major indices (Dow, NASDAQ, and S&P, Sheila explained in a quiet whisper) had been in decline for two years, many of the women had made money by virtue of careful and well-researched stock picking. I went home determined to do a crash course in investing, so next time I'd understand the whirl of terms being tossed around like peanuts.

I scanned the *Journal,* happy to note that I was making progress at decoding the lingo. Like the article titled "Ahead-of-the-Curve Investing: Ten Stocks with Good News in the Pipeline." "Pipeline," I knew, was investor speak for hot products about to debut.

The name Canfield Brands leaped out at me, number two on the list, right behind Nextel's coast-to-coast walkie-talkie. My stomach dropped as I read that, sometime in the fall, Canfield's Au Chocolate would hit the stores, "in direct competition with IM's hugely successful, smartly marketed Better Than Chocolate." Despite making its debut more than half a year after ours, the writer felt Au Chocolate had a shot at stealing a significant portion of IM's business. Unlike Better Than Chocolate, Au Chocolate utilized an aspartic acid-free sweetener, one Canfield had been making for years. Although the sweetener on its own was far less satisfying than the aspartic-acid version, rumor had it that, when blended with the artificial chocolate and fats, a fortuitous chemical reaction took place, producing a creamy, rich-tasting, thoroughly satisfying result. This, the article writer inferred, would appeal to the significant number of consumers who mistrusted aspartic acid.

A chilly little blade of recognition went through me. I remembered Glen Milton's phony—and still unpublished—article for *Nerve & Tissue,* and Nils Holmquist's confidence that such articles were often funded by competitors. Someone who makes a less popular sweetener that isn't based on aspartic acid, Nils had told me that day, or someone who has a product that uses the alternative sweetener.

I called Kate immediately. To my amazement, she was absolutely unruffled.

"Oh, that," she said. "Nothing for us to worry about. Canfield would love to knock off BTC, of course, but I don't think it will happen."

"Why not?"

"They're not going on the market for another nine months, for one thing."

"How do you know that?"

Her voice dropped almost imperceptibly. "I have my sources, Annie."

Kate had *sources?* I felt unnerved. "At Canfield?"

"It wouldn't do much good to have them at IBM, would it?"

She seemed amused by my naiveté. I took a deep breath. "Do you think Canfield has their sources with *us?* I mean, that whole business with *Nerve & Tissue*—it would have been an awfully fortuitous time to get the aspartic-acid ball rolling again. We would have been tied up in that for months, enough time for Canfield to beat us to the market with Au Chocolate."

There was a moment of silence. Then Kate said, "I've considered that, Annie. And I tend to agree. I've got some ideas and some leads I'm checking out." She paused again, as if crafting her next sentence. She'd begun picking her words carefully, I noticed. God, our phones were probably bugged. "I think the best way to handle this for now, Annie, is not to appear overly concerned about Canfield. If we make our suspicions known . . ."

We could end up on meat hooks, I thought. Giving our print-ad tag line, "chocolate to die for," a whole new meaning.

"Right," I said. "I never saw today's *WSJ*."

"You know, Annie, it probably *is* all just a coincidence. Ideas in the air and all that. You'd be surprised by how often nearly identical products debut within months of each other, just because everyone has access to the same raw materials, the same research, the same list of consumer demands. But I'll stay on top of the situation anyway. Nothing for you to worry about."

I was more than happy to forget the whole thing and went back upstairs to check on Janusz's progress with my computer. As I climbed the stairs, I rejoiced in the way the winter sunlight fell over the newly repainted hallway, turning the saffron to a deep, mellow, and, to be honest, breathtaking shade that I had no words for. But the molding and trim, my God, how could I not have noticed it before? It had looked fine with the muddy nutmeg of yore but now—well, it was an affront to my gorgeous saffron. It was too stark and much too cold. White. *White?* What on earth had I been thinking? Baker's Square served a pumpkin-chiffon pie that came with whipped cream shaded with the lightest dash of amaretto. That's what was needed here.

The bench under the hallway window, the one IM's decorator had talked me into, that would have to go too. It looked so . . . so *earthbound*. I wanted this hallway to float. Hadn't I seen just the right thing in that decorator's showroom downtown? Or maybe we should replace the bench with a window seat. Thank goodness I'd saved all the decorator's slips and numbers.

"I'm finished, Mrs. Wilkins," Janusz called. "You're completely networked, so have fun. Flash-message everybody in the house. Listen to Radio Japan at cable-modem speed. Go nuts!"

"Thanks, Janusz."

I checked my e-mail—nothing from Lucie, thank God—and surfed to finepaints.com, a site that specialized in custom-color wall finishes. I flipped on HGTV as well. Maybe I'd see a bench I liked while I was straightening out the paint situation. Instead, I saw a living-room couch that took me in a whole new direction.

Chapter 11

HOUSE THEORY

On Valentine's Day morning, Lucie phoned at four-thirty A.M.

"Look out the window. Thirteen states. I'm on top of it. Tell Tom," she said and hung up. I had to replay the call in my head to even figure out who it was.

"Wrong number," I murmured, and waited until Tom went back to sleep to tiptoe to the window and press my face against the glass. White flakes were whirling through the dark, as they did three out of five mornings in Minnesota in February. *Thirteen states?*

I went back to bed and contemplated the possibilities of a blizzard. Last night at midnight, Tom and I had stood in front of a giant, heart-shaped clock at the Mall of America and counted down the seconds to February 14. Surrounded by cameras, TV news, and at least one reporter I recognized from *USA Today*, we distributed samples of Better Than Chocolate from heart-shaped boxes.

It was a marketing coup of unprecedented proportions. Kate had negotiated a series of twenty-four-hour leases to sell boxes of BTC from Valentine-bedecked kiosks in malls across America. IM proclaimed February 14 BTC day. *Ad Age* was planning a front-page story, and Lucie had gotten video clips to *Fox & Friends*, *Good Morning America*, and *The Early Show*. By the end of the day, millions of husbands and boyfriends were supposed to be buying last-minute boxes for the women in their lives. Calorie free, fat free, and popularly priced to fall neatly between the price points of Russell Stover and Godiva. (That was Kate's idea. The Russell Stover crowd would move up a notch, the Godivas would trade down to get the fat-free benefit. The woman was a genius. Why she wasn't running the place I'll never know.)

Thirteen states. A blizzard through the candy-eating heart of the country would cost us millions. Malls might even close early. And we'd lose the publicity advantage. Footage of crowded kiosks and people walking away with red-ribboned boxes would get picked up as a kicker for local news shows everywhere, but in a blizzard, there'd be wall-to-wall footage of people sleeping in airports, truckers holed up in diners, and cars skidding across interstates, not a BTC box in sight. I actually felt a pang of sympathy for Lucie. She'd worked so hard on this she'd been too stressed to even bother color-coding my e-mails.

But lying drowsily on my side in our warm bed, staring at the floor-to-ceiling windows that framed our curve of lake, I wasn't in complete despair. Part of me was thinking, *Snow day!* I imagined listening to the radio as the WCCO announcer got to the *M*s and informed us that Minnetonka District 276 was closed for the day, along with the Curious Minds Preschool. I saw myself calling Minka and telling her to stay home. It would be Tom and me and the kids, just the four of us, building a snowman and eating tomato soup and grilled-cheese sandwiches for lunch. Our first play day in our new house. I drifted back to sleep inhaling the imagined scent of wind-freshened children and melting snow.

Then the alarm was going off and Tom was getting up.

"But the snow—it's going to blizzard. That was Lucie on the phone before."

"What did she say?"

"That she was on top of it, whatever that means." He glanced at the phone and saw that I'd left it off the hook. "Oops." The minute I put it back in the cradle, it started to ring.

Thank goodness it was Kate.

"I hear Lucie's been faxing up a storm to you." I mouthed the word "fax" to Tom and he disappeared down the hall to my office. "Don't worry, I've calmed her down. And don't worry about the snow, either. The forecasters went overboard—*quelle surprise*—and it turns out there's going to be just enough slush on the ground to keep people from going out to dinner or the movies or wherever they were going to go. So I think it will actually boost our kiosk sales. They'll do a quick swing by the mall instead of dinner at Le Crepe and rent some chick flick—most husbands will jump for joy."

Kate's voice was pure lanolin. We were going to sell thousands of boxes of BTC today after all. A snow day—what on earth had I been thinking? I thanked her and got off the phone just as Tom dropped a sheaf of papers in my lap.

2/14/02: 4:40 A.M. *Your phone is off the hook.*

2/14/02: 4:50 A.M. *Your phone is off the hook!! Need to speak to you!!*

2/14/02: 5:05 A.M. *YOUR PHONE IS OFF THE HOOK!! SEE MAPS (NEXT PAGES). CALL ME!!! (Lucie)*

This was followed by several radar maps and more pages informing us that our phone was off the hook and finally:

2/14/02: 6:30 A.M. *KATE HERE NOW. SAYS ROADS NOT BAD.*

2/14/02: 7:15 A.M. *STAND DOWN. NATIONAL WEATHER SERVICE DOWNSIZING PREDICTED SNOWFALL. TURN ON WEATHER CHANNEL, AND TELL TOM OUR 9:30 MEETING IS STILL ON.*

I got out of bed and, thanks to the foresight of Janusz, pressed a button on my laptop that caused a wake-up song to start playing on the computer in Jeff's room. It was nicer and more effective than poking my head into his room at two-minute intervals and heckling him out of bed. Of course, some fine-tuning had been involved. My first pick, "Start Me Up," had just left him grooving in bed, although he did admit that the choice proved I was cool. "Wake Up, Little Susie" introduced him to the world of golden oldies or, as I heard him describe it to one of his new friends, "Music for really, *really* old people." My third pick—Debbie Reynolds, Donald O'Connor, and Gene Kelly braying "Good Morning"—did the trick. To Jeff, it was so cataclysmically uncool he leaped out of bed to shut it down.

If he went back to bed, the program reopened and played every five min-utes until, satisfied that my son was up, I sent a secret shut-down command racing through the network. Janusz had thought of everything.

The home phone rang—yes, we also had our own in-house phone net-work—and I picked it up.

"Are you up?" I asked Jeff, on the other end of the line.

"Mom, it's Valentine's Day. There's no school, remember?"

I did now. But who could blame me for forgetting? When I was Jeff's age, February 14 meant decorated shoe boxes, chalky-tasting hearts, and a party with chocolate milk and sugar cookies. Now the holiday had become a touchy, free-fire zone. What if somebody got better Valentines than somebody else? What if parents on the food committee failed to heed the warning about pork and peanut products? What about lactose-intolerant children who would be left out of the chocolate-milk orgy? And children whose Ritalin dosages would conflict with the sugar cookies? Not to men-tion (as a recently filed lawsuit asserted) the fact that Valentine's Day was about *Saint* Valentine and, therefore, a thinly disguised attempt to establish state-sponsored religion. Faced with this minefield, Minnesota had called it quits and replaced February 14 with something called a Home-learning Day. It joined several other Home-learning Days, ones that had replaced Halloween (blatantly pagan), Election Day (blatantly patriotic), and Pres-ident's Day (blatantly white, blatantly male).

"Sorry, Jeff." I groped on the bedside terminal for the little button that would stop Debbie, Donald, and Gene.

"And, Mom, we're having hockey practice on the lake today, right?" My son had the exasperated tone of a well-organized executive saddled with a none-too-bright assistant. "You said we could have lunch here."

"Oh, um, sure." *Had* he mentioned it? Oh, now I remembered. I'd been looking at fabric samples for the new love seat and he'd said some-thing about hockey and a lake. How was I to know he meant *our* lake? Really, I had to get back on top of this mother thing. "What would you like? Anything special?" Please say Pizza Hut. *Please.*

"Pizza?"

Bingo. "Just tell Minka to order whatever you guys want."

"*You* have to order, Mom. Remember what happened last time?"

Oh, yes. A week ago I'd told Minka the kids could have pizza, but before placing the order she'd calculated the cost of a large sausage, mushroom, and sun-dried-tomato pie and rebeled. "Eighteen ninety-five," she told me later with a piercing glance. "In Poland, half a month's rent."

So began my day. Another day in paradise. I'm not being facetious. In spite of everything, it *was* paradise. Once I dispensed with Lucie's color-coded task list, a skill I was becoming remarkably adept at, I could indulge in the fantasy that I was a stay-at-home mom sans career, something I'd never been before. Now I saw what all the fuss was about. As lifestyles go, it was great. I could watch endless hours of Lynette Jennings and HGTV. I could learn to *Quilt in a Day* and create *Curb Appeal*. I could see how our abode stacked up against *Spectacular Homes* and stop by *Caprial's Café*. How had we ever lived without DIRECTTV? It was like living without electricity. While I'd been wasting my time writing about artisanal breweries of the greater metro region and cheese-curd festivals, a whole new world had sprouted on the screen. All over America, women in the know had gotten a jump on me. Now I was playing catch-up. Just yesterday I'd learned how to make herbed custard and raspberry mascarpone kisses. I hadn't, of course, actually *made* them, but I'd downloaded the recipes. In fact, the fastest-growing part of my computer was a cluster of new folders labeled "Recipes," "House Ideas," and "Shopping." The wonderful thing about all this was that it felt *productive*. After downloading fifty recipes and ordering all-new silicon bakeware from kitchenetc.com, I felt I'd actually worked. And really, in a way, hadn't I? At some point, wouldn't I have to bake BTC chocolate-chocolate-chip muffins? Or show some curious interviewer the piece of porch furniture I was planning to distress with an interesting crackle glaze?

"I really see what you like about staying home," I told my friend Lyn later that day. "I envy you. Pizza?"

I'd had to give our credit card number in advance to assure the local Pizza Hut that the order for eight large pies wasn't a prank. When Minka had seen the bill, she'd snorted something in Polish and rolled her eyes, but had nevertheless pitched in with the hockey team, Sophie, and Emily to eat

her share. Janusz would be proud. He was delighted that Minka was working for us because it gave her exposure to, as he put it, the "full capitalist
experience."

Lyn pushed the cardboard box away from her. "I can't. Still trying to
lose that baby weight."

"Oh, go ahead. You look great," I said. "Healthy." I wanted another
slice but didn't want to eat alone.

"Thanks, but—" She hesitated. My head snapped up. Were we getting
to that sharing-secrets stage of our friendship? I felt a tingle of pleasure.

"But?"

She furrowed her brow and smoothed back her white-blond hair,
which she'd recently had styled to turn up slightly at the tips. She looked
like a worried Dutch girl. Katrina Van Tassel on the horns of a dilemma.
Then her brow smoothed and her face lit up with soft happiness.

"Dan and I want to have another baby. So whatever weight I don't lose
now, I never will."

"Oh." What was that pain jabbing at me? And the sudden prickle
behind my eyes? Did *I* want another baby?

"Are you all right, Annie?"

"Pepper," I said, and gave a little cough. "I got a hot pepper, sorry.
That's wonderful, Lyn. When are you going to start trying?"

"We're trying now."

"Well, you *need* the pizza, then. Isn't there something about dieting
being a deterrent to pregnancy? Isn't there a critical mass of calories
you're supposed to eat or something?"

She reached for another slice, but I no longer wanted any. I was left
with the sensation you get when you see your reflection in a store window
with your hair blown out of place and your jacket rucked up, someone you
hadn't expected at all and were surprised to realize was you. I'd just discovered, a little to my surprise, that I actually did want another baby. A lot
more than I'd thought.

It wasn't as if Tom and I had never discussed it. We had, half joking,
half serious. One more for the road. One more, so Sophie would have
someone to boss around. One more because Jeff was the best big brother

in the world. One more to keep those tax credits rolling. One more because we *wanted* one. But all that was before chocolate, and now we hadn't talked about it for months.

Why had I wanted a baby so fiercely for that moment in my kitchen? I wondered. For the right reasons or the wrong ones? Did it play into my new stay-at-home-mom fantasy? Or was it because I could see Jeff and Sophie slipping away from me? Since we'd moved, Jeff had acquired a whole new circle of friends. For the first time in his life, he was popular. One of the crowd. He'd even, somehow, managed to befriend Bengt Mackenzie without making a pariah of himself. But with his newly acquired cool, a little of his sweetness had slipped away. Which, I reminded myself, it was bound to do anyway. In another year, he'd be a teenager. And Sophie. Every Tuesday and Thursday, after French for Fours class, she came home babbling like a Parisian. The other day, she'd asked me how much an apartment in the *huitième arrondissement* would cost, and if I could start holding back some of her allowance so she could get one. Apparently, that was where *petite* Marie-Laure, the heroine in their videos, lived.

"An apartment? Don't you want to buy a house?" I asked. Naively.

Sophie wrinkled her nose. "Houses are in *banlieues,* Mommy. I want to live *à la cité.*"

I felt like a Tolstoy peasant listening to Natasha Rostov chattering away in *le français*. Soon—the handwriting was clearly on the wall—both my children would be looking on Tom and me as the uncoolest couple since Dwight and Mamie Eisenhower. Jeff used to gaze at me as if I held the keys to the universe, just because I could make cereal out of hot water and some Cream of Rice. The only member of the family who looked at me that way now was Scout when, armed with nothing more than a simple can opener, I produced food from a metal cylinder. Was this all because I needed someone to idolize me again, as only a baby can? The prospect was so pathetic I decided to think about it later. And, in the meantime, to make the most of life with Jeff and Sophie before they *both* moved to the *huitième arrondissement*.

The day Kate called to tell me the sales figures were in, I was browsing through the "Curious Minds Spring Forward!" catalog from Sophie's preschool, trying not to be distracted by the *Martha By Mail* glossy that had arrived with it. Curious Minds urged parents to "Hurry! Guide your child in making his/her course selections by March 6 to ensure enrollment in our most popular offerings! We don't want your Little One to miss out on the Learning Experience he/she wants most!" One of which was a workshop called How Many Trees? How Many Bees?: What You Can Do to Save the World, which didn't sound like our Sophs at all.

Much more up her alley was The Curious Minds' Players Presents, a six-week course in which Minnetonka's littlest thespians would cast, rehearse, and stage a complete one-act play, to be presented "at a sumptuous dinner-theater evening in the East Playroom. Mommies, daddies, friends, and other members of the Curious Minds family are invited to attend. Tickets will be sold at a nominal fee to cover food costs and to acquaint budding performers with rudimentary concepts of sales and marketing. Please specify meal preference of kosher, vegan, or lo-salt/lo-cholesterol." I wondered what the tots would be staging. *The Death of Bessie Smith?* Some cutting-edge gem by David Mamet? A scaled-down version of *Long Day's Journey into Night?* Should Tom and I go kosher for the night? Or vegan?

"So the sales figures are promising," Kate was saying, "but we need to do some fine-tuning for phase two. Tom's clear on Friday. Is that good for you?"

I was about to say Monday would be better because on Friday, *Passport to Design* was featuring homeowners who, after a pledge-drive marathon viewing of *I, Claudius,* wanted to create a Roman bath off their master suite. Fortunately, I got a grip and told her Friday afternoon would be fine. I did call Lyn, though, to ask her to bid in two eBay auctions for me. I'd recently decided to redo my office in an ironic retro theme, and there were two absolutely primo pieces of bark cloth I wanted to have made into slipcovers for the chairs.

When I walked into the conference room on Friday morning, the first thing I saw was a magnum (or was it a jeroboam?) champagne bottle molded in chocolate sitting in the middle of the table. The cork was off and it was spouting miniature truffles wrapped in gold foil.

"It's from Jacques Torres," Kate explained. "He made it out of the BTC we sent him. And he definitely wants you to do his show."

"Are you kidding? Really? That's fantastic!" I sounded like a culinary groupie, completely undone by the prospect of having my chocolate hand-melted by the cutest chef in the four-star firmament. Fortunately, Kate and I were the first to arrive, so no one else heard me gushing. "Well, I mean, I don't watch much television, but I hear his show is very popular."

Food Network, Wednesday afternoons at three, as well as various PBS stations. I was a walking almanac of daytime television.

Kate grinned. "Yep, he's a hunk, isn't he? I've already volunteered to make the trip with you. Absolutely worth the flight time. Oh—remember those red slippers you liked? The ones I had on the flight to New York? I ordered a pair for you. They should be in your mail any day now."

The red silk slippers! I felt a surge of childish glee. "Can I pay you for them?"

Kate shook her head. "Courtesy of IM. We're about to put you and Tom to work, big time. Here." She tossed me one of the gold-leaf truffles and motioned to a chair. "Sit down. Fortify yourself."

I sat down but waved the chocolate away. I'd been eating BTC for almost five months now, and I was getting jaded. And oddly enough, in spite of the meal-replacing quantities I was consuming, I hadn't lost any weight because of it. Was it my imagination, or did I actually feel hungrier after polishing off a bar or two? My imagination, surely. How could it possibly affect my appetite? There was nothing in it, after all.

"The reports are good, then?"

Kate tapped her Mont Blanc against her legal pad. "Essentially good, yes."

I was still puzzling over the "essentially" when Lucie whirled into the room.

"Annie!" She gave me a quick head-to-toe appraisal. "Why don't we get together next week? We can do an afternoon at my gym. They have killer spin classes. You'll love it!"

How was it that Lucie's legs seemed to have actually lengthened in the two weeks since Valentine's Day? Or was it her *couture du jour* of demure gray skirt, sheer white stockings, and navy V-necked pullover with white cuffs and collar peeking primly forth? She looked like an exceptionally coltish Catholic schoolgirl. A look, I well knew, that was sure to ring my husband's bells. Lolita in the front row, in danger of failing a class, was one of his favorite fantasies. Sometimes we bartered over my grades, and what I could do to improve them. Suddenly I wondered if Lucie *knew* about Tom's Lolita daydream. How? Was something going on here?

"Hey, Annie." And there he was, squeezing my elbow as he sat down beside me—*not* beside Lucie—and everything was all right. What was wrong with me? I was turning into one of those paranoid, housebound women who drive their husbands batty with accusations. I was out of the loop, and it showed. Instead of the energetic, flab-blasting swim I'd envisioned for myself each morning, I settled into a lounge chair with a stack of magazines—*Home, Creative Home,* and *Metropolitan Home*—leafed through them for an hour or so, took a quick paddle across the pool, and made it back to the kitchen in time to eat lunch while watching Christopher Lowell create a romantic canopy bed from PVC piping and some inexpensive gauze.

"So," I said brightly, "how are we doing?" Tom had told me he thought our numbers were good, so I felt confident.

"It was a terrific launch," Lucie said, "and we got some amazing focus-group data. Not quite what we expected, but that's what focus groups are all about, right?" She thumped thick, spiral-bound books onto the table. Tabbed and color coded. I hefted mine and turned to the happy blue section marked "Sales."

"Wowie zowie."

Lucie had charted BTC's performance against some of IM's most successful rollouts—Nipper Chips, Spuds a-Go-Go, Flustered Custard, and several other items, all of which resided on pantry shelves across an estimated 35.7 percent of America. We were well in the hunt, placing below only Pizza Poppins, a recent craze, and the astronomically successful watershed product of the century, Whip 'n Stir, America's first premium-quality instant mashed potatoes, introduced in 1948 and the product that had catapulted IM from a regional company to an international behemoth.

"The chart you're looking at is unit sales," Lucie explained. "Of course, the revenue is lower due to the lower per-unit price and narrow profit margins." Lucie flipped the page and directed my gaze toward the "Profits in Millions" chart, which didn't look nearly as impressive.

"Oh."

"But we're very pleased," Kate interjected. "Better Than Chocolate launched well and is essentially on track." There was that "essentially" again. "We feel there's ample opportunity for growth."

"For BTC to become truly successful," Lucie said, "we need to double our unit sales."

Double? "Couldn't we just raise the price?"

Kate frowned. "Not before we've established ourselves firmly in the customer's mind."

Tom looked as bewildered as I was feeling. "But didn't we just do that? New York? The Mall of America? Wasn't that getting established?"

Lucie looked at Tom and gave a gentle shake of her ringlets. "The first year of any product is a winning-over period. It's like building a TV audience. There's premiere-week hype, and if you're lucky, you get a lot of exposure. But to keep viewers coming back, and to add more viewers, you need a sustained assault."

"What Lucie's saying is that our sales numbers are impressive, but our profit margins aren't yet self-sustaining."

Did I actually say "*oof*" as I leaned back in my chair? I don't think so, but I certainly felt it. I don't know if Tom grasped the full meaning of what Kate was saying, but I did. Unless we could become a "self-sustaining" moneymaker for IM, BTC, despite its initial splash, would fizzle.

Kate gave a slight smile. "Due to the capricious nature of synthetic oligosaccharides, BTC has turned out to cost more to produce than we projected. There are two ways to address that. Increase unit sales, allowing our production lines to run at full capacity, or raise prices. We can't raise prices until we've become indispensable to our customers, and that will take a good nine months."

"Like being pregnant!"

Tom shot me a startled look, and I'm sure I looked startled in return. I had no idea why I'd said it, either.

"But I thought you said the news was good."

"It is!" Lucie cried. "Because right here, in the focus-group feedback, we have the information we need. A road map for dramatically increasing unit sales."

"Not quite what we expected," Kate said, and we all turned to the marigold-colored pages in the section marked "Consumer Response."

With a jolt, I saw that there were a lot of women out there who didn't like me. They thought I should "stay home," "spend time with my children," and "get a hairstyle with more height." In evaluations of Tom and me as a couple, I was perceived as a tagalong. Stay-at-home moms and single women over forty were palpably angry in their perception that I was "pretending I was a writer." A woman named Flo in Butte, Montana, wrote,

> It seems to me she is trying to build a career on her husband's success. She is like Hillary Clinton. Has she ever written anything? (The chocolate woman, not Hillary.) I never heard of her before, so why would I want to read an article by her?

Flo, like most of the other women in her focus group, thought Tom was dreamy, "like Harrison Ford when he played the cop in *Witness*. A little nerdy, but someone you'd fall in love with."

"They hate me."

The tip of Kate's Mont Blanc tapped down the lines. "*Some* of the response has been disappointing, yes, but look down here. Your Q rating on the Northeast corridor is excellent. They could identify you after just one media exposure, and wanted to see *more* of you. With self-motivating omni-competent career women, college women, and repeat-cycle dieters, your Q is actually *higher* than Tom's. They saw you as"—Kate glanced down at the report—"a successful wife and mother who is just coming into her own."

I wasn't sure what it meant, but I felt complimented. In fact, the only negative comment on the Northeast-corridor page was from someone named Stephen in Short Hills, New Jersey, who felt, rather strongly, that I needed to pluck my eyebrows thinner in order to "open up" my face. On the "Personal Information" section of the questionnaire, Stephen had bypassed M and F to mark "Other" in the gender column.

"There were surprises about Tom too," Lucie said, looking up with a twinkling smile. At *my* husband. "After our experience in New York, we expected him to score well with women. But look at this. Men west of the Rockies love him too. I mean, who knew? We may have something the world has never seen before. A man who can get men to eat—or at least buy—chocolate."

"We think it's the high-tech aspect," Kate said. "Most men feel chocolate is women's food. In their minds, it falls into that dubious category with sushi, crepes, rice pilaf, and shrimp toast. But Tom's broken through."

I studied the comments:

A scientific approach to food—about time.

Wouldn't mind eating this.

Now my lard-ass wife will have to stop making excuses.

Lovely.

"Obviously, we needed to do some fine-tuning." Lucie flipped to the lavender-hued section. "We needed to find a way to take advantage of your individual viabilities with very different consumer segments. To capitalize on popularity without incurring unintended negative blowback. *Quite* a challenge. But we did it. We found a way. Ingenious, really." She held her breath for the briefest second, just long enough to give us a mental drumroll. "We're splitting you up."

Tom's head shot up. "What?"

"I know this isn't exactly what we planned," Kate said soothingly. "But Lucie's right. We had quite a challenge on our hands. In some markets, your appearance as a couple was actually detrimental. Women related more strongly to Tom when Annie wasn't present."

"The house theory."

I looked at Lucie. "What?"

"House theory. You know, like in decorating magazines? They photograph all those dream houses without people in them, so readers can imagine that the house is theirs. If you show the rooms with their owners, readers don't relate. In fact, they find fault with the room and pick apart the decorating."

"Amazing."

Lucie shrugged. "A simple defense mechanism, actually. No one wants to envy someone else, so they see the room as unenviable."

As an inveterate reader of those magazines, I realized she was right. I had yet to see a person in any of those pictures. "So you're saying Tom is the house? And I'm the owner no one wants to see?"

"Exactly. Which is why we've got to separate you."

Tom looked worried. "You don't mean you want us to *legally* separate, do you? Because there are some things we just won't do, Lucie."

Surely there wasn't anything in our contract about divorcing in the best interests of the product, was there?

"Oh, Tom." Lucie's laugh was a little too silvery, and for a fleeting second, she gazed at my husband a little too fondly. "Of *course* we don't want you and Annie to break up. Not in reality. But for now, we feel the best way to make this work is to showcase you separately. If you just go to page eighty-eight, you'll see your schedules."

And there they were. Tom was headed west, for Jay Leno and the Calgary Stampede and a BTC weekend on a riverboat. I was doing a *Parade* magazine spread and a series of mall and women's business-association appearances that Lucie's notes described as "a cutting-edge blend of cooking demos and motivational speaking."

I looked at the schedule dates. "But this is unbelievable. Tom and I— we're almost never home at the same time."

"Isn't it perfect?" Lucie said brightly. "We've scheduled it so one of you will always be home with your kids."

Well, yes, there was that. "But—" I looked helplessly at Tom.

"It's not that bad, Annie," he said. "Look, there are some weekends we'll both be home. The week after Easter. Labor Day."

Lucie cleared her throat. "Yes, well, of course, these schedules are always subject to change. If we get a hot opportunity, naturally we'll pounce."

"Good. Maybe something will come up in time and I can cancel that damned gourmet night."

"What gourmet night?" Lucie asked. I explained how we'd been roped into Estelle Mackenzie's circle of gourmands, and how this morning I'd received an e-mail reminding me that, as we'd taken the Esterlys' place, our turn as hosts came up in March.

"Estelle Mackenzie of Mackenzie Clinics?" Lucie asked.

"You know her?"

"No, but . . ." Lucie's voice trailed off, to be replaced by the disturbing clicking sound of the gears in her brain whirring.

"What?"

She made rapid notes and punched something into her Palm Pilot. "It could be . . . never mind for now, I need to think about something."

I went back to studying the schedule. Next to July it said, "Summer event for Camera 10 Media? July 4?" "What's this? Who's Camera 10 Media?"

"A production company. They do a lot of lifestyle TV stuff—*Sixty-second Remodeling, Midlife Makeovers*. Have you ever seen *Guess What's in It?*, where they send people around the world to eat the local cuisine then try to describe what it is?"

I had, but wouldn't admit it. My favorite had been the Manhattanites who'd enthused over a Hawaiian dish they described as "authentic pan-Asian stir-fry with a nod to Italy evident in the morsels of crisped pancetta." They'd eaten Rice-a-Roni stir-fried with Spam, and threatened to sue for public humiliation until the producers offered to send them on an all-you-can-eat truffle hunt.

"We want them to shoot Annie entertaining, using BTC in various dishes. We need enough good footage to get one of the lifestyle syndicators, like HGTV or the Food Network, to commit to a pilot. Which will hopefully begin a series. Then, with the series as a platform and Annie's writing credentials, we could shop around a BTC cookbook. Establishing BTC as an everyday cooking and baking ingredient is vital to increasing unit sales. Conservatively, a series would boost sales by fifteen to twenty percent." Lucie stopped pyramiding and tapped her teeth with the tip of her pen. "We need an event to build around for the shoot, and I'd thought maybe a Fourth of July picnic would work. But tell me more about this gourmet night thing. I've got some other early July leads to work anyway, and it's still all very fluid. *Very* fluid."

So, very fluidly, I told her about the Minnetonka gourmet group. I wanted to warn her about Estelle's addiction to Blackberrying, but I was sure she'd see this as a positive thing.

"That's fabulous," she said. "It'll be a perfect backdrop. Much better than a picnic. I'll need to book Camera 10 right away. And get on those other July leads. And get someone to start on chair and table rentals."

"Really? There are only about a dozen of us, and our dining room is more than big enough to—"

Lucie swatted my words away and chuckled at my utter lack of imagination. "That's *so* five minutes ago, Annie. If IM's going to get behind this, we're going to make it really big."

Like IM's Apple Fluff Puffs and the thighs of all who ate them.

"But—"

"Don't worry, Annie." She flashed me a serene, even queenlike smile. "It's all out of your hands now."

Obviously. I went back to scanning the color-coded schedule. "Thanksgiving Day: Tom, Macy's Parade, NY. Annie, Mummer's, Philadelphia." Now hold on a minute. Thanksgiving was my favorite holiday, the kind of holiday I suspected Christmas had been meant to be before it was commandeered by Isotoners and the Chia Pet company. "We're not going to be together on Thanksgiving?" I heard tears in my voice, even if no one else did.

"That's still fluid too," Lucie said. "We're trying to lock you both in to different events. Great camera op, with the TV coverage and food focus that day. Of course, if we can't find events for both of you, IM will be happy to pick up the tab so you can be together, wherever it turns out to be."

I stood up and looked at Tom. "I need to talk to you," I said.

"Actually," Lucie said, consulting her watch, "you can't. Tom and I have to be somewhere, and we're already running late."

"But—"

"Sorry. We really have to go or we'll be late."

Ten minutes later, I was in Kate's office. Which, like Kate, had the uncanny ability to soothe. At least the ice from the mini refrigerator and the three fingers of Chivas poured over it did.

"Not Thanksgiving," I said firmly. "Any other day, just not Thanksgiving. I want one perfect holiday with my family. In my home. Alone."

"Done," Kate said. "You've got it."

"I can tell Lucie that? Really?"

"*I'll* tell Lucie. Don't worry about it."

For a moment, the cloud lifted, then settled again. "I don't suppose there's anything you can do about the rest? About Tom and me on separate schedules?"

Kate looked sympathetic. "I know it's hard, Annie. But, really, Lucie's right. Splitting you up is the shortest, surest way to build our customer base."

"But I'll never see my husband."

"Of course you will."

I riffled through the lavender pages. "You know what Lucie's like. This is just the beginning." She'd already told me that expanded, updated files were sitting in my e-mail. I could just imagine.

"Leave Lucie to me. If she goes over the edge, I'll reign her in."

"Promise?"

"Absolutely. You can take it to the bank." Kate leaned back and smiled. "On the subject of banks, did you buy any of that Exxon?"

I nodded and swirled my ice cubes. The week after Valentine's Day, over cucumber salad and a chicken fricassee the likes of which hadn't been seen since the mid-1960s, Kate had strongly recommended XOM as a likely breakout. I'd bought ten thousand shares at $39.12, and I still remembered the flying, frightened, exhilarated feeling I'd had when I tapped the buy into our Scottrade account. The dividend yield alone made it seem like a good buy, and certainly the market was done bottoming. What could possibly go wrong?

"Look at this."

Kate swiveled her monitor toward me and I saw a line of jagged ascending mountains. "What's that? The Brooks Range?"

"Exxon's chart for the last two weeks. Haven't you looked?"

I set down my glass and leaned closer. "Is that today's quote—forty-four dollars?"

Kate nodded and, reading my mind, handed me her calculator. Even rounding down, the stock was up $4.88 from where I'd bought it. I felt a prickling in my scalp. In less than twenty days, we'd made almost $50,000. Tom and I were *in*. We'd cracked the secret code—after two years of downturn, this market was going up. At least that's what everyone said. We'd climbed aboard the perfect wave. All we had to do now was ride it in to shore. We could just place our bets, leave them on the table, and go on about our business.

In a few years, we might not even have to work anymore. Remember that year with IM? we'd ask each other with knowing smiles. *But really*, I heard myself telling a future *Fortune* magazine reporter, *after studying a lot of market cycles—my Ph.D. was in history after all—I knew by March 2002, that we were in for a new bull market, one that would make the nineties uptick seem like a blip. So Tom and I just committed ourselves ... What? No, I've never considered managing money on a professional level. I handle my parents' account and have done some investing for my sister's family and Tom's mother, but that's it. Now I'm just, well, enjoying life. We've got our hundred acres up north and will start building up there next spring. Let me tell you, getting the right plans and the architectural team together has been an absolute nightmare ...*

And there it was, half-framed and hazily perfect in my mind, an arts-

and-crafts house that embodied every good idea Frank Lloyd Wright had ever had, hovering above the shore of a pristine, pine-edged lake so fresh and clean my mouth filled with the sudden taste of wintergreen. I would choose every feature in it, sign off on every fieldstone fireplace and open-beamed ceiling, select every scrap of fabric and stick of furniture and . . .

"Annie?" Kate was looking at me quizzically. "Are you okay? Do you want me to get someone to drive you home?"

"Of course not." I set my glass down so she could see how little of the Chivas I'd actually drunk. "I'm fine. Walk a straight line, breathe into a balloon, all that."

"You just seemed a little . . ."

I glanced pointedly at the XOM chart, which was still glowing on her computer screen.

"It's just the money," I said. "I got a little weak in the knees. You wouldn't believe what I . . ." My voice trailed off. I wasn't ready to share my north-shore house with anyone yet. "Money takes people in the oddest directions, doesn't it?"

"Yes, it does," Kate said soberly. "More than you know."

Chapter 12

TOYS "R" US

Days later, I was still thinking about my flash vision of what I now thought of as our vacation home. Hadn't I just read that second homes were the fastest-growing add-on for families in our age and income bracket? Of course we should have one. Not this year, though. Not until we really got our footing, but that didn't mean I couldn't start planning.

I flipped through the stack of pictures and articles I'd torn from various home magazines and spread them across the dining-room table. Somewhere in the stack was an ad for Anderson windows that had distinctly prairie-school lines. I had three accordion folders and was busy labeling and sorting. Really, this was more fun than paper dolls. We'd have this house for city living and our second home—rustic but sleek—for private getaways.

I glanced down the length of the table, imagining how it would look with autumn leaves and a cornucopia spilling casually at Thanksgiving, with our family and Barb's family and maybe even Lyn and Dan and Emily and a turkey and—suddenly, I realized something was desperately wrong. We had no dishes. Not really. There was our everyday blue Pfaltzgraff stoneware, but that was hardly up to scratch. Not to mention the fact that our original service for eight had been reduced to service for five and a half, provided the half would be content with a cereal bowl. Other than that, our new china hutch was so bereft that Sophie's purple Barney set was proudly on display, along with an impressive collection of mismatched Arby's Christmas glasses. Good God. We were living like cave dwellers. I was far more familiar with the spectrum of patterns offered by Chinette than, say, by Lenox and Mikasa.

I drove to the nearest Marshall Field's and was soon staring at walls of softly gleaming china. China that looked even better in the sample place settings on display, where it was framed by Waterford stemware and decent silverware. And I'm not being extravagant or overly materialistic here. By "decent" I just mean forks and spoons that haven't been a) purchased in a blister pack at Wal-Mart, b) mangled in the garbage disposal, c) used by Sophie to dig mud pies, or d) buried by Scout and rediscovered at random with the Weed Eater. It took me five minutes to pick seven china patterns, and another two hours to narrow it down to Lenox's Firelight. It was a little more money than I'd planned to spend, especially when you added the soup tureen and trencher-size meat platter. On the other hand, ever since Kate had promised that we'd have Thanksgiving at home, I'd been fantasizing about a big, perfectly laid table, the kind you see in magazines, the soft flicker of candlelight gleaming faintly. These were just the kind of gorgeous, elegant pieces we needed, pieces we could use forever. I fast-forwarded to Jeff bringing a fiancée home for the first time, to a baby shower for Sophie. *Your mother has such classic taste.* So why not get them now? Especially when, by Thanksgiving, they would probably cost even more. Ditto the subtly gold-trimmed silverware that went with them. I was on my way to the cash register when I saw a dinner plate in the Porsgrund alcove on the far wall, white, bordered with sprigs of pine punctuated by red hearts. The perfect Christmas dishes. Once I'd seen them, I couldn't picture my cool, elegant Firelight pattern on our Christmas Day table at all. It would have been like asking Grace Kelly to lead a polka—which, since my mother was a native of New Ulm, home of Wally Pickle and his magic trumpet, was a frequent part of our Christmas revelries. But the hearts-and-pine plates were so casually cheerful, so perfect for Christmas on the edge of a snowy lake . . .

I went ahead and bought the stuff, two sets of dishes, place settings for twelve, as well as the silver. I knew Tom and I had decided to put the investment earnings aside, in college and retirement funds, but we'd gotten into the market at one of those once-in-a-lifetime bottoms. Our Exxon winnings were already huge. Would a few thousand off the top even matter?

"Mommy, is this *chic?*" Sophie had pulled a fishing hat, emblazoned with Budweiser logos, low over her head. "Or is it *de trop?*"

I laughed. "Where did you learn that? *De trop?*"

"At French. It was on the Fashion Week list, remember?"

I was still undecided about French for Fours, the preschool's "dynamic new approach" to language. I could never decide if they were preparing young Minnesotans for a lifetime of ugly-American-style tourism or simply equipping them with the self-satisfied command of minutiae needed to blend in as true Parisians. I mean, whatever happened to straightforward phrases like *il fait chaud* and *ou est le dentiste?* During Perfect Pronunciation week, Sophs had driven all of us to distraction by chirping *chic, les artichauts* on a near hourly basis. She did, however, end up with an intimidatingly flawless way of spitting out menu items, and if we ever made it to La Pyramide, she'd be the one doing the ordering.

"These?"

Having given up on the Budweiser hat, she was riffling through the sunglasses. *Violette, cerise, puce, brun, gris,* pair by pair, so I snatched them out of her hands and stuck them back on the spinning plastic rack. We didn't have much to work with here. In fact, now that we'd hit the hat-and-sunglasses booth, we'd exhausted all the *couture* the Minnesota Boat Show had to offer. This was the high point, this and the Save Our Smelt booth with its diorama of the smelt life cycle.

I'd decided to come to the boat show with Tom and Jeff in a flood of gemütlichkeit, determined to make the most of our newly prized family time. I stayed onboard with the idea even after Jeff asked if two of his friends could come along. We could still have a family day, I told myself, and it would give me a chance to see who my son was hanging out with these days. But after ascertaining that Sam and Anthony, sons of the Martins and the Culpeppers from the gourmet group, were absolutely normal and without any Blade-like tendencies, and after two hours of listening to the boys—I'm including my husband here—discuss the merits of various fish finders, my gemütlichkeit had begun to fade, and Sophie and I drifted off in search of some girl-friendly fun.

"How about another juice?" I asked, and was almost relieved when Sophie shook her head. The food booths were located near the live-bait rows, and the idea made me a little nauseous. If you could peddle fried walleye on a stick, how long would it be before someone decided minnows would be even better?

"How many boats is Daddy buying?"

The answer turned out to be two. And when you thought about it, it made sense, really. Tom and I had settled on the idea of a cabin cruiser, a *family* boat, behind which we would tow our tanned, athletic offspring as they mastered first the water board and later, water skis. We would spend carefree afternoons juttering around Minnetonka—*our* lake—and becoming the healthy, picture-postcard family we'd always meant to be. After years of receiving Christmas photocards showing our friends and their children cross-countrying on newly purchased acreages and playing water polo in their in-ground pools, we were going to drape ourselves across the bow of a thirty-six-footer and spell out N-O-E-L with red and green beach towels.

But there was a problem, Tom explained.

"I found the perfect cabin cruiser. Nice size, last year's model, good price, and the dealer's right here in Minnetonka. But Jeff saw this little red bass boat. Really nice, compact. Bright red. The perfect little fishing boat."

"Fishing," that was the operative word. Not waterskiing. Not family boat. "And Jeff would rather have it than a cabin cruiser?"

"No, he'd rather have it *and* the cabin cruiser."

"Look," I said, "we can fish off the cruiser, right? But we can't very well ski off the bass boat. And didn't we decide to get a family boat?" I didn't really see what the debate was.

"Right, but . . . You know, Annie, I'd love to teach Jeff how to handle a boat. He's a responsible kid, and living on a lake, he really should know how. The cruiser is just too much boat—two-hundred-and-sixty-five horsepower inboard for starters. But the bass boat, with a forty-horse-power outboard, that'd be just right for him."

I'd never really understood horsepower and always pictured something like the golden horse statues that reared and galloped in troikalike formation on the top of the state capitol building. I did understand the look on Tom's face, though. Jeff wanted both boats—but not nearly as much as Tom did.

"Let's get them both," I said.

"Annie, you don't know how expensive—"

No man on earth sports a look of concern as attractively as my husband does. His brow creases slightly, his eyes go to storm-on-the-Baltic depth, his hair actually seems to riffle. The overall effect is a look so artlessly earnest, you just know this is a man who will never try to tell you what the meaning of "is" is. No wonder our phone had been ringing off the hook ever since we got back from New York. Women all over the country had looked us up and found a reason to call my husband. They wanted Tom to speak at their clubs, they wanted to send him money to invest in BTC for them, they had recipes to share, they wanted to know if he'd write their science-inclined sons and daughters recommendations for MIT and Cal Tech. One suggested he work on a "bedside" box of BTC, Viagra-laced for Him, birth-control freighted for Her. Mostly, they just wanted to talk to him, my husband. One caller even asked how we got along and, if there was a chance of us getting a divorce, would I pass her number along to him? Nothing personal against me, she'd added.

"We'll get them both," I repeated. "Look, we were going to get a cruiser anyway, and the bass boat, well, remember that Exxon stock I bought?"

And so I told Tom about the Exxon stock now, and showed him how the profits would easily pay for the bass boat. I didn't mention the Lenox china or the Gorham silverware, much less the Porsgrund, of course. There was more than enough profit to pay for everything.

"How much did you say Exxon went up, Annie? Maybe we should sell some. Because, you know, you don't actually *make* the money until you sell the stock. Stock doesn't always go up, Annie. Sometimes it goes down. Sometimes it completely tanks."

"Well, Exxon isn't going to 'tank,' and neither is this market. We've just been through two down years in a row, which almost never happens. There's no way we're going down another one. Three in a row is just unprecedented. The fed is going to cut rates again, and housing starts are still ticking up. But okay, if you want, we'll sell enough stock to pay for the boats, worrywart."

He hadn't been to Kate's investment afternoons. He didn't understand the ground floor we were in on. I did, though. Which was why I planned to carry the boats on credit and sell shares *next* month, when XOM was worth even more. The increased value would more than make up for the finance charges. Why bother him with the details?

I reached up quickly and touched his cheek. "Stop worrying. You're right about the boat, it's perfect for Jeff to learn on, and something the two of you can do together. He'll always remember the summer his dad taught him to run an outboard motor."

"I guess he would, wouldn't he?"

We ordered both boats and went home to wait for the ice to melt, with Jeff high-fiving his friends and Sophie singing the theme song from *Gilligan's Island* in French. "*Le Minnow s'est sauvé . . . le Minnow s'est sauvé!*" What were they learning in that class, anyway?

I was unpacking my new dishes and thinking we might need a second china hutch when my sister, Barb, called with the good news. Rob had been accepted into the D.V.M. program at Iowa State—no small matter, since for some reason, it was harder to get into veterinary school than med school.

"We're going to try to make this happen," Barb said, her voice an even mix of determination and strain. "He's already lined up some loan money, and Mom and Dad said they can help a little. Jay's going to take on more private students, and I can get a part-time job at the mall, and . . ."

And I was swept by a wave of guilt. Clearly, Rob's education was going to be a family effort. And where was I in the equation? Unpacking loads of dishes. Speculating on a custom-made sideboard. Browsing for new toile for the guest room. And I didn't even *like* toile.

I brooded about it all afternoon, then realized that the answer was right in front of me. It was truly incredible, how perfect my solution was. All I had to do was get Tom to see it that way.

I waited until later than night, when the kids had gone to bed and Tom and I were in our bedroom, having a drink for the road. Literally. The suitcase was open on the bed and we were packing for his first week-long BTC jaunt. Two days with some wheat farmers in North Dakota, a one-day stop at an IM processing plant in South Dakota, then three days at a Beef Belles convention in Billings, celebrating the lives of contemporary ranch women.

"So which shirt looks more western?" Tom asked. "Lucie said wear something 'Rio Grande.' What's that supposed to mean?"

"I think it means her geography's a little off. What's she wearing?" Lucie and her people were shepherding my husband through Big Sky country, and I was torn between selfless happiness that he wouldn't be alone and visions of Lucie in a frisky bolero and chaps, shooting the lights out in the last-chance saloon while my husband watched in helpless admiration. "Never mind, I don't want to know what she's wearing. Take your regular clothes, hon. I don't think they're going to ask you to do any roping or branding. Besides, the reason those ranchers' wives like you is because you *don't* look like their husbands."

"You think?"

"Yep, pardner, I do." I took a deep breath. "I've been thinking something else too."

"Good, Annie. That's good. How many pairs of socks? Does this tie look okay with my gray suit?"

"No, go for the red. Could I get your attention here for a minute?"

"Sure. What's up?"

"I've been thinking about Aunt Edith's property."

Aunt Edith wasn't, technically, my aunt. She was my father's aunt by marriage, and it was just as well that she wasn't a blood relation because she'd been, in Minnesota speak, peculiar. She and her husband, Walt, had lived a hardscrabble life up north, and after Walt's death, Edith rocketed off the deep end. First it was a conviction that the Communists would win the Cold War. At the very least, they were certain to take Hawaii, which may have explained the sixty cases of canned pineapple we found in her house after she died. Along with several rooms full of Carharts overalls, Coleman camping equipment, toilet paper, toothpaste, instant ramen, batteries, insect repellent, charcoal briquets, and—most surprising of all— six dozen pair of silk panties and a department-store-display-size bottle of Joy perfume by Jean Patou. Who would have guessed that Aunt Edith, who used to entertain Barb and me with her ability to strike matches on her work-callused fingers, was underneath it all a sensuous little pleasure beast?

Also not so cracked as we all thought, or at least cracked in a productive way. Because, eager to prevent anyone from encroaching on her privacy, she'd bought up a whopping amount of property, which we never really saw because the very last time my father tried to visit, she'd accused him of trying to bilk her out of the "estate" and fired warning shots. Her paranoia leapfrogged my sister and me, apparently, because when she died she left the two of us everything—the pineapples, the five-gallon vat of perfume, the house that was barely winterproof, and 247 acres of uncut wilderness. What a great thing to have. Something Barb and I pledged we'd keep in the family forever, a house we'd refurbish and make the site of long, summer holidays, a hunk of forest that in a hundred years would be commemorated as the last surviving scrap of pure north woods in the whole state. Except that, since we'd owned it, all we'd done was struggle to come up with the steadily rising property taxes.

"What about your aunt Edith's property? Should I buy a shearling jacket, do you think? Is that Rio Grande?"

"You know how we always say we're going to vacation up there and never do?"

"Mmm." I followed Tom out of our bedroom and down the hall to the office, where he started surfing the Net for shearling coats. "Wow, look. There's an Eddie Bauer in Fargo. I'm just going to e-mail ahead and have them set aside some stuff for me to look at."

"Where'd you learn that?"

"What? Surfing the Net?"

"No, using personal shoppers."

Tom looked up. "Is that what they're called? I don't know, it was Lucie's idea, and it just seemed efficient to me." He smiled, and, suddenly, we were exchanging guilty glances. "It's kind of fun though, isn't it?"

"Yeah, it is." I wondered what else he'd been buying. Then I remembered the new watch. The all-terrain four-wheeler (*How else can you drag a deer out of the woods, Annie? It'll actually save money not having to call someone to do it anymore.*) The calls from Stub's Ice House Builders and Hansen's House of Hi-Fi. Not to mention sales reps from LabX and SciQuest who were "following up" on my husband's inquiries about creating a home laboratory. And the thing is, it made me glad. What kind of wife would begrudge her husband the spoils of his big win? "You know how we always say we're going to spend time up at Aunt Edith's but we never do? Have you ever wondered why?"

"Mmm, because it's colder than all get-out up there? Because the road to it is a mosquito-filled mud trough? Because the one time we did, Jeff got strep throat?"

"The August snow was a fluke. And that's not the reason anyway. It's that house. It's old, it's musty, and the roof leaks."

"Okay."

"But the land itself—it's gorgeous, isn't it?"

"Yep. Best duck blinds I've ever seen."

"So the answer's obvious. We should tear down the old house and build something new." The image of my stunning Falling Water–type house rose up before me, as it had that afternoon, sitting where Aunt Edith's riven cavern now sat. "With a new house on it, we'd use that place all the time."

"But, Annie, we just bought this—"

"I don't mean right away. Of course we have to wait a few years, when we have more money."

"And what does Barb think about this?"

And here's where my plan reached perfection. "I haven't talked to Barb about it yet. But you know, with the whole vet school thing, they're going to be really broke. So why don't we buy them out? We could buy the land now and take over the taxes ourselves, then it would be ours to do whatever we want with when the time comes. And, of course, Barb and Jay could use it whenever they wanted. It'd still stay in the family. And the money . . ." I looked at him imploringly. "The money would really, really help with Rob's tuition. It's a win-win for all of us."

Tom's face went serious. "I don't know, Annie. It's a big commitment."

"But we'll have plenty of money. I'm sure Barb and Jay won't expect it all in one lump. But if they *knew* it was coming . . ."

"And we have two kids to put through college too, you know."

"Not for several years, and by then we'll have tons of money. Buckets of it."

"What if we don't?"

"Oh, honey, don't be such a worrywart. What can possibly go wrong? Between BTC and hitting the stock-market roll—remember that book I read last week, *Dow 36,000?* Think about it. It means everything we invest in will be worth more than three times what it is now."

Tom looked startled. "You're kidding."

"Do the math. The market is hovering around ten thousand. Thirty-six thousand is three-point-six times that."

"But all stocks don't go up equally. Some go down. Some sink out of sight. You can't believe that just because you invest X amount of dollars you'll end up with X times whatever."

"Of *course* I know that," I said impatiently. "But with a balanced portfolio and a representative selection of stocks, maybe a few index funds and some muni bonds and—"

"Look, Annie, can we talk about all this another time? I need to finish packing. And get some sleep."

"But Barb is so worried, and if we could just let them know . . ."

"Annie, another time, okay?"

I sighed. "Okay."

I meant to bring it up again the next morning, after he'd had a good night's sleep. But in the morning it was sleeting and Lucie called to say the car would pick him up two hours earlier than planned, to make sure they took off before the weather turned really bad. So I stood in the foyer in my robe and slippers and kissed my husband good-bye at five-thirty A.M. Then I closed the door and stumbled back to bed.

When I woke up again, Tom's plane was landing in Fargo. I felt oddly detached, as if I was the one who'd flown off into the dark morning sky. In all the time we'd been married, Tom and I had never spent more than two nights apart. For some reason, I thought of a scene from my favorite war movie, *The Best Years of Our Lives,* where the war hero takes his artificial arms off to show his girlfriend how helpless he is without them.

I got out of bed and walked over to the closet. Not my closet, his closet. And I reached out my arms, pulled his clothes close to me, and buried my face in them as if they were actually him. I inhaled deeply and waited for the special smell to embrace me, the smell I could never quite describe but could pick out of a thousand other smells. It was no good, though. The smell of his clothes wasn't the same without him in them.

I got dressed and started down the stairs just in time to hear Minka enter the house, singing a Polish song about snow on a roof on a house on a brook on a hill in the middle of a meadow.

Chapter 13

HOW DO THEY DO IT?

How *do* single mothers manage? By the time Tom had been gone four days, I was ready to pull my fillings out just for the diversion of it. Even with Minka helping, I slipped almost immediately into a LaBrea tar pit of ineffectuality.

First, I almost forgot about the spring school conferences, which Tom and I usually went to together. I hadn't thought going alone would make all that much difference until Julie Hart, Jeff's teacher, tilted her head sympathetically and asked in a walking-on-eggshells voice, "Is the father in the home?"

"No, he's in Fargo." Her look of concern deepened. Over her shoulder, I could see a bulletin board displaying "Global Warming: A Ticking Time Bomb." The board on the other side of the room was freighted with pictures of antelope, bighorn sheep, bison, and elk. "Extinction: Who Will Be Left?" Oh great. I was in the hands of a twenty-five-year-old neurasthenic. "He's on a business trip," I added.

"I'm so sorry," she murmured. I wasn't certain if she was sorry for prying or sorry our marriage hadn't yet evolved into one of those healthy, we're-still-good-friends-who-respect-each-other's-shared-custody-rights type of arrangements. "It's just that, well, let's sit down, shall we?"

My knees bumped against the pint-size desk. Hopefully not the desk of a kid who deposited gum—or worse—on the underside. "Tom and I are very *happy* together," I said defensively. "Is there a problem? With Jeff?"

I felt a smidge of guilt. Had I missed something? Because, to me, it seemed that he was doing fine.

"Not a problem, exactly, but . . ." She paused and her head dropped even lower. "But, well, your son seems almost preternaturally good-natured. He actually seems to like everyone in the class."

"Oh, that's just Jeff. He usually really does like everybody. Kind of like Lassie."

"You think of your son as a dog?" She made a note in Jeff's file. "Interesting."

I leaned forward and read upside down. I could just make out the words "species/gender confusion??"

She saw me and slammed the file shut. "And you're aware of the Bengt Mackenzie situation?"

She had me there. Had Bengt's reputation as the Jeanlin of Minnetonka spread beyond our neighborhood? How did she even know who he was?

"Doesn't Bengt go to that alternative school downtown?" I asked blandly. "The Carl Jung Academy?"

Yes, I was sure of it. Estelle had proudly shown me the brochure— "Try Jung, It's Fun!"—which boasted a program guaranteed to "assist the delimited child in learning via a freely structured, wholly self-directed exploration of the unconscious and its unique languages—symbolical, prelogical, and allegorical." Whew. "Of course," Estelle had noted quietly, letting me down gently in case I was thinking of enrolling Jeff, "they can only accept a very few, very exceptional children."

Julie's saddened sigh snapped me back to the present. That and the intoxicating smell of school paste mingled with damp sneaker.

"Apparently, I gather, there's a bit of a *locus parentis* problem in Bengt's home. He's been showing up here after school and"—her eyes widened—"trying to pass himself off as one of our students. Last week he crashed a game of pom-pom pullaway. The week before, he got involved in a Bring Home the Bacon tournament."

Poor old Bengt. I actually felt sorry for him. I pictured him in his snugly belted, double-lined Burberry coat, trying to lose himself in a crowd of down jackets and bright-colored stocking caps.

"And your son seems determined to befriend him."

I stared at her, waiting in vain for her to continue. Finally, I asked, "How is this a problem?"

"It may not be troublesome in itself." Meaning, of course, that disaster was looming. "But when the other boys make fun of him for his efforts with Bengt, Jeff doesn't seem to care. I must admit, that's troubling."

What was I missing here? "Look, I'm afraid I'll have to be leaving in a few minutes, so if you could just—"

"When a prepubertal boy is as even tempered as your son, it can be a trouble sign. A warning flag that deep anger is being suppressed, at least at some level. There may be some *issue* in the home, between the parents. Can I ask—has there been any abuse between you and your husband?"

"Of course not."

"Because that can lead a young boy to decide that it's not okay to express his displeasure. Boys like this sometimes hook up with an alter-ego peer, an angrier, less repressed persona, often a delinquent. In some cases, the two go on to evolve into a symbiotic—"

"Oh for heaven's sake," I said, standing up and banging my knees. "This is ridiculous!"

"Of course," Julie added hurriedly, "we don't think that's what's happening with Jeff and Bengt. If we did, we'd be far more proactive. But it's a possibility you need to be aware of. So if you and your husband would just read this—"

She thrust some pages into my hand, which I stuffed into my purse without looking at them. In fact, I forgot I even had them until I was in the car and digging for my keys. Then I smoothed them out and realized she'd given me a reprint from a psychological journal. The title loomed up at me in accusatory twenty-point type: "Psycho and Sycophant: The Eric Harris—Dylan Kliebold Story."

And this was a public school. Heaven only knows what was going on out there where Jung is fun.

The next day started off more smoothly. I spent the morning writing, a good thing since a month earlier IM had made a deal with a publisher to reprint my dissertation with glossy artwork and an addendum chapter on artificial chocolate, and the work was due soon. With no husband to greet, no dinner to get (we still had leftovers from Leeann Chin's), and Sophie playing Smurf ball with Lyn's daughter, Emily, in the great room while Minka refereed, I was able to make real progress. In fact, it began to seem that our separate schedules might be beneficial after all.

Then I heard shrieking and the sound of an airborne Sophie hurtling up the stairs. "Mommy! Mommy! Mommy!" The door swung open. "Emily's sick! Emily threw up!" And as she lunged forward with the news, Minnetonka's tiniest town crier threw up herself, an aurora borealis of cereal, graham crackers, chicken fingers, carrot sticks, and apple juice that jetted across the carpet to land on Scout, me, my desk, the computer printer, the pages I'd just written, and the bolt of $90-a-yard tea-dyed silk I was having a chair upholstered with. Later, I even found a semi-digested Cheerio stuck to the lampshade. While Minka cleaned up Emily, Sophie, Scout, and I took a group shower.

An hour later, they were lying like pale little rag dolls in Sophie's room watching television, each of them armed with a bucket, a glass of ginger ale, and a damp Handi Wipe. Sophie wanted to know if she was going to die. When I told her it was probably only the flu, she announced, *"J'ai la grippe,"* and turned her face to the wall with a dramatic flair that Eleanora Duse would have envied. Emily just wanted to know when her mommy would be back from shopping to come get her. Then Minka called up from the basement to tell me that there was something wrong with the washing machine. It had digested the girls' clothes and now was spewing water all over the floor. Which meant I would have to keep an eye on Scout or put him outside for a while, because there was nothing he liked better than lapping up sudsy water. Kind of his own version of a canine colonic.

We mopped up the water and rescued what shreds of the girls' outfits remained. It seemed that one of Sophie's sneakers had gotten wedged firmly under the agitator, turning it into a sucking vortex that could not be stopped. The washer ground on, pulling more clothing into the tangle, until the agitator came to a complete halt and the computerized digital panel shut down. This was the kind of thing Tom usually took care of, and when the panel stayed blank even after I pried out the clothes and the sneaker and attempted to reset the machine, I decided it would remain the kind of thing Tom usually took care of. I muttered about not being able to do any laundry until next week.

Minka turned to me, hands on her hips, and cried almost joyfully, "I wash by hand! I wash, we hang outside. Much cheaper!"

I was about to explain how we lived in a residential zone that restricted public displays of laundry when the phone rang and I ran upstairs to get it.

"Annie? Can you hear me?" It was Lucie. Speaking, apparently, from the middle of an early spring tornado.

"Where are you calling from? Where's Tom?"

"Are you okay, Annie? Because you sound like you're out of breath. I *told* you you should start coming to my gym with me—"

"Lucie, can you put Tom on? I need to talk to him."

"Tom can't talk right now."

I froze. "What's wrong? Lucie? Lucie! Has there been an accident?"

She laughed. "Of course there hasn't been an accident. Tom's touring one of our sorghum plants and I'm on my way to pick him up. We rented the coolest red convertible and—well, never mind. I called because I've got some great news for you! You're going to die!"

With Lucie, a real possibility. "You've discovered Tom would poll better if he were a widower? You're going to set him up for a season on *The Bachelor?*"

"Wait, let me make a note—oh, you're kidding. Sorry. Not that it wouldn't be *great* TV but—no."

"I can't hear you," I screamed.

"Can you now? Is this better? Wait, I'll pull over to the side." The roaring-wind sound stopped suddenly. I could hear meadowlarks. "Okay. That's better. Remember you said you were hosting that dinner thing for your neighbors, and how we decided it would be the perfect op to shoot some footage? Well, it took some doing, but I got IM to sign on—we've increased the guest list to three hundred and fifty! We're making it a truly VIM event!"

"V-I-M?"

"Very Influential Minnesotans. Are you thrilled?"

"But it's only two weeks away."

"I know. And don't think it hasn't taken a lot of work to get everything clicking. I mean, a guest list of three hundred and fifty—"

She must have gotten back on the road. There was an unmistakable roaring in my ears. "*Three hundred and fifty?*"

"Yes, and we'll get tons of great footage of you in the kitchen, pulling cakes and hors d'oeuvres and all sorts of things out of those stunning double ovens. It'll be fantastic!"

"Lucie! I can't possibly—"

"Don't worry. We're going to get staff to do the actual serving. *And we've jumped this project to the front burners*, so Jean-Paul has developed some fabulous recipes for you. There's one for BTC genoise thimble cakes filled with hazelnut butter-crunch cream that I know everyone will want two or three of at least! What could be easier? It'll be a snap!"

Let's see, 350 times two—or three—genoise thimble cakes . . .

"And, Annie?" Lucie went on. "You'll need to come in to the kitchens so Jean-Paul can give you some lessons. I e-mailed you a new schedule. Your first session is tomorrow. Have a good time!"

"Lucie, could you ask Tom to call—" It was no use. She'd hung up. And I was giving a party for 350 people. It'd be a snap.

"Cucinaphobia." Was there such a word?

I looked around my kitchen and fought the urge to flee. *Get comfortable* was Kate's advice. *You have two weeks.*

Across America, women were afraid to leave their homes, afraid to go to malls, restaurants, beauty shops, and libraries. I was afraid to go into my kitchen. Not the manageable and friendly kitchen we used every day. The behemoth lurking behind it—the airplane-hangar-sized work kitchen I was intended to take command of and look completely at home in. The glinting, polished, overequipped, overdesigned work space millions dreamed of but only a professional chef could love. *Cucinaphobia.* Maybe I was on the cutting edge of something here, and if all the couples saving to build their dream kitchens ever succeeded, they'd be as unnerved as I was about it.

Standing at one of the two immense islands, a shiver ran down my back. For starters, this was the coldest room in the house, no doubt because at least one of its heat-building ovens—gas, electric, convection, wood burning—was expected to be in use at all times. I was also utterly alone. Jeff and Sophie were at school. The kittens, Bonnie and Clyde, had been banned after several loud and noisy cat chases through the place, sending utensils and bowls and small appliances clattering. Scout refused to enter because the glossily polished floors made him nervous. *It's like toenails on ice,* you could see him puzzling; *whatever were those people thinking?*

I glanced down at the loose-leaf notebook the designers had thoughtfully assembled for me. Titled simply "The Wilkins Kitchen," it was a mapped and numbered guide to virtually every item in the place. I'd finished with the blue floor plan—"Built Ins"—and no longer had to scan the room to know which oven was where or which panel concealed the "Flour & Grains Pantry" and which concealed "Whisks, Spoons & Spatulas." I was now ready to move on to the green-tinted plan, "Small Appliances," and eventually to the mind-boggling pink one, "Tools and Gadgets."

With a surge of confidence, I slid open the door beneath "Island #1." God, what was *that?* I pulled out what looked like a double-decker flying saucer, with a griddlelike top and the handles of little trowels sticking out underneath. Maybe some new-style hibachi, and the trowels were used to shovel in the briquetts? Or the s'mores maker? No, that had been item #167. I lifted the contraption, located the peel-and-stick label that said "#568," and consulted the cross-reference list in the notebook. Raclette maker. Of course. What exactly *was* raclette, anyway? I'd always thought it was the same as fondue.

Right beside the raclette maker was something that looked like a small, insulated coffeepot with two sputniklike projections coming off the top.

Who dreamed up this stuff? I wondered, and how had I lived my whole life without #672, which turned out to be an automatic cream whipper. And the tubed stainless handle attached to a plastic ball and oval pivot? Of course! A Rösle can opener. The thing that looked just like it but stood upright was a professional egg topper. And since I had no idea what that was or did, even after looking up the name, I consulted the alphabetically indexed instruction manuals stored in the oak-finished filing cabinets flanking the recessed computer alcove. "Used in high-end restaurants for professional presentation, Mr. Topper is placed on top of an egg to make a perfect hole in the top of the egg. The egg is drained out and rinsed, and the shell used as a serving vehicle for caviar and other gourmet foods. Very elegant!"

And so it went, from handheld blenders to rice cookers to truffle slicers to something that looked like a cubist cookie press but in fact made butter come out in a thin, rippling ribbon. The whole kitchen was a bridal registry dumping ground. No gadget too obscure, too expensive, or too pointless.

"Island #2" was referred to in the manual as a "Camp Chocolate." Here were molds and melters and shavers, tempering machines, breaking forks, dipping forks, spatulas, spreaders, thermometers (did we really need a dozen?), and double boilers. Having spent so much time playing with BTC, I felt more at home here. And just to reassure myself that I wasn't completely incompetent, I made a pan of brownies using the newest BTC product, artificially sweetened BTC cocoa powder. The brownies came out fine, once I consulted the manual and figured out how to work the oven touch panel. But cooking alone at home and narrating your way through a recipe in front of cameras and strangers were two very different matters. For starters, I'd have to stop licking the spoon.

Why couldn't Jean-Paul De Navets, IM's famous chef, just come out and cook for me, at least for the party? When I'd suggested this to Kate, she looked at me as if I'd suggested that the pope drop by after Sunday mass to say grace. "Jean-Paul *never* leaves the IM kitchens," Kate said sharply. "Everyone knows that. It's part of his mystique."

When I showed up for my lesson with the master of mystique the next morning, I was feeling distinctly shaky. I hadn't slept well. I'd had night-mares in which I'd lost Jeff and Sophie in my kitchen and couldn't find them. In the most horrifying scene, I'd snatched in vain for Sophie's baby-size hand just before it vanished down the drain. It was the kind of night-mare Tom used to talk me down from, but I hadn't talked to my husband for more than five minutes at a time in the last three days.

On top of everything else, the housekeeper told me the kittens were using the potted trees in the great room as litter boxes, the washing-machine repairman told me it would be cheaper to replace the machine than to fix the digital panel, I wasn't sure I'd escaped Sophie's flu, and, oh yes, the new love seat with the right upholstery—replacing the new love seat with the wrong upholstery—had arrived with a tarlike stain and was, once again, waiting to be picked up and redelivered to the factory. It now seemed like a permanent part of our entryway. Swathed in bubble wrap and about five hundred yards of crumpled brown paper, it should make the perfect "Welcome to the Wilkinses" statement for our party.

As tired as I was, I made certain to arrive in the kitchen before the renowned De Navets. Kate had forewarned me: IM's VIP cook was always the last to enter the kitchen. She'd also pointed out that he preferred to be referred to simply as "Chef," no first or last name. She advised me not to panic if he seemed to stand too close, as he was French and they had an altogether different sense of personal space. And, if he threw food, swore, shouted, incinerated his toque (it had happened), or had any other form of a divalike tantrum, the best thing to do would be to pretend nothing had happened. Above all, I shouldn't mention Mangeons les Paysans, the restaurant he'd once operated in downtown Minneapolis.

As I waited in the specially designed Better Than Chocolate kitchen, the one Lucie had shown me weeks ago, I longed to lay my head down on the countertop. My energy was ebbing by the minute, and if Chef didn't appear soon, I was going to fall asleep. The bright glare bouncing off the white tiles needled into my eyes. When I closed them, the sensation of rest was heavenly.

"Madame?" My head snapped up. Was it my exhausted state or did the floor actually tremble as De Navets entered the room? He was enormous, a

Swiss Alp of a man in his chef's whites. Paul Prudhomme was a sylph by comparison. De Navets stared at me for so long, I began to feel like a lamb chop without my paper frill on. *"Bien,"* he said at last. "Are you ready?"

I nodded and tried not to cringe as he drew near me. Brut? Hai Karate? Giorgio? He was enveloped in an overwhelming miasma of scent that brought back memories of many an unhappy, fumbling, no-I-*don't*-want-to-just-touch-it high school date.

"Let's cook," I chirped, in a voice I hoped sounded game and cheerful yet frosty enough to discourage the chef-size paw that had come to rest on my backside. He's French, I reminded myself. *Gallic.* Seduction is second nature to them. Egad! The afternoon bristled with nightmarish possibilities, not unlike those high school dates. I stepped away, leaving his paw to float in the air.

"Kate told you I'm giving a big party, right? And I need to come up with some impressive-looking hors d'oeuvres that I can master well enough to demo on tape. For two or three hundred people."

"Of course." With the flourish of a coquette snapping her fan, De Navets produced his reading glasses, settled them on his nose, and consulted a list. "We are going to start with a *mousseline de veau au persil* on toast rounds, then proceed to a *tartine tartufate* and a *parfait de canard,* which will give us an excellent opportunity for some puff-pastry work. Very simple, you will see."

And the amazing thing was, I *did* see. For the next four hours, I was spellbound. De Navets moved with a quick, hypnotic grace, filleting, mincing, sautéeing, pirouetting his four-hundred-plus pounds around like spun sugar. I grew accustomed to his looming nearness, the way people living near mountains accustom themselves to deep shadows. True, I felt increasingly feverish, but surely that was just the intensity of our work.

During the *mousseline* making, I slipped into a hyperzone of concentration, focusing so intently I barely noticed Chef's hands swooping—and occasionally resting—on my shoulder, my waist, my hip. And if they did, so what? I thought as I toasted crostini and cut cornichon stars with a tiny aspic cutter. It was innocuous. It was his way. Far more alarming to me was the knowledge that, engaged though I was, there was simply no way I could reproduce these wonders in my own kitchen. Not for a dinner party of eight, and certainly not for 350. Each time this thought knifed its way into my consciousness, I shoved it violently aside. What on *earth* was I going to do on that upcoming night in April?

It was while Chef was showing me how to drizzle melted BTC over miniature profiteroles that I felt the first real wave of nausea. I ignored it and continued to concentrate on the chocolate. Really, who knew you could have so much fun with an ordinary squeeze bottle? Then a wave hit me with such force I closed my eyes and gripped the edge of the counter.

"You are all right, *madame?*"

Any moment now, the room should stop heaving. You cannot throw up in front of a three-star chef, I told myself. Cannot do it. My grip on the counter tightened. I forced myself to smile. "I'm fine. I'm just, mmm, impressed. The delicacy of those profiteroles. Genius!"

"Ah, *madame,* I knew you would understand me! The moment I saw you in my kitchen, I realized that we were . . . were . . . yes?"

His voice came from slightly behind me, close enough for me to actually feel the warmth of his breath against my neck.

"Yes." I had no idea what I was agreeing to or he was mumbling about, but I was willing to say anything that might make him move his furnace-like body away from mine.

"Ah," I heard behind me, "ah, ah, *ah!*" The last of these burst directly into my ear and the smell of whatever it was he was wearing dove into my mouth. I could actually *taste* the stuff. His bearlike arms encircled me and, glancing down, I saw two enormous floury hands plant themselves firmly on my breasts.

"Please, Chef! I have such a fever!"

I should, of course, have said "temperature."

Ten seconds later, still struggling to extract myself from the playful but firm embrace of a man who was now panting, *"D'accord! Un coup de foudre!, "* into my ear, I vomited across the profiteroles, across the Silpat sheets, and onto the glistening countertop. Yes, indeed, I had caught Sophie's flu after all.

De Navets let go of me and I fell forward like a limp rag doll.

"Call someone," I croaked. I was about to pass out. I couldn't possibly clean this up myself.

"What?"

I pushed myself upright and turned to look at him. "Call someone!" I gestured toward the mess. "We need to call someone!" My voice rose to a shriek, making De Navets go deathly pale. Before my eyes, he turned into a quivering blancmange, a billowing white truffle beginning to sprout beads of perspiration. He looked stricken, convinced that the mere prospect of his massive virility had terrified me to the point of illness.

"No. *Non!* Please, *madame*, I beg you. There is no need to tell anyone! It was a jest, an accident, a mere brush of the hand, a complete mistake. I am sincerely sorry. *Je regret!* But to call someone? To make an incident of a mere gesture? *Non, non!* You must allow us to be friends again."

"Could I have a glass of water?"

"Of course, of course!" He watched me take a tentative mouthful. "You are feeling better? Yes?"

"No." I started to dust the floury handprints off my breasts, then thought better of it, the same way Monica must have thought better of getting that blue dress dry cleaned. Why not let the goofball twist a bit longer? "No, Chef, I am *not* feeling better. In fact, I need—"

"Anything! Anything, *madame!* Tell me what I may do to reunite our friendship."

I'd only been about to ask him to call a company car to take me home, but really, why stop there? "If only it were possible . . . no, you would never—"

"You have but to ask! Surely there is something."

And so I suggested, as coherently as possible with what I later discovered was a temperature verging on 102 degrees, that since I could not possibly master his perfectly divine recipes in the two weeks before the party, I would so much appreciate it if he would abandon his rookery at IM and come to my kitchen to cook that evening. He demurred at first, showing more alarm than hauteur, but when I glanced meaningfully down at my handprint-marked person and murmured something about the terrible complications of sexual-harassment suits, he consented.

"*Merci*," I said graciously, dabbing my mouth with the handkerchief he'd handed me. "I'll be looking forward to it! You won't change your mind?"

"Of course not."

Just to make sure, I wore the apron home.

So, party for 350: problem solved.

Surprise booking to speak at the spring meeting of Golden Valley Girls, followed by a demonstration involving Better Than Chocolate and a fondue pot—problem! What was Kate thinking?

For a solid twenty-four hours after IM's limo driver helped me into the house and Minka put me to bed, I'd been too weak to do anything but vomit and drink 7-Up. As soon as I mustered up the strength, I called Kate with the good news, saying only that I had persuaded the legendary De Navets to chef the party. I'd thought she'd be stunned by my coup, or at least subtly impressed. But the edge of victory had been blunted when she told me she had to take an urgent incoming call, and by the time she called me later, the element of delighted surprise was gone and all I got was a polished *Well done*. The next morning, after ascertaining that I was nearly back to 100 percent, she told me how well everything had worked out. With the weight of worry about the party off my shoulders, I'd be free to accept the speaking opportunity that had just come up. Attempts to backtrack and say I wasn't *really* as well as I'd said were futile, as were protestations of being unready for a cooking demo. *It's just melting chocolate and dipping some strawberries and angel food cake, Annie.* As to the speech, it was being written now and would be e-mailed to me later in the afternoon. Plenty of time for me to read, rewrite, and rehearse.

So two days later, the day I'd planned to spend primping and plucking for Tom's return that night, I found myself in a church-fellowship room in Golden Valley. I was so light-headed Kate had agreed to come with me, and she sat at the back of the room reading *Fortune* and *Business Week* while I did my thing. How the speech went, I couldn't judge. I still had that floating, fragile feeling you get from not eating (the silver lining in the bout of flu—I'd lost five pounds!), but Kate said I was fine. Dipping strawberries in BTC, then showing the Girls how easy it was to give them professional panache with a finishing squiggle of our new white BTC glaze— it wasn't exactly brain surgery, so I suppose I didn't do too much harm. Even so, I was exhausted by the time it was over and relieved that Kate was driving me home.

"I feel like I just played the lead in a Broadway show," I said, closing my eyes.

"You did," Kate said. "And you got great reviews. Those women were *interested*. Bet they have you back."

"If I ever get the energy."

Kate gave a sarcastic snort. "You've got four more talks like that next week."

"You're kidding."

"Nope. It was genius of you to free up your time by getting Jean-Paul to cook. I thought it was one of Lucie's few wrong turns to have you do that anyway. I mean, we can get all the so-called cooking footage we want without you knowing a thing about cuisine, high *or* low. Into the oven. Out of the oven. How hard is that? An orangutang could do it, for heaven's sake. No offense. But your time is much too valuable to squander on vol-au-vents. And I've been really pleased by how easy it's been to book you. Once the buzz starts to build, you'll be out there every day of the week."

Oh, fabulous. How could she possibly do this to me? But of course, I reminded myself, it was her job. And mine.

I was sound asleep when Tom came home at seven P.M. The joyous reception he received wasn't from me but from Minka, who was thrilled to relinquish custody of me and the children. He tucked Sophie into bed and watched television with Jeff for an hour, and by the time he woke me up it was almost ten. Still tired and a little buzzed from everything that had happened, I began weeping at the goodness of it all. How many husbands could manage not to come slamming into the bedroom right away, or making such a racket they woke you up.

"I love you," I said, pushing myself up and trying to smooth my rumpled flannel pajamas. "I missed you so much, and every time I tried to call, the cell faded, or you were in a meeting, or——"

"Ssh," he said, climbing in beside me and stroking my hair. "I know, I know. I tried to call you too. Were you really speaking to the Golden Girls today?"

"Golden Valley Girls. I think Minka got it wrong."

Tom sighed and put his arm around me. "This is rough, isn't it, being apart?"

For the first time, I noticed how tired he looked. "Yeah, it's rough." I forced a smile. "We'll get through it, though, won't we? I mean, this won't last forever, this part of it."

We kissed and I think we meant to make love. At least *I* meant to—he may have been put off by my slept-in pajamas—but we fell asleep. The last thing I remembered was burrowing my face against his chest and finding it, that comforting, warm scent I'd missed so much.

When we woke up, it was one A.M., the bedroom lights were still on, and the doorbell was ringing wildy.

Chapter 14

MI CASA ES SU CASA

Tom bolted upright. "What the—?"

He'd never even made it out of his clothes, I noted as he sprinted down the stairs. When gunshots and cries didn't ring out, I followed him at my own, more cowardly pace. Well, who wants to get home-invaded in their tattered pj's, after all?

"Annie! Darling!"

Good God, it was my mother.

"We're not waking you, are we?"

And father.

"What are you doing here? You're in Spain."

"We found cheap tickets on-line and we just thought, why not?"

Why not indeed.

"But, Mom, why didn't you call to let us know?"

"We tried, darling, but there's something wrong with your phone. Every time we dialed, we got a recording about your number being changed."

It *had* been changed. In the face of the hundred or so calls a day Tom was getting from women who'd seen him on television, and the ten or twenty far less friendly calls I was getting from women telling me I ought to be home with my children, not gallivanting around the country, we'd had to go for an unlisted number.

"Remember the e-mail I sent you last week? With our new number?"

My mother frowned slightly. "Oh dear, did you e-mail us, sweetie? I just got so tired of those darned ads to enlarge your father's winkie, well, I just got fed up and deleted everything. Have you got a blanket handy?"

Hang on, here. I was fully awake now. Awake enough to wonder why my mother needed the blanket Tom had promptly gone to fetch. Then I noticed that the yellow roof light of the taxi was still visible in the driveway.

"Tell me you didn't bring—" Oh, what *was* the named of that damned parrot? "You didn't bring Don Diego with you, did you?"

"No, we found an au pair quite to his liking," she explained as my father gathered the blanket and headed back to the taxi. "The Don—that's what we've been calling him lately, it suits a king parrot don't you think?—The Don didn't care for the first two, but the third girl we interviewed he took a real liking to. I think it was her hair. She was very blond, and he seemed to enjoy plucking strands of it. But then, coming through customs, there was a bit of a ruckus."

"A ruckus?" This did not bode well. My mother is not one of those people who only seemed big when you were a child, she *is* big—big voice, Cliffs-of-Dover bosom, and the kind of fast-moving vigor that makes people half her age step aside. "What sort of ruckus, Mom?"

"Some awful man was trying to smuggle exotic animals into the country, and—"

"And your mother just *had* to see what was what." My father was back, carrying an ominously large, blanket-draped something.

"And here was this gorgeous, darling . . . anyway, the animal-control people said they were overflowing already, and since Sophie's birthday is coming soon—"

"Mom, what did you—"

There was a squawk as my father unwrapped the blanket and opened a shipping box with ventilation holes punched in it.

"Come on out, little fellow," my father coaxed.

Little? Out climbed a scarlet parrot the size of your average Thanksgiving turkey.

"Isn't he a beauty?"

"But, Mom, we don't have a cage or food or—" Any desire to own a parrot whatsoever.

"Parrots don't really need cages, they don't fly all that far." Far? How far was far? "Although you might get one just so he can have a bit of personal space. He can perch on a branch tonight, and tomorrow your dad will make a proper stand for him. None of those purchased affairs. He'll need something much bigger, with natural branches. You know, they need something varied to grip. Those standard dowels just give them arthritis, from holding their claws in the same position all the time. And look, isn't it lucky, they were selling bags of sunflower seeds at the airport store, so we're fine for tonight."

"But what about our other pets? We have two cats now, you know."

"Oh, don't worry, he can take care of himself." Looking at the talon-size claws, I didn't doubt it. I was more concerned about him swooping down and carrying Bonnie and Clyde off to his aerie on top of the china hutch. Not to worry, my mother explained a little scornfully, that was falcons and eagles I was thinking of. Parrots didn't *do* kittens. They did, sometimes, chew through phone cords, but that was just their way of saying they needed more toys to play with. I tried a different approach.

"Mom, I'm not so sure this is the right gift for Sophie. You know, small animals don't live all that long. That's why we've never had gerbils. I don't want to put her through the trauma of losing a pet a year or two from now."

"But that's the best part," my mother said with her winning smile. "Parrots can live anywhere from thirty to fifty years! He'll probably outlive us all!" There was a cheering thought. "By the way, in all the hubbub, I forgot to ask, we're not coming at a bad time, are we? We just got to thinking how much we missed you, and how much we wanted to see your new house, so—"

"It's great to see you, Mom," I said, hugging her. "How long can you guys stay?"

"Oh, two weeks at least, after coming all this way. Of course, we'll spend some time with Barb and Jay and the boys too."

"You'll be here for the party, then," I speculated none too happily.

"Party? Fantastic! I'll make my spinach dip in a bread bowl. Everyone always loves it. And your father can tend bar!"

"Just show me where the ice bucket is!" My dad grinned.

What was it they'd taught me in Lamaze classes? Deep, cleansing breaths? It was no use. Just as in childbirth, I'd forget everything the minute the parrot feathers hit the fan.

I worked up several ways of putting it. *Mom, I love that spinach-bowl thing, but we're having so many people, I hate to see you do all that work . . .* Or, *IM's supplying everything, so why should we?* And my fail-safe fallback, *Tom's boss is coming and he has a terrible allergy to spinach and several other foods, so let's let someone else poison him.* But I didn't need any of them. As soon as she saw the *mousseline de veau* and *parfait de canard* on Chef De Navets's menu, she sighed and said, "Well, maybe another time," in a way that made me hug her and positively beg her to make her special spinach bread bowl just for us, even though I hate spinach in almost any form, including that one.

Unfortunately, my dad and the bartending was a different thing. He had his bow tie and signature red vest all ready to go, and there was no dissuading him. When the first platoonlike squads of cleaning people and glass and tableware rental companies began to descend, he swung into General Patton mode. And once Jeff handed him our walkie-talkies and showed him how to patch into the computer network so he could relay questions and commands throughout the house, it was a completely lost cause. *Party Planner number two? This is Bartender number one. I have a van here with four hundred champagne glasses from a*—pause, scrabbling, mumbled voices—*a Tip-Top Table Toppers of Bloomington. Are we clear for delivery? Repeat: are we clear to accept delivery?* Mom must have seen me roll my eyes because that afternoon she convinced my dad that now would be the perfect time to visit my sister, Barb.

"Don't you worry about a thing," Dad assured me as I handed over the keys to my car. "We'll be back bright and early the day of the party, in plenty of time to get the wait staff organized."

Kate, meanwhile, had been right about my success with the Golden Valley Girls, and I was booked for a speaking engagement every day leading up to the party.

"Can't we space these out a little?" I asked.

We were sitting in Kate's office at IM. She looked calm and almost annoyingly comfortable, sipping an espresso fresh from her personal, desk-side machine. I'd thought the office IM gave me was pretty nice, until I got acquainted with Kate's. The more you poked around, the more little surprises there were. A cabinet slid open to reveal a TV/DVD hookup. On stressful days, Kate said, she would turn the lights down and watch a few minutes of some movie—her eclectic mix included *Wall Street*, *Woman of the Year*, *Working Girl* (she *did* look uncannily like Sigourney Weaver), and *Gone With the Wind*. More often, she surfed briskly from the Food Network to HGTV to Discovery Daytime to daytime soaps. Kate was always on the prowl for product-placement opportunities, checking to see which shows were doing it, and if there was an opening for IM and its five thousand top-selling products.

"Space out your personal appearances?" She looked at me in full surely-you-jest mode. Kate had a low threshold for whining and weaseling out, and I was rapidly approaching it. From time to time, she reminded me of what a big deal, big investment, big opportunity this was, in a way that made me feel distinctly second string. And I didn't want to be second string.

"It's just that there's so much going on this week, getting ready for the party. Somebody should be there to sort of oversee things, don't you think?"

And that somebody, I gathered, was not about to be me.

"I'm sorry, but it just isn't possible, Annie. Look." She pushed one of Lucie's color-coded calendars my way. "You're booked solid. The week after the party, you're off to Chicago, Boston, and Toronto. Then you're back for just four days before you do that Women in Food conference in Atlanta. On the twentieth, there are those congressional hearings on synfoods. I got you on that, and since it hardly makes sense for you to come home between Atlanta and Washington, I'm working on a mall opening outside Philadelphia to fill the gap."

The gap? What gap? I felt tired just listening to it. And had she said something about a congressional committee? Visions of Oliver North and Linda Tripp being grilled flashed in my mind. "What about congressional hearings? Do I have to take an oath? I don't think I can——"

"You just have to read a statement. Easy. But I *do* see what you mean about someone being at your house to supervise. Let me see what I can do about that."

So just when I was thinking that I might be miraculously freed from making chocolate crepes *à l'orange* for the Restaurateurs of the Greater Twin Cities—which I admit was a fantastic opportunity for our product line—I got an e-mail from Lucie saying she'd come up with a fantastic solution. The Hastings-Delano Labs' proposal to use BTC in a weight-loss drug had gotten a tentative green light, and they'd just begun working on insert pamphlets to accompany Better Than Thin. She, Tom, and a whole fleet of higher-ups from the advertising, sales, and marketing divisions were meeting daily. Lucie's genius idea was to move the meetings to our house so she could personally oversee both the progress on the insert and the party preparations. Who better, she asked, to field questions from the kitchen and supervise Camera 10, to reconnoiter their setup? It made so much sense that I couldn't protest, but the idea of Lucie flitting around my house with her headphones, cell phones, PDAs, and long legs made me feel inexplicably glum.

Each afternoon or evening I came back from wherever I'd been talking, usually spattered with chocolate, to find a fresh and perky Lucie—and, I might add, an annoyingly fresh and perky Tom as well.

"Annie! Are you home already? You look *awful*," she would say, jumping up. "Here, take my seat." *Get all that weight off your feet,* her slight frown would say. I swear she scanned my legs for puffy ankles and varicose veins.

"No, don't let me interrupt you guys," I'd say and stagger off. The sooner they finished for the day, the sooner she would leave.

Stranger in a strange land, I'd make my way through our sprawling house looking for a familiar face. In the family room, people were draping buffet tables with white linen tablecloths. A team of florists was working with six-foot-tall Chinese urns and two delivery trucks' worth of forsythia. I didn't see my children and could only hope Sophie had not fallen into one of the urns. Bonnie and Clyde had been banished to an upstairs guest room for the duration, where they were no doubt happily shredding the thousand-count Egyptian cotton sheets, and Scout, who was terrified of the parrot, was sulking in Tom's study. Where the damned bird was I didn't know, but from time to time I could hear a loud and distressingly healthy squawk echoing through the house.

Ah, the kitchen. The heart of the home. So *here's* where the action was.

"Mommy! Look! He likes macadamia nuts!" For Sophs and the parrot, it had been love at first sight, perhaps because there was only a slight difference in their sizes. She promptly named him Sparks and, from Sparks's point of view, this was the best gig going. When Sophie was at preschool, he'd lounge on his perch in the great room, enjoying the early spring sunlight that filtered through the windows and, when the mood took him, sampling the rare and exotic trees that Outdoors Indoors, our houseplant service, spent hours watering, spritzing, potting, and feeding. When Sophie was home, he'd ride around the house on her shoulder, surveying his domain like a vividly dressed pasha visiting the bedouins. No wonder he looked smug—he spent more time enjoying the place than any of the rest of us had time to. Now he glared at me arrogantly and took another beakful of the macadamias I'd paid $23 a pound for at Byerly's. No wonder rich people went broke. There were so many unanticipated ways to do it.

I walked over to where Jeff was sitting and ruffled his hair. He'd started to hate having me do that, but today he was so engrossed he didn't even flinch. "Listen to this, Mom. 'When the wind kicks up and the water is choppy, this is the boat to have. The Triton TR21 is designed to ensure a soft, dry ride, and even on the most blustery days will maintain stability in the water.' Did you hear that, Mom? The blusteriest days! Dad says we can try it out as soon as the ice goes."

Jeff's eyes glowed; his hair picked up the light. My bright boy, so vivid it almost hurt to look at him. He'd practically memorized the bass-boat manual, and there was something so lovely and innocent in the way he scanned Minnetonka for signs of open water.

"Mom?"

"What?"

"If I get, really, really good with the bass boat this year, can I have a bigger one next year?"

So much for innocence.

In the kitchen, Minka was making cinnamon toast for Jeff, Sophie, and, no doubt, Sparks as well. Her blond braid swished in indignation, her white-blond brows were grimly lowered.

"Is it the parrot, Minka?" I asked. It had taken only one or two nanny horror stories from other mothers to convince me I'd do almost anything to keep Minka happy. "I'm sorry, I know it's a nuisance."

"Parrot is A-okay!" she said, slamming down the plate of toast and whirling around. Really, the end of that flying braid could leave cuts, like the tip of Zorro's whip. "It's that woman with the wires! Look, look! *Look!*"

She jerked open the refrigerator door and I saw deli trays littered with leftover fresh fruit, cold cuts, sushi, salads. "Every day, she orders so much food! Those people eat just a little, leave all this, the next day she orders more food!"

"Don't worry, we're not paying for. It's all expensed to IM."

"Expensed is right! America is so expensed! People throw half of everything away! In Poland we—"

Oh no. I couldn't bear another story about factory workers in Krakow, transportation strikers in Warsaw, or her parents in northeast Minneapolis, especially when I'd begun to suspect that these Perils of the Polish fables had been heavily embroidered for maximum effect.

I jumped up quickly and grabbed the Saran Wrap. "You're right, Minka. It really is a shame to waste this, no matter who paid for it." She shot me a look of sulky triumph. "So why don't we wrap all this up and maybe . . . maybe, mmm . . . would you like to take it home? Do you have friends you could share it with?"

Her face lit up, her smile accentuating her broad Slavic cheekbones. "Oh, Mrs. Wilkins! So generous of you! Wonderful! So wonderful! With so much food, I will not have to buy groceries ever! Can put more money in the bank!"

I helped bag and bundle everything into her car and she drove off singing. I envied her her easy happiness, as she probably envied, however scornfully, the sheer excess of my life. Quite a country, this America.

I heard voices, a warning that the IM contingent meeting in Tom's office was adjourning for the day. Eager to avoid Lucie, who often handed me a preview list of tomorrow's to-do items, I sprinted up the stairs. I had just enough time to take a lovely, reinvigorating shower before dinner. With luck, Tom and I could squeeze in half an hour of illicit adult behavior before the effects of the cinnamon toast wore off and the children started clamoring for dinner. The mere prospect of having sex began to reenergize me. Whatever could be said in terms of maximizing our time and growing our customer base, one thing our new schedule didn't do was improve our love life. Here, fingers crossed, was a golden opportunity.

I peeled off my clothes and headed for my bathroom, enjoying the sensual feel of the thick carpet under my bare feet and wondering if I had long enough for a luxurious soak in the tub or should go for the quick shower. It hardly mattered. Just being in the bathroom was a spa experience in itself. The lighting was gentle, the air perfumed with fresh flowers that appeared biweekly, the towels warmed in a glistening hamper that gave you your choice of a warm, dry towel or a steaming, eucalyptus-scented *oshibori* at the drop of a hat. The shower, which I opted for in the interests of maximizing our romp time, had not one showerhead but a battery of them, each shooting a massaging jet of water set to your personal temperature preference. I dialed to 1, my personal code, prepared to enjoy, as I always did, watching the nozzles lower and twist to my preferred settings.

Wait a second. What was this? Flung over the towel rack of my bathroom—*my* bathroom—were two slender strips of marigold cloth with strings dangling. It had been so long since I'd worn anything even remotely resembling a bikini that I had to hold it up to ascertain that that, indeed, was what it was.

I heard Tom's footfall in the other room and charged out of the bathroom, waving the marigold scraps. "What are these?" I asked.

"Those? Um, I think it's Lucie's bathing suit."

"Lucie?"

"Yeah. She went for a swim. This afternoon."

I'd spent the afternoon under hot lights, a microphone clipped to my shirt, making crepes like someone in an infomercial while Lucie had been scissoring her long legs back and forth across the pool I'd swum in exactly twice.

"Did everyone else go swimming too?"

"We were working, Annie."

"As opposed to Lucie, who was here doing what? Taking a personal day? Checking out Spa Wilkins? Why was she in my pool?"

"She's been under a lot of pressure," he answered. "She was planning to go to her gym to de-stress, had her bag and gear in the car, so I suggested . . ." *Oh, don't defend her. Please. Do. Not. Defend. Her.* But he went right on. "With the long hours and the situation with her brother and—"

"She told you about her brother?" Two or three times since Lucie had confided to me that moment in the garden I'd asked how her brother was doing. Each time I got a shutdown, glossed-over response.

"Yeah, he's been in and out of the hospital the last three weeks. Do you know she's been to Madison and back, round-trip, three times in the last ten days?"

I shook my head. I didn't know. And I fleetingly wondered if it was even true.

"Did she ask you to go swimming with her?"

"Uh, I guess."

I put my robe on and cinched the belt. "She has a crush on you, you know." Tom tried to look shocked. His mouth opened, but the hoped for denial didn't pour forth. "Don't tell me you haven't noticed."

"Um, Annie, I . . . it isn't mutual. How could you think that? I can't help it that Lucie's infatuated." *Infatuated? I'd only used the word "crush."*

"You saw how those women in New York were. And you should have seen those ranchers' wives in Montana. I mean, one of them tried to crawl through the window of my motel room. A woman in Fargo made me sticky buns in the shape of a heart. In Minot, they had to call the police!" He smiled slightly. *Oh, don't smile. Do not.* "There's just something about me, I guess, that has this kind of effect. I guess you'll have to get used to—"

I went back into the bathroom, slamming the door behind me. I paid no attention whatever to Tom's muffled voice calling, "What? *What?*" after me.

Chapter 15

THIS NEVER HAPPENED
TO SCOTT AND ZELDA

Years ago, I saw the episode of *Thirtysomething* where Hope gives Michael a surprise party. On the surface, everything goes wrong. Michael arrives hours late and the guests get bored. Plumbing bursts. Strange Japanese businessmen appear. And yet the party is a success. Everyone bands together to staunch the flood and eat stuffed grape leaves. A fortune-teller assures Ellyn that love is just around the corner. Miles Drentell pours his meds down the drain.

My party was exactly the opposite. On the surface, picture perfect. Underneath, a seething disaster.

On any normal morning at six A.M., I was still sloughing off sleep. If I was particularly alert, I might do a quick, top-o'-the-morning surf through the home-decorating channels. On the day of the party, I was jolted out of bed at five when my parents, returning from Barb's early *to help you, dear,* set off the security alarm system while trying to get into the house. Which was just as well because it meant I was already up when they set off the smoke alarm an hour later.

At eight A.M., the first landing craft were spotted. Camera 10's twenty-four-foot moving van backed up our driveway, and a crew of at least a dozen began unloading cameras, light panels, reflectors, prompters, monitors, sound equipment, and enough coaxial cable to wire Hennepin, Ramsey, and Dakota counties.

Lucie arrived at nine, and by nine-fifteen she was in full producer mode. She was wearing a pair of DKNY stretch jeans, red cowgirl boots, a yellow shirt with tiny bronco busters galloping across it and—I did a double take when I saw it—an actual hip-hugging gunslinger's belt. Two cell phones were rammed into each holster, and pens were slotted through the cartridge loops. One headset was nestled in her curls, the other three were looped around her neck. Her Palm Pilot dangled from a bolo lanyard and she was wearing a watch on each wrist, one normal one and one countdown clock that beeped as each mini-deadline approached. By the time I caught up with her, my dad was duct-taping one of our walkie-talkies to her forearm and looking at her as if she was the war games pal he'd never had.

"Command Central? . . . This is Bartender number one. This is Bartender number one calling Command Central. Testing . . . testing. Do you read me, ComCent?"

Lucie raised her forearm and punched the keypad. "Read you loud and clear, BT number one. This is ComCent signing off. Will be in studio if you need me. Repeat urgent: will be in studio if you need me."

She vanished into the kitchen while my dad got busy supervising early arriving members of the wait staff. Everywhere I looked, there were strangers—strangers uncrating champagne glasses, strangers doing last-minute dusting, strangers ironing tablecloths, strangers replacing the dog-eared books on our shelves with a glossier selection of best-sellers. I had an urge to go after the stylist who shoved my Shelby Foote Civil War trilogy out of sight in favor of *The Cake Bible* but restrained myself.

On my way to our bedroom—now known as "Makeup/Wardrobe"— I saw Minka out of the corner of my eye. She'd returned from the school run just as the florists were bringing in fresh tulips, pussy willows, and forsythia to replace the stand-in sprays in the Chinese urns. This was the third furtive trip she'd made to her car with an inexpertly disguised bundle of the still beautiful but no longer wanted foliage. Two guesses—either it would be resold at busy intersections by various members of the Minka-

Janusz enclave during tonight's rush hour or it was destined for an overnight flight to Gdansk and Cousin Ludwik, who'd no doubt already lined up three or four potential buyers. I pretended not to see her. Not only was it futile to argue with her, but I'd grown genuinely fond of Minka and her frugality. Why spoil her fun?

I sat down in the bedroom—when had they moved the giant, adjustable chair in?—and let them go to work on me. I had a few qualms about what "flyover chic" might mean and half-expected to see myself with big hair and blue eye shadow, wearing a dress with puffed sleeves and a bow at the neck. So I was pleasantly surprised when I found my made-up self looking as if I were sporting no makeup at all, just flawless skin and a great set of cheekbones. My outfit was similarly casual—well, casual if your idea of cooking togs was indigo-slubbed silk pants and an oversize Anne Klein silk charmeuse shirt. I was about to peek in the zipped-up bag tagged "Annie: Party" when my shirt spoke to me.

"Annie, we need you in the studio. It's 10:58."

"What the heck is that?"

One of the dressers darted forward and lifted the collar of my shirt to reveal a plastic button the size of a sewing-machine bobbin.

"Isn't this cool?" she asked. "They've just come on the market. Wireless micro mikes. They send *and* receive, so watch who you bad-mouth. Lucie had to pull a million and one strings to get them."

"Annie! It's 10:59!"

"I'm on my way," I told my collar, twisting my head until I felt vertebrae pop.

"Just speak normally," someone hissed as I hurried out of the room. And, behind me, added, "She hasn't a clue. This is *never* going to work."

"Stop!" Lucie shouted. "Annie . . ."

"I know, I know," I said apologetically. "Sorry."

This was not going well. We'd been taping for two hours and had—optimistically—about twenty seconds of anything usable. I'd had my makeup reapplied twice, and one of Lucie's assistants had made an emergency run to Lenscrafters for nonglare contacts. And I still couldn't read the damned prompter without flubbing my lines.

I took a sip of Diet Coke and automatically parted my lips as someone dashed forward to blot and reapply my lipstick. "Let's try again. I'm ready."

"Roll tape," Lucie called.

"Hi, I'm Ann Wilkins, and whether I'm cooking an intimate holiday meal for thirty or hosting a large party for three hundred and fifty, as I am tonight, I want to provide my guests with the very best of everything. It's the little details that matter most. The orange-flower water I *always* wash my table linens in"—at least, that's what the laundry service told Lucie—"the centerpiece bouquet picked in my garden just minutes before my guests arrive"—In Minnesota in April? There weren't even buds on the trees yet—"the individual boxes of chocolates I love to give each guest as they leave . . . These are the touches that turn ordinary into extraordinary, and that's what I'm here to share with you today on the Best of BTC!"

Oh, this was absolute drivel. Who had written this anyway? And now I'd lost my place on the damned prompter. Again. I signaled Lucie that I needed to talk to her alone.

"This isn't going well."

"You're telling me." Lucie looked grim. The pilot was her baby. In her mind, it was already on her demo reel, the one that would get her out of IM and into television commercials.

"Look," I said. "Let's try something. Turn off the prompter."

"What?"

"Turn off the prompter. Let me just talk."

"Without a script?" She looked panic-stricken.

"Give me three points you want to make in this section. Just three. No best of everything, no orange-flower water, no individual boxes of anything. Just the two or three most important points you want to get across."

"All right, let's try it. I want them to understand that BTC is special, and they'll be special using it."

"Okay, I can work with that."

For the next ninety minutes, we rolled tape nonstop. I don't remember exactly what I said, but I remember saying it smoothly and confidently, and giving myself silent little high fives along the way. After a week of fonduing all over town, I could dip enormous strawberries with the flick of a wrist. I demonstrated how easy it was to make elegant, no-guilt almond bark using my own secret proportions of BTC (two parts bittersweet, one part milk). I felt positively competent in a way I hadn't while reading someone else's words, and when the dipped strawberries set, I gave them all a signature squiggle of BTC white. For a few minutes in there, I was as one with the Barefoot Contessa, ready to enter the arena with Martha and Julia, Emeril and Mario.

"You were fantastic! Fabulous!" Lucie said when we finally finished. "With this and some footage from the party, I should be able to put together something really impressive. You're a born cook, Annie!"

No, I wasn't, I realized, coming back to earth. I'd read the almond-bark proportions years ago in someone else's cookbook. Chef De Navets had made the profiteroles and sent them over. As for the strawberries, well, with a little practice anybody could dip a strawberry. What I *was* born to do was stand up and talk. Convey ideas. *Teach.* Something I missed more than I'd ever imagined.

When I got back upstairs, Mom was sitting in "Makeup/Wardrobe" enjoying a pedicure and facial, courtesy of IM.

"This is lovely." She sighed. "You and Tom really have hit the jackpot." She took a closer look. "Are you all right, dear?"

"I'm a little tired. I think I'll lie down for a few minutes."

"You've got fifteen," said Cindi briskly. She began stroking foundation on my mother's face. "Check the schedule," she added in answer to my raised eyebrows.

While I'd been with Lucie's crew, the blue-coded entries had yielded to yellow.

3:00   Annie shower, shampoo.

3:10   Food delivery #2.

3:15   Annie pedicure, manicure, facial.

4:00   Annie hair.

4:30   Buffet available: sandwiches, fruit, soup, juices.

5:00   *Annie makeup. Tom shave/shower.*

5:15   *Third setup (lighting, blocking, placement, etc.).*

5:30   *Annie dress. Spot pressing/alterations as needed.*

5:45   *Tom dress.*

6:00   *Annie stills & video in kitchen, w/ and w/out Chef.*

7:00   *Guests!*

Stills, video (candid). Thematic: We're giving a party!

I laid the schedule down and sprinted for the guest room.

There's a moment just before a party begins that is so full of perfection and promise you want to call the whole thing off and live in that moment for the rest of the evening. You want to spend every second floating around your unrecognizably clean and beautiful house. You want to enjoy the feeling of being freshly dressed in clothes you hardly ever get to wear. You want to nibble hors d'oeuvres with your husband and say, "Hey, we should do this *every* Friday night." You want to believe that this is your life and the previous years of eating cold spaghetti out of the fridge, of pretending to have just noticed the dog hairs on your coat, of pressing 6 now to hear your available credit/checking balance/last payment received, of saying all right, all right, we'll buy the *Marcy Goes to the Moon* video—that was someone else's life into which you'd accidentally stumbled.

That was how I felt when I floated down the stairs. And I know, from Tom's look when he saw me, that that was how he felt too. I'd been hoping for an elegant little black cocktail dress, or perhaps one in deep crimson. In fact, I had a fantasy of Lucie proclaiming that garnet would, from here on, be my signature color. So when I unzipped the garment bag pulled out a silvery white sheath, I was a bit disappointed. But only until I got the dress on. The ghost-colored silk slid over my hips with a whisper. Thanks to my bout of flu, I was very close to my BTC fighting weight. The best part was the overdress of sheer pale fabric covered with a design of delicate palm fronds. The long trumpet sleeves fell almost to my fingertips. The floaty hem rippled in scallops. Once I stepped into the strappy, barely there sandals and had a last-minute adjustment to my hair (up, not down, the stylist cried when she saw me), I looked glamorous and almost model tall.

"As soon as this is over," Tom whispered, "I'm kidnapping you and we're running away together."

"Promise?" It was the most playful exchange we'd had in days, ever since I'd stuffed Lucie's bikini in an interoffice mailer and driven to IM to drop it off.

"Yeah, see you later. Around midnight? Our bedroom?"

Now *this* was more like it. I gave him a quick kiss and hurried down for my stills with De Navets. I'd been dreading them all day, but, I told myself, with so many people around, what could he possibly do?

My cavernous and usually chilly kitchen was warm with food and people. De Navets loomed at the center in his chef's whites, and as I drew closer, I saw nervousness and perspiration on his face. He looked almost phosphorescently pale, an irradiated rutabaga.

"Are you all right, Chef?" I asked between supposedly candid shots of us conferring over ingredients and trays of canapés.

"*Un peu de nerveux.*" He wiped his forehead with a cloth. "You know my condition. Can you not understand? It is *your* fault—"

I clattered a tray before he could declare his undying lust and gave him a *let's never mention this again* look that I wasn't entirely sure he understood.

"Hold. Good."

The camera clicked, and as we hovered over *parfait de canard* and the more pedestrian pea pods with taramasalata, I noticed his hands trembling visibly. He almost seemed frightened of me. I wanted to pull him aside and tell him to buck up and get with it, but before I got the chance, Lucie came looking for me.

"Guests!" she announced, making a checkmark on her clipboard.

Thank goodness the early arrivals were people I knew—my sister, Barb, and her husband, Jay, Lyn and Dan and two other couples from our gourmet group, and a few dozen IM people.

"This is spectacular," Lyn said. "Definitely a high-water mark for our gourmet club."

"Almost as good as Charleston." Tiny Culpepper sighed. "Are those real potted magnolia trees? I'm in heaven. In fact"—she grabbed a glass of champagne from a passing tray—"I'm never leaving. I'm going to drink champers till my panties melt, and I plan to pass out right under those trees."

What was it about Southern women? They could say almost anything and sound completely innocent, as if passing out sansculotte in the floral decor—which in Tiny's case was more than likely to actually happen—was simply an endearing little caprice.

Lyn took Dan's hand. "Let's dance, hon."

And that's when I noticed that a few people actually were dancing. Dancing! In my great room-cum-ballroom, where a jazz quartet was playing underneath a canopy of blossoming magnolias. Now *that* was major.

People were arriving in greater numbers now. Unmanageable throngs, it seemed as I greeted them. Where were we going to put them all? In my old house, dinner for six had required a major furniture rearrangement. But every time I looked up, things seemed to be going remarkably smoothly. A team of three was taking coats, tagging them, and hanging them on racks. Guests dispersed throughout the entire first floor, as if they were strolling through a museum. IM had even hired a lifeguard so we could open the pool room. I'd glimpsed it from the window in Tom's office. Decorated with blossoming orange trees, tiny lights, and café tables, my mother said it was just like being home in España. The orange trees were some rare variety, and probably the only ones available in the entire Twin Cities. That was the subconscious theme of the party, Lucie had told me, uniqueness. A unique party for a unique product. And while the branches of forsythia cascading through the house weren't unique, the six-foot-tall Chinese vases they stood in were. They'd been borrowed—with guarantees of a personal guard for each piece—from a St. Paul antiques dealer.

It's a lovely party, people kept telling me, *you've done a fabulous job.* But really, it was hardly my party at all. The down-to-the-last-toothpick planning had been done by Lucie and Kate, the money laid out by IM, and BTC—the reason for the whole thing—invented by Tom. What had I done other than show up, wear the dress, and blackmail the chef who'd groped me into making my hors d'oeuvres?

"Annie, I just confirmed that Mark Dayton and his wife are coming. Will you recognize them?" Lucie had shucked her urban-cowboy outfit in

favor of a devastating lilac slip dress edged in satin. Her ever present headset was disguised as a silver headband, although heaven only knew where
she'd hidden her phone.

"I'm not sure. No, I don't think so. Where's Kate? She was supposed to
be here half an hour ago."

Kate was in charge of what Lucie referred to as CRUD, celebrity roundup and delivery. All week she'd been stroking and cajoling the biggest
names in our part of the world, and making it absolutely impossible for anyone to refuse putting in an appearance. It was Kate who'd arranged for the
fleet of limousines continuously arriving and departing outside our door,
and Kate who was supposed to clue me in as to who all these people were.

Lucie disappeared to dial her cell phone. Fifteen seconds later, I
noticed that the Palm Pilot behind a vase of lushly drooping double tulips
was glowing faintly. "On way," the screen said. "ETA 7 min."

Thank goodness. Kate breezed through the door ten minutes later,
removing her coat as she walked and coming rapidly to my aid. It wasn't
until after I'd chatted with a famous (I was told) French playwright whose
one acts were in rehearsal at the Guthrie that I even had time to ask her
why she'd been late.

"Just some last-minute fire fighting over the Canfield thing," she said.
"Worst possible timing for BTC, but I think we'll be okay."

"What Canfield thing?"

Kate looked mildly startled. "You don't know yet? It was everywhere,
even the front page of the *Star Tribune*, above the fold."

I felt a warning lurch in my stomach. "Give me the bullet."

"Don't be so dramatic." She laughed lightly. Genuine? Hollow?
Forced? Against the hum of the party, I couldn't tell. "Stop frowning like
that, Annie. It's nothing for you to worry about. I'll give you the details
later. Really, we'll be fine, so just enjoy the party."

I managed to circulate for another fifteen minutes before I broke away.
Locating our copy of the day's paper was no easy matter—I finally found
it, completely unread, in the recycling bin. Tucking it under a towel, I
dashed for the bathroom.

It was even worse than I'd imagined.

CANFIELD BRANDS ENTERS
CHOCOLATE WARS: STRIKES BIG

Edina-based Canfield Brands announced Friday that it will debut
Au Chocolate, a no-fat, no-calorie chocolate taste-alike bar on
July 1 of this year, three full months ahead of plan. The product is
designed to compete directly with International Milling's highly
successful Better Than Chocolate, whose Valentine's Day splash
netted the company its biggest ever one-day profit. "It's been
tough watching IM sweep the market," said Canfield's VP of specialty foods, Jerry Beuhl, "a little like sitting out a big football
game with an injury. Now we're back." And back big. Simultaneously with Canfield's announcement came news that the Disney
Corporation will make Au Chocolate the official low-calorie treat
of its parks, resorts, and cruise lines through at least 2005. That's a
lot of candy bars, Mickey!

I actually leaned over and put my head between my knees. What had
happened? Kate's sources had assured her that Au Chocolate was slated for
a Thanksgiving rollout, by which time we would have established BTC
throughout America. But here it was, a fait accompli, and with a three-year
Disney contract that made our Valentine's Day kiosks look like lemonade
stands.

"Annie? Are you in there? It's Kate. Let me in."

"You look remarkably calm considering that all hell has just broken
loose," I told her, opening the door. You'd think she spent all afternoon
browsing through magazines and getting manicured, not fighting for
BTC's life.

"Annie, you've got to stop being so goddamned dramatic." That got
my attention. I watched as she ripped out the story, flushed it down the toilet, and stowed the rest of the paper behind my half-inch-thick Egyptian
cotton towels.

"What happened to your sources? I don't understand. How could they
have been so wrong, when just a few weeks ago—"

"This is a problem, Annie, but it's not a *disaster*. It's bad timing and it

means we'll have to word extra hard to get BTC embedded in the market-
place. And that's exactly what we're going to do. Do you understand me?
Good. Now get back out there."

She hauled me to my feet, thumbs pressing painfully into the balls of
my shoulders. Kate, I thought, would have made a great Catholic-school
nun. The kind several friends of mine still had nightmares about. I hadn't
been talked to like that since I'd handed in a grad school paper a week late
and been told I was looking at a long career at McDonald's, the shared fate
of mediocre Ph.D.s everywhere. That was why there were so many
McDonald's all over the world, in fact. To absorb the Ph.D.s who couldn't
get jobs. I returned to the party with an odd floaty feeling—not the happy,
heady floaty feeling I'd had before but a surreal one, a sense that the whole
canvas spread before me was a stampeding machine, completely out of my
control and just as likely to chew me up and spit me out as not.

The surreal feeling intensified when I heard a vaguely familiar voice
exclaim, "This room! It says . . ."

I turned to see Claire Holmes, the semiotics expert who'd led me on
the search for the perfect message house. "I'm so glad you could come,
Claire. And, of course, I'm dying to know what this house says to you."

"You've done a *won*derful job," she said, eyes scanning as she sipped
her champagne. "It says warm, it says family, but it also says"—she held
her breath in that exasperating way of hers—"it also says *tomorrow*. It says
next century. Kubrick sumi-brushed by the Pacific Rim. I mean, those
glazed urns are just so fabulously Ming."

"Dynasty?"

She looked confused and slightly annoyed. "No, Ming Tsai, of course!
Fusion! East meets West! I mean, pea pods and taramasalata, Annie! *Think*
about it!"

So I moved off to *think* about it, preferably with another glass of Veuve
in my hand. This was turning into a truly bizarre evening. I'd stepped into
a suburban version of *Guernica*.

"Mrs. Wilkins!"

For a moment, I thought the coat person was talking to Tom's mother.
She must have come after all. She'd said she would if she could get away,

which of course meant *I'd rather clean the cow barn than spend a night in panty hose*. But maybe she'd changed her mind. After all, even the Mississippi had flowed backward once.

"Mrs. Wilkins, there's, hmm, someone who would like to speak to you."

Oh. The coat person meant me, not Tom's mother. I followed him to our entryway and found Bengt, dressed in his school clothes and carrying a small, Bengt-size briefcase, soft sided and bulging.

"Mrs. Wilkins? My mother asked me to explain that she had an emergency patient but will be here soon."

"Thank you, Bengt. I'm afraid Jeff isn't here. He's spending the night at Tony Culpepper's."

"Oh. Well, my mother asked if I could wait for her here, because my father won't be coming tonight and because Mrs. Vickers, where I usually go, is here and . . ." His plump little face began to show marked signs of unhappiness. Dangerous. Especially as there were candles and matches in almost every room in the house.

"Of course you can stay, Bengt! We'd be very happy if you did." What on earth was I going to do with him? I couldn't very well leave him alone, and Minka and Janusz had taken Sophie and Emily Vickers to see *The Little Mermaid*. Wait a second . . . "Come with me, Bengt. Actually, we need you."

His face lit up. "You do?"

"Absolutely."

We wove through the crowd, through the family room and company kitchen and back to the working kitchen.

"Wow!" Bengt said.

Servers were coming in with empty trays and leaving with laden ones. Prep chefs arranged hors d'oeuvres four at a time, while others were spreading and filling at a breakneck pace. Chef De Navets was nowhere in sight, so I grabbed one of the prep people.

"This boy can cook—use him!" I released Bengt, adding in a low voice, "No sharp knives, though, and keep him away from the flambé."

I wove and mingled for another hour, trying to forget Canfield Brands and Disney and looking, usually in vain, for people I knew. In the great room, the jazz quartet was still playing, and people were still dancing. In fact, my mother had requested "Tico Tico" and was demonstrating her version of the tango. The crowd around the bar was constant, and I saw several men walk by drinking my father's signature gin and tonic double-lime highballs. Tom, I noticed, was reprising the I-am-a-hunk role he'd perfected in New York, and, more recently, taken on the road to the Dakotas and Montana. Every time I spotted him, he was surrounded by a different crowd of women, which made me feel like India Wilkes watching Scarlett grab all the attention at the barbecue.

The plain truth was, I couldn't forget about Canfield. Everybody was having a better time at this party than I was, and all I could do about it was smile and talk about how proud and happy I was to be part of the IM team.

"Hello, darling." My mother waved, breaking through the crowd. "I just popped into the kitchen for a minute and saw the strangest young man in there." I explained all about Bengt and asked if she'd gotten a gander at our chef as well. "Oh no, I don't think I saw him. I'm sure I would have remembered."

"Hmm. I wonder where he is. I didn't see him when I dropped Bengt off. I hope he's not throwing some temperamental tantrum, just because he's De Navets."

My mother froze. "De Navets? Jean-Paul De Navets? Who had that restaurant in the seventies?"

"Yes. Did you and Dad ever eat there? Was it good?"

"It was fabulous. But then there was that horrible incident, and deaths—or so they said, but I never believed that part of it."

You'd think I would have learned, by this point in the evening, to keep smiling and not ask questions. But, of course, I had to know, so I asked. That's how I learned that, not long after Mangeons Les Paysons had earned an unprecedented (for the 1970s Midwest, anyway) two stars, there'd been an incident involving Brie and killer bacteria, giving a whole new meaning to the restaurant's name. It wasn't De Navets's fault, but he took full responsibility. He'd even tried to commit suicide, leaving a note that read "*Viens,* Vatel!"

"And then," my mother continued, "he disappeared. Became a recluse.

Remember the Eberts, who lived on Fairchild Lane? Her daughter's a tax attorney in St. Paul? I still write to them at Christmas, and Bev says her daughter says De Navets won't go out, he's so terrified of being recognized, of cooking for the public. And if he does go out, he gets the most horrific palpitations. Tell me, dear, how did you persuade him to—"

I handed her my champagne glass and ran. What had I done? Where *was* De Navets? And where was Lucie? Come to think of it, I hadn't seen her for quite a while, either.

"Chef!" I cried, sprinting through the kitchen. "Chef! Chef! *Chef!*" But the spot where Chef was supposed to be standing was occupied by Bengt. Bengt standing on top of three empty glass racks and piping mousseline onto toast rounds as if he'd been doing it all his life. I tried to sound commanding as I demanded, once more, to know where my chef was. Nervous nods and apprehensive glances guided me toward the dry-goods pantry. The door was ajar and in the dim light the first thing I saw was Lucie's lilac slip dress kneeling on a large, rolled-up mattress. The mattress, of course, was De Navets, sweating, gasping, and curled into a fetal position.

"Why didn't you call me? How long has he been this way?" I knelt down. "And what are we going to do?"

"I've got it under control, Annie."

It didn't look as if she did, though. "You should have told me right away, Lucie."

"Oh really? Do you have some special insight into what we should do here?"

I shrank back. She was right, I didn't have the slightest clue as to what to do. She, at least, had experience dealing with her brother's medical emergencies.

"Are you sure he isn't having a heart attack?"

"He's having an *anxiety* attack, Annie."

"Can't breathe," De Navets gasped.

"I know, I know," I said guiltily. "Hang in there. Would you like to go to a hospital?"

The hideous, choking gurgle that rumbled through De Navets's body suggested that this was not, perhaps, the best suggestion I could have made.

"Wait a second," Lucie said. "Didn't you tell me that that big-deal shrink Estelle Mackenzie was coming?"

"But she isn't here yet."

"Well?" Lucie said, giving me a look. "Get her!"

"Bengt!" I called over my shoulder. "What's your mother's cell number?"

Lucie extracted her phone and headset and handed them to me.

"Estelle? This is Annie Wilkins. Lovely, thanks, but I'm wondering if you could come as soon as possible. We have a bit of a crisis here and— half an hour? Could you possibly make it twenty minutes? Wonderful!" I glanced at Lucie. "Do you think he'll be all right until she gets here?"

"Put it this way. Since I've been with him, he's tried to grope my breasts twice and put his hand between my knees once. I think he'll survive. So get back to the party. And don't tell anyone about this!"

Estelle arrived in less than ten minutes, concluding her session with the emergency patient via Blackberry as she flew through the door. "You can count on my complete discretion," she assured me. "I'm a virtual Pandora's box of secrets when it comes to the rich and famous. Now, what do we have here?"

She squeezed into the pantry and sat down beside De Navets. I knew I should go back to the party, but my parents were now showing everyone how to jitterbug, so really, who would miss me?

Estelle took De Navets's hand. "I'm wondering, now, even though you're not feeling well, if you could tell me a bit about your home."

"My home?"

"Yes. I've always been curious about what it might be like to grow up in France. Ever since I read *Le Petit Prince*. What color was your bedroom? Was it blue, or perhaps gray?"

I waited for De Navets to gasp, to break out in a fresh round of sweating and rigid tremor, but instead he said, "Puce, *madame*. And there was an old yellow armoire." He sighed pleasurably and closed his eyes. "And a little blue rug with a fringe."

Fifteen minutes later, we knew about Chef's beloved dog, Matisse, and his sister's fiancé who sometimes brought him chocolates and sometimes brought him cigarettes. It was the most amazing litany of drivel I'd ever heard. Remarkably, it seemed to work. Within half an hour—after recounting, in excruciating detail, how *grand-mère* had taught him to make *pommes frites* and *anguille en ail*—his breathing was so normal that Estelle managed to get him up and on his feet, one huge arm draped around her like a stole.

"I'm going to take Chef over to my house and have him lie down for a while," she said.

"Thank you." This was the absolute capper, not just on the evening but on my life as a hostess: I was grateful to Estelle Mackenzie. "Can I, mmm, do anything to help you?"

"I don't think so," Estelle said, "although it would be better if we could leave by a side door."

"Of course, of course." Just as they were disappearing into the night I saw De Navets pinch her bottom. She didn't even flinch. In fact—was it my imagination? Did she actually move closer? "Wait a minute!" I cried, starting after them. "What about Bengt?"

"Bengt?" For a minute, I wasn't entirely sure she remembered who he was. "Oh, send him along in the morning. It wrenches my heart to do without him, even for one night, but I have my hands full here. *C'est la vie!* I have my responsibilities and he has his. He'll understand. He's extremely perceptive and gifted that way. And lucky you—he'll probably insist on making *pain perdu* for breakfast!"

So, after coming to grips with the fact that I'd forced an agoraphobic to confront his single worst fear, after I'd led Estelle through a brief but humiliating explanation of my folly, and after I'd left her eleven-year-old pyromaniac of a son in charge of the most expensive kitchen in town, I rejoined what was left of my party.

"Annie, where were you?" Tom asked when the crowd of women around him thinned enough for us to make contact.

"Mmm, a little mix-up in the kitchen." A tray whirled by. I nabbed my fourth glass of champagne in the last fifteen minutes and gulped.

"Your hair's starting to come down." He leaned close. "It looks sexy."

More Veuve! I needed at least two more glasses to even begin to put the evening behind me. Oh good, there was the waiter, he'd seen me.

"Why don't I just leave this here with you?" The waiter smiled at me and I smiled back. There were only three glasses on the tray.

"Why not indeed?" I asked, taking the tray from him.

By the time all my guests left, I felt almost as if the party had been the success everyone kept telling me it was. Only my parents and Barb and Jay remained, along with Bengt, who was helping the kitchen staff clean up.

"This really is the most gorgeous house," Barb said, giving my hand a quick squeeze. "You've done a wonderful, wonderful job, Annie. I'm so proud of you."

I wanted to explain that I hadn't done anything. My life had been seized by IM and tinted, teased, and coiffed into a fantasy I barely recognized. But her eyes were so full of innocent pride in me I couldn't possibly tell her that. Instead, I squeezed her hand in return and said, "Well, I may have the house, but you're going to have the veterinarian son!"

Barb's face tightened. "If we can ever afford it."

And that's when it popped out of my mouth. "But you can!" I picked up another glass of Veuve. There *was* something I could do after all. "This calls for a toast. Because Tom and I were talking, and we've decided, now that we finally can afford it, we'd like to buy your half of Aunt Edith's property."

Suddenly everyone was looking at me. Including Tom. Especially Tom. Well, we *had* talked about it, hadn't we? And hadn't he seemed to agree with me?

"We'd take over all the taxes of course, and of course you could still use it whenever you wanted to. It would be just like owning it, only you'd have the money to use. And . . . and we'd create a clause in our wills so that it would eventually pass to all our children, in a kind of trust and . . ." Okay, so this was something we hadn't talked about. But it was still a good idea, wasn't it?

"Oh, Annie!" There were tears in Barb's eyes as she flung her arms around me. "Oh, thank you, thank you, thank you! I'm going to call Rob right now and tell him, even I have to wake him up! This is the best thing anyone's ever done!"

Over her shoulder, I saw Tom set down his glass and walk to the other end of the room. Even through my haze, I could see how angry he was.

Chapter 16

PAIN PERDU

Bengt did insist on whipping up a batch of *pain perdu* the next morning, taking us all further into the heart of darkness. I found him clattering around in the kitchen shortly after sunup, an hour at which I would have much preferred to be working on my marriage. But my marriage was avoiding me. Tom had hunkered down when I got into bed the night before, feigning sleep and rolling so far away from me on our raft-size pillow top that I was actually as alone as I felt. Whole families of medieval peasants could have bedded down in the space between us.

"Good morning, Mrs. Wilkins. Where do you keep your cinnamon?"

"Good morning, Bengt. And why do you want cinnamon?"

"For the hard sauce that goes with the *pain perdu*. I will also need a double boiler, half a cup of Southern Comfort, and demerara sugar if you have it."

In the sloping morning sun, a note in my mother's handwriting lay on the counter. "Dad and I have gone for a power walk around the lake, back in a few hours." No one wanted to be in my house this morning, not even me.

"Tell you what, Bengt. We aren't really a hard-sauce kind of family. Let's just have syrup."

"What kind of syrup, Mrs. Wilkins?"

"Whatever's in the fridge."

I felt so indebted to Estelle for removing De Navets from my pantry that I figured keeping her peculiar—*gifted!*—child occupied as long as possible was the least I could do, so after a brief negotiation, Bengt agreed to forego the hard sauce if I would take him to the store for Jamaican ginger syrup. But SuperValu had never heard of ginger syrup, Rainbow was out of it (Who bought this stuff in the first place? How could they be *out* of it?), and the parking lot at Cub was so packed I chickened out (Were they coming in from the Dakotas to shop these days?). Bengt would not be dissuaded, however, and when he observed, as we drove along toward Byerly's, that the Aunt Jemima's Butter Rich Lite we had at home was "rather hopeless," I understood afresh why the other boys took such pleasure in hurling him to the ground.

The mission lasted well over an hour, Bengt having decided that he also needed a new battery for his watch and, as long as we had the car out, some hard-to-find caffeinated mints. It must have been about the time we were cresting toward what Bengt described as a "head shop" in Dinkytown that Lyn called our house to see when we wanted Sophie back. At least that's how I reconstructed it later. I pictured Tom waking to the ringing phone and realizing that a) he was completely alone in the house, and b) he had no real idea where I was. I wondered if he thought, even momentarily, that I'd persuaded my parents to leave for Spain and take me with them.

I didn't have the courage to ask. As we forked up our *pain perdu* with Jamaican ginger syrup (discovered at last at a natural-foods store across from the caffeinated-mint head shop), a sort of deathly silence hung in the air. Tom and I barely exchanged ten words, and Bengt was completely lost in the excitement of his butter rosettes. He didn't seem to mind or even notice that Tom and I weren't speaking. Maybe it seemed normal to him. Or maybe just having two parents in the same room was enough to make it a better-than-ordinary day. As soon as he polished off the last butter rosette, he suggested we inventory and database the nonperishables in both kitchens, entering the precise quantity, location, use, and date of purchase in cross-indexable fields. I declined, but was wondering what we *would* all do next when Jeff came home from Tony's. The sigh of relief Tom and I breathed was the only thing we'd done together all morning.

"Oh, super, Bengt's here!" Jeff cried. "Can he stay? I want to show him the mpeg editing program Janusz is teaching me, and how you can make Britney Spears sing with a guy's voice."

"Of course, if Bengt calls and it's all right with his mother." I made a stab at living up to my son's graciousness. "You know Bengt is always welcome."

A few minutes later, I had to grab the phone when I heard Bengt saying, "Mother? Mrs. Wilkins has invited me to live here."

"Did you see this?" The sound of Tom's voice addressing me in a nearly normal tone was so startling I almost dropped the syrupy plates I was stacking in the dishwasher. He was reading Saturday's recap of the Canfield Brands story.

"Last night. It broke yesterday, but I think IM was keeping it from us until after the party."

"Don't you think it's sort of a coincidence? This story comes out the same day as the party?"

I told him about the conversation I'd had with Kate after the *Wall Street Journal* article, and how she suspected there might be a corporate spy.

"Does she have any idea who?"

"She said she had some possibles, but she never talked specifics. But this could be anyone, couldn't it? Not even a spy. I mean, everyone at IM knew about the party weeks ago. And tons of people outside IM knew too—rental people, the florists, the guys who delivered the liquor, the security guys. What if one of them's married to someone at Canfield? I mean, it's the kind of thing you'd share with your spouse, wouldn't you?"

As soon as the words were out of my mouth, I realized my mistake.

"I don't know, Annie." He closed the paper. "I don't seem to be too up on what you do and don't share with your spouse these days."

There it was. Did I pull the Band-Aid off with one clean jerk or did I leave it and hope it floated off in the tub?

"Let's talk about this," I said, and sat down before he could get up and walk away. "I know I was wrong last night. So I'm going to call Barb and tell her it was a mistake. We can't follow through, at least not now. We don't have the money."

"It isn't the money, Annie."

"And I realize we should have talked about it again and made the decision together."

"So what happened?"

"I don't know. I really do not know what got into me, other than the Veuve, that is. I just wanted to *do* something."

"Mission accomplished."

"I told you, I'll *undo* it. I'll call Barb now."

He looked at me. "You can't call and tell Barb that. You saw their faces, we can't go back on your word, especially since they've already told Rob. We made the offer, we'll stick by it."

"Really?"

"Yeah. It's basically the right thing to do."

Relief made me giddy, playful. "So you're not divorcing me? As a wife, you think you'll keep me around a little longer?" I ran my finger over the top of his hand.

He stood up. "It's the right thing to do. That doesn't mean I like the way you went about it. So you'll just give me some time, Annie."

"But—"

The morning after my parents headed back to Spain, Tom left for California. I saw him on the Jay Leno show. Lucie—I was sure it was Lucie—had had his hair subtly spiked for the L.A. crowd. He was wearing a shirt and tie I didn't even recognize. When I called his room after the show, Lucie answered. I could hear laughter and music in the background, and, not having been invited to the party, I hung up without saying anything.

I opened Excel to my portfolio spreadsheet and booted up the Quicken program, pleased to see I had almost two hours before I had to show up at I Do '02!, the bridal expo being held at the Minneapolis Convention Center. I would be promoting personalized, decorated-in-the-bride's-choice-of-colors BTC bridal-favor chocolates, a personal appearance that at least would not involve melting, dipping, or swirling anything. Nor would it involve, as Lucie had suggested, me dressing as Mother of the Bride as I strolled among the sylphlike models. Kate had intervened on that one and gotten me a lovely pale linen suit with *broderie anglaise*. It was hanging upstairs, pressed and ready to go. More than enough time for another cup of coffee with the CNBC *Squawk Box* boys.

The truth was, being a single parent wasn't all bad. I don't just mean rolling up to Broadway Station to eat the best pizza on earth for dinner. A certain latitude of freedom held sway all round. Laundry went unsorted, makeup went unapplied. Books didn't quite make it to the library on time, and when I missed an appointment with Jeff's prospective orthodontist, I took such a lofty and beleaguered tone that the receptionist didn't even charge me for failing to cancel in advance.

With no husband around and a general inattention to detail, I could really take my time with certain tasks, like keeping the books and paying the bills. I'd always been the one to do it, mostly because I liked fooling around with numbers. I liked my lined ledger book and the *ka-ching ka-ching* sound the Quicken cash register made whenever I entered a transaction. When I paid all the bills and took stock of our savings, holdings, and debts at the end of each month, I felt like Carol Kennicott's husband in *Main Street,* surveying the coal and potatoes snugly binned in his white-washed cellar.

This month my sense of satisfaction didn't quite reach those Kennicottean levels. How had we managed to spend so much in such a short time? Boats, love seats, glassware, china, silverware, new furniture for the pool room, a John Deere riding lawn mower. The credit statements read like the consumer price index. So many things I'd bought—or urged Tom to buy—with the reassuring thought that I'd pay for it with our stock profits. Or, if worse came to worse, I'd just cash in the stock. But this morning, bill-paying day, almost every stock I'd bought was worth less than I'd paid for it. Even Exxon, which had moved up to $44.38 in the first month I owned it, had done a surprising turnaround, sinking almost back to what

I'd paid for it and temporarily wiping out $49,000 of our $53,000 profit. I did some figuring and realized it would be cheaper to pay the card minimums and hang on to the stocks for another month—or even two—until they went back up. Even with the heavy interest rates, we'd still make money.

Besides, I now had Inside Information.

It had happened at Kate's last IM luncheon. Attendance had not dwindled with the sinking market, and I suppose everyone else kept coming back for the same reasons I did—financial anxiety mixed with dietary escapism. Who in their right mind passes up a chafing-dish dinner? It would be like passing up a trip in Mr. Peabody's time machine. At Kate's, there was never so much as a single bean sprout in sight, which I suppose is why Lucie never attended. The eggs Benedict fumes alone would have felled her, not to mention the ham loaf. There was usually a dessert table as well, and the first time I saw Kate's footed cake plate adorned with white angel food cake filled with a tunnel of raspberry mousse, I'd shrieked with delight. Embarrassing but true.

"Raspberry Road to Ruin!" I cried as if greeting a long-lost friend. The cake had been a Pillsbury Bake-Off winner somewhere around 1975. I remembered begging my mother to make it for my birthday and her telling me not to be ridiculous, it took three pints of fresh raspberries. "Do you know how much our electric bill was last month?" she'd added, as if I were supposed to connect the dots.

Of course, Kate was probably billing everything to IM.

"I thought we'd have something light today," she'd said last Saturday, gesturing toward a sandwich loaf layered with tuna, egg, and ham salad and frosted with tinted cream cheese.

There was more, of course. Baskets of ripple chips and a big relish tray. A layered chicken salad. Famous chocolate wafer cake and checkerboard cookies for dessert. Layered food seemed to be the theme of the day. And sure enough, that was what Liz Sienko, from finance, had chosen to talk about. Investment layering. I wondered if anyone besides me got Kate's wry joke. And I wondered if anyone besides Liz, a woman who could juggle multiple columns in her head, understood what investment layering was. I took notes when she said that, with the market now in a "valley-peak-valley" mode, investment layering could be applied to individual investors, yielding enormous benefits at tax time. I struggled to understand exactly how this would come about. I wasn't even sure it applied to me, since my peaks were turning out to be almost as low as my valleys. From where I sat, it was mostly Death Valley Days, with buzzards circling overhead and the Old Ranger nowhere to be seen.

After half an hour of listening to Liz, squinting at her silhouette against the blue-white glare of Lake Josephine glittering beyond Kate's sliding balcony doors, I had a splitting headache. I slipped to the back of the group and discreetly tiptoed up the stairs to Kate's bathroom.

My head was pounding. I slid back the glass of the cabinet above the sink. I couldn't find Kate's aspirin, but I did learn she was a fan of Shiseido's High-Performance Care line. There were no aspirins on her dressing table, either, or in any of the drawers. Maybe she was like me and just kept them where they were really needed, at the computer. I stepped across the hall to her office.

Kate was the only person I could think of other than J. R. Ewing who actually kept decanters of liquor, glasses, and an ice bucket in her office. Other than that, the place was a model of boring tidiness. A dark, polished mahogany desk with a green banker's light, maroon leather in and out boxes—ho hum. There was an accordioned bank statement lying beside the keyboard, which my glance fell on during my aspirin sweep. According to the statement, she was doing a lot better than we were. There was a whole list of deposits. Big ones. $9,500, $9,950, $9,750. And beside each deposit, in Kate's no-slant script, were two- and three-letter notations. "CB," "PFE," "HD," "MYG." And sometimes there were notations beside them. Like "___GM" and "[AMD]."

All at once, I got it. Kate's investments. She must be day trading. And boy, was she making a lot of money. I wanted to write them down, but that felt too sneaky. If Kate wanted to share her strategy with us, she would. Besides, there were at least a dozen symbols I already knew and could remember, at least until I got to the car and could write them down— Chubb Corporation, Pfizer, Home Depot, Maytag. She was making a lot more money in the market than I was. I wondered what the sideways arrow between "WAG" and "GM" meant. Oh, she must have traded Walgreen for General Motors. I made a mental note to look up AMD.

"Oh, there you are, Annie." Kate was standing in the doorway.

"Do you have any aspirin?" I asked. "Or Advil? I looked in the bathroom and couldn't find any, and I thought maybe there'd be some in here. You must think I'm snooping."

What made me say that? If I'd lived during the French Revolution, I'd probably have run after a tumbrel and fought to climb on.

Kate laughed. "You'd make a hell of a snoop. The Advil's right there in front of you." She picked up the bottle I'd overlooked, nestled right beside the statement, and tossed it to me. "I'll get you some water."

That night, when I got home, I created a spreadsheet with Kate's stock symbols. I spent hours, the next few days, looking up charts on-line and plotting Kate's picks against my own. Some had performed marginally better, some hadn't. But Kate didn't throw her money around, those bank deposits didn't lie. After sleeping on it overnight, I sold most of my portfolio and bought Kate's. The only thing I kept was the Exxon. If it had gone up and down five points in a month, surely it would make them back. Wouldn't it?

The week after Tom returned from California, he came home from work in the middle of the day driving a new car. I was among the first to know because I too came home early that day. I'd done a particularly nasty and stressful cooking demo at the Mall of America, where I'd been heckled by a freakishly burly group of women who claimed that BTC caused "rebound hunger." "I Gained Fifty Pounds Eating Better Than Chocolate!" said one woman's XXL T-shirt. "Synfoods—the Agent Orange of the Pantry!" cried another's. A third woman had affixed a bumper sticker to her backside. "*Avoir du Pois* Courtesy of International Milling." Two or three of the larger women even tried to charge the platform I was standing on. A truly fearsome sight—all I glimpsed were glazed eyes, frizzed perms, and Care-Bears strained over breasts the size of frozen turkeys. I was rescued by a cadre of TCRM women who formed a protective cordon around me. Members of the Total Caloric Replacement Movement had been showing up more and more often when I spoke or demoed, and the presence of these sticklike, overexercised, feverishly enthusiastic women was almost as distressing as the Lane Bryant crowd. The curious thing was that the two groups dressed almost identically, in huge tops, spandex bottoms, and marshmallowlike New Balance shoes, even though their collective body weight differed by hundreds of pounds.

"You're such a pro at these now, Annie, you don't need me to hold your hand," Kate had taken to saying. She meant, *I've got better things to do than watch you make more chocolate tacos at the Crystal Community Center. Let me know if anything exciting happens.* I didn't blame her, but I did feel justified calling her from the sheltering murk of the A&W Patio Restaurant while I waited for my hecklers to disband.

"Oh dear," she said when I'd finished my plaint. "Poor Annie."

The day Kate had taken Sophie and me to lunch at the Rainforest Café and treated us to girlish manicures at L.A. Nail seemed to have happened a long time ago. Now it was just me and my chicken strips.

"So I'm going straight home," I said, picturing the oasis of her office, an office that had recently acquired a lovely, hand-tied Aubusson rug. "I know, I was going to come by to work on those *Story of Chocolate* galleys, but really, I just need a shower and a Cinnabon. So could you send the galley pages home with Tom? Or messenger them?"

"Absolutely. I'll get them right out. As, long as we have them back the day after tomorrow. I'm sorry, Annie. I know it's a short turnaround, but it's the publisher. I got you as much time as I could."

As an act of rebellion, I stopped at the garden center and bought several flats of bedding plants. Spandexed women and impossible deadlines aside, spring had arrived—or at least the mild, sullen, and sunless weather that passes for spring in Minnesota. I would blast through those galleys and spend tomorrow afternoon in the backyard, troweling up the unwarm earth while Scout loped around and got himself muddy.

The thing in the driveway was so unexpected and so blindingly red that I almost ran into it. A Porsche. A Porsche 911 Turbo in Zanzibar Red to be exact. I knew my husband's dream car when I saw it.

Tom was polishing it with a scrap of suede I recognized as Sophie's Pocahontas costume. Outgrown, but couldn't he have used a sponge? She'd looked so cute that Halloween.

"Gee, hon. To think we'd been talking Toyota Supra."

"Don't get excited," he said. "I didn't buy it. IM leased it for me—for us. How great is that?"

How great is that? One of Lucie's phrases. But I didn't say anything. It was the first time he'd looked happy since the night of our party. I was willing to set aside the Pocahontas issue too.

"Well, you must have been a very, very good boy for them to get you a toy this expensive."

"They were pretty happy with the California trip. Plus, I've come up with something Lucie thinks can really work for us."

Plus. Another Lucie construction. "What?"

"Remember how upset we all were about Canfield's deal with Disney? Well"—he unloaded a bag of mulch while I picked up a flat of pansies— "I've been working on a power bar using BTC and—get this—Lucie thinks she can make a deal with the IOC to get it named the official sports bar of the next Olympics."

When we got all the plants unloaded, I took a close look at the Porsche. The Zanzibar Red finish was as thick and smooth and flawless as the best nail polish there was.

"So, if I'm a good girl, will you take me for a ride?" It was the first time I'd ventured into let's-be-naughty talk since the party.

"Sure," he said, returning my glance. "But if you're a bad girl, I'll let you give *me* a ride."

We left the kids with Minka and scooped the loop in Minnetonka. Everything about the car was fun. Fun to sit in, fun to ride in, fun to be seen in, fun to look at. But it wasn't just the machinery that buoyed me. It was sitting beside my husband and laughing, it was switching places and having him lean over to show me what was where. It was the spring wind and the feeling of *start* that surrounded us.

Chapter 17

THE OUTER BANKS

I looked at the dashboard clock. I *did* have enough time to get to Jeff's school, didn't I? The First Annual Truffle-Off at Just Truffles lasted twice as long as Kate had told me it would. Nor had she mentioned that the panel of judges was a first-grade class from White Bear Lake Elementary—a plan someone, clearly, had not thought through. *Bradley sneezed on my candy! My tooth came out in the sticky one! I forgot my consent form! Melissa wet her pants!* Not only did the woman from the Just Truffles shop have home-court advantage, but she'd produced a peanut-butter-and-jelly truffle against which my mocha mist held little sway with six-year-olds.

Now, splattered with chocolate and bested in the truffle wars, I was stuck in traffic on Grand Avenue. And I'd promised—*promised*—to pick up Jeff and his friend Tony after school and take them to the Ridgedale mall. Today was the last day the Minnesota Twins would be there signing baseballs, and I'd already had to cancel yesterday and the day before. So this afternoon was *le ultimo*—my last chance to prove my worth as a mother.

How had this happened to me? What had happened to that vision of the busy yet flexible parenting experience I'd been promised? Tuesday, I'd put Jeff off because I was urgently needed at a pretzel-dipping event at the

Apple Valley Kmart. Wednesday, I'd spent office time at IM working on advertorials for *Bon Appetit*'s Thanksgiving issue, then gone to address a group of senior Girl Scouts (described by Lucie as a "women's business group") whose primary interest was knowing how many calories you saved if you used BTC in s'mores instead of Hershey's.

The slower we crept along in the giant bottleneck, the more impatient I became. I'd spent so little time with my children lately. My friend Lyn had been the one to point out that Sophie's shoes were too small, and Minka had had to remind me—twice—that Jeff needed an eye exam. Worst of all was the afternoon I'd had to send Minka to Sophie's parent-teacher school conference. This is how I learned, via a written note, that Sophie's issue was that she had no issues. She had consistently "failed to show signs of the verbal rudeness or sassiness that signaled a healthy challenge of authority." If I'd been there, I would have pointed out that Sophs challenged authority plenty, she just did it on a more sophisticated level. But I wasn't there. I was telling executives at the Nor'star Dairy Company that I was looking forward to promoting their BTC ice cream, yogurt, frozen yogurt, and chocolate milk more than I'd ever looked forward to anything in my life.

How long could this go on?

I slid my hand into the white bag beside me and pulled out a handful of Just Truffles—dark chocolate, caramel, maple nut. Nice of that woman to give me a consolation prize. And handy, since I was starving and BTC no longer did the trick. I'd begun to secretly sympathize with the women who complained about rebound hunger and wondered if BTC would eventually have to carry a warning label: "Prolonged use may lead to eating contents of large-size family refrigerator."

Beneath this welter of discontents, another discontent had begun to throb of late, one I kept tamping down but was, day by day, increasingly nodding a quick hello to. I was beginning to feel the way the rebound-hunger women looked—frowsy and marginalized, done up in a slogan-bearing T-shirt and sent on my way. All of my married life, Tom and I had been partners. Now I was feeling distinctly distaff. Why was I the one dipping pretzels and flacking yogurt while he was talking to CEOs and being interviewed by *Fortune?* I knew the answer, Kate had told me a hundred times. Based on focus groups, consumer-generated feedback, and mappable buying patterns, this is the way it was. There was no grand plan, only a business plan. The more strawberries I dipped in Premium BTC White, the more yogurt I handed out, and the more Girl Scout groups I addressed, the more I felt like one more female worker bee buzzing hopefully around my husband, fighting with all the other bees for his attention. And let's face it—on a day-to-day basis, as far as BTC was concerned, Lucie was a more important bee than I was. So was Kate, but she didn't buzz around Tom the way Lucie did.

And so my thoughts went on, one problem tailgating the next, just like the traffic morass around me. I glanced around and knew everyone in every car, every single person, was going through the same thing I was. Details, worries, unfinished business, ordinary problems that for one reason or another would never be solved. It was only a matter of time until America, engine of democracy, ground to a complete halt. The same way my washing-machine agitator with Sophie's shoe caught underneath it had eventually pulled in all the other clothes and blown the circuitry of the whole machine. When you thought about it, it was a great metaphor.

What time was it again? I was never going to make it to Jeff's school. I scrabbled for my cell phone and dialed Minka, who of course did not answer. She never answered on the first three attempts, to make sure whoever was calling was serious and not a telemarketer, wrong number, or some other miscreant bent on wasting our anytime minutes. If I could get her to answer, she could pick up Jeff and Tony after Sophie's school run, a little late but better than never. When I couldn't get her to answer on the fourth try, I knew she'd already left to pick up Sophie. Once Minka was behind the wheel, you could hit redial until your fingernails fell off and never raise a response, a safety-first policy that made me suddenly want to rip my hair out by the roots. Which I might as well do. At the rate we were inching forward, it would have plenty of time to grow back.

It took me another forty-five minutes to get to Jeff's school, and by the time I arrived, even the last of the teachers was leaving. Jeff and Tony were nowhere to be seen. I executed a U-turn in the parking lot and headed home.

The minute Sophie heard my key in the lock, she came bowling down the hall, a sheaf of papers in her hand. "Mommy, look!" she cried, flapping the papers. "This is my portfolio!"

Ever since I'd convinced Minka that Sophie wasn't wasting film when she played with the digital camera, the presses had been rolling. Janusz had installed an elementary version of Photoshop and now Sophs was layering, cropping, and tinting with abandon. She presented me with a Marilyn-by-Warhol-ish series of Sparks the parrot in fluorescent red with a yellow background, chartreuse with a purple background, azure with a plum background, and orange with a gray background.

"I like these, Sophie."

"I'm going to sell them."

"Oh really? How much? I'll buy one." A nickel? A dime? An extra week's allowance?

"One hundred dollars," Sophie said. Seeing my dismay, she added, "You can put it on a credit card."

I looked over her head at Minka. "Did Jeff come home from school?"

She shook her head, and I knew exactly what he'd done. He and Tony had walked three blocks from the school, hopped a city bus, and gone to the mall on their own. Even though Tom and I had told him, on several occasions, that he wasn't allowed to do either one of those things without permission. A year ago, if I didn't show up, he would just have come home. But this year wasn't last year, and that willing little person had begun to slip away from us.

I grabbed my car keys and headed for Ridgedale. This was the first time Jeff had ever defied a rule we'd laid down, and I was going to have to deal with it without Tom. It didn't help to know that the whole thing could have been avoided if I hadn't had to do that truffle-off, if I hadn't been stuck in traffic, if I'd shown up like I'd promised.

I spotted Jeff and Tony almost immediately. They were under the "Meet the Twins!" banner, eating corn dogs and waiting in line. I lurked in the background until they got their balls signed because I didn't have the heart to drag them out of the line. Or the energy. Mall smell—that vivid mix of stale air, new merchandise, food, and cleaning chemicals—was making my head pound. Or maybe it was the dozen Just Truffles I'd eaten in the car. If only we could go the wait-until-your-father-gets-home route. But Tom wouldn't be back from Seattle until the day after tomorrow, and although I flirted with the idea of a family phone conference, I just didn't think it would work. For one thing, Tom was rarely in his hotel room. Unlike my personal appearances, which ended with me packing up my gear in forlorn silence, everyone who met Tom seemed to want to take him out to dinner.

I shot out of hiding as soon as they passed through the line and tapped Jeff on the shoulder. He whirled around and his eyes widened, not with fear but with the sheer embarrassment of having his mother touch him in public in a mall. Tony, embarrassed for him, looked away.

"We're going home," I said. "Right *now.*"

I waited until we dropped Tony off before I said anything else. Then I let him have it. "How many times have Dad and I told you you're not allowed to take city buses alone?"

"I wasn't alone. Tony was with me."

"Don't talk back to me. And don't play dumb, because you know exactly what I'm talking about." There it was. The script my mother had read me twenty-five years ago. The one I said I'd never read to my own children. My own children, who would never do anything even remotely defiant, because I would have raised them in a completely different way. My own children, with whom I would always calmly talk things over. "What did you think you were doing, Jeff?"

"I was being resourceful."

"Yeah? How do you figure that?"

"You *told* me, remember? You said that with you and Dad so busy, I was going to have to be resourceful. Do things for myself. So I did."

I glanced at him in the rearview mirror. He had on his Lassie look. Bright eyed, attentive, completely guileless. This was a problem. I *had* told him to be resourceful. Now I cringed, remembering how competent I'd felt that day, how smugly certain I'd been that I'd handled the challenge without resorting to Estelle Mackenzie–style speeches about the family as corporate enterprise.

"But that didn't mean doing things we've told you not to do. You know better than that. Didn't you know how worried I'd be when I showed up and you and Tony weren't there?"

"But how was I supposed to know you'd show up?"

"I promised I would."

"You promised yesterday too. And the day before that."

"Yes, I know. I'm sorry, Jeff. Something came up with work."

"Something *always* comes up with work. You and Dad might as well not even live here!" He turned his head to stare sullenly out the window. "Hey, why'd you turn here? You never turn here."

I hadn't meant to make the turn onto Mudjekeewis Lane, but for the last few days—ever since Lyn had told me a car with IM plates was parked in Estelle Mackenzie's drive—I'd been cruising the house. "Oops," I said. "I guess I goofed."

Surreptitiously, I snuck a peek. Yes indeed. Through the smoked windows of the town car, I could just make out the slumped form of a bored chauffeur.

"Bengt's mom is having an affair with that cook, if that's what you want to know."

"Jeff!" Do not swerve off the road, I commanded myself. Deep breaths. Positive outlook. No rash assumptions. "Do you even know what that word means, Jeff?"

"It's what married people do. Like, when they've been married awhile and they don't spend time together anymore. Then they sleep with other people."

My knuckles whitened on the wheel. "Not all married people, Jeff."

"So am I grounded?" he asked when we got home. And added, "Mom, you've got chocolate in your hair. *Gross.*"

Whose child *was* this?

———

The person I wanted to ground over the next few weeks was me. Or Tom. One of us needed to be put under house arrest or we might never see each other again. Someone—and I can only suppose it was Lucie—had crafted a schedule for us that was a marvel of time management, as coldhearted as a five-year plan from the old Soviet Union. In May and June, we spent less than one day a week under the same roof. I missed Sophie's debut as the lead in *Sky Blue Jellybeans*, Curious Minds' year-ending dinner-theater event. Tom shared a table with Lyn and Dan Vickers, and said Sophs brought an unmistakable dimension to the role. Emily Vickers, as a cherry-licorice whip, also got good reviews. More serious was Tom's missing Jeff's sixth-grade graduation, something he'd been looking forward to for months. Tom called from Omaha, but of course it wasn't the same. When Jeff opened his present—skybox tickets to the Vikings home opener in September—he started fretting about who would take him if Tom and I were both busy. My assurances that our schedules would surely be calmer by then didn't convince any of us.

I reached a personal low point one night in Atlanta. It was in the middle of a marathon week spent hopscotching across the South, doing mall appearances and noontime news shows from Biloxi to the Outer Banks. I'd had to suck the head fat out of a crawfish in New Orleans, which didn't turn out to be nearly as objectionable as the 236 times an Emeril wanna-be shouted *Bam!* into my left ear, the one I was now going deaf in. By the time I arrived in Atlanta, I was disoriented and sleep deprived, and felt so much like a dispossessed person I could have brought whole new insights to the course on twentieth-century diasporas I used to teach. As I stepped off the happy-talk news set, I realized that I had no idea where I was. I searched for a name tag, a logo, anything. Was I at ABC? NBC? Fox? CNN? Who had I just talked to? Had I called the talking heads by their right names? I now understood why so many powerful, stressed-out executives found it necessary to maintain a flock of personal caretakers.

Someone shoved a cell phone in my hand.

"Surprise!" cried Lucie. "I've got the greatest news. Do you have a pencil? Never mind, I'll e-mail you. You're going do a quickie guest food column for the *Journal-Constitution*'s Sunday section. Isn't that fab? But you've got to get it in by tomorrow, five P.M. Call Doris Gaights, she's the editor, and tell her when you'll be e-mailing."

My protests—that I was exhausted, that I'd agreed to do something (though I no longer remembered what) that involved getting up at five A.M. tomorrow, that I had hoped to maybe leave Atlanta on an earlier flight so I could spend a few extra hours with Tom—carried all the weight of empty BTC wrappers. *It's only fifteen hundred words, Annie. You've got plenty of time. You're not scheduled for anything more tonight, are you?*

So I slogged back to my hotel, pouted through a room-service meal, and opened my laptop. Lucie had sent me the *Journal-Constitution* info, along with an attachment ominously named "new schedule," which I decided to lose in the downloading process. Jeff had also e-mailed me an attachment, which I opened immediately. The screen dissolved in a field of stars and neon streaks that morphed into footage of Jeff and Sophs.

"How cool is this?" Jeff called. "Janusz taught me!"

Sophie waved at me with sparkly blue fingernails.

"Hi, Mommy! Look at my fingers! 'Bye, Mommy! I miss you! Sparks pooped on my shoulder!"

I watched the minute-long mpeg three more times, touching my fingertips to my children's shifting faces on the screen. How had two such beautiful and perfect beings sprung from my body? I went to work on the food column with a lump the size of a golf ball in my throat.

"This schedule is a nightmare," I complained to Kate days later. "Tom and I never see each other. My children are growing up without me. Do you know what Sophie did last night? I set the chicken and carrots on the table and she said, '*Maman, on a oublié le caviare.*'" Kate laughed. "It isn't funny. When I asked her why she thought we'd be having caviar for dinner, she told me it was expected among the upper classes. Only she didn't say upper classes, she said BCBG. I honestly think she believes we live somewhere in Paris. Thank goodness I can send her to public school next fall."

Kate was still smiling, so I plowed on. "I have new furniture I haven't sat on, mountains of paperwork I haven't done, bills I haven't paid—when's that market going to make that turnaround, by the way?—and I can't remember the last time the four of us ate a meal together. I haven't had sex with my husband in a month, and I'm not sure I could stay awake even if I got the chance. I'm serious, Kate. I don't know how much longer I can keep this up."

Kate leaned back in her chair, no longer smiling. Concerned, in fact, which gave me a tug of satisfaction. I spread my wings and ranted on. "Tom still has his work—his *real* work—and even when he has to travel, Lucie and a cast of thousands are there with him. What am I doing? I'm on the great American mall tour, alone. Do you know, according to Lucie's schedule, I'm supposed to drive to Ely next week and back in one day? Do you know how long it takes to drive to Ely? I mean, why not just give me a suitcase and make me sell the damned stuff door-to-door? Why does Tom get all the great appearances out of this? Why does everyone love my husband?"

Surreptitiously, Kate nudged the door closed with her foot. "You mean the Lucie situation?"

I felt my skin contract, like the skin on a burn victim. *The Lucie situation?* It was one thing for me to know that Lucie had a crush on Tom, but the idea that everyone else did too stung me. I remembered Lucie's bikini, slung like a territorial marker over my shower railing. Should I have protested more? Less? Tom and I had always been so solid, so absolutely sure of each other, one of those couples who told each other about their crushes.

But that was before.

For the first time, I realized that there was a *before*, a line we had all crossed over without realizing it. Before BTC and IM. Before the almost perfect house we inhabited alternately, as if sharing its custody. Before the toys we still hadn't paid for. Before Jeff began giving me the *So what?* shrug and Sophie began insisting that Minka, not me, brush her hair in the morning. Before product demos and Q ratings and separate schedules. Before the time—*now*—when I could seriously wonder if there might be more between Tom and Lucie than a fleeting one-way crush.

"Kate—" But I couldn't finish. It was too pathetic, sniffing around for clues about my husband.

Kate intervened adroitly. "Look, Annie, don't worry about Lucie. I've got my eye on her. For several reasons, not the least of which is that she's bucking for my job." Kate gave me a wry smile. "I'm sorry about the mall marathon. This isn't the way we planned it, as you know. And we've had a tougher time than we anticipated selling a cooking show, which we hoped would let you stay home more. Lucie thinks we can still make it happen, but we have to keep you out there, make you better known, create some buzz."

"Do you think it will work?"

"Yes, but sometimes our Lucie tends to overlook the human element. To tell the truth, I didn't realize things were quite this bad for you. Let me see what I can do. Maybe there's a way to lighten things up a little." She flipped open her day planner and looked at the calendar. Like me, Kate had an ingrained dislike of Lucie's color-coded schedules. "We can't cancel the Des Moines thing next week—we've been trying to get that meeting with BHG for months. Then there's the shoot for *Martha Stewart Living*— you'll be home for that, but Tom will be in Seattle. The first week in July— well, that's the good news."

I brightened. "Summer vacation?"

"Sort of. Calder Payne wants you to come to New York to do his show."

What show? I'd never heard of Calder Payne and was instantly suspicious. For a dizzying split second, I imagined myself on some kiddie show, pelted with chocolate or, worse, dressed as a giant, child-friendly chocolate marshmallow. "Who's Calder Payne? I thought you said Jacques Torres wanted me?"

"Calder Payne's the *new* Jacques Torres. Came here from London two years ago. Now has restaurants in New York, L.A., and Boston. He's just starting to franchise his line, otherwise he'd never bother with the Food Network *or* us. Believe me, Annie, we're lucky to get on with him. He's the next big thing. Cuter than Torres too. And the best part is, the whole thing will be a twofer for us—the Food Network is doing a daylong taping that's going to air on Labor Day weekend, and the Calder Payne segment is "Red, White, and Chocolate." We can't very well cancel on that. So hopefully we can do the show *and* get a meeting with the Food Network head of programming. We've been holding back on that footage from your party, looking for the right opportunity to approach them. This could be it. If the shoot goes well and they take an interest, we might get them to commit to a pilot. And if a series catches on, or even filler spots, your mall days will be over."

I felt relieved. I should have talked to Kate weeks ago. I was going to make it through this after all.

I drove home in a cloud of optimism, went straight to my office, shut the door, and switched on the computer. This was a good time to tackle my bill paying. Now, while I at least had the illusion that my life was under control. I switched on CNBC too, to see if the market was ending the "small, corrective," downturn that was now well into its second month. Nope, it was still heading down. In my newly clarified state of mind, this no longer bothered me. In fact, last week at Kate's, Peggy from market research had talked about using market dips as buying opportunities, thus lowering your cost basis. I'd missed the get-together but got the point from the recap e-mail Peggy had sent—if you bought 100 shares of J&J for $50, and another 100 when the price dipped to $40, you'd actually lowered your overall purchase price to $45. With this in mind, I got on my Scottrade account and bought more of the stocks in my Kate portfolio. Even if they just returned to where they'd been when I bought them, I'd make money. What a fantastic system.

As always, trading made me feel happy and secure. The stock market was like Tom and me. It had bumpy patches and lows, but they were only minor glitches in a long series of ups, an overall trajectory of climbing steadily to higher ground.

I got out my checkbook and started opening bills. AmEx was demanding a six-figure sum due on a nonrevolving account. How primitive! What had I been thinking? How shortsighted I'd been not to accept their generous offer to upgrade from green to the realms of gold and platinum, where Tom and I truly belonged. All because I'd balked at paying a heftier annual fee. But it wasn't too late. I went on-line, hit "Apply Now," and five minutes later received a new American Express Platinum account number. Then I rolled the whole six figures over onto it and paid the minimum due. I hadn't felt so smart, so efficient, or so completely in charge of my life for months. For good measure, I picked up a few new MasterCards and Visas as well, and rolled half the balance of our current cards onto them, thus lowering our interest rates for a six-month introductory trial period, not to mention scoring more credit. On the interest savings alone, I was making money hand over fist. And when you considered how much our investments were due to rebound over the next few months, carrying the debt forward in order to sell into a fall rally was really the only prudent thing to do. More than prudent. It was the kind of gutsy, contrarian move you needed to keep afloat in a market like this. I mean, the Dow closed down another 128 and it didn't even bother me.

Chapter 18

BREEZING UP

"I'm sorry my husband wasn't here for this."

"No problem," said Sid, the stylist for the Martha Stewart shoot. "We got some terrific stuff. Besides, we're used to shooting around the husbands." He glanced mischievously at the location director. "Husbands are *so* last century."

"Pay no attention to him," said Caitlin, shaking back a mane of dark auburn hair. She was so young she sparkled. As did the cocktail-onion-size diamond on her finger. "He thinks I'm retro for taking the plunge."

"Not retro, darling, just in the wrong business."

"Magazines?" I asked.

"*Lifestyle,*" Sid said. "Do you know, nine out of ten readers would much prefer knowing the intimate details of a celebrity's house than of her marriage?"

"And you've certainly got a lovely house here," Caitlin interposed swiftly.

Well, yes. And it was even lovelier after the crew from *Martha Stewart Living* got done with it. Ditto the house's owner. Now it was late afternoon on the longest day of the year, and for eight solid hours my house and I had been the center of a dozen people's attention—brushed, buffed, cosseted, rearranged, and set to sparkling. It had felt wonderful. More than wonderful. *Important.* For whole minutes at a time, I'd felt exactly like Martha herself, the impeccably coiffed head of a glowing consumer empire. Now the shoot was over, and when my little coterie departed, I was going to be left with a pumpkin instead of a carriage.

I offered everyone sun tea and served it in the pool room, the coolest room in the house on a warm day.

"Go for a swim if you want," I said expansively. "We've got extra suits galore."

Sid looked at the pool wistfully, but Caitlin shook her head. "Thanks, but we've got to get going soon."

I noticed she'd found my file on Aunt Edith's property, which I'd been going over the night before. We'd had to have the land resurveyed and reappraised to buy out Barb's share, and the firm of Grinnell & Lutz had sent us comprehensive photos of the acreage that was now wholly our own. The land itself was more beautiful than I remembered. As for the house—let's just say the years hadn't been kind.

"I hope you don't think I was snooping," Caitlin said, smiling. "I just noticed the pictures of this house and . . . well, you know the magazine always does a huge Halloween issue, so I'm always on the lookout for a truly rundown, falling-apart place like this. Haunted houses are such fun, aren't they? Besides which, the land around it is gorgeous. Where is this? Is it yours?"

I nodded. "About four hours north of here. It's usually snowed in by October, though. We want to tear down the house and rebuild."

Caitlin studied the pictures for a few more minutes. She was one of those tall, smooth young women who seemed to have been born polished and sophisticated. Fingernails as perfect as almonds, teeth without a single discernible flaw.

"Can I make a suggestion? If you're going to rebuild, this other location would be much better." She handed me a shot showing a black pine hill that sloped down to a wide terrace. The terrace ran flat for a few hundred feet before the downward slope continued, as if the hill was taking a little break. "You could do a great arts-and-crafts rustic here. It would look as if the house was flowing right out to that hill. Besides," she said, handing the picture back to me, "the hill would insulate the whole back of the house. It would cut your winter fuel bills in half."

I felt a little flush of excitement. "I was thinking of something arts and crafts," I told her. "Nothing too grand, more bungalowish. But I'm not sure how it would look."

Caitlin whipped out a small tortoiseshell case that flipped open to reveal a scratch pad and a tiny pen. She wrote down a name and number and handed me the slip of paper. Rice paper, I noted. Thin and delicate but durable. "This is Martha's architect. He's an absolute genius. He's in New York. Call him, see what you think. And I'd like your recipe for sun tea."

I stared at the slip of paper, not unmindful of the fact that I was now on a recipe- and architect-swapping basis with someone in Martha's inner circle. "Actually, I'll be in New York the week after next," I said, trying to sound as if the Big Apple was a regular stop for me. I wanted to add that I was doing a show with Calder Payne, but her cell phone started vibrating and it turned out to be Martha, wondering how the shoot had gone and why they weren't on the road yet and could someone please scan and fax the pictures as soon as possible because the art department wanted to see what they'd have to work with. Caitlin never did get that sun tea recipe.

"You look happy," Tom said when he came home two days later. "That Marsha thing go okay?"

"Martha, not Marsha." I wasn't completely sure my husband even knew who Martha Stewart was, which made me feel lonely. How could anyone not know Martha Stewart?

"Whatever."

I wanted to tell Tom all about the shoot, but was afraid I'd end up blurting out that I'd gotten the name of Branston Arche, Soho architect, and had made an appointment to see him while I was in New York. Tom and I had talked in a vague way about "doing something" with Aunt Edith's house "someday," but I don't think Tom would interpret that as yes, let's hire an architect. So I decided to keep my mouth shut, at least until the stock market rebounded. Which of course it was certain to do any day now. Kate had told me all the indicators were there.

Whistling, brushing his ever lightening hair back, he flipped open his suitcase and began tossing soiled shirts into one heap, dry cleanables into another. As he tugged a favorite old T-shirt over his head, I noticed that he had achieved the first glimmer of a washboard torso. And when his head popped out of the top of the T-shirt, I noticed that he was grinning.

"You look pretty happy yourself," I noted.

"We've got the deal, Annie. Almost. We have a few more things to iron out, but it's beginning to look like the BTC Bolt Bar will be the official sports-nutrition bar of the Olympics."

No wonder he looked so happy. Where was the next Olympiad? Greece? He'd probably get to go. I'd be home showing elementary school teachers how their first-, second-, and third-graders could make teddy bears and Christmas tree ornaments from BTC miniature chocolate marshmallows, toothpicks, and flexi-straws. Lucie had recently discovered that there were twenty million potential customers in this buying niche. At five finished teddies per bag of marshmallows, convincing el-ed teachers to do just one marshmallow craft per school year could result in an additional revenue flow of millions.

"That's great, honey." I was happy for him, of course. I just would have been happier if I thought there was any chance of me getting to go to the Olympics too.

He sat down on the bed beside me. "Yeah, it's great. But the really great thing is this. We're going to Paris. You and me. For a whole week. Well, almost a whole week."

"You're kidding." But I knew he wasn't, and a slow champagne tingle started perking through me.

Born about a decade too late, Tom and I had missed out on the drugs-sex-rock-and-roll travel odysseys of the baby boomers. By the time we finished grad school and got down to the business of repaying student loans, having kids, and getting a mortgage, there was exactly enough money left for a trip to the Wisconsin Dells. The closest we'd ever gotten to international adventure was the Sunday travel section. Until this minute,

I hadn't minded, except when faculty peers would bring out hideous wine-glasses with attention-demanding explanations like, "Suzanne and I bought these in a little *villaggio* in Neive-Alba, from a dude who ran the *cucina locale* and made his own grappa . . ." Which always made me want to serve *my* hors d'oeuvres out of a plastic Barney dish while reminiscing, "I got this in a Kmart outside Stillwater the day we stopped for corn dogs and the kids threw up on the way home. Cocktail meatball?"

I hadn't missed Europe—or hadn't thought I had—but suddenly I wanted to be alone in Paris with my husband. I wanted to wander for hours and discover some little café we'd remember forever. I wanted to ride those thrillingly Euro-looking boats on the Seine. I'd save whatever Euros were in our pockets when we came home and carry them around with me for months. I'd bring Sophie a copy of *Bonsoir, Lune,* and Jeff some cool French video game. And most of all, I'd make love to my husband in the sexiest city in the world, far from the reaches of BTC, Lucie, and all the other women with crushes on him. It would be exhilarating, like reclaiming territory after an enemy attack. For the rest of our lives, Tom and I would be like Rick and Ilsa and four hundred million other couples, able to look at each other with secret smiles that said *Yes, but we'll always have Paris.*

"When are we going? August? Everyone says Paris is mobbed with Americans in August, but I don't care. I can't wait."

"You don't have to. We're going now. Lucie and I have a one-day meeting with the IOC people on July first, then a breakfast meeting with some French food conglomerate the next day. Do you know, they think demand for BTC Bolt Bars will be so heavy during the games that IM won't be able to ship fast enough? So they're looking for a manufacturing partner who can ship throughout Europe. You can amuse yourself for a day and a half, right? Then everyone else is flying home and we get the rest of the week to ourselves. IM's picking up the tab, and if Minka can't stay over, we can leave the kids at my mom's, or Barb and Jay's if you'd rather. I checked with them both." He was beaming, clearly proud of his detail work. "Are you surprised?"

"Yeah." Shock was more like it. The kind of shock Pearl Harbor folks out for a Sunday stroll must have felt when they noticed that the planes overhead all had zeroes on their wings. "Did you say July first? And we'd come home, like, what, the sixth or seventh?"

"Okay, so we'll miss the Fourth here, just this one time. We'll make it up to the kids."

"We can't."

"Sure we can. Everyone else bribes their kids, why can't we?"

"No, we can't. *I* can't." There was a knot in my stomach the size of a BTC Toys 'n' Prizes Easter egg. "I have to be in New York on the third through the eighth. There's that live cooking thing on the Fourth, then I speak to the Independent Chocolatiers of Connecticut on Saturday morning, and Kate has us meeting with the Food Network people on Monday. Did you check my schedule at all?" I was going to cry. Or throw something. How had this happened?

"I asked Lucie. She said she didn't see a problem."

"Not a problem for her anyway," I muttered.

"What does that mean?"

"Nothing. Can't we make it a week later?"

He shook his head. "Sorry, babes. This is the window, the week of the Fourth. It took Lucie ages to set up the IOC thing, and the next week we go into high planning for the Olympic campaign. I'm supposed to develop some special-flavored chip to go in the Bolt Bar so the ad department can market a special Olympic Power Chip Bolt Bar. What do you think? Cinnamon? Cherry? According to Lucie, women who don't work out and eat Bolt Bars between meals will account for a third of our sales, so it has to be a female-friendly flavor. What do you think? Orange, maybe?"

"Banana," I tried to say, but the word came out with jagged edges.

"I'm sorry, hon." He put his arm around me and kissed my hair. "We'll go to Paris another time."

I gave vent to a full-fledged pout. "I don't want to go to Paris another time, I want to go *now*." I should have felt juvenile and embarrassed. In fact, I felt much better.

"I know, Annie," he said again. "We just have to make the best of the time we do have together." He pulled me a little tighter and slid his hand under my blouse. "I don't suppose you feel like fooling around, do you?"

"No, I don't suppose I do." It wasn't his fault. But I couldn't go from Paris to frisky playmate in 2.5 minutes. Especially when I was still wondering why Lucie had told him there was no conflict with my schedule. I stood up quickly. "You won't stay on in Paris without me, will you?" I had a sudden, alarming vision of Lucie slotting herself into my place, convincing Tom that there was no reason to let a paid-for suite go to waste.

"Of course not."

"Good."

In the murky light of dawn, my sinuses clamored with the ache of disappointment. The na-na-na-na-na-na refrain of *You're not going to Paris* had played all through my sleep. In fact, it had hit the top forty and assumed golden-oldie status. I could not get over it. I was *not* going to Paris. Of course, I hadn't been going to Paris two days ago, either, but it didn't matter then. Now, every time I thought about it, I saw Lucie gamboling down the Champs-Elysées with my husband. I pulled the covers over my head.

"Maman! Maman! Leve-toi!" Sophie shrieked, bursting into the room. She was wearing her blue-and-white-striped T-shirt, the white clamdigger pants my mother had bought for her in Spain, and, in lieu of a beret, her white sun hat with the brim turned down. Half Apache dancer, half Gilligan. I turned to catch Tom's reaction and realized that Tom wasn't in bed with me. He came in behind Sophie and Jeff. They were all signing "Frere Jacques," only instead of Brother John, they made it *"cher Maman."*

"What is this?"

"Since we can't go boating on the Seine, we're doing the next best thing. Get up."

Fifteen minutes later, the four of us were out in the middle of Minnetonka in the bass boat. The cabin cruiser would have been more *à l'esprit de Paris,* but Tom had been giving Jeff lessons and they were both so eager to show off that I couldn't refuse *le bateau rouge*. And it was a beautiful day, the kind of day when the land of sky blue waters really lives up to its name. There *is* a special blue to most Minnesota lakes, although I don't know why, and, to tell the truth, we'd rather not have too many outsiders realize that it's more than just a good photo-tint job. Minnetonka can be a water-bound traffic jam on summer weekends, but that morning the lake was nearly empty, so unpopulated that we felt a jolly camaraderie with our fellow boaters, totally unlike the *Hey, eat my wake!* attitude that sometimes prevailed.

Sophs and I sat up front, ostensibly watching for rocky outcroppings but, in fact, pretending we were voyageurs. *Ce n'est pas chic!* she'd protested, picking at her orange life vest. Which was almost like red. Which, I told her, was the preferred color of the voyageurs who paddled all over Minnesota singing not only "Frere Jacques" but "Sur le Pon d'Avignon" and "Alouette" as well. So now our bass boat had become a canoe, and Sophie—*je te plumerai!*—was scouting *rendezvous* sites for our luncheon portage. I saw that Tom, amidships, was watching for rocks, and I relaxed as the warm sun settled around me.

There was a glow coming from the back of the boat and it was my son. He was trying to slouch casually on the wide seat, as he'd seen older boys do, but he couldn't quite manage it. His shoulders were tense with excitement and the pleasure of adult responsibility; his hand never came off the throttle.

Like most lakes in this part of the world, this one had been scraped out by glaciers. Forget the tidily curved, bowl-like rims of Iowa lakes, ours were frilled extravaganzas of bays and inlets and barely tethered coves. From the air, it looked like a spilled thermometer, mercury beading off in all directions. There were parts of Minnetonka that weren't even attached to Minnetonka, and parts that you could reach only by threading your way through a necklace of bays, circling for miles when the crow-flies distance was less than half a mile from the part of the lake you were already in.

It was a tricky lake, with its shallow waters, boat-crunching shingle reefs, and unmarked islands. I wouldn't have tackled it for a hundred bucks, but my son was fearless. As we left our bay and struck open water,

Jeff opened the throttle. We skimmed across the lake, the front of the boat lifting and bumping, the water flying up in drops that made Sophie scream with delight.

"How am I doing, Dad?" Jeff asked. The sun was bright and he squinted into it.

"Here, navigator," Tom said, taking off his Oakleys and handing them across.

Jeff slung the cord reverently around his neck. The preteen sullenness vanished from his face and for a fleeting second the shadow of the man broke through. I couldn't take my eyes off him. Tom caught my eye.

"The once and future," I said.

"What does that mean?" Jeff asked.

"That you're a good sailor," Tom told him.

"So, like, after this I can take the boat out alone?"

The adult vanished. My boy was back.

"Not until you're older."

"Jeez, Dad." But he was laughing, and Sophie was singing, and our red bass boat was a throb of glory beneath the summer sky.

We beached on a sandy-shored island, stripped down to our swimsuits, and splashed into the water. The statewide inability to swim always baffled visitors almost as much as the sight of toddlers on ice skates. All these lakes and all you do is paddle around? I told them it was *because* of the lakes. Swimming pools stood in direct opposition to the number one tenet of Minnesota child rearing: *Get outside and get some fresh air!* But you didn't learn to swim in lakes. You learned to splash, float, stay out of the way of boats, get pushed off a dock and paddle back to it, but you never got a shot at those long, clear lanes pools offered. Even my husband swam with his head above water. I made a mental note to sign both kids up for swimming lessons. Especially Sophie, who would be heading off into deep water if Tom hadn't been hanging on to her.

He saw me watching. "Go on," he urged. "I'll keep an eye on them."

So I dove under and let the world slide away. I kicked, surfaced, and felt as sleek as a seal. I rolled on my back and watched my arms cartwheel, flinging diamond drops at the sky. The backstroke was the only athletic skill I'd ever possessed, and for weeks after winning a blue ribbon at Camp Tanadoona in 1978, I'd nurtured a fantasy that involved gold medals, my picture on Wheaties boxes, and being on a best-friends footing with Nadia Comaneci. I did a few more strokes, waiting for the surge of freedom I remembered, but it didn't come. I kept listening for my children's voices, lifting my head to make sure they were all still there. I flipped over and swam back to the boat.

Jeff surfaced beside me. "You know what, Mom? There are minnows here. I can see them. Look."

He pulled off his swim goggles and made me put them on, but all I could see was blond shafts of light and the white flash of his feet and legs. Jeff made me duck and look again and again until I finally saw them, darting like tiny silver leaves. I grabbed his toe and pinched it, hearing his *Yowwwch* before I even surfaced.

"What was that?"

"Snapping turtle," I laughed, splashing him.

He splashed me back and tried to dunk me. I tried to pick him up to dunk *him*, but he was too heavy and we went down in a tangle, laughing so hard we were spitting water when we surfaced.

"This is fun, isn't it, Mom?" He looked unguarded and anxious, waiting for me to choose.

"The best fun," I assured him. "What are your dad and Sophie doing?"

"Sophie wanted to swim like you, so Dad's trying to teach her the backstroke."

On the other side of the boat, Tom was floating Sophie in waist-deep water. When her arm shot up out of the water, I noticed its slimness, its defined shape. *"Maman!"*

So we portaged our picnic basket to shore and got out our sandwiches and cans of pop, grapes and cheese and a big bag of IM's Cornacabanas, popcorn clusters with "an exotic hint of island sweetness." It was heavenly. Not a single BTC bar in sight. In the middle of it all, Sophie put down her sandwich, darted into the trees, and reemerged sans swimsuit. She sat down smugly and picked up her sandwich, waiting for us to catch on.

"What is it, Sophs?" I asked. "What?"

"Le Déjeuner sur l'Herbe!" she cried triumphantly.

Really, as soon as I had time, I was going to take her out of that French class and find a swimming class for her. Or tap, ballet, and baton. Surely they still taught those, didn't they? Even in Minnetonka?

"I don't get it," Jeff said.

"I'll explain later."

Tom was laughing.

"Don't encourage her. She'll end up in the Folies-Bergère."

I found Sophie's clothes and wrestled her into them before she could treat us to a rendition of the cancan au naturel.

Chapter 19

THE BEST YEARS OF EVERYONE ELSE'S LIFE

At the foot of the yard, where the lapping blue of Minnetonka met the stunning green of Lawns by Biltmore, the Lawn Company That Gives You More, Jeff and Sophie were playing either *Baywatch* or *Rescue 911*. Whatever it was involved sending Scout out to retrieve a stick, Sophie shouting *Il se noie! Aide-le!*, and Jeff taking a running dive off the end of the dock and onto an air mattress. Followed by shouts, splashing, and frantic paddling in knee-deep water until the triumphal rescue of Mssr. Le Scoute. Safely on land, Sophie draped an old beach towel around Scout, who'd morphed into Rose from *Titanic*, and offered him a doll's teacup of hot chocolate. The chocolate being BTC's ChillOut!, based on availability and the personal preferences of all involved.

Don't give him any more, I wanted to shout, remembering Scout's rather notorious lactose intolerance. But I kept still, the book I wasn't reading on my knees, the smell of Coppertone in my nostrils, my toes—freshly pedicured and painted a color called Sex on the Beach—winking at me from the end of the rose-upholstered deck chair. Watching my children made me happy. Lawns by Biltmore could deal with the aftermath of Scout's rescue tomorrow.

I'd started out with the idea of reading Sophie a *Madeleine* book. I'd laid the scene out in my mind yesterday standing in the cash-only line at

Barnes and Noble. Daddy's in Paris. Not so far away. Let's see what Paris looks like, Sophs. Why, there's a little girl just like you there! But Sophie declined, saying that Mademoiselle Swanson had already read them the *Madeleine* books in class—in French, of course. Then she brought me her *Little Traveler's Guide to the World* and pointed out exactly where Paris was. We turned to the New York page and I explained that Mommy was going there tomorrow and would be there for a few days while Daddy was in Paris and she and Jeff would be right here on the edge of Lake Minnetonka. I spanned my fingers to show how we made a neat triangle and then brought them together to show how we would soon all be together again.

Sophs looked a bit glum, but then her face suddenly brightened. "So will I be in charge?" I told her Minka would be staying overnight until Daddy got back, whereupon she lost interest in me and romped off in search of Jeff and Scout.

I read *Madeleine* by myself, sunglasses on. Tom had left Sunday night. Now he was off having Paris with Lucie, a phrase whose words I kept subconsciously rearranging. I glanced at my watch. They were done pitching BTC for the day and were probably now listening to *le jazz hot* in a slinky little club where businessmen hung out with their *haute Parisienne* mistresses. France was the country that had had no trouble with Bill Clinton, after all; the country where Mitterand's wife and mistress had swapped funny old Francois stories over his coffin. Who knows what all that might suggest to my husband? I calmed myself by focusing on the antics unfolding down there at the edge of the lake. It was impossible to look at Jeff and Sophie, streaked with sunlight and holding up the sky with their laughter, and believe that anything could possibly go wrong between their parents.

Scout was just finishing his fifth cup of ChillOut! and I was thinking it might be time to intervene when I looked out across the water and saw what seemed to be a reenactment of Washington's Christmas Eve crossing of the Delaware. Only Washington was wearing an enormous sun hat, sunglasses, and a billowing caftan, commanding the deck of a pontoon boat that was equipped with a gayly striped awning, table, banquette seating for six, captain's chairs, a Weber grill, and a sizable refrigeration unit.

Cleopatra's barge was a dinghy in comparison. And was that Bengt at the helm in a smart nautical blazer?

Estelle gripped the pontoon rail with one hand. The other, I saw as she raised her arm to wave, was tightly clutching her Blackberry. "I've been e-mailing you for almost the last two hours. Is your connection down?"

If only, I thought. There was a splintering sound as Bengt attempted to dock. Estelle wobbled but remained upright. I wondered if our homeowners insurance covered contingencies like Bengt, who was now completely tangled in the mooring lines. Scout paced the shallows nervously, ready to effect a water rescue.

"Do you need some help, Bengt?"

"Oh, don't worry, he has a *flair* for boats," Estelle called out brightly. "A born navigator!"

Jeff shot me a look that was easy to read even at this distance. *You see? I told you!* There'd been a heated discussion, before Tom left, about Jeff not taking the boat out alone. We were both surprised by the fight he put up—two against one had always been a fairly effective strategy for us. But Jeff informed us that we were lame and that all his friends could take boats out whenever they wanted. Tom, yet to notice that his son's personal boat was steaming toward the Outer Banks of surly adolescence, told Jeff to cut the backtalk. Jeff missed the warning flag and asked why we'd bothered to buy boats if we could never actually use them—a well-aimed barb that found its mark in the soft target of parental guilt. I watched the two of them glare at each other and felt the same bystander helplessness I did during nature programs when bull moose locked antlers and bears ate their own cubs. But these were *my* moose, so I dodged in among the horns and told Jeff that it wasn't that we didn't trust him, just that he hadn't had enough lake experience yet. Tom grabbed the exit strategy and hurried in reinforcements, telling Jeff that I was right and even jet pilots needed flight time before they could solo. Jeff was the last to back off, mumbling about being out of college by then, but it was only a halfhearted grumble.

"I am on the horns of the most exquisite dilemma," Estelle announced, collapsing into the lawn chair beside me. "Sunblock."

I passed over my La Mer SPF 18 and watched her sniff. "I usually never use below thirty-two, fifty preferable." She uncapped the tube and squirted a good $20 worth onto her hand.

"I read an article that said everything over sixteen works more or less the same."

Estelle halted in mid-swipe, then squeezed out another $5 quarter inch. "Oh, well, you're lucky, you don't have to worry, being swarthy."

Swarthy?

She adjusted her sun hat and arranged her caftan sleeves over her lavishly La Mer'ed arms. "I have to be so careful. Bengt too. Even with his dark hair, he burns practically on contact."

Bengt materialized beside us and stood quietly, eyes squeezed shut, as she streaked more of my La Mer over his cheeks and chin. I looked quickly toward the water, expecting to see the pontoon drifting free. To my amazement, he had managed to tether it to the dock. Way to go, Bengt.

"Play, Bengt," Estelle commanded with a finishing swat. "*Now*."

We watched as he joined Sophie and Jeff by the water. He carefully removed his blazer, socks, and Top-Siders, then unfastened his cuffs and folded back his sleeves. I thought I saw him slide a little pair of cuff links into his pocket before, at last, he offered himself up for play.

"Bengt really seems to be, hmm . . ." What? Less weird? No longer destined for court-ordered therapy? "Getting along well these days."

"Well, he's *always* been exceptionally gregarious. It isn't hard to see why the other boys look to him as a leader. Amazing, really, since usually the ones with the high IQs are shunted to the side." She looked at me brightly. "It must be wonderful to know your children will always be solidly in the middle of everything!"

Yes, we swarthy types and our sons loved the middle, and spent our lives searching for a leader like Bengt.

"Actually, Jeff was recommended for advanced placement." A lie, clearly. Jeff was at this moment trying to catch minnows with his toes. "Tom and I thought it was more important to give him a normal childhood." Who was I kidding? We would have jumped. The problem with

Estelle was that she deftly maneuvered you below her level. Then, when she looked at you pityingly, as if she were superior, you experienced the humiliation of knowing she was right.

"The horns of a dilemma," she repeated. "And I simply must confide in someone." She stretched out a hand and waited for me to clasp it. Stupidly, I did. "And since you know Jean-Paul, well . . ." She withdrew her hand, leaving me with empty air. "The fact is, I've been leading a double life. Oh, I know, I know what everyone thinks of me."

"You do?"

"Oh yes, I've been hearing it since I was five. So smart. So brilliant. So *intellectually gifted*. It's not been a bed of roses. When you function at this level, people tend to overlook the fact that you're also a woman."

"But—"

"Oh, I know you can't really understand. Your life has been so simple and direct, so uncluttered by the obligation of ambition. I envy you, I really do." She paused, generously giving me time to toy with the unexpected gift of her approval. I wondered if I could exchange it at Marshall Field's for something useful. Like fireplace matches. She shook her head crisply. "The truth is, I've been living a lie. Bengt's father and I—and I know this will come as a shock—no longer have a real marriage. We've played our roles—rather impeccably, I think—for the sake of Bengt and the clinic. But Bengt's such an intuitive child, sometimes I think he's begun to sense that something isn't quite right. And now the most surprising thing has happened. Ever since your soiree . . . since I met Jean-Paul . . . well, he's reawakened my anima."

"But that's wonderful, isn't it?" I asked quickly. I wasn't completely certain what an anima was, but I was fairly certain I didn't want to meet up with Estelle's. Especially since the awakener was Chef De Navets and his magic whisk.

"It *would* be wonderful, if I were an ordinary person. And, of course, Jean-Paul is fabulous with Bengt. Do you know, they made the most incredible osso buco last night. For no reason. It took hours. They said the spirit just moved them." She brought herself back sharply. "But what about the clinic? What about my patients? You have no idea how entrapping it all is, being so much in the public eye. The press would have a field day. 'Brilliant Therapists Caught in Marriage Fizzle.' I can just imagine."

"But divorce can happen to anyone. And new love can happen too. Don't you have to make room for that? To accept endings and celebrate beginnings?" God, I sounded like a radio shrink, vapid yet deeply sincere. This was frightening to me. "Wouldn't it maybe help your patients to see that life goes on in spite of setbacks?"

Estelle smiled quietly. "I've always been something of a role model," she confessed. Suddenly, she caught my wrist. "A book! I could help *millions* with a book. In diary form. Life-saving psychological advice couched in daily experience. *Renewing Love.* Do you think that works as a title? Maybe it should be *From Old to New: Reflections on a Life in Love.* Or *Love Soup for the Soul.*" Her cheeks filled with pink. She looked ten years younger. "There'll have to be workbooks, of course, and self-testing quizzes. Maybe motivational tapes as well. I should do seminars! Bengt! We're leaving now."

She stood up, caftan flaring, and looked down on me. Literally, this time. "I knew I was right to confide in you. Sometimes, the simplest minds *are* the best. I'm such a thinker, I just see too much, all the details, all the ramifications. Thank you, Annie. For listening. For *being there.*"

"No problemo," I answered in my simple folkloric way, unburdened by any complexities of thought.

"And I hope," Estelle added, "you won't feel awkward."

"Awkward?"

She swooped down and patted my hand. "That's the spirit. Jean-Paul told me that there'd been a little spark of interest. Between the two of you. Perhaps you had expectations?"

I sat there, speechless, until I realized Jeff was standing beside me.

"Mom, can I go with them? Bengt and I want to do stuff this afternoon."

I contemplated the many boating accidents that could occur as Bengt played dodgem with various boats and Ski-Doos.

"We're going to have lunch, Jeff, but I'll run you over after. When Sophie and I go on errands." To tell Lyn Vickers Estelle's news, for starters.

Estelle swooped down the lawn and allowed Bengt to escort her onto the pontoon. As they pulled out into oncoming boat traffic, Estelle waved. "Maybe I'll let you have a look at it as I go along," she called back, beaming. "I'll Blackberry the outline over to you—you can be my first reader!"

Except for the lime green sunglasses, she looked like Katharine Hepburn in *The Lion in Winter*. And well did I understand the joy that surged in Peter O'Toole's heart as he waved her back into exile.

I brooded about this episode, and the one that followed it, on the plane to New York. Because the minute Sophs and I pulled up at the Vickers's, and Lyn answered her door, the day took its second turn. She looked different, yet familiar. To be honest, the picture that flashed in my mind was the time Scout got some form of canine-style flu and had to be rehydrated at the vet's. "He's still leaking," the attendant said when she handed his leash to me and dabbed at a damp spot of fur between his shoulder blades. He'd looked plumped up and juicy. That was how Lyn struck me. Wait a minute, I was thinking, I know this picture. And I was on my way to figuring it out when Lyn practically shouted, "I'm pregnant!"

I quickly got a handle on the wish-it-was-me feeling that came surging up, congratulated her, and asked all the right questions about due dates and how she was feeling.

"March twenty-sixth, and I feel terrific."

She had it already. That was what I'd seen when she opened the door—that set-apart glow, that free-pass-for-the-next-nine-months look. That and a certain amount of water retention. Oh, how I wanted to say *me too* and sign myself up for aerobics and yoga relaxation at Ladies in Waiting, Minnetonka's Mom Salon. Hey, everybody, I'm pregnant too.

Except I wasn't.

We had a little celebration with cinnamon toast and decaf. Lyn, who bowed to none of the superstitions about announcing early or making plans, already had paint chips and fabric samples strewn across her kitchen table. She was looking for just the right baby yellow, she explained. Ah, something I could relate to, despite my empty uterus. Emily took Sophie off to show her where the baby's room would be. "He can live here," I heard her say, "but he can't have my Barbies. That's the law."

After we'd polished off the toast and I'd asked her to consider a white base with a pale yellow wash, I told Lyn about Estelle. Like me, she was glad in spite of herself. The prospect of no longer pretending we didn't know that Estelle's marriage was more IPO than I Do cheered us. The idea that our little curve of Minnetonka would once again present a united marital front to the world made us feel more secure. The fact that a true chef would be part of our gourmet group struck us as a good thing. The idea of Bengt having a partner for his Evening in Tuscany dinners was to be cheered. And we were both unaccountably happy for Estelle. To our surprise, tears gathered in the corners of our eyes. Lyn, at least, could attribute it all to the tsunami of hormones bathing her synapses. Tears? What was my excuse?

Like a child who'd been unfairly spanked and decided never to speak to Mommy again, I trudged onto the plane. Kate was busy making all the adjustments and demands business class allowed and didn't notice my mood. She sipped her second Chardonnay and asked the stewardess for a fluffier pillow.

The plane took off, but I didn't soar with it. I felt as if I was standing still, mired, while lives were flowing forward around me. For the first time since I was five, when I'd realized in the middle of a summer night that both my parents would eventually die, I felt frightened about my own life. It wasn't even a hot, proactive, let's-take-out-that-tumor kind of fear. It was a frozen chill. And it wasn't just feeling left out while Estelle and Lyn planned weddings and nurseries—well, divorces and weddings and nurseries. It was a moment I'd been suppressing since the *Déjeuner sur l'Herbe* boating day.

In the summer, when sunset doesn't come until nine o'clock, the sky bleaches to near white in the middle of the day. Then, gradually, tints of blue appear and deepen with the evening. Eventually, there's an amazing moment when the sky becomes darker than the lake, and for one breathless, spinning glance, you feel the world has capsized and you're seeing it from a breathing space beneath the water. When that moment came, that night, we were crossing the lake on our way home.

"Look! There's *our* house," Sophie cried.

In the second it took to lift my head, expectation detonated within me. I imagined myself looking across the water and seeing our magnificent house against the backdrop of spellbinding blue. I anticipated a rush of well-being such as I'd never felt before, a cumulative burst in which the present would catch fire and, for a flickering moment, reveal our perfect future. But when I looked up, I had a hard time even distinguishing our house from a dozen others hugging the shore. When I did pick it out, and was still doggedly struggling to have my climactic moment, something entirely different happened. It was like one of those movie shots that begins with a spinning blue earth seen from outer space and in the space of seconds zooms in to a corner bistro in New York or a cornfield in Indiana. When I looked at my house, I saw a spreadsheet of sinking stock values, a folder stuffed with credit card statements and jammed out of sight in my desk. I saw two children whose parents were about to leave them with a nanny. I saw half-upholstered chairs and a storeroom full of lovely objects that had somehow never found their way to their final destinations. That was when fear settled around my shoulders, like a sweater I couldn't take off. I could pull my arms out of it, tie it jauntily around my neck, pretend for hours at a time that it wasn't still there. But it was.

The plane engines thrummed and the ground vanished beneath cloud cover. We'd reached cruising speed.

"Have some wine," Kate was saying. "This is going to be a *fun* trip."

Why not? I held up my glass. When it was empty, I held it up again. And yet again. Which was how, five miles up, somewhere over Michigan, I decided I really, really wanted another baby. I would talk to Tom about it as soon as we were both in the same spot for more than twenty minutes. Obviously, I was going to need to approach this desire as an adult, put my shoulder to the BTC wheel to earn maternity time off, clean up those credit cards. Which would be a snap if only I could get those investments back to even.

I noticed Kate was reading *Investor's Business Daily* and felt suddenly, irrationally angry. Every stock she'd profited on—the ticker numbers I'd copied down that day in her computer room—had done nothing but sink.

And I couldn't even complain about it because she'd never recommended them or even known I was buying them. It seemed unfair.

"When is that Dow going to snap back?" I demanded, sensing at once that my voice was too loud. I had a vague awareness of having drunk too much, or too much for a stomach that had known only BTC products for the last seven days. As always, I'd taken the crash-course approach to trimming down for the TV appearance. Lucy had Ethel and a steam cabinet, I had BTC. I lowered my voice to a genteel whine. "I mean, you can't make a cent in this market."

She turned a page and looked at me over the top of her reading glasses, a serene smile on her face. "Sure you can. I've done fairly well with some picks. Of course, the opportunities to lower my cost basis by buying on those huge down days have been a real boon. You were there the afternoon Peggy did that presentation on cost averaging, weren't you?"

No, I was with a group of diabetic seniors showing them the range of healthy snacks and beverages to be made with our product.

"I got the e-mail."

"Well, you *have* been lowering your cost basis, haven't you?" Kate asked again, looking somewhat concerned.

"It's a terrific strategy," I told her. A genius strategy, actually. And I would have done it, if I'd had anything left to invest.

Kate went back to *IBD*, I hit the call button for more wine. Another few glasses and everything seemed to smooth out. The market would rally. This was America, after all. Rallies 'R' Us. The upward spiral would begin any day now. It had to.

The pilot announced that we were over Niagara Falls, which seemed like a favorable omen. I closed my eyes and saw Tom and me with three children, the littlest one of indeterminate sex. We were decorating a Christmas tree, not in our Minnetonka house but in an arts-and-crafts-style solarium aglow with northern light. I smiled sneakily to myself, congratulating clever Annie Wilkins for wangling a meeting with Branston Arche, Soho architect It hadn't been easy. His office manager had mentioned to me that he was one of Manhattan's Top Ten Architects, and wouldn't I be just as happy to meet with one of his assistants, at least at this preliminary stage? No, I was only in New York for a few days and I wanted Mr. Arche. Then I'd mentioned Caitlin and Martha Stewart and the seas parted. I got the appointment and had forwarded a half dozen scans of Aunt Edith's property to him. By the time I met with him, on Saturday afternoon, he would have some preliminary sketches for me to look at. And one of them, I knew, would be perfect, a jewel of a bungalow. Then, if only we could afford to build it, our life would be complete.

Chapter 20

SHE KNOWS CHOCOLATE

"How can it take twenty minutes to go two blocks?"

The cab, locked in a sea of other cabs, was at a dead halt somewhere on the west side of Manhattan. In the months since our first trip to New York, they'd changed the entire city. The crisp, clear-eyed, swank New York I'd seen back then had been replaced by rabbit warrens of buildings that radiated heat. Around the corner from our hotel, hundreds of vending carts were frying things—doughnuts? *dog?*—around the clock, filling the air with a miasma of grease. The intersections were melting, as I discovered when one of my heels became mired, and the first thing I'd heard on the radio that morning was a gleefully Satanic weatherman chuckling, "We've got another gorgeous one on tap for you today, New York, with highs topping out at ninety-nine across the tri-state region and humidity down to a manageable ninety-four percent. Quite a relief after last week . . ." Clearly, I was in hell. And now our driver was leaving us.

"Wait a minute." I leaned forward and squinted through the scratched plastic divider to read his photo ID. "Where are you going, Sageer?"

"I crack hood. Otherwise, radiator."

While Sageer was outside the cab, he had time for a lively, hand-waving conversation with another driver three cabs away.

"My cousin," he said, popping back in. "Okay, let's go."

We crawled forward another ten feet.

"Could you turn up the air-conditioning maybe?"

" 'S'no air-conditioning. You don't like heat?" He grinned. Fiendishly, I thought. "I am from Punjab!"

And I am from Minnesota! And doing TV in an hour. Live and sweating. I checked my watch. "Kate? Maybe we should get out and walk."

She looked as if her side of the seat was cooled to a comfort-cushioned seventy-two degrees. "Relax, Annie. We'll get there."

Yes, but would I have time to dry off, that was the question. I rode the rest of the way with my hands pressed to my head, literally trying to hold down my hair to keep it from frizzing in the manageable 94 percent humidity.

"You have headache?" Sageer asked.

There was a huge crowd surging around and around the outdoor stage set up in front of Macy's. It looked like Mecca during the hadj. It was so crowded, there was no way of knowing if these were people milling around until the show started or were thousands caught in sustained pedestrian gridlock. From what I'd seen so far that morning, it was possible that the entire island of Manhattan had ground to a complete halt. It would be hours until anyone freed themselves to phone in the news. On the upside, we had an audience.

I looked around for the makeup booth, and when I looked back, Kate had already paid Sageer, found her way to the Barefoot Contessa's cluster, and with a merry laugh seized one of the Contessa's mimosas. I brightened instantly.

"I'd love a mimosa!"

"No time. We have to get you into makeup and ready to go. Oh, look, there's Calder."

Well, it was one of those moments. My head swiveled and I think I actually did a double take. Calder Payne, who I'd been picturing as Kate's age and slightly graying, turned out to be Hugh Grant's separated-at-birth brother, right down to the crinkly corners of his eyelids. The world lallapalooza sprang to mind. God, but he was cute.

A rail-thin girl wearing Minnie Mouse shoes introduced herself as

Burt. I stared at Calder while she pulled back my hair and sprayed me with the makeup gun.

"Stop sweating," she ordered, starting on my eyes. "Your mascara's running."

It occurred to me that these people had become genetically altered by their climate. They were like tube worms clustering around ocean-floor hot springs. Burt wasn't even damp.

"Am I frizzing?" I asked, anxiously touching my hair.

"Yeah, but it's windy up on the stage, so it won't make that much difference, it would be whipping all over anyway. I mean *really* windy, so watch out. Rachel Ray almost went over the edge."

"Thanks," I said, and felt a blast of wind-driven grit embed itself in the lipstick she'd just applied.

"Don't talk into the wind" was Burt's parting advice.

Which was no help at all because, as far as I could tell, the wind was coming from all directions. I made a beeline to where Kate was chatting with Calder. The word "Cool" might just as well have been written above their heads in fat blue letters dripping with snow. I stood beside them with my own cartoon bubble—"Hot, Flustered"—hovering over me. Until Calder turned to me and smiled.

"Ah, you must be Annie." Ten degrees cooler. Instantly. He turned back to Kate, eyes dancing. "You have a truly lovely product here."

He said it in just the right way, suggesting that maybe it was BTC that was lovely but more probably it was myself. Gentleman's flirting. This might not be so bad after all, I thought. And that was when I saw them.

"Oh no."

"What is it?"

"Right over there. Look. Rebound-hunger protesters."

Kate looked startled. "Are you sure?"

I nodded. I recognized them instinctively, on a soul-to-soul level, even though their clothes were different. They were the New York version of rebound-hunger protesters—thin and bitter looking, with tight-fitting leather jackets and black, matte-dyed hair. They all looked like Katrina vanden Heuvel.

"They're going to ruin this."

Deftly, Calder grabbed a plate of truffles and sailed over to the group, the plate balanced on his fingertips as if he were a waiter. We couldn't hear the whole conversation, but we caught enough. Surely these beautiful women understood that other women lacked their self-confidence and beauty? Their lovely thinness? So surely a small ray of hope, even false hope, could be forgiven now and then? That was the gist of it. Calder held out the truffle plate. His body language said *I am a supplicant. Yet killingly attractive*. The women snatched the truffles. By the time he left them, they had the syrupy eyes of dim-witted cocker spaniels.

"That's them sorted," he said. "And we still have time to do a walk-through."

Kate left, probably off in search of another mimosa, and Calder led me behind the stage to a relatively becalmed set-up area. He looked down at a clipboard and handed me three hand-printed note cards. "I made these for you last night. See, step by step? I don't like my guests to feel nervous or confused. So it will be simple, you'll see." His thoughtfulness stunned me. No one had been this nice to me in months. "We're going to start with the individual molten-lava cakes; I melt the chocolate, you beat the eggs and sugar. I wrote what you do in red and what I do in blue. Easy. Then some simple *mendiants*, which are actually already made; all we do is press some roasted nuts and candied peel onto their tops, and then I finish by making a firecracker from your Better Than Chocolate. I use white for the wick, so you will melt some of both for me; it's already measured." He paused and looked at me. "Nothing to be nervous about, Annie. Or is something wrong?"

"No, I'm just not used to this heat. I have a headache." Also a hang-over, from all the wine I'd drunk on the plane and the bottle of Pouilly-Fuissé Kate and I had polished off at dinner. Why hadn't she taken the glass out of my hand?

"Oh, a headache." He stepped behind me and began touching my temples. Not massaging, exactly, just applying gentle pressure with his fingertips. Then his fingertips moved to the sinuses beneath my eyes and gently kneaded. I felt a rush of oxygen. The scent of his sun-warmed chef's whites flooded my nose. He smelled like clean sheets. By the time he finished, I was practically purring. I wanted to curl up in him, like a cat in a basket of laundry.

"You have beautiful skin," he said. "Is the headache gone?" Amazingly, it was. "So we'll go have fun now."

And we did. For the first time in my life, I actually had fun in front of a camera, fun cooking. Even the things that went wrong—like losing one of Calder's carefully printed cards in the crevice between the cooktop and the faux counter—didn't seem to matter. He just tilted his set so I could see them. Calder's sheer happiness over the food pumped me up, put me on top of my game. So on our first recipe, when Calder was melting BTC for my molten-lava cakes and it seized, I was able to jump in.

"Actually, Calder, I'm glad this happened. Can you get this?" I asked, tilting the pan toward the camera. "It looks like a disaster. But because BTC doesn't actually have sugar in it, all you need to do is set this aside, let it cool completely, and then simply remelt it. Keep the temp a little lower than for ordinary chocolate." A mistake—I was always supposed to say "fat-filled chocolate"—but a tiny, forgivable one. "BTC will come back smooth and glossy on the reheat. If it seems a bit thick, you can add a drop or two of water."

Calder melted a second batch of chocolate for me, perfectly this time, and we got the molten-lava cakes in the oven just four minutes off schedule. We made up two of the minutes on the *mendiants,* then Calder cut three minutes off his firecracker, which was truly extraordinary. A man who can roll a perfect cylinder of tempered BTC with the fingers of one hand while piping raspberry mousse into it with the fingers of the other makes you glad to be alive. His dexterity gave us enough time to reheat the seized BTC, showing folks across the land how easy it was to do. The last America saw of us was a spoon held aloft, displaying a satiny waterfall of BTC.

"That was great," I cried when we got off.

"It was good for me too. Let's have a cigarette." I must have looked startled. "A joke," he assured me. "It's just that I liked cooking with you. You *know* chocolate. And the way we moved together—brilliant!"

This struck me as the sexiest possible thing he could have said. I could hardly wait to get back to the hotel and sit chin deep in a tub of cool water and think about it.

"Tell your husband he is a lucky man."

Husband. I plummeted back to earth. For almost an hour, I'd forgotten I had a husband. And if a man I'd known for fifty-six minutes could make me forget I had a husband, how much further could Lucie have gotten in making Tom forget he had a wife?

That afternoon, I tried to call Paris. Sixteen times, according to the bill that Kate eventually signed off on, tactfully not mentioning what looked like a roiling international crisis. No one was in Tom's room. Sometimes I just hung up; other times I tried to leave a message with the concierge, who didn't seem to possess any English. Have Mr. Wilkins call his wife in New York, please, I asked Monsieur Bienfait—we knew each other's names after my seventh call—but I was using my high school French, leaving both my room phone and cell phone numbers. So for all I knew, I'd instructed Tom to bring me a telephoto lens and left numbers that made alarms ring all the way up to the highest levels of homeland security. If only Sophie were here to handle this.

Between two of these calls, Kate phoned to tell me she'd wangled reservations at Nobu.

"It's stifling out. Let's go eat some cold soba" was her way of justifying a meal that would cost IM a good $300, and that's only if we stuck to the noodles, which of course we didn't. There was also the salmon tartar with Sevruga caviar, and the duck with eggplant appetizer and the avocado tempura. Several mango martinis also figured in it. I was like a sponge, taking on ballast after my week of BTC binge dieting. It was as if, instead of allowing your stomach to shrink, it settled in your gastrointestinal tract, expanded, and vaporized, creating one huge, long, empty feed trough.

I ventured this theory to Kate. "Probably it does work something like that. I don't involve myself too much with the ramifications. Personally, I never touch the stuff."

Very candid. I felt a thrill of kinship, as if she'd dropped the final veil.

But, of course, she hadn't. I felt disappointed, realizing for the first time that our friendship had never quite flowered the way I'd thought it would. I didn't even know if she'd ever been married, or in love with someone.

"There's so much about you I don't know, Kate," I said, in a leaping non sequitur.

"Oh, there isn't really that much to know." She poured more wine. "Think of me as a fairly uninteresting person. Not to myself, but to the world. I show up, I do my work—do it well, I like to think—and I go home. Everything that would make me remotely interesting to anyone else—sky diving, season tickets to the Guthrie, a desire to walk the Great Wall of China before it disintegrates—strikes me as boring. I like the stock market because it's so purely psychological, which is what people always miss about it, but my investment style is so contrarian I don't really get much out of swapping information with others. I only hold those IM afternoons because it's an easy way to keep tabs on everyone. I'd really rather be sitting there reading, alone."

I believed her. And felt I'd learned a great deal about her. "Only the women," I said after a while.

"What?"

"Those afternoons at your house. It's only the women you keep tabs on."

"It's the women you *have* to keep tabs on. Men are so transparent you needn't bother. Women are subterranean. All that estrogen in play can eat the foundation right out from under you. I've seen secretarial pools bring down whole corporations."

We shared a bento box of dessert tastings. I ate everything that wasn't chocolate, Kate ate everything that was. While I was savoring my miniature shiso crepe with strawberries, Kate let me know that I'd be venturing to Connecticut alone in the morning to deliver my speech to the Independent Chocolatiers of the nutmeg state. She'd gotten the raw tape of my appearance with Calder, but since the show wouldn't air until Labor Day, and we were meeting with Food Network programming Monday, she was having editing equipment sent to her room so she could cut footage herself to add to the reel Camera 10 had shot at our party. In the afternoon, she thought she might go binge shopping at one of Manhattan's vast Barnes and Noble. There was a book on William James she'd been looking for that none of the Minneapolis stores ever had.

I felt like she was trying to emphasize just how boring she really was, but I didn't care. I had my afternoon meeting with the architect Branston Arche, which I hadn't wanted to tell her about since even Tom didn't know about it. No one knew. Just me and the new MasterCard account I'd put the deposit for the consultation on.

We picked at the bento box for a while longer, then had a nightcap and found our way to a cab. I felt deliciously full and relaxed. Kate had that effect. As I sank down onto the bed, I realized it was too late to call Paris, and there had been no messages for me.

My mission to Connecticut went pretty well, although the train back to New York stalled somewhere south of Stamford, meaning I was both frazzled and half an hour late by the time I got back to Manhattan. I sprinted out of Grand Central, commandeered a cab, and gave him the address of Branston Arche's offices.

Soho was a trendy part of town, especially if you were an art dealer, a jewelry designer, a vendor of 1950s furniture, or an up-and-coming-no-more-glass-boxes architect. It also boasted an unusually high number of art-wear shoe stores with names like Sneë Finndly, Miss Otis Regrets, and Mistletoes, which made me picture captive elves in back rooms, cobbling out shoes one by one. On the whole, I just didn't get the whole Soho thing. In the Midwest, you couldn't give real estate like this away. Whole blocks of buildings seemed to have been cast out of a single, huge piece of iron, then painted over so many times, with so many layers of dust and handbills plastered in between, that doors and windows no longer opened or closed completely. Around the swankier rentals were holdovers from the pre-trendy period—novelty stores with wind-up plastic toys swimming merrily in dishpans of water plunked down on the sidewalk, Chinatown outposts that hadn't been resupplied since Mao, locksmiths and wheat-grass juice vendors whose shops were so narrow traffic was strictly one way. I had an opportunity to explore all this because my driver, Calaban, let me out three or four blocks from my actual destination. It made me long for Sageer.

Frazzled, I arrived at last and was ushered back to Arche's office by a young Audrey Hepburn look-alike in a severely tailored black linen suit. Her short black hair had lovely blue streaks that looked like feathers.

"He just popped out for a sec because there's a one-hour-only tag sale at Merriweather Pickle."

"Shoes?"

"Vintage toys. Make yourself at home. We're a little laid back here on Saturdays, but I'm sure he won't be long."

She handed me a beverage menu and I immediately ruled out the Jamaican ginger beer, leaving a showy bottled water from a newly discovered spring in Kazakhstan, freshly squeezed orange juice, or, clustered together at the bottom of the page for the true plebeians, a "selection of sodas." I asked for a diet cola and Audrey disappeared, not seeming to mind at all that she was wasting a summer Saturday at the peak of her beauty fetching selected sodas for a perspiring woman from the Midwest.

Her assistant delivered the drinks on an ironic vintage cocktail tray trimmed with faux leopard. The assistant was younger than Audrey and, though he looked about fifteen, I thought he was probably an intern, or even a recent graduate. He wore a very skinny knit tie, which suited him, and cuffed, 1950s-style trousers, which also suited him.

"I guess you can leave the water on his desk," I offered helpfully, taking my Diet Coke. "He's supposed to come back soon."

The kid looked confused. Then he laughed and thrust out his hand. "I'm Branston. Sorry you had to wait, but the sale—there was this mint-condition Creepy Crawler set I absolutely had to have. I can't wait to go home and play with my Thingmaker."

He was completely serious, which didn't seem like a good sign.

"Now, Annie, I've looked at the slides you sent me, and the tear sheets of the kind of prairie house you're considering. I have to tell you, I don't think it's quite a match."

I felt a little stab in my heart. "But I love arts and crafts."

"Obviously." He said it the way a doctor would say it to a four-hundred-pound patient who'd just confessed a fondness for cream pies. Obviously, you have no restraint whatsoever. Obviously, you've never heard that less is more. Obviously, you need a firm that specializes in honeymoon hotels and brand-new Victorian McMansions with faux leaded-glass windows and add-on carriage houses. "So I've tweaked it just a little bit."

He reached behind him and brought out a cardboard tube, from which he removed several large scrolls of drafting paper.

"This is really a stunning location. You should forget the site the house is on now and build up here instead. It would be fantastic. You could stand up there and shout, "I'm king of the world.' " He threw his arms out wide, like Leonardo DiCaprio in the movie. "But this is really a Nordic country setting. You need something that complements it instead of fighting it. So I've sort of married arts and crafts with Swedish country for you."

"Really?"

"Don't look worried. It's a very happy marriage." He unscrolled a sheet and there it was. Not my dream house. *Better* than my dream house. Instead of a wide-winged horizontal spread, it seemed to flow down out of the pines and rocks, a clean, sparkling waterfall of a house.

"Two levels?"

"Three, actually. You can't see the third one from the front because it drops back into the hill. Here, look."

He unscrolled the second sheet. This one showed interiors, not just floor plans but meticulous colored-pencil sketches of how each room would look. Curved arches and exposed beams and built-in bookshelves flowing into clean blond wood and simple lines. It was so . . . me. So *us*. It was the house we'd been meant to have all along, and I felt absurdly proud for having found it, like a golden needle in a stadium-size haystack.

"It's fantastic."

Young Audrey stuck her head in the door at that moment and told Branston that Chris Capers was on the phone.

"Thanks, Lorelei. I'll call him back in five. Brokers," he muttered, which reminded me.

"I should tell you, my husband and I won't really be ready to build for a year or so. We've had some losses in the market."

"Yeah, tell me about it. Dot bomb."

"So could we slow this down and go step by step? I'll pay up to date before I leave today, of course. And then"—we were years from affording this, but I couldn't resist it—"if you could just tell me how much more it would be for some estimates?"

He grinned. "An estimate on estimates? God, this economy sucks. People like us weren't meant to be poor. We weren't meant to have to get estimates on estimates. But absolutely, whatever you want."

I took my cardboard cylinder, which he capped with smooth gray plastic disks that said "Arche & Assocs.," walked to the front desk, picked a credit card from the ever growing deck that now had its own wallet in my purse, and handed it to Audrey-Lorelei. What I wanted was, like him, not to have to get estimates on estimates.

Kate had found the William James book and wanted to hang out with it, so no Nobu redux evening for us. We had a fast, early supper near the hotel, and when we came out, it was pouring rain and someone had put all the taxicabs away. I seemed to be the designated flagger, floundering out into the street time after time to try to snag a cab while Kate waited, snug and dry, beneath a portico. The rain was so thick I actually had a hard time breathing. There was no space at all between the drops. Had anyone ever died this way? I tried to remember if I'd ever read stories about New Yorkers drowning in rainstorms. Of course not. They were tube worms, after all.

When I got back to my room, there was a message from Audrey-Lorelei with the estimate for the estimates, saying if I was up for it to call the office because they were working all night and could probably messenger the final estimates to me before I flew home Monday afternoon. It was expensive, but I still had headroom on that particular card, so I called back. Branston answered the phone himself.

"I thought you were going to play with your Creepy Crawler Thingmaker tonight."

"We are. Lorelei made some fantastic beetles. Almost scarablike. Work is play. You have to remember that."

Right. Work is play. Until you're my age. Then work is work, and play is also work. I authorized the estimates, then hung up and dialed Tom's number in Paris. No answer. I didn't have the energy to chat with Monsieur Bienfait, so I hung up, waited twenty minutes, and redialed. I tried three more times before I remembered that, in addition to it being three A.M. in Paris, Tom and Lucie were no longer there. They'd flown out of Charles de Gaulle hours ago, and if I could manage to stay awake for a few more hours, I could call Tom at home.

I woke up to the ringing phone. I really resented this. I pictured Kate having been up for hours, sipping coffee and nibbling at croissants, idling away with the Sunday *New York Times* crossword until she decided it was late enough to call me so we could go over the edits and she could go back to the crossword and more coffee and croissants.

It was 6:45 A.M. My hand froze around the phone the minute I heard Minka's voice. She would never call unless something was wrong.

"Mrs. Wilkins? They are not here. I woke up, to use bathroom, and your children *are not here*."

My heart broke free of its arteries and did a slow cartwheel, emptying all the blood out on its way down. I could only see the edges of things. I sat up quickly, then hung my head forward, between my knees, gripping the phone hard.

"What do you mean, Minka? Minka? What time was this?"

"A little while ago. I looked in their rooms. I always do. They weren't here. Not Jeff, not Sophie. Gone."

I voted her the death penalty for using the word "gone." No mother should hear that word in any sentence with her child's name in it. But maybe they were already up. They loved to drag quilts into the family room and watch TV.

"Did you check both family rooms, Minka? Is the TV on? Can you hear a TV anywhere? Did you look in Tom's office?" My stomach lunged. Oh God. "*Did you check the pool room?*"

"No TV. I checked the whole house. Of course. Of course I checked!" She seemed miffed that I would doubt her efforts. "Mrs. Wilkins? I am sure they are somewhere okay. The police are here now. I have to go."

The line went dead. *Police?* Police as in I called them and now they're here to help, or police as in we have some bad news for you, ma'am? I dialed Minka's cell and got no answer. I dialed every other phone in the house and got I-can't-take-your-call-right-now messages from all of us, including Jeff and Sophs. My mind exploded with the fifty other questions I should have asked. Did she check the locks? Could anyone have broken in? Where was Scout? Scout barked at everything, including ants that appeared on kitchen counters. Had she punished either of the kids? Had they possibly run away?

I crashed around the room balling up clothes and throwing them toward my suitcase. I called Kate and told her what had happened and that I was going straight to LaGuardia to get on the first plane I could find. She was at my door in three minutes flat and took charge. Forget the packing and just go, she said, she'd take care of the loose ends. She'd call Northwest and try to book a flight for me and alert them to my arrival. I shouldn't be too hard to pick out. The woman whose hair was standing straight on end. Kate would call the Food Network people too, who I hadn't even thought about.

Fifteen minutes after Minka's call, I was in a taxi, clocking my heart rate at 120 beats a minute. It was only when it dropped below 110 that I wondered with a jolt why it was Minka who had called me. What about Tom? He should have gotten home by midnight last night. Why hadn't he called? Where *was* he?

We took a curve at what seemed like fifty or sixty miles an hour and I slid across the seat, snagging my slacks on sharp, torn edges inexpertly mended with duct tape. I felt as unrooted as a lone green pea, brushed off the plate and tumbling toward the garbage disposal.

Chapter 21

THE LAST TIME
I SAW SOPHIE

God and I made deals all the way back to Minneapolis. Well, I made deals. I had no way of gauging God's participation. I tried to envision Him, who I'd always believed in in a vague kind of way, as an actual entity, someone who would look like Gregory Peck as Atticus Finch. Someone whose eye was ever on the sparrow.

The truth was, the world was littered with downed sparrows.

At the moment, though, He was my best bet. Tom and I had clearly failed, as had Minka. The all-connected promise of technology had also gone down in flames. At some point, I'd managed to destroy my cell phone. I have no recollection of how it happened, I just started to dial and realized that the LCD was black and there was a deep, San Andreas–like crack spanning the case, spitting out shards of plastic. I tossed it in a garbage can outside LaGuardia. The air phone worked, after I calmed down enough to slide my credit card, rather than my library card, through the slot, but no one was answering. I had a terrifying flash of them all standing around letting it ring. *No, she should hear it in person, not while she's still flying.* I pushed the image away so forcefully the person next to me jumped. If I could imagine the words, then the words could be said. Only Scout was still in the mix, as yet unaccounted for and therefore hopefully doing what his breed was supposed to do—*retrieving*. This was what my defense system had boiled down to on a July morning in 2002—a golden Lab, the Minnetonka police department, and God. You can see why I went with God.

I tore open my little bag of Sunchips and sipped my plastic cup of Diet Coke. God and I were at a party. He was the cute guy in homeroom I'd had a crush on but had never had the nerve to approach. Hi, remember me? We met that time in the emergency room when Jeff fell off a swing and there was so much blood I couldn't see if his eye was okay or not? And then the doctors said they needed to do a brain scan?

Oh, this was ridiculous. God was probably dating somebody else anyway.

I got down to brass tacks. Okay, say we do this. See this plane? This sparkly 757? It's yours. Take it, take me, take the whole kit and caboodle, just let Jeff and Sophs be all right. And if they aren't all right, well, in that case you absolutely *have* to take the plane, it's the only merciful thing to do. I smiled smugly, thinking I'd called God's bluff. He was God! He had to be merciful! He *had* to do what I asked! The fact that these negotiations were undoubtedly unfair to the other passengers held no water at all with me. Anyone who has children will understand.

With fun like this, my three hours in the air virtually sped by.

Kate had come up aces for me, I will say that. When we landed, a Northwest agent stood at the gate with my name on a placard. He walked me outside and put me in a waiting Town Car. I remember how carefully he walked beside me, as if I might detonate. And I remember thinking how hard it must be for him not to urge, from force of habit, that I enjoy my stay in Minneapolis, where the ground temperature was seventy-nine degrees and the skies were partly cloudy with winds gusting to twelve miles per hour. I appreciated his restraint. If this turned out all right, I would write a letter praising him. I never did.

There were police cars in the driveway when we pulled up. I ran straight through the house to the backyard, where voices were bubbling. Oh God. There in a pool of summer sunlight, surrounded by police officers, was Jeff. And Bengt. And Tony Culpepper. Minka and Janusz were there too. And Estelle Mackenzie and Jim and Tiny Culpepper. And two people in EMS outfits. They parted for me the way the crowd at the Sventitsky Christmas ball parted for Pasha Antipov after Lara shot Komarovsky in *Doctor Zhivago*.

"I'm all right, Mom," Jeff said.

I felt a surge of relief so profound it was physically painful. "What happened? Where *were* you?" You could hear crickets chirping. All the way from Hawaii, where it was still dark. "Well?"

Jeff wouldn't meet my eyes. "We, uh, went boating. We snuck out after everyone was in bed. Minka didn't know. It wasn't her fault."

"*You* went boating after dark?" I could barely speak. In fact, I might need someone to poke my ribs to get my breathing action back.

"It was okay. I had the lights on."

"*You* had the lights on? You mean you took *our* boat out? After what your dad and I told you about not going out in it alone?"

"I wasn't alone. Bengt and Tony were with me."

He was my son—surely I had the right to kill him? I didn't think there was a court in the land that would convict me. Not if anyone on the jury had kids. I felt a sudden hand on my elbow, both restraining and reassuring.

"The important thing is, these boys are safe," one of the policemen said. His name tag IDed him as "Officer Lumley."

Yes, that was the important thing. Jeff was unharmed. God had taken my bet and called me. Yes, I will save your son, but for the next ten years he will be a teenager.

"What exactly happened? Why were you gone all night?"

Jeff looked embarrassed, clearly more distraught over losing face in front of Bengt and Tony than over releasing heart-attack-inducing stress hormones into his mother's bloodstream.

"I got lost. I couldn't figure out where we were and got worried about running out of gas. So we found this island and stayed there for the night. Isn't that what you would have wanted me to do?"

The last sentence had a defiant edge. He'd become Blade after all. This was one of those trick stories where someone is given a tip from the future

and spends weeks heading off disaster only to realize, in the last para-
graph, that everything he's done has engineered it. If you were the reader,
you saw this coming long before the sap in the story did.

"What I wanted, Jeffrey, is *not* to have the police have to locate my son."

"They didn't. Janusz did."

Still with the smart mouth, the hitherto unknown voice of a wizened
Jewish—or Irish, or Italian—godmother whispered in my head. She must
have popped in while I was in New York and hadn't had time to scramble
out again. Or maybe she was curious about what went on in that big
empty patch west of Hoboken, the last known point of civilization because
Sinatra was born there. *Look, Morris, they have fancy-schmancy backyards
but no sour pickles. Who ever heard of such a thing?* Isn't this the kind of
thing trauma victims reported? Voices? Visions? Soon I'd be flashing on
Vietnam.

No, I wouldn't.

"What do you mean, Janusz found you?" I turned toward Minka.

"Before I call you, I call Janusz," she said. "I call Janusz *before* I call
police." She seemed proud of this.

"Your husband had me put a global positioner in the boat," Janusz
explained, holding up something that looked vaguely like a Palm Pilot. Or
a Blackberry. Or an iPod. How did people tell all these gadgets apart?
Pretty soon, we wouldn't have real things anymore, no televisions or tele-
phones or stereos or computers, just big baskets of mini-things that all
looked alike. You'd grab a handful on your way out the door and be set for
the day.

"After the installation," Janusz continued, "I stored your serial number and scanned your product code into my database. Cousin Ludwik in
Gdansk has been working on a program so one GPS can find another
one. Beta version, but guess what? It works! Cousin Ludwik will be a
millionaire!"

Do you hear that, tatela? My godmother was back. It disturbed me that
she used words I didn't know, like *"tatela."* So let Cousin Ludwik get rich,
I wanted to tell her. It's no big deal. In fact, I'm pretty sure he'll probably
live to regret it.

I looked around at everyone looking at me. Something wasn't right here. More not right than I'd let myself in on. Wait a minute. Where was Scout? Why wasn't he barking? Why wasn't he racing around in antic circles with that stupid if-there-are-this-many-people-it-has-to-be-a-barbecue grin on his face. Where was he? And where, I wondered, feeling my fingers uncurl and let go of the ledge, *where was Sophie?*

I must have said this aloud, because another officer, Lindberg, said, "We're looking for her."

"She wasn't with you?" I asked Jeff.

He shook his head. "I wouldn't take Sophie out in the boat without you or Dad, Mom."

Only just this one time, Jeff, I wish you had.

I broke away and ran down to the dock. I squinted as far as I could see in both directions, looking for a little girl playing with her dog by the shoreline. Looking for a little bundle of clothes and Sophie snagged in among the weeds.

Minka came up beside me. "Police searched here already. Nothing." She had my arm and was drawing me back to the group. "Scout was not here either. When I woke up."

I looked at my watch. It was 11:07 CDT. Four hours after chatting up God over Sunchips, my hopes were pinned on a golden Lab.

If anything had happened to Sophie, nothing else would matter because we'd be finished anyway. I saw Tom and me living on forever, long after we wanted to. I saw Jeff crushed by guilt he didn't deserve, and how even though we'd tell him it wasn't his fault, we'd never be able to feel the same way about him again.

"I'm sure she's all right," Tiny Culpepper assured me.

"If there's anything we can do," her husband offered.

"I'm here if you need me," Estelle said without her usual brightness.

"Police will find her!" Janusz declared. "I know so!"

But they were all drifting away from me. Heading off. Not wanting to be here. The chickens. I wished I could go with them. Except for the police and EMS crew, only Minka remained, fair game for torturing.

"Where's Tom?" I demanded in a way that made her flinch. "Where?"

"He called last night, from long-distance parking."

"Long-term parking, you mean?"

"Yes, yes. Where his car was. He said he and that woman he went with, Lucie, had to finish work they were doing and fax it to Paris before noon, and could I stay one more night. I said fine, no problem." She stopped. I saw that she had no intention of going on.

"And?" I stepped closer. She stepped back. But I had the upper hand because there was a glacier of terror behind me, propelling me onward. "What happened this morning? Did he come home?"

She shook her head. "I call his office, his cell phone. I call and call. I can't find him." Her beautiful blue eyes filled with tears. "I am so sorry, Mrs. Wilkins."

Not only bereaved and terrified, but humiliated. Minka, Janusz, and probably most of Gdansk knew about my shaky marriage. Someone reached in and cut the sinews between my shoulder blades. I stopped trying to stand and felt myself collapsing. "It's all right, Minka. It's not your fault." *Steer into the skid.* Now Morris, my new godmother's husband, was butting in. *Go with it, the car'll be totaled either way.*

Officer Lumley, radio buzzing, came up beside us.

"Got 'er," he said.

I thought, I really am fainting if he's catching me. But I had to stay awake so I could be punished some more. "I'm all right," I told him.

He grinned. "Of course you are. They found your kid."

"They did?"

"Yeah, Hank and Lou got her. She's fine, fell asleep under an apple tree about ten houses down. Owners weren't home or someone would probably have spotted her sooner. Next-door neighbors complained about a barking dog and we checked it out."

There it was. Perfect police work. They'd found Sophie. And in less than fifty words, Office Lumley had told me exactly how it happened. My cheeks were suddenly wet. I knew because I felt the air on them as I ran through the house to get to the driveway. A police car had just pulled up.

"Mommy!" Sophie tumbled out, wearing the Powerpuff Girls sleeping shirt my mom and dad bought her when they were here. Mom had pushed for the sweet pink one trimmed with hearts. Sophie had insisted on chartreuse with a bright red ruffle.

"Oh, Sophs, Sophs." I kneeled down and hugged her.

"I slept under a tree! Scout put his head on me all night long."

"But where were you going, sweetheart?"

"I saw Jeff go in the boat and I wanted to go with him. Scout and I walked all around the edge of the water, then I couldn't see the boat anymore and wanted to come home. We were lost."

Almost, I thought.

"Sophs!" Jeff grabbed her away from me and swung her up. "You scared us, Sophs!"

"*I* wasn't scared!" she cried.

The police cars were taking off one by one. The EMS people had disappeared too. "I guess that's about it," Officer Lumley said. "Everybody seems to be fine."

"Wait a minute. Aren't you going to charge my son? Isn't there a juvenile-court date? Or some kind of penalty?" I was hoping for a hefty fine, something that would eat into his allowance slowly and painfully over the next fifty years.

"He didn't actually break any laws. According to the other boys, he had the running lights on. They all had on life vests. And he's old enough to run a small boat like that without a license, so—"

"You mean he just walks away from this whole thing?"

Lumley chuckled. "You're the first parent I've ever come across who *wants* her kid prosecuted. Which suggests to me he'll be fine. You seem to have a handle on it."

No, I just wanted the Minnetonka Police Department to do my work for me.

"You're grounded for life," I told Jeff on my way into the house. "And that's just for starters."

"I figured," he answered.

I would have gone on to *Just wait till your father gets home*, but I had no idea when that would be.

Inside, I paid Minka and told her we'd see her Monday morning.

"I'm not fired?"

"Of course not. You didn't do anything wrong, Minka. My kids snuck out on you." In a screwball kind of way, she'd even done exactly the right thing, calling Janusz and his magic GPS. But I didn't tell her so. Today was a day on which we should all suffer.

A few minutes after she left, I heard the soft cat's-paw tread of Porsche tires on our driveway. Now the suffering would really begin. I sprang down the front steps like Cujo the rabid wonder dog. Tom was going to be the couple trapped in the broken-down Pinto.

"Hi, babes." He looked rumpled but refreshed. "What're you doing back?"

"Where the *hell* have you been all night?" I shrieked. There it was, in one split second. I, Fishwife. I could hear windows popping open all over the block.

Tom looked puzzled and sleepy.

"Working. I called Minka."

"And Minka called you. About seven times. You were nowhere near your office."

"Look, hon, I don't know what's wrong, but let's go on inside, okay?"

"You weren't *at* work, so don't give me that crap."

"Sssh. What's wrong with you? Why are you talking like you grew up in a pool hall?"

We got inside. He hadn't bothered to take his suitcase out of the car. Maybe he was thinking of a quick getaway. He sat me down in a kitchen chair and poured a glass of bottled water for me. Right. It was the impurities in tap water that were behind this.

"I'm not thirsty."

"Okay, okay."

"Why did you tell Minka you were working if you weren't?"

"I *was* working. We worked at Lucie's. It's four times closer to the airport than IM, and we had to have a proposal addendum faxed to the Olympics by this morning. They were threatening to go with Canfield's Grain-A-Roo bars. They were that close to walking."

The electrocardial rhythm of my anger was momentarily interrupted. "You're kidding. What happened?"

"No idea. But your Kate was no help. Lucie kept faxing and leaving messages, asking for stuff we needed to make our final pitch. Were the phones out in your hotel all weekend? Anyway, we never got it, and Lucie finally convinced the IOC to give us a twelve-hour extension."

My electrorhythm snapped back. I folded my arms and gave him a withering look. "And all this information you needed so badly just happened to be at Lucie's?"

"Yeah. You should see her apartment. It looks like an office. Except for the exercise equipment, you'd think you were actually at IM. She had her kitchen taken out and turned into a second computer room."

"Where does she sleep?"

"Gosh, I don't know. Hanging upside down like a bat, maybe. I never saw a bed."

"I'll bet."

Finally he caught on. "Don't tell me . . . You don't think . . . How could you think *that*, Annie? One, I didn't, and two, it doesn't even make sense. If I wanted to sleep with Lucie, I had a whole week in Paris to do it. Why would I fly back home, jet-lagged to the bone, and think, Hey, right, let's do it in Richfield."

I walked to the sink and poured my water down it. Through the French doors, I could see Jeff and Sophie and Scout playing in the backyard. It was a game they called loop-de-loo. I had no idea what the rules were.

"I didn't know we had these kinds of problems." Tom's voice was quiet behind me.

"We've got bigger problems than that," I answered. "There are our biggest ones, right out there."

"Jeff and Sophie?"

"Sit down, Tom."

I took him through every miserable minute since 6:46 that morning. I wanted him to feel as tortured and desperate as I had. It was no use, though. He could look out the window and see the happy ending. In the end, I settled for him just understanding how close we'd come.

"We are going to have to make some changes around here," I finished.

"I agree. We are going to have to do things differently."

But what? I don't think he had any more of a clue than I did. We couldn't blame today on Minka. Not unless we wanted to hire sentry nannies to patrol the halls on rotating shifts. And what about Jeff? We could go ahead and ground him for life, but part of what he'd done had been out of sheer frustration. It didn't take a Dr. Spock to see that. It didn't even take Mr. Spock, just a Tribble or two. We'd surrounded Jeff with all sorts of big-deal toys, then walked off and said don't touch. Coming down too hard would only make him figure out more ways to get around us.

"I'll talk to him," Tom finally said.

What about? Bobber fishing? The Vikings' chances of making it to the Super Bowl? The importance of taking basic science? Tom got so little time with Jeff, I couldn't picture him blowing it on a lecture. But I held my tongue.

"I'm sorry I wasn't here, babes. No wonder you were upset. Are you okay now? I need to go take a shower. I've been in these clothes for twenty-four hours."

Left alone, I felt empty but oddly buzzed, like a ham actor who couldn't wait for the next matinee. I wanted to tell my story all over again. I wished I'd called my parents in Spain when the kids were missing, so now I could call them with the good news. But of course I hadn't called them in the first place. Who would inflict that kind of pain on someone if there was a chance they'd never have to know?

I tracked down my day planner and called Kate in New York. She was right by the phone.

"They're fine. They're home," I told her. "Jeff's in trouble for taking the boat out and we may have to get an electric fence for Sophie, but physically they're fine."

"You must be so relieved, Annie."

"You wouldn't believe what I've been through. The whole thing."

"And I want to hear all about it."

Great. Welcome, Kate. You're in the orchestra section, row D, seat 24. I felt like handing her a *Playbill.*

"Can you hang on a minute, Annie? Or wait, I'll call you back in ten. Make it fifteen."

So I was the one sitting by the phone, waiting for the star to break her leg so I could go out there and become the star. Kate called back half an hour later.

"This has worked out fantastically," she said, apparently forgetting her desire to hear my story. "I took a chance and called March Sapperstein."

"Who's March Sapperstein?"

"The woman we were supposed to meet with tomorrow morning. Food Network programming, Annie? I called her at home, explained everything, and she said there'd be no problem switching our meeting from morning to tomorrow early afternoon. Then I called IM's travel people and they're getting you on a morning flight back here. Only it will have to be a touch early, there's the time difference and March could only push the meeting back to one P.M. I'll call in your flight number and times when the travel people get back to me."

My adrenaline supply had been depleted hours ago. I could barely hold the phone up to my ear. It was slightly better than being underwater with a lead vest. "Wait a second. You mean you expect me, you actually expect me, to go back to New York? Tomorrow morning?"

"Absolutely."

"But this was an emergency."

"Yes, it was, and I did everything I could to help. And it all worked out, so we can pick up where we left off. Now, I've been looking at weather forecasts and we may have to cut things close if your flight's delayed, so wear something that travels well in case you don't have time to change."

I could believe it. She was out Lucieing Lucie.

"Kate, I can't just get back on a plane and—"

"Yes, you can, Annie. You will. This Food Network meeting is vitally important to us. To *you.*"

I tried to explain all the unfinished pieces left lying around, teeny-tiny pieces that Tom and I were going to have to go around for weeks on our hands and knees picking up.

"But it's a crisis," I repeated.

"*Was* a crisis. Now it's over."

Here was another answer to my questions about Kate. Clearly, she'd never had children or a husband. If she had, she'd know that it's never over. Ever.

"You'll be on that plane tomorrow morning, right?"

"Right," I said, finally giving up. I was too exhausted to deal with her anymore. I was too exhausted to deal with my husband and my children too, so maybe it was just as well that I was headed back to New York.

I laid my head down on the cool kitchen table and closed my eyes. I wished it was nighttime so we could all go to bed. I wished I was Polish so I could call Cousin Ludwik in Gdansk and turn everything over to him.

Chapter 22

UNDERWATER IN
A LEAD VEST

Later, on the flight back to Minneapolis, Kate told me I'd done a good job at the Food Network meeting. Those were her words. *Good job, Annie.* Not fantastic, not shoe in, not get out your ya-yas, you're going to be a TV star. Good job. Acceptable. Reasonably coherent. By that point, I was more than willing to settle. My adrenaline had yet to replenish itself, I'd had almost no sleep, and I'd flown back and forth so many times I had whiplash. Literally. My neck felt like it was about to crack. I began to fantasize about being strapped onto one of those spine-stabilizing boards EMS workers cart around. I wondered if there was one on the plane for emergencies. I was an emergency.

Then, just as the pilot told us we were over Green Bay and would soon be starting our descent, I remembered Branston Arche.

"What is it?" Kate asked.

"I totally forgot. Someone was supposed to fax me something important. This morning."

Kate smiled placidly and turned the page of her book. "Oh, that. His office called yesterday. They rang my room, so I gave them your home fax. It's all taken care of. Not to worry."

Not to worry? I could only hope I got home before Tom saw the fax with those estimates on it.

I didn't.

"What's this, Annie?" was the first thing he said to me. "Who're Arche and Associates?"

I told him about the referral and said they were just a few estimates, making it sound like Branston Arche, $400-an-hour architect, had noodled up some figures as a friendly favor.

He frowned. "I don't think we can afford it this year."

No kidding. I wonder if he'd had a peek at our portfolio. "Of course we can't. I was just getting an idea."

I didn't mention the cost of the estimates, and as I talked I juggled my carry-ons so he wouldn't notice the cardboard tube with Arche's sketches inside.

"What's that?" he asked, noticing.

"I bought some posters for the kids."

Which meant I now had to drive to the mall to buy posters.

"I talked to Jeff," Tom said. "Laid down some rules. He's going to start doing some work around here. Taking care of the house. The yard."

"Tom, we can't even take care of the house and yard. They're both too big. That's why we have cleaning people and lawn people. This isn't 1980 and you with your dad's Toro doing the yard of the farm, you know."

"Why are you sticking up for him?"

"I'm not sticking up for him."

"Yes, you are. I know he's a good kid, but look at what he did, Annie. I'm not going to stand by and let him spin completely out of control."

I saw a hardness in Tom's face I'd never seen before. It frightened me. I wanted to thread myself between him and Jeff

"We're not going to do this." I gathered my luggage and started for the stairs.

"Do what?"

Make Jeff our scapegoat. Make him the repository of every other problem we have.

"Annie?"

I didn't turn around. Going back would have meant setting Jeff aside and saying what I thought our problems were. And the truth was, I wasn't completely sure what they were. Tom was flirting with Lucie. Or I was insanely jealous of my husband's life. Neither prospect flattering. I kept on going.

In the middle of the month, Lucie's brother had another sickle-cell crisis. Lucie, Tom told me, was flying to Madison each night and back to Minneapolis each morning. Two and a half hours each way, when you counted getting to the airport and fussing around with airport security. You had to hand it to the girl. She didn't crumble. Besides, she had other ways to work out her anxieties. Like the day she summoned me to her office and looked me up and down.

"Really, Annie. That outfit. Did anyone see you on the way in? I hope. *Not*."

I'd been snacking nervously ever since those Sunchips with God five miles up. I no longer felt like tucking my blouse in. Was this the end of the world?

"Hang on a sec." She turned her head slightly toward the computer. "Pick up from 'special sales and marketing opportunities include.' " Then she hit a key and a dialogue box asked if she wanted to save untitled. She did. "You'll be getting voice memos from me from now on. Isn't that great?"

Yes, indeed. Few prospects were as delightful as the idea of Lucie's voice reaching into my very dreams.

She was continuing to stare at me. Hard. "Are you off your diet, Annie?" Suddenly, she smiled. "Tell you what. I've been wanting to do this for a while. Let's go together and get our BMIs done."

"Our what?"

"Body-mass index. You know, for seeing what your percentage of body fat is."

I already knew. Hers, zero. Mine, well, let's just say significantly more.

"Do they take an average?"

"Huh?"

"Never mind. What did you want to see me about?" I sat down and folded my arms across my chest, my favorite pouting pose.

Lucie ran a teardrop fingernail down her list of notes. Anyone who could keep up a perfect manicure in the midst of a family crisis was on some level a better woman than I was. It was like a gladiator saluting Caesar, not a care in the world.

"I've been looking over your schedule," she said. "I think we haven't been making the best use of you."

At last. Someone appreciated me. And Lucie, of all people. I unfolded my arms. "Really?"

"Mmm-hmm." She brought up my schedule and Tom's for June, July, and August, and tipped the flat-screen monitor toward me. "Look. When Tom's home, he's working. When you're home, you're more or less on downtime. You haven't done a local event since mid-June. You're underutilized."

I felt my glow fading. But the burn was just beginning.

"I work very hard, Lucie."

She rolled her eyes. "We *all* work very hard, Annie. That's what this is about. That's why they call it 'work.' Now, I've outlined some avenues for us to explore, and . . ."

The long and the short of it was this: for the back-to-school season right through the first snows, I was to tour the Twin Cities in a specially designed vehicle called the BTC-Mobile—it looked like a twenty-foot candy bar on wheels—handing out BTC products in school parking lots and football practice fields.

"Are you out of your mind?" I asked Lucie. "Some of those rebound-hunger women have kids. They'll follow us all over the city."

"Great! We can count on press coverage, then."

"But you've never seen them. They're vicious. They'll murder me."

Lucie offered an exasperated sigh. "It's a bulletproof car, Annie. Really, you are *so* way too emotional."

———

The third week of July was a financial disaster. Our portfolio deflated at an average rate of 3 percent a day until, after a staggering ten-session loss, we'd lost so much that what had been 3 percent was now 5 percent. It wasn't just the stocks I'd bought after copying Kate's notes, it was everything, even the allegedly safe mutuals our broker had herded us into. We were going down like the *Hindenburg*. Why did everyone connected with Wall Street seem so chipper? The CNBC crowd was still quipping away, as was our broker the day he called to suggest we bail on a 40-percent-down-and-still-falling tech fund.

"They fired that fund manager," he said proudly, as if he'd personally waded in and flattened the bully, "but I don't think we should fool around. Let's get you into something a little more promising."

And presto, just like that, our paper losses became real. Three hundred thousand dollars alchemized into one-twenty. It was as if we'd both spent our first two years teaching for free. Meanwhile, the fund manager was probably lying on a beach somewhere looking out for number one, fielding new job offers by cell phone.

Well, two could play the new economy game. I turned on the computer and sat down with a box of chocolate-covered cherries.

I was getting good at this. Two new credit cards, 2.5 minutes. It was amazing. I didn't even have to go look for them, the offers just poured into my e-mail. It was as if someone had put in a good word for me. Annie Wilkins could use a little credit. And getting it was such a cinch. Often I was preapproved. Even when I wasn't, I got instant approval on-line. That was the thing no one ever told you. You didn't actually have to *be* rich. You only had to get rich once, put the money in some highly visible, easy-to-check bank account, and then you could do more or less whatever you wanted. You could live on credit for months, maybe even years. Really, why there wasn't a market for falsified bank references, I'd never know.

Not that I intended to carry around this much credit forever. I planned to scale down as soon as possible. For one thing, it was hard to keep track of all the dates the bills were due, and I'd had to buy one of those accordion folders with pockets for each month. Then there was the time it took to pay them. Not to mention the monthly interest.

Click here to accept terms.
I clicked.

In mid-August, Tom came home with the news that they'd not only gotten the French food distributer to sign on to the IOC deal, but had brought along an Australian firm to handle the Pacific Rim. BTC Bolt Bars would be the official bar—excuse me, *energy food*—of the next summer Olympics, with worldwide distribution. Six months ago, we would have popped champagne corks. Now I just said, "That's terrific, hon," and he said, "Yeah, I guess," and we didn't mention it again until we were getting ready for bed.

"I suppose you'll get to go to Athens."

"I think Lucie's putting together some sort of tour. She wants to follow the course of the Olympic torch, so we can take advantage of the crowds."

I pictured me following along behind them in the BTC-Mobile, flinging Bolt Bars left and right. Probably not. Probably it would just be Lucie and Tom. "It would be nice if we could all go," I ventured. "It would be great for the kids. And Mom and Dad could meet us there and—"

"It's not a vacation, Annie. It's work."

I finished pulling the display pillows off the bed and began folding back the bedspread. Tom helped me. It was too heavy and the bed was too wide for me to do it alone. "But wouldn't it be great, Tom?"

"I suppose so."

Right. We got into bed and turned off the lights.

"Tom? Are you mad at me?"

"No, babes, just tired."

That was all. He turned over and went to sleep. We didn't even touch hands. I found my earplugs and connected them to the Bose. More and more often these days, the last voice I heard at night was Art Bell's.

The happiness express kept rolling on past us. A few days later, my sister, Barb, called to say they'd driven Rob down to Ames and he was now officially enrolled in the veterinary medicine program.

"Rob's doing handsprings, and we couldn't have swung it without you and Tom. You have no idea, Annie, there's just nothing like seeing your kid that happy."

The pure joy in her voice made me feel melancholy. I remembered joy like that. Didn't I?

Two days later, Minka took Jeff to register for the seventh grade. It was his first year of junior high and I'd wanted to take him, but he told me that only really, really hopeless dweebs had their moms with them. Apparently, there was no problem with a beautiful twenty-four-year-old nanny loitering in an SUV. This is how men rehearsed for trophy wives, I thought. But since Jeff had been on his best behavior since the incident with the boat, I gracefully stepped aside.

Sophie told me not to feel bad (how did she know I did?) because *she'd* play with me. Which is why, when Lyn and Emily walked over, Sophie and I were down by the lake, teaching Sparks to say, "Yo-ho-ho," as he paced up and down the dock. This was Sophie's idea, not mine. She'd finally picked a career—pirate—and wanted to get started.

She'd picked it for practical reasons. "I have a boat. I have a parrot. I only need a treasure chest."

"You know, Sophs, you don't really have to pick what you want to be right now. Just because they asked you at that school interview. I mean, there's lots of time to decide . . ."

"*Je le sais, Maman.*" It sounded like "jealousy" to me, but I was probably oversensitive. "I only picked it because no one else did. I'm not really going to be a pirate."

"No?"

"I'm going to be a mermaid." She looked at me seriously. "So I have to start growing my hair *right now*."

That's when Sparks flapped to the top of a dock post and called out, "Welcome aboard, welcome aboard," and we saw Lyn and Emily coming toward us. Lyn wasn't showing yet, but her walk was gravid, rolling and backward leaning. If you'd put a daisy in her belly button, it was the daisy that would have reached you first.

Lyn kicked off her flip-flops, plunked down on the dock, and swung her feet into the water.

"Ah." She sighed, leaning back on the heels of her hands. "This feels like heaven. I'd forgotten the FIF."

"The what?"

"Fluid inferno factor. You know, the way two minutes into the pregnancy you're sweltering. I think it's the extra fluid, but maybe it's hormonal."

We sat for a while on the dock saying nothing. Scout had unwisely come down to join us and was now playing Seabiscuit to Sparks's Red Pollard. Sophie and Emily were looking for a saddle blanket.

"Did you get Estelle's announcement?" I asked and we both laughed. It had arrived by Blackberry a few days ago.

DVRCD BNGTS FTHR

NGAGED J-P DNAVETZ

@HOME WDG 12-19-02

PLS CM

"I almost wish I could go," Lyn said, looking at me.

"What do you mean? You *have* to go." I noticed that she was glowing. "Lyn? What is it?"

Her glow split into a smile, spilling sunlight all over the dock. "We bought the farm. Literally. It's been something we've been wanting to do for years, and this fantastic offer came along, so we just went for it."

I was baffled. "A farm? Tom grew up on a farm. Believe me, it's not what you think. It's hard, hard work. Or are you just going to live there? Where is it?"

She held her breath for a split second, then her words tumbled out in such a rush her white-blond hair lifted. It was like watching milkweed down catch the sun. "Virginia. It's a horse farm, Annie. A working, honest-to-god bluegrass horse farm. We have to get down there as soon as possible. You should see how much stable managers charge. I mean, boy, are *we* in the wrong profession. It's like a license to print money. Anyway, we're flying down three weeks from today, and the moving company will come finish the house. When I told Em she could have a party before we go, she wanted to come ask Sophie herself."

I felt incredibly lonely sitting on that dock.

"Mommy," Sophie told me later, "Emily gets a party and a pony *and* a baby brother or sister."

That's right, Sophs. Some people hit the trifecta.

"You can have a party too, honey, for your birthday, in November."

"Emily won't be here, though."

"No."

She was quiet for a while. "I want a baby brother or sister. For my birthday."

"It doesn't work like that, Sophs."

"How does it work?"

"Well, for one thing, it takes longer. And Daddy and I would have to be home more, to take care of everyone."

"Is that all?"

No, Mommy and Daddy would have to be having sex too.

Why couldn't she have gone for the pony?

Chapter 23

YELLING THEATER TO W
A FIRED-UP CROWD

That September was beautiful in Minnesota. Fall—or Fall Week, as we called it, to distinguish it from Spring Week, Summer Fortnight, and Winter Ten Month—was swept with sunlight and a beautiful stillness. There were no mosquitoes. Or Iowans. Children went back to class, and the school year looked promising. The shock of Miss Strannack suggesting that the brown-eyed children mistreat the blue-eyed ones as part of Prejudice Awareness Week was yet to come. As was winter, which you could feel lurking just beyond your sight line. Floating under the dock like a witch whose icy fingers braceleted your ankle when you dipped your foot in, or puffing frost onto dark green chrysanthemum leaves. Live it up, everything said, take your last look until the April snowmelt.

We did. One Saturday afternoon, we drove up to Lake Mille Lacs to marvel at the foliage. Sophie kept up a constant backseat chatter. She had brought a book home from school, her first reader, and would not let it out of her sight. Jeff listened good-naturedly to *How Many Hats?* at least half a dozen times. In the face of our children's goodness, I kept waiting for the eggshell silence between Tom and me to crack and melt away, but it didn't. I wondered whether he was wishing he were on this ride—the one through life, I mean—with Lucie. Like a good lawyer, I didn't ask questions I didn't already have the answers to.

Everyone at IM was excited about the BTC Olympics deal. In fact, brands and advertising had already shifted into high gear, even though the Athens games were over a year away. "You want to go for the *build*" was the way Lucie put it. Storyboards appeared with sketches of a Famous Athlete holding a BTC Bolt Bar aloft like an Olympic torch. "Bolt to Athens!" the sell line read. An MTV campaign was also planned, with kids of all ages screaming, "Jolt the Bolt!" as they surfed across the screen on neon lightning bolts.

Looking at the orange and purple lightning bolts, Lucie said, "Wouldn't it be fun if Jeff and Sophie—"

"No," I answered, cutting her off before the question was unleashed. Jeff and Sophie were *not* going to be on MTV, even though Sophie might later sue me for thwarting her showbiz career.

Lucie also wanted our input on Famous Athletes. "Any ideas?" she asked. When I looked closely at her earrings, I saw they were like charm bracelets, each tiny charm a piece of junk food—a hot dog, a doughnut, an ice-cream cone. "Who do you think we should approach as spokesathletes?"

"Bret Favre?" I suggested.

Lucie rolled her eyes. "Not someone old," she said. *"Someone young."*

"How about that skateboard guy," Tom said.

What skateboard guy?

"Right! Tony Hawk." Lucie made a note. "Extreme boarding. He'd be perfect."

It was the last Bolt Bar strategy meeting I was asked to attend.

"Oh no," I said. "There are limits."

I was standing in IM's kitchen, the one they'd made just for BTC, with Chef De Navets and a dozen people from recipe development. We were all staring at a plate on which was laid a darkish lump that looked like the shriveled lung of a lifetime smoker. It was a Binkie, the chocolate version of a Twinkie, over which IM had just made a huge deal with Hostess. Only this was a Binkie with a difference. It had been deep fried.

"I am not going to stand out in the broiling sun selling *that*."

Next summer, IM had decreed that I was to tour America, touting the pleasures of deep-fried Binkies at every state fair, Renaissance festival, and rodeo to be had. From Guernsey County, Ohio, to Saugerties, New York, to Rio Verde, Arizona, I—like Tom Joad in *The Grapes of Wrath*—would be there.

"But this will be *huge,*" a girl named Debbie from snacks and specialties said.

"Maybe bigger than the corn dog."

De Navets prodded the Binkie. I had to hand it to him. Since his engagement to Estelle, he'd been a complete gentleman to me. "Legion of Honor," he'd said, thumping me on the shoulder. "You are taking this very well. And who knows, perhaps one day . . . ?" I'd assured him that I would never betray a friend, even in matters of the heart. The magnitude of my sacrifice seemed to move him, and now he came to my defense.

"Perhaps she could just bake the Binkies?"

"What's a baked Binkie? *We* bake the Binkies, so why would the customer *re*-bake them? Whereas fried—"

"And I'm not wearing that, either." I pointed toward a Dolley Madisonesque costume in brown-dotted Swiss with panniers and puffs and ribbons all over it. It was the proposed Miss Binkie outfit. They were still working on a first name for me. Barbara Binkie? Beatrice Binkie? Bo Binkie? "We have to get the name right," a memo asserted, "because we're hoping for character/doll retail activity in fiscal '04." They saw Bo Binkie as "a hip, youngish Mother Goose type" who would spin modern fables *(The Binkieland Chronicles)* while promoting product to beat the band.

This was how far I'd fallen. And the day wasn't over. It had begun badly, when Lucie and her crew had shown up at our house to do some shots of Tom for the BTC Bolt Bar campaign. They wanted to get him relaxing on the deck of our cabin cruiser, dressed in tennis whites, and having come in from a jog. *Honey, where are the Bolt Bars? I sure am hungry!* According to the storyboard, my voice would be stripped in later. Clearly, house theory was still firmly in effect. Tom sold better without me, in scenarios where women could mentally call out, *They're on the table, dear,* and walk through my house to claim my husband.

"You might be more comfortable working at IM today," Lucie had said brightly at seven-fifteen. "We're going to be making quite a fuss over your husband." She pulled her headphones off and tapped the microphone clip on her blouse. "Are you getting me, Ed? Because I'm getting a hum on this end. Okay, let me try different headphones. 'Bye, Annie."

Now it was two P.M. and I was trying to convince Clint from advertising not to dress me in brown-dotted Swiss with a coal-scuttle bonnet.

"But the outfit focus-grouped really well," Clint was saying.

Beyond him, I saw Debbie gesturing, holding up her cell phone. "Kate wants to see you, Annie. Right away."

Good. I could go get Kate on my side. Surely she wouldn't let them go ahead with this ridiculous Bo Binkie thing, would she?

"You won't believe what they want me to do," I cried, bursting into her office. Adrenaline—or maybe it was the BTC s'mores I'd eaten in lieu of lunch—had taken hold of me. I was moving so fast, I almost crashed into a side table. "I *refuse* to wear that ridiculous outfit!"

"So Debbie said." Kate was smiling. "Sit down, Annie. I have terrific news."

What? We were going to grill the Binkies instead of fry them? "Kate, almost anything would be good news at this point."

I couldn't stop pacing, and Kate stopped trying to make me sit.

"I just talked to March at Food Network. They're picking you up for thirteen episodes. Half-hour show. The premise they went for is that each week a celebrity chef comes by with a favorite chocolate recipe, and together you re-create the recipe using BTC. Food Network will use celebrity chefs from their own lineup—Emeril, Gale Gand, Jacques Torres. It'll be terrific."

I couldn't believe it. We'd pulled it off! Surely someone with her own Food Network show wouldn't have to go around deep-frying Binkies.

"When do we start production?"

"I bought you some time. Not until November. They're going to shoot from mid-November through mid-January, and debut the show on Valentine's Day. Now, I've already started looking into residence hotels for you, and of course we'll pay for you to come home at Thanksgiving and Christmas, unless you'd rather have Tom and the kids come to you."

Wait a minute.

"What are you talking about, Kate?"

"You. New York. Isn't it great that Food Network's studios are in Manhattan and not in New Jersey? You'll have a terrific time."

"You mean *I* have to go *there?*" My voice cracked with disbelief. "But—but what about the kitchen here? What about the work kitchen in my house? I thought that's where we'd shoot from."

Kate sighed. "That was the plan, Annie. But since the celebrity chefs are based in New York, it makes sense to do the show from there. And, frankly, the network is a bit nervous about committing. They want oversight."

I snapped. "No. No! I've had it, Kate. I am *not* living alone in New York for two months—or even two weeks—so we can sell more of this crap."

She leaped from her chair and forced me down into it. "Sit, Annie. Calm *down*. Everything's going to be fine. Two months isn't so long, and then you'll have a nice break at home before the Binkie cakes tour."

"You don't mean they're still sending me on that, do you?"

"I expect so. Why wouldn't they? It's a great chance to bring the six-to-twelve age group onboard."

I stared at her. "You have no problem, do you, selling this fried crap to kids?"

"It's up to their parents. We're not force-feeding anyone."

She'd gone over to the dark side. Completely.

"Well, I'm not going to do it. Have you ever eaten this stuff? Those rebound-hunger women have a point, you know. No one here admits it, but they're right—the more of this you eat, the hungrier you get, all out of proportion. What's the chemical setup here? Has anyone ever studied *that?*"

I must have been flailing my arms. She leaned forward and moved something on her desk.

"Every ingredient in BTC has been approved for human consumption," she reminded me.

"But that doesn't mean BTC is good for you, or that there isn't some interaction that's lethal. As far as we know, it could kill us all in twenty years!"

I realized I was shouting. My last few words actually seemed to echo in the office.

"Slow down, Annie." She handed me a glass of water. Why did people always give me water when I was upset? "Let's not make any rash decisions. Why don't you go home, have a hot bath, and relax. We can talk about all this later."

"I can't go home. They're shooting Bolt Bar with Tom today."

She looked surprised. "The shoot was canceled. There was a power outage in your neighborhood around ten this morning."

"Then where's Lucie?"

"In her office, would be my guess."

Home with my husband, would be my guess. Alone, since the kids were both at school. I don't even remember leaving Kate's office. I don't remember anything until a horn was blasting because I'd crossed two lanes of highway at once. Since the horn wasn't from a police car, I just kept going. In fact, I probably accelerated.

On the drive home, I morphed into full-out jealous-wife mode. I pictured Lucie scampering through my house with Tom in hot pursuit. I imagined her having an afterglow cigarette in my bed, a quick shower in my bath. I imagined grabbing a handful of her adorable ringlets and dragging her out the front door, tossing her clothes behind her.

Inside every woman is a Colombo, waiting to be touched to life. Having decided to make my approach on foot, I parked in the driveway of Lyn and Dan Vickers's empty house. A "Sold" sticker was plastered over the FOR SALE marker, and I wondered who'd bought the place. Someone happier than I was, I hoped. Someone who wasn't about to sneak into her own home.

Scout came bounding toward me the minute I cracked open the front door. Before he could start his heavy-pawed welcome dance, I reached in my pocket and fished out a package of Ham 'n' Bees, IM's shelf-stable, honey-coated ham morsels. Scout took his prize to the kitchen rug. I slipped out of my shoes and tiptoed in the opposite direction.

The ground floor was absolutely silent. Because of the shoot, Tom had told Minka she could go home after Sophs left for school, a detail that now glowed with malice aforethought. It was almost two-thirty. Sophie wouldn't be home for an hour. Jeff had football practice and would be home even later. Just enough for a rumpled-sheet romp, I thought. But as I started up the stairs, I heard sounds coming from the pool room. Gentle, lapping sounds. I turned away from the stairs and started down the hall-way. It was so murky I almost fell into Tom's office. I was about to pull the door closed and move on when I saw in the dim, reflected light the curve of my husband's shoulder. He was sitting in the winged leather chair at his desk, facing the watch window that opened onto the pool. In the dusky room, the window was a bright azure square, Tom's own pri-vate movie. And the featured attraction was Lucie, as lovely as a gazelle, swimming nude.

It was photographic, the way her body stretched in the blue water. I saw a hundred shifting pixels—the delicate beige-pink of her heels kicking the water, the swell and flash of a breast when she reached for the next stroke, the dolphin curve of her back and flanks.

Suddenly, my anger ebbed. I felt the wind die behind my sails. I'd been ready for rumpled sheets, not Humbert Humbert.

"Well," I said quietly. "Has the main feature started, or is this still the coming attraction?"

I still couldn't see his face, only his shoulder, which flinched. Whether from surprise or guilt or the relief of those who sought to be caught I couldn't tell.

"It's not what you think, Annie. She didn't know I was in here. I came to get a pen and—"

"And you stayed." I heard the hard, brittle edge to my voice. "What did you think, Tom? That you'd get lucky? That you'd sleep with her?"

"No."

"But you *want* to sleep with her."

"Maybe. No, not really."

"So this is—what?—just kind of an anatomy-appreciation class?"

"Annie . . ."

"The truth, Tom."

"I was thinking about us."

"Oh, please."

"I was, Annie. Maybe not at first, but Lucie . . . Lucie isn't what I want. You are. So why isn't it you and me in the pool? Why was that one day—that day before we moved in—the only day?" His sigh was deep. "That's what I was thinking. Not that you're listening."

"What does *that* mean?" I came all the way into the room and stood in front of him. His face was lit by the light from the pool window. For a split second, I saw hardness there. Then our eyes met and there was only sadness.

"It means there's something wrong here, but I don't know what it is. Every time I turn around, you're mad because you think I'm fooling around with Lucie. Or mad because I'm on some god-awful road trip."

"Adored by thousands."

"Plucked at is more like it. The point is, I'd rather be here. Except that when I am, even when we're together, you don't seem that interested. You seem more interested in the house. How many chairs and love seats have you bought, Annie? And lamps and drapes and god only knows what? And have you ever asked me or Jeff or Sophie what we want?"

"But—" I felt attacked. Everything I'd done had made the house *better*, hadn't it? The soft, yellow silk drapes of our bedroom? The seawater green tiles in the third guest bathroom, the ones it had taken me weeks to find? "It's our dream house, Tom. I wanted it to be perfect."

"Is that what we've got? A perfect house? When was the last time we made love here, Annie?"

It had been seeping into me slowly as I stood in the darkened office, the realization that I'd hurt my husband. I'd left him a sitting duck for the nymphet swimming on the other side of the glass. I turned sharply on my heel and headed toward the door. Just for the hell of it, I hit the light switch on my way out. Instantly, the room was bathed in light.

"What do you know. The power's back on."

"Wait a second, Annie." I could hear Tom's voice behind me. "Lucie had no idea—she's been under a lot of stress—"

You could practically hear the water rocking to a halt in the pool room. The instant the light came on, Lucie realized we were in the office, watching her. She didn't have time to scramble out of the water before I reached her. She sank back, crouching in the shallow end. With her hair stuck to her head and her jutting collarbone visible just below the waterline, she looked all of thirteen years old. You're not even his type, I thought.

I grabbed a robe, my own, and tossed it to her, in the water. "You're needed at the office," I said.

She looked confused. "For what? Kate told me there was nothing happening there, to take the rest of the day off if I felt like it."

But hadn't Kate thought Lucie was in her office? "Let's put it this way, then. You're *not* needed *here*, Lucie. And the next time you try to seduce my husband . . ."

Lucie had struggled into the robe, now heavy with water, and waded up the pool steps.

"Seduce your husband?" She cinched the belt around her waist. "Your husband is one of IM's biggest investments. And my responsibility. And sure, he's nice, but"—her nose wrinkled—"not exactly my type. I told Kate that when she suggested we split you up—"

"When *Kate* suggested you split us up? But that was your idea."

"I wrote the strategy paper and Kate let me have the credit, but it was her proposal. She insisted we'd get more mileage out of you separately than together. The focus-group data backed her up, although I thought there might be better value in educative selling—setting a level and bringing your customer up to it—but Kate prevailed. My part of the deal was that I keep Tom's ego stoked. BTC as subliminal sex. And it worked. Your husband is a coast-to-coast sensation, isn't he?" She was gathering up her clothes. Beyond her, I saw Tom's face—and his ego—go down like a soufflé. "Really, you people cannot tell sales from reality, can you? Kate was right from the beginning—we should never have made BTC such a major product line."

Kate? Why did Kate's name keep coming up? Somewhere a bell was tolling. For thee. Kate. Kate. Kate.

"Kate didn't back BTC?"

Lucie shook her head. "Not at first. She was dubious, wanted to go conventional. Three-year product rollout, minimum." She'd managed to get her underwear on under the robe and now shrugged into her blouse.

"But if you'd done that—"

"Right," Lucie said, zipping up her skirt. "Canfield's Au Chocolate. Without the mass-onslaught approach, we never would have established the name recognition we have. We'd have a much harder time holding on against them."

"Amazing."

She stepped into her shoes. "It is. I've never known Kate the Great to be wrong. Maybe she's losing her grip."

Or maybe she never wanted Better Than Chocolate to succeed in the first place. My mind telescoped to a dozen seemingly unrelated incidents. The way she'd initially ignored me until I'd come up with research to block that potentially disastrous paper in *Nerve & Tissue*. The way she hadn't returned Lucie's faxes from Paris during the Bolt Bar negotiations. The way she'd been behind the strategy to send my husband and me in different directions. The way she kept promising that things would get better while they spun further and further out of control. The way she kept putting Lucie in Tom's path and hoping for the best—or worst. For Kate, that was a real win-win. Either Lucie would split Tom and me up, badly tarnishing BTC's image, or I would made a fuss and get Lucie fired, leaving Kate in sole control of BTC's fate. Poor Lucie. Like Tom and me, she was just another pawn on Kate's big board of life.

"For what it's worth, Annie, I've never had designs on Tom. It'd be like sleeping with my father."

I heard a *flump* as Tom's ego finished its collapse.

"And I hate the Binkie campaign as much as you do. That's why I didn't go back to the office today. It's just too tacky. And that outfit Kate got for you is *hideous*."

"You think so?"

"Oh yeah. It makes your hips look like the Mendota Bridge."

After she left, Tom and I stood for a few minutes in silence. What do you say to a husband whose vanity has just been scrubbed with a steel-wool pad? *I've got you where I want you?* Not if you love him. So instead, I told him my suspicions about Kate. Then, suddenly, my head filled with a Munch-like scream. I saw white light. Bright, white light. Maybe I was dying. Maybe it was the hoop crinoline of my Binkie outfit coming to smother me.

"Oh God," I said.

"What is it?"

"Just before I came home, I had a tantrum in Kate's office because of the Food Network schedule."

"What Food Network schedule?"

"I'll explain later. But I was shouting. About BTC."

"So?"

I remembered that motion Kate had made—sitting me down in her chair, then fiddling with something on her desk, pushing it aside or turning it a different way. I remembered a nub of black plastic.

"I think she recorded me."

He looked uncertain, as if deciding between the lone-gunman theory and the grassy knoll.

"If she did, Tom—"

"We're dead," he finished.

I took his hand. "Do you trust me?"

"More than you trust me, apparently."

"I'm sorry about that, Tom."

"So am I. But yes, I trust you."

"Good. I've got a plan. I need Jeff. I'm going to go get him at football practice. Sophie'll be home any minute. Fix her something for dinner, okay? Jeff and I'll be home as soon as we can."

As soon as Jeff got over the humiliation of being pulled off the football field by his mother, he listened attentively.

"But isn't that illegal, Mom? Like corporate spying?"

"Think of it as corporate *anti*-spying," I said, hoping he would see it that way, "We're the good guys."

"We are? Cool. So tell me what it is again that you want me to do."

I told him.

"But it isn't that simple, Mom. Even if we find the file and delete it, even if we flush it out of her recycle bin, someone really good on computers, someone like Janusz, could still recover it. Plus, we'd leave a footprint. Someone could figure out what time we'd entered the computer, when we'd deleted the file, that kind of stuff. Every single keystroke could be tracked."

I handed him my purse. "Dig out my cell phone and call Janusz."

"Mom, don't you remember? Janusz and Minka's friends are getting married. They're going to the wedding."

"That's tomorrow night."

"In Poland."

"Poland?"

"Yeah, they're leaving tonight."

"What time is it, Jeff?"

"About three-thirty."

"They haven't left yet. Hang on, I'm going to make a U-turn. If the police stop us, I'm a diabetic with a rare form of insulin intolerance. We have to get to the airport to pick up a specially formulated life-saving insulin. Call Janusz and find out what their flight number is."

Jeff got no answer. "They must already be at the airport," he said. "Janusz switched his phone off."

"Okay, start calling airlines. Find out who has flights to Poland, and what time the planes leave." I hoped the police didn't stop us. They'd never buy that insulin story. "What are you doing?" Jeff was jackknifed over the seat, digging for something in his backpack. "Start calling. I'm afraid we'll miss them."

"We don't need to call, Mom. Janusz wanted to see how good his cousin's GPS tracking software was, because he's thinking of investing.

He gave me a GPS with the program in it. I'm supposed to see if I can pick up his signal when he's in Poland."

"Well try now."

"I am, I am. Got it! They're at the airport."

We were doing fine until we hit the new and improved homeland security wall. We had no tickets and no luggage, my son was carrying a dubious handheld device, and, to top it all off, the underwire in my bra set off some sort of alarm. Apparently, we looked like international terrorists.

"If you could just step over here, please."

The security agent looked serious. This was no time for my diabetic insulin story. After a strip search and a lot of talking, I persuaded them to page Janusz. They let Jeff speak to him across a metal divider. I saw Jeff pull out his spiral-bound notebook and write something down.

"We're set," my son said as we headed back to the main concourse.

"You got instructions?"

"Instructions aren't enough, Mom. I got something better—Ludwik's super-secret number. And Janusz's password."

It was dark by now, which was just as well. Kate always left work at five on the dot, and the emptier IM was, the less chance we'd have of being noticed.

"Any idea how long this is going to take?" I asked.

"It depends on how big her hard drive is," Jeff said. "A few hours, at least. And, Mom? I'm hungry."

We screeched into a McDonald's drive-through, barely coming to a full stop. I threw a twenty into the window and didn't bother with the change.

Getting into the building was no problem, since my clearance scan showed that I could bring guests in and out. But when we got to Kate's office, her door was locked. Of course. Offices were supposed to be left unlocked for the cleaning crew, but Kate had decided to protect her day's work. Damn.

"Don't worry, Mom," Jeff said. He pulled out a wafer-thin nylon wallet, extracted a blank white plastic card, and ran it through the slot. The door opened.

"Did you get that from Janusz too?"

"No, from Blade. Remember? From the old neighborhood? It was like a going-away present. I can get into any hotel room in the country."

Terrific.

Jeff turned on Kate's monitor and munched a cheeseburger while he started searching her files. "It's probably a .wav file," he said. "Unless she wants to swap with a Mac user." A screen filled with file names. The screen started scrolling. "This is amazing. It's like the world's biggest jukebox. Let me try something." Windows opened and closed. Programs I'd never heard of flashed by. Jeff clicked on various files. "She's really smart," he said. "Half of these are decoys."

"But which half?" There were thousands of files. We could be here all night. "Can you search them by date?"

But Kate had changed all the dates too. On her computer, it was 1935. Jeff told me it looked like she reset the date each night before she left work, choosing a random year, month, and day every time.

"You sit here, Mom. Scroll. Look for a file name that would have made sense to her. Even someone smart forgets file names, so if it was important, she might not have risked it. She would have picked something she wouldn't forget."

I looked at the clock. It was 6:30. How long was this going to take? How long did I have? Because finding the file was just the beginning. While I started scrolling, Jeff called Cousin Ludwik. On Kate's phone.

"Won't the call be traceable?" I worried. "Won't it show up on IM's phone records?"

"Give me a break, Mom. This is Ludwik's deep-cover number. It goes to a local number—I think it's Janusz's other cousin's bakery—and he patches me to Ludwik. Cobra," he said. He raised his eyebrows at me over the receiver. "That's Janusz's password. Cool, huh?"

I went back to looking at file names: a.wav, aa.wav, aaa.wav, abb.wav, abc.wav, abbadabba.wav, ace.wav, action.wav. I scrolled down. It would take me all night just to get through the *a*s, and the more file names I looked at, the less sense any of them seemed to make. It was hopeless.

"Okay," Jeff was saying. "I'll tell her."

"Tell me what?"

"Ludwik can help us. But he wants a thousand dollars."

And there it was, as if I'd rattled it into my vision. amw.wav. Anne Manning Wilkins. I was sure of it.

"Tell Ludwik yes."

Of course, Ludwik wanted the credit card number first. I dug one out and took the phone from Jeff. While I relayed the number, Jeff played the file I pointed out to him. Yes, there I was, shrieking away. I watched Jeff delete the file and search for copies. Then he deleted all copies, all the .bk!s, and emptied the recycle bin. Ludwik told me my card had been accepted and it was a pleasure doing business with me. I handed the phone back to Jeff, who wrote some numbers on the back of the McDonald's bag, thanked Ludwik, and hung up.

"Okay, we're ready."

"Great. What are we going to do?"

"We're going to upload Kate's hard drive to a mirror site. Then we're going to wipe and reformat her disk, so no one will be able to retrieve that deleted file or find out where it went. Then I'm going to call this number, press this code, and the mirror site will download her drive right back onto the disk. It's Ludwik's newest program. He calls it Instadisc, because he's got a supercompression program for the download. But, Mom?"

"What?"

"It's still in the development phase, and Ludwik thinks Microsoft is trying to steal his source code. So if we get caught"—he picked up the paper with the numbers on it—"one of us has to eat this."

"No problem," I said.

Kate's drive turned out to be enormous—she seemed to be reconstructing the whole world of William and Henry James on it—and it took almost an hour to upload her data and over two hours to wipe the disk. No wonder Janusz charged an arm and a leg for working on our computers— it was incredibly boring sitting there watching a blue progress bar creep slowly across the screen. I wanted to go down the hall to my own office and start working out the thought that had been swimming in my head ever since I'd seen that amw.wav flash in front of me. But I couldn't leave Jeff alone. After all, if he was caught, who'd eat the McDonald's bag?

"When did Ludwik come up with this program?" I asked.

"I don't know for sure. A week or so ago, I think Janusz said."

"So why does it take Windows years to update their platforms, do you think?"

"They try to work out the bugs, Mom."

"You mean this program has never been debugged?"

"It's never even been used, Mom. We're beta testers!"

"What if it doesn't work? What if it's loaded with bugs?" *What if it loses her jamesworld folders?*

"Relax, Mom. It'll just look like normal file corruption. You know, like when for no apparent reason some program that was working before isn't working now? There are so many millions of things that can get screwed up, probably not even Janusz could figure it all out."

I wasn't sure whether that was reassuring or not.

It was almost midnight when we got home. Tom had put Sophie to bed hours ago. "I was starting to worry," he said. "Mission accomplished?"

"Half of it. Now I've got to write a research paper."

"What?"

"I'll explain tomorrow. You might as well get some sleep."

"Oh no, babes. If you're pulling an all-nighter, so am I." If we weren't on such a tight deadline, I would have had a little cry and told him I loved him. "You go do whatever you need to do. I'll be here if you need me."

"Can I stay up too, Mom?"

"Jeff—" Tom began, but I caught his eye.

"It's okay, don't you think? It's already late and tomorrow's Saturday. Besides, he earned it. We would definitely have been SOL without him."

"This rocks," Jeff said, grinning. I wasn't sure what rocked—staying up all night, me saying "SOL" in front of him, or him realizing he had finally, completely, worked off his bad karma from the boat adventure this past July.

Chapter 24

SO LONG,
FRANK LLOYD WRIGHT

Had I known it all afternoon? Or only when I saw the amw.wav file on Kate's computer? Or had part of me suspected it for months and kept looking the other way—looking at new furniture, at pots of melting chocolate, at glossy pictures of glossy me, and at curving vistas of sky blue lakefront water? I honestly don't know.

But I knew that night. As I went upstairs to my office, my vision was completely clear. I felt that alone but exhilarated feeling you get driving through farmland at night, when there's no one else, just you. The road is black and white, as empty as the surface of the moon, and you imagine that you can see straight down the blacktop to your final destination. Exhilaration hits and you gun the engine.

Kate had named my file amw.wav. Anne Manning Wilkins. To the investor class, of which I was, sadly, one, the ticker symbol for Merrill Lynch. The day I'd looked for aspirin in Kate's apartment, I thought I'd come across a real find in her computer room. And I had—I'd just been wrong about what it was. Or thought I'd been wrong. I booted up my computer and opened the spreadsheet of stocks I'd bought after that day at Kate's.

From the moment Tom had submitted his formula for Better Than Chocolate, everyone at IM had treated him as the second coming of Barney Oldenfield, creator of everything from MudSpuds to Dip-*IN*-Chips. Except, according to Lucie, Kate. Kate alone had been skeptical, and had argued for a suicidally lethargic three-year product rollout. Kate, who I'd believed was my best friend at IM. Well, as Sophs would say—*non*.

When I thought about it, it all came down to a pair of red silk slippers. The Chinese slippers with embroidery on the toes, the ones of Kate's I'd admired so much that she'd gotten me a pair just like them—that was the one, unencumbered thing she'd given me. Everything else had been a live grenade whose pin I'd unwittingly pulled. How cheaply I'd been bought. And how certain she'd been of my greed. If anything at all had surprised her, it had probably been how long it had taken me to snap. She'd known it would happen eventually, if she kept pushing. Either Tom or I, and probably I, would implode, taking Better Than Chocolate down with us. If I'd challenged her in any way, it was probably in thinking up new and ever more demeaning activities for me. Any sane person would have quit after having her truffles judged—and found wanting, I might add—by the first-graders of White Bear Lake Elementary. But I, convinced that I was on the road to happiness, had hung right in there.

Why *had* Kate been so eager to block Better Than Chocolate? The answer glowed on the screen in front of me. Chubb Corp., which I'd bought for $78.11, was now trading in the low 60s. If I hadn't been so quick to see Kate as a repository of market savvy, I might have thought twice about Chubb's ticker symbol. CB. If you were making notations, it would be an awfully handy stand-in for Canfield Brands. Just for the hell of it, I went on-line at fool.com and looked up the ticker for Canfield. CFLD. I wish I'd paid more attention to Kate's jottings. There'd been several brackets and parentheses, and at least one arrow.

I jerked open the drawer of my desk. Hadn't I saved that piece of paper? The one where I'd written down as much as I could remember the minute I'd gotten into my car that day? I pulled out handfuls—armfuls—of paper. Credit card agreements, bills, swatches of fabric, paint samples, insurance for the boats, the annual reports on mutual funds and stocks that, for some reason, seemed to be published on a monthly basis. Nothing. I got on my hands and knees in front of the marble-topped French country cupboard and pulled more paper out, all the way back to my *Minnesota Menus* article on walleye a year ago. The room was awash in paper and I still hadn't found it. Damn. My foot slipped as I got up, fanning the contents of a hanging file. And there it was, rumpled and winking up at me, like a penny in a stream. I dove for it before it disappeared back into the primordial paper swamp.

I'd written down a lot more than I remembered. There were seven bracketed "AMDs," an "HD–GM," and a "WY–GM." Stupid of me to assume she kept buying stocks with her winnings from Merrill Lynch, and even stupider to assume she'd sold Home Depot and Weyerhaeuser to buy General Motors. The money hadn't gone to buy GM. It had flowed through Kate's hands to pay Glen Milton, author of the blighted *Nerve & Tissue* research study that had almost sunk BTC before it even hit the shelves. "HD" and "WY" were, I suspected, shorthand for whoever Kate had gotten the money from.

Thank goodness for all those research skills I'd spent the first thirty years of my life honing. Within ten minutes, I had the roster of Canfield Brands top employees on the screen in front of me. Hank Daniels, CFO. William Yablonsky, vice president of sales. Paul Felzer, corporate operations. I could match up all of Kate's symbols to someone or other at Canfield. She'd gone to some effort to make her abbreviations conform to legitimate ticker symbols—using "PFE" for Paul Felzer, for example. No wonder she hadn't been ruffled when she discovered me in the computer room that day. Maybe she'd even hoped I'd seen her notations, knowing I'd sink even more of our money in her market wins.

I opened a fresh document screen and went to work.

From time to time, there were knocks on the door, and, at three A.M., fumes of chocolate chip cookies wafted through the room. I thought I was hallucinating, but a few minutes later, Tom and Jeff arrived with a plateful.

"Dad and I are having a blast," Jeff told me.

Ten cookies and a pot of coffee later, I was done. I made one final phone call to Cousin Ludwik, told him what I needed, and forked over my credit card one last time. I printed out three copies of my work, left two on my desk, put the third in a manila envelope, and went downstairs.

It was almost seven A.M. Tom and Jeff were watching my collection of Tivoed Christopher Lowell shows.

"Are you okay, honey?" Tom asked. "You look a little, umm—"

Jeff cut straight to the chase. "Your hair's sticking out in funny places, Mom."

I pulled the scrunchie off and ran my hands over my hair. "Better?" I grabbed my purse and fished out my keys.

"Don't you think maybe you should get some sleep? Or have a shower?"

"I'm too tired to sleep."

"But shouldn't we at least talk about—"

"Tom, I'll explain everything when I get back, I promise. Right now, I have to get to Kate's."

"I'm coming with you."

"You can't come with me. You need to have plausible deniability. Just in case."

"In case of what? This isn't Iran-Contra, Annie."

Oh yes, it is. I held up the manila envelope. "There's a copy of this on my office desk. Read it. We'll talk when I get home."

Tom's brow furrowed with worry. "Are you sure you want to do this, Annie? Maybe we should go to the authorities, or at least come up with a strategy."

"But it might be too late by then." I didn't know exactly what Kate planned to do with that file. As Jeff had pointed out last night, it wasn't large—she might already have sent it to herself at home as an e-mail attachment, and could even now be burning it onto CD after CD. But there was another factor propelling me forward. I was in the middle of good history. I wanted to see what happened next.

"If you're not back in two hours, I'm coming to get you."

"What's she going to do, Tom? Drown me in a chafing dish?" I pulled my coat on and headed toward the door. "Don't worry," I called back to him. "I have a plan!"

More or less.

Kate seemed amused rather than surprised to see me. "Come in, Annie. I was just having breakfast. Can I get you some fruit soup?"

"Maybe later."

She was probably the only person I knew who owned, much less wore, lounging pajamas. I was going to miss that.

"Have a seat, at least, Annie. What's on your mind?"

"I was fairly overwrought yesterday afternoon at work. I said some things in your office, things about BTC, I didn't necessarily mean."

"Ah. Well, I wouldn't give it too much thought, Annie."

"But I have to, Kate."

"Why? The door was closed, after all."

"Yes, the door was closed. But your computer was recording."

She looked startled. "Wherever did you get that idea?"

"From listening to your .wav file."

She put two and two together swiftly. It was unsettling to see how quickly she worked it out—that first I would have had to suspect, then I would have had to go back to IM to confirm my suspicions, and having confirmed them—

"And you deleted the file?"

"Of course."

She poured more coffee. "Just as well. I thought it might be fun to play back, at a party, but just as well, those things *do* have a habit of finding their way into the wrong hands."

"Like Canfield Brands?"

This caught her off guard. She set her coffee cup down with a jolt, then tried to recover with a trilling laugh. "That *would* be disastrous, wouldn't it?"

"Not as disastrous as the press."

Normal color came back into her cheeks. She was congratulating herself for getting past the tricky part. "You're right. Once the press gets their teeth into something—"

Suddenly, I slid the manila folder to her. "I think you should read this, Kate. I've done a bit of the press's work for them."

She considered the title I'd written in all caps, boldface: "THE VARIETIES OF CORPORATE EXPERIENCE." "Very clever, Annie, and quite observant of you too." But a thin line of worry was bridging her eyebrows.

I still regretted that Kate was a William James enthusiast rather than an Anaïs Nin fan. I hated losing a good headline, and "A Spy in the House of Chocolate" would have been perfect.

I helped myself to some coffee and watched her face as she read. Except for the line between her eyebrows, you'd never guess she was reading a magazine article in which she was fingered as Canfield's number one corporate spy.

"And who," she asked when she'd finished, "do you plan to shop this to? The *New York Times* business section? *Fortune?*"

"Actually, I was aiming for something closer to home. *IM Today,* maybe."

Her smile grew, her self-confidence spread its cobralike hood. "As you might imagine, there are other copies of that .wav file floating around. Turn this paper over to IM and I'll see that it's played over the company loudspeakers. You'll never convince anyone there's an ounce of truth in your accusations. You can't. There's absolutely no paper trail, no checks, no wire transfers from Canfield, not a single shred of evidence that I even know anyone from there. IM won't even dig too deeply. Because I do trade all those stocks, you know. Small but myriad buys and a lot of portfolio churning. Seeing if all the numbers match would take a fleet of accountants. I'm inclined to think IM isn't interested in making that kind of investment.

"Think about it, Annie. I've been their terrific employee for over ten years. They have a lot invested in me, and they need me. If push comes to shove, you and Tom will be toast. In fact, if you look at the conduct clause in your contract, you'll find you've agreed not to, and I quote, 'speak, write, or act in any way that could prove detrimental to IM or its brands.' That little outburst of yours could have a huge personal-liability price tag on it. Believe me, IM will put a lot more energy into pursuing that than they ever will into investigating me."

She slid "THE VARIETIES OF CORPORATE EXPERIENCE" back across the table to me.

"Of course, as you point out here, my particular take on corporate life *has* been very lucrative. If it continues to be, I'm sure there are certain arrangements that we could make, between us."

"I guess you're right, Kate." I put the pages back in the envelope. "Maybe it would be better if this stayed between you and me."

"I'm so glad we understand each other, Annie."

"You and me and the IRS."

"IRS?"

The look of confusion was worth every miserable thing she'd put me through. I tried to suppress the rush of excitement, the sheer thrill of gotcha, I was feeling.

"Yes, the IRS. What did you think, Kate? That I'd settle into an amicable standoff with you? That you could try to ruin my marriage and we'd call it even Steven?" You've been depositing large amounts of money in your bank account, just a few hundred missing each time to bring the amount below the bank's mandatory reporting threshold. Which means, I'm guessing, that you haven't paid taxes on any of this, have you? IM might not be interested in what I have to say, but, believe me, the IRS is a whole different story. They have all the time and resources in the world, and you're just the kind of person they're look-ing for."

"You'll still be toast at IM, Annie. I've got six copies of that .wav file, all attached to e-mails, all ready to fly the minute I hit send. And I burned some CD backups for good measure."

"But you won't hit send, Kate. In fact, you're going to delete the e-mails and destroy the CDs."

"Why would I do that?"

I looked around. Even the breakfast nook we sat in was padded with unobtrusive luxuries, from the apricot shantung silk chair cushions to the antique Victorian asparagus dish she was using as a butter dish.

"Because jail's a cold, hard place, Kate, not you at all. I don't even know that you get your own toothbrush there, much less slippers and the Saturday-morning paper. I'm pretty sure the prison library doesn't have William James on tap, either."

"You think the IRS would send me to jail? The IRS wants money. That's its sole purpose. Money, not sending people to jail."

"Yes, usually. But they take a dim view of people who evade taxes. Especially people who do it so blatantly for so long. And look at all the interesting things that would come out of their oh-so-thorough investigation, Kate. Even if you could make a deal with the IRS, your Canfield work would come to light. Corporate spying is, I think, a federal crime. All in all, Kate, I just can't see you being very happy in prison orange for the next ten to twenty years."

Kate was beaten and we both knew it. Which made her refusal to whimper almost admirable. "I suppose there's something you want?" she asked, eyebrows raised slightly.

"So many things, I haven't thought of them all yet. For starters, you're going to write Canfield a letter explaining why you'll no longer be useful to them. I know you'll do this because I'll deliver it myself. Then you're going to start thinking about early retirement, and you're going to start grooming Lucie for your job. You can ease out of IM. I think a year would be about right, don't you? As for all those unpaid taxes, I foresee a burst of remorse leading to some well-chosen and incredibly generous charitable contributions. Be sure to get the vouchers because I'll want to see them."

"Is that it?"

"Only for now. I'm sure I'll think of some others. You might want to cancel the Binkie tour, for example. You're lucky I'm a fair person, Kate. I've got you, you know. If I wanted to, I could own you."

A cool mask settled over her face. "And how do you know I'll put up with this indefinitely? You apparently think the worst of me. This is a big-stakes game, Annie. Aren't you the least bit frightened? How do you know something won't happen to you?"

"As fond as I am of you, Kate, this isn't indefinite. There'll come a day when we part ways, and what you do after that I couldn't care less. Until then"—and here I sent up a hosanna for Cousin Ludwik and his recently perfected OuttaSite Storage software—"everything—this paper, your bank finaglings, every move you made to sabotage Better Than Chocolate—it's all out there in cyberspace. Safe, invisible, and immortal. You couldn't find it if you looked. And if anything even remotely bad happens to me, if Tom's reputation is damaged by some bogus research paper, if my dog so much as rips a toenail, Cousin Ludwik knows who to take the data to."

"Who's Cousin Ludwik?"

"Kate, you don't want to know."

The house was quiet when I got home. Jeff had finally crashed in the family room, where *Aliens* seemed to be playing in perpetual rotation, and Sophie was getting Sparks the parrot's opinion on a Barbie outfit she'd made entirely out of cupcake papers.

Exhausted, rumpled, and probably even smelly, I passed them and started up the stairs. How deep could I fill my bathtub? I wondered. And how long could I soak in it before falling asleep and drowning myself?

"Is that you, Annie?"

Tom's voice reached out from my office. I'd forgotten about leaving my Kate article for him. Good, I thought, because I no longer had the energy to explain.

"Hi, hon. Did you read it?" I swung the door open.

"Oh, yeah."

That's when I noticed the neat piles on the marble-topped console, on my desk, and on the floor. All the papers I'd hauled out in my search for the note I'd made at Kate's. The old articles, the pieces I'd written for IM, the memos in response to Lucie's memos. And, oh my god, my bills. All the credit agreements and applications, all the cash advances, all the checks written on one card to pay the minimum due on another. I sat down slowly. I couldn't bring myself to look at him.

"Am I looking at what I think I'm looking at, Annie? Is there any remote possibility that this is a mistake or a hoax?"

"No." My throat was so dry it sounded like a bark. I wished I'd had Kate's fruit soup.

"Well." That was all he seemed able to say. I looked up just enough to see his mouth opening and closing but not, as far as I could tell, taking in or letting out air.

"Are you going to leave me?" I asked finally. When he didn't answer, I asked if he wanted *me* to leave *him*.

"No," he finally managed, looking faintly bluish. "I have something to tell you too, Annie. My Porsche. You know, my red one?" To distinguish it from the silver one and the black one, obviously. "When I told you IM leased it? It was a lease with an option to buy. I bought it. About a month ago."

Now my mouth flopped open. How could you do that? I wanted to ask. But I knew exactly how he could.

"And the hell of it is," he said, "I didn't even really want it. I wanted lab equipment."

My head snapped up. "Lab equipment? Honey, you work in a lab."

"Not lately I don't. Not since I discovered that damned chocolate. I had this fantasy about renting some lab space somewhere and fooling around. And I had all these equipment catalogs I was browsing through. But even if I had that stuff, I'd never have time to actually use it, and so, I don't know, I bought the Porsche instead."

"Let me get this straight. You *miss* being locked in a room without windows all day? You miss pipettes and centrifuges and all that?"

"Yeah, I guess I do. Yesterday, when you told me what happened in Kate's office, I was relieved. I thought great, now they'll fire us. And I sort of tried to tell you that, but you were in such a hurry to get to Kate's."

"But—but you *love* being America's sexiest scientist, don't you? I mean, they're sending you to Europe next summer. You'll be an international sensation."

He looked sheepish. "I guess I'd rather just be a scientist. I mean, it was flattering at first, but as Lucie said yesterday, it's business when you get right down to it. For the last few months, I've only been doing all this because it's what you wanted."

"What I wanted? What I wanted was for all of us to be happy together."

"In a dream house."

"Well, yes, but . . . but . . ." I took a deep breath and looked at him. Not past him, not at a point on his collar, but into his eyes. "We've screwed up here, haven't we?"

"Looks like."

I felt the ache of filling sinuses. I needed a bath *and* a good cry. "I wish we could give it all up."

"Why don't we?"

I held up the stack of bills. "We can't. We're broke. We're *worse than* broke. We have no liquid cash. Nothing I invested in is worth even remotely what I paid for it. And we owe. Big time."

He thought for a minute. "What if we gave up the house, got our equity out, and sold some of the stock, would we have enough to pay it all off?"

"Maybe. About. Yes. But, hon, we wouldn't have enough for a down payment on even a tiny little house. We have to live somewhere, after all." I'd managed not to cry so far, but now my nose was dripping. "I need a Kleenex."

"Good luck finding one."

He was right. My office really was a hopeless mess, much like my life. I'd be lucky to ever get either of them back to a level of functionality. I spotted the box of tissues and reached for it, knocking over a stack of furniture brochures and the cardboard tube from Arche and Associates.

It came to me all at once, in one deliciously sweet moment—a vision of the future I really wanted.

"Wait a minute, Tom. We've *got* a house. Not a very good one, but a house. Up north. Aunt Edith's place." Tom stared at me. I felt blood flow into my cheeks, like sap into a tree in the spring. Was that right? Was that when sap flowed? I'd have to learn. "We could quit this whole thing, Tom. We could get out relatively clean and go up there."

"IM would sue the pants off us."

"I don't think so. Not if Kate thought up a better way to sell BTC and convinced them to negotiate a dissolution."

"Why would she do that? I read your article, Annie, but I'm not sure we've got enough ammunition—"

"We've got more than enough ammunition, Tom, so let's just say, for argument's sake, that she'll do it." I was feeling the clean, astringent sting of a northern summer breeze against my face. I was inhaling pine trees. I definitely wasn't remembering the Fourth of July snowflakes. "Tom, we could be a family again. Look at Jeff and Sophie, is this really what we want for them? Rotating single parents? Getting too much too soon? Living like little adults? Do you know what Sophie was singing the other night? '*Voulez vous couchez avec moi, ce soir.*'"

"She doesn't know what it means."

"She called it the slumber party song, and it's only a matter of time."

Tom laughed, which gave me just enough courage to slide into his arms and hug him.

"This is our window, Tom. Let's get out of this mess while we can. Otherwise, we might never do it."

"But what about jobs? I mean, northern Minnesota isn't exactly a metroplex wonderland of white-collar jobs."

"There's always U. of M. Duluth. It's not that far away, and I'm sure they'd hire you in a minute. Or—this is the age of telecommuting, isn't it?—you could work freelance, do your own lab work, be a consultant."

"What about you?"

"Anything, so long as it doesn't involve chocolate. I could teach again. Even if I couldn't get on at UMD, there's high school. Or I could call up my old editor at *Minnesota Menus.*"

"We'd have to live pretty frugally, Annie. You'd have to shop at JCPenney, not . . . not . . . wherever the heck it is you've been buying twenty-thousand-dollar love seats."

"I know. But we'd be together. That's what really counts, isn't it?"

"Stop crying, Annie."

"I can't."

"Stop crying, because we're going to do it."

"We are?"

He kissed me. "You bet we are. But we really *are* going to have to pinch pennies, no matter what Kate works out for us with IM, because I want to come out of this with some of that portfolio intact. No living off it."

"Of course not."

"So we'll have to be self-sufficient, make our own fun." He had a Daniel Boone look in his eyes that melted me.

"We could do that. We could make our own fun." I held my breath a minute. "We could even make another baby."

That's when I knew he still loved me, and that we really would be all right. Because he didn't point out how much another baby would cost, or how we should talk about it later. Instead, he stroked my hair, the way he hadn't in months. I closed my eyes and inhaled him. The indefinable smell, the one I'd never had a name for, I finally understood. It wasn't just the smell of him, it was his soap and my shampoo, his cotton and my silk. It was us mingling together. And this is what we smelled like: contentment.

Acknowledgments

There are two people whose support and input were vital to the making of this book. First, my agent and friend, Robert J. Markel, whose wisdom, support, and luncheon companionship have lighted my way. Next, my editor, Carolyn Marino, whose faith and patience allowed this book to emerge. If there were more agents and editors like this in the world, there would be more good books for the rest of us to read.

I would also like to thank alpha and omega reader Steve Hogan, for whom I am dying to return the favor; my sister, Peggy Nylin, for interrupting her workdays to answer many questions about Minneapolis; my supportive and enthusiastic friends; and the important families in my life—the Waggoners, Nylins, and Bowers—for keeping me in the fold.